Where
 Willows
Grow

Where
Willows
Grow

A NOVEL

Kim Vogel Sawyer

DOUBLEDAY LARGE PRINT HOME LIBRARY EDITION

BETHANY HOUSE PUBLISHERS
Minneapolis, Minnesota

This Large Print Edition, prepared especially for Doubleday Large Print Home Library, contains the complete, unabridged text of the original Publisher's Edition.

Published by Bethany House Publishers
11400 Hampshire Avenue South
Bloomington, Minnesota 55438

Bethany House Publishers is a division of
Baker Publishing Group, Grand Rapids, Michigan.

Printed in the United States of America

ISBN-13: 978-0-7394-8051-9

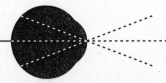

This Large Print Book carries the
Seal of Approval of N.A.V.H.

*For Daddy,
who coaxes new life from withered plants
and broken lives.*

For I will pour water upon him that is thirsty,
and floods upon the dry ground:
I will pour my spirit upon thy seed,
and my blessing upon thine offspring:
And they shall spring up as among the grass,
as willows by the water courses.

ISAIAH 44:3–4 KJV

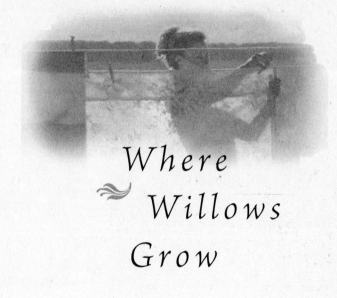

Where
Willows
Grow

1

Spencer, Kansas—Late April, 1936

Dear God in heaven, please let me be wrong.
Anna Mae Phipps hung her head over the sink basin as another bout of nausea tried to turn her belly inside out. She heaved, but nothing came up. Wasn't anything in there to come up—she hadn't even had breakfast yet. It wasn't a good sign, getting the heaves first thing in the morning. Especially three days running.

With a shaking hand, she grasped the corner of her apron, raised it to her lips, and wiped away bits of spittle. She straightened just as Harley rounded the corner from the bedroom. He snapped his suspenders into place and sent her a worried look.

"You okay, Annie? You're white as a ghost."

Please, God, we just can't have another one right now.

"I'm okay." She pressed her hands to her belly. "The heat is a bit too much this morning." She had hoped it was only the unseasonable heat that had caused her missed cycles. But now, the heaves . . .

Harley nodded. Grabbing two biscuits left over from last night's supper, he crossed to the back door. "Gonna go out an' get the mules hitched. Headin' to town. Need anything?"

Need anything? She nearly laughed out loud. There were so many things they needed! Dorothy's shoes pinched so badly the little girl cried every time her mama got them out. The lye soap she used on their laundry gave baby Marjorie a rash. A soothing cream from the doctor would help, or maybe just a box of Dreft to use instead of that horrid lye soap. But Anna Mae knew it was pointless to give Harley a list. How would he buy the things she named? Fifteen cents a bushel for corn couldn't possibly meet the needs of a family of four. Or five.

She shook her head. "I suppose not. Except maybe a bag of beans. I've got a meaty hock in the cellar. I'll cook up a mess of ham and beans for Sunday's dinner." A meal like that could stretch to cover supper Sunday and lunch on Monday, too.

Harley stuck one whole biscuit in his mouth. "Jus' beans?" He spoke around the lump in his cheek. "Don't nothin' else sound good?"

Anna Mae clutched her stomach. No, nothing else sounded good. But if Dorothy were in the room, she would have some suggestions: white sugar, a peppermint stick, some bologna. How that child liked bologna on white bread. Anna Mae felt her stomach tilt.

"No, I can't think of anything. Just . . . just take care of your own errands and bring me those beans, okay?"

She held her breath as he scowled at her, his lips parted as if ready to speak. *Don't ask, Harley. Don't ask what's wrong again or I'm liable to tell you.*

"Annie, if you could have one thing from town—something you really, really wanted— what would it be?"

She straightened her shoulders, her brows shooting upward. Harley wasn't one to play whimsical games. Not since the banks collapsed and the drought struck, making it almost impossible to eke a living out of the land. She wasn't sure why he was asking, but she had an answer. "I'd get a fine new hat to wear to church on Sundays. A straw one, with little wax cherries or some silk flowers on it."

A grin tugged at Harley's whiskered cheeks. "Cherries on a hat? Only place I want to see cherries is in a pie."

Anna Mae frowned and looked down at the scuffed linoleum floor. If he was going to poke fun at her answer, she wished he hadn't asked in the first place.

"Bet you'd be the purtiest gal there, wearing a hat like that."

Her heart caught in her throat.

" 'Course, I always thought you was plenty purty, hat or no."

Had he paid her a compliment? How long had it been since Harley had paid her a compliment? She slapped her chapped hands to her face. "Oh, Harley . . ."

His grin broadened. Snatching his battered hat from the peg beside the door, he plopped it over his shaggy brown hair before heading outside.

Anna Mae crossed to the open doorway and watched him stride toward the barn. Even in those worn-out clothes, there was no disguising the handsome man beneath. Wide shoulders tapered to narrow hips. Strong legs carried him across the dusty ground. Firm arms swung with determination, as if he were heading to a meeting of diplomats instead of their weather-beaten barn to hitch up mules to an old wagon.

It was Harley's way of walking that had captured her attention when he'd wandered onto the Elliott property eight years ago and asked her daddy for a job. There was such pride in the way he carried himself. And then she'd looked into his eyes—those twinkling blue eyes that made her want to look into them until everything else faded away. It had been a long time since she'd allowed herself to get lost in the depths of Harley's eyes.

Sighing, she turned away from the sight of her husband and closed the door against the wind that carried bits of grit into the house. Her gaze fell on the remaining dry biscuit on the table. She picked it up and nibbled an edge. Her stomach rolled. Maybe she should ask Harley to buy a tin of saltines. Saltines had helped her get through the early weeks of carrying Marjorie.

Dropping the biscuit onto the plate, she hurried through the back porch, swung open the screen door, and called to Harley. Wind whipped a strand of hair into her mouth. She tugged it loose and anchored it behind her ear.

He appeared in the wide doorway of the barn. "Yeah?"

"Can—" She pressed her hand against her stomach. Maybe she was wrong. Maybe it was just the heat. Maybe . . . No. She knew. "Can you pick up a tin of saltines from the store?"

She couldn't tell since he stood in shadow, but she thought she saw him frown.

"Saltines?"

She swallowed. "Yes."

With a nod, he turned away.

Closing the door, she slumped against it and pressed her fist to her trembling lips. *Dear God, they're supposed to be blessings, but this time it feels like a curse.*

Anna Mae held Marjorie on her hip and battled to throw diapers over the sagging clothesline one-handed. The wind caught the wet cloth and slapped it against her face. The strong smell of lye soap filled her nostrils. With a snort of disgust, she threw the diaper into the basket and set Marjorie on the ground. The baby squalled in protest.

"I'm sorry, angel baby," Anna Mae cooed as she grabbed a handful of diapers and fastened them to the line with wooden picks, "but I can't hold you and hang clothes at the same time. Just sit there for Mama and be good until I'm done."

Instead, Marjorie pulled herself up on Anna Mae's leg and continued to bawl, reaching with chubby hands to be held.

Anna Mae scooped up the baby and stomped around the side of the house to where Dorothy played beneath the drooping limbs of a monstrous weeping willow. A small smile tugged at her lips as she approached her daughter's favorite playing spot. How she'd loved playing in the shaded shelter of those same limbs when she was a little girl. She found it comforting that, despite so many other things changing, the weeping willow's welcoming branches remained the same.

Pushing one straggly limb aside, she addressed her daughter. "Dorothy, watch Marjorie for Mama so I can get the laundry hung."

The five-year-old sat on her knees in the dirt, her fine blond hair sticking out in feathery wisps. At her mother's question, she scrunched up her face. "But, Mama, I just got ready for tea with Dolly."

Anna Mae's gaze swept across the chunks of tree bark and rocks set up as substitute plates and cups on the smooth ground. She wished she could give her little girl a china tea set, but at least she had been able to give Dorothy her own doll.

"Can't Marjorie come to tea, too?"

Dorothy's lips pooched out in a pout. "She messes it all up."

"I know, darlin', but I can't—"

"Annie?"

Anna Mae turned sharply toward the voice. She hadn't heard the wagon rumble in. With Marjorie still riding her hip, she rounded the corner of the house to find Harley in the backyard, a crate in his arms.

She scanned the area in front of the barn. Where was the wagon?

Harley's grin stretched from ear to ear. "Look here what I got."

Anna Mae inched forward and peered into the crate. She gasped. "Harley!"

"Thought you'd be pleased." He set the crate on the ground and bent down on one knee, shifting things around as he recited the crate's contents. "Got your beans. Plus sugar, coffee, cornmeal." He grinned up at her and winked. "Gotta have corn bread to go with that mess of ham an' beans, right?" He poked around some more. "Pound an' a half of bologna, some cheese, canned peaches, the biggest tin of saltines I could find . . ."

The list went on, while Anna Mae's amazement grew.

"And"—he picked up an odd-shaped, tissue-wrapped package and stood, holding it out to Anna Mae in his work-roughened hands—"I got this for you."

Anna Mae tipped her head. "W-what is it?"

Harley tousled Marjorie's wispy hair before peeling back the tissue paper. "Didn't have one with cherries on it, but I thought these daisies were real purty."

Anna Mae's eyes widened as Harley placed a tan straw hat with daisies all around the brim on her head. "Harley! What's it for?"

A boyish grin tipped up one corner of his lips. "Oh . . . just because."

Was she dreaming? She touched the hat with one hand. The silk petals of the flowers tickled her palm. Yes, it was real. She pushed Marjorie's hand down as the baby reached for the hat. "But . . . but it must have cost so dear!" Tears sprang into her eyes. When had Harley ever bought her a present "just because"? Not since their courting days, for sure.

"It wasn't so much." His blue eyes sparkled with pleasure. "An' it looks real purty on you, just like I knew it would."

Dorothy ran around the house, her cotton dress flying up to reveal her dirty knees. "Daddy! What'cha got?"

Harley bent down to capture the little girl in a hug. He rubbed his whiskered cheek against her smooth one, making her squeal. Then, kneeling in the dirt beside the box, he answered, "Got all kinds of goodies. Lookee here." He pulled out a small brown bag and handed it to the child. "Peek in there, Dottie."

Dorothy unrolled the top, peeked in, and squealed again. "Gumdrops!"

"That's right. But you gotta make 'em last. Don't eat 'em all at once."

"I won't!" Dorothy popped a green gumdrop into her mouth and beamed at her father.

Anna Mae shook her head. She took off the hat and held it against her hip. "Harley, this is all wonderful, but—but where'd you get the money?" Her heart pounded in sudden fear. "You didn't take out a loan, did you?" If they lost the house, what would they do?

Harley shot her a frown as he straightened to his feet. " 'Course not, Annie, I got more sense than that. No, I—" He scratched his chin. "I sold the mules."

"You did what?" Marjorie squirmed, reaching for the hat again, and Anna Mae plunked it back into the crate. Suddenly she couldn't bear to hold it.

"Sold the mules." Harley's voice sounded gruff.

Marjorie slipped lower on Anna Mae's hip, and she jerked the baby upward so abruptly the child began to howl. Anna Mae raised her voice to be heard over the ruckus. "Those mules were the only thing we had to keep this farm going! You can't work the land without those animals. What were you thinking to sell them off?"

Harley's jaw thrust out. "I was thinking my family needed fed. It was either butcher 'em or sell 'em. Didn't figure you'd be willing to cook 'em up if I did butcher 'em, so I sold 'em and bought enough grub to get us through the next month at least."

"It was a fool thing to do, Harley."

Harley's face drained of color, then filled with red. He pressed his lips together so tightly they nearly disappeared, and his hands balled into fists. Anna Mae sucked in her breath. Never had she seen Harley so angry. Instinctively, she shrank back, cradling Marjorie's head in the crook of her neck. Even Dorothy stopped sucking on her gumdrop and peered at her father with round, frightened eyes.

But Harley didn't storm at her or raise his fist to strike her. He stayed rooted in place with his neck arched so taut the tendons stood out like rope. For long seconds he stared into her face, his eyes narrowed, fury seeming to spark from him. Then, slowly, he relaxed his shoulders. His hands opened to pick up the crate.

Resting the crate against his belly, he rasped in a low, tight voice, "Don't ever call me a fool, Annie." He pushed forward, and she slid sideways to avoid being bumped with the crate. She watched him stomp into the house and heard the thud of the crate hitting the table. When he stomped back out, he passed her without a word, heading for the barn.

"Mama?" Dorothy looked upward, her blue eyes—so much like Harley's—wide and fearful.

Anna Mae tweaked her daughter's tangled ponytail. "It's okay, darlin'. You eat your gumdrops and don't worry."

The little girl ambled back to her play area, the bag of gumdrops in one dirty fist.

Anna Mae patted Marjorie, who hiccupped with her crying, and looked toward the barn. Should she go talk to him? Apologize? Then she raised her chin in stubborn pride. No, she hadn't said anything that wasn't true. Selling those mules *was* foolish, and only a fool man would do such a thing! Why hadn't he asked her about it first?

Those mules had belonged to her daddy. She remembered the pride in her father's eyes when he'd brought the team home, claiming he was moving up from driving a milk cow in his fields. Harley had no right to sell those mules without talking to her.

Leaving the remaining wet laundry in the basket beneath the clothesline, she stormed into the house and slammed the door as hard as she could. But when she turned, she spotted the crate on the table. The new straw hat sat on top of the other contents. Her heart turned over. He'd meant well.

But what would they do without those mules?

2

Harley jerked the pitchfork from its spot in the corner. *Callin' me a fool.* Turning, he thrust it into the soiled straw from the mules' stalls. *Man tries to care for his own only way he sees fit, an' what kind of thanks does he get?* He shook the fork until the dry straw loosened and drifted to the hard-packed dirt floor. *Fool woman doesn't know beans about the fears in a man's heart.* Stomping out to the side of the barn, he banged the soiled straw into the manure spreader. *What good's a pair of mules when the land ain't fit for farmin'? Just take up space and eat hay I can't afford to buy.* He thumped back into the barn and repeated the process until the mules' stalls were clean.

He threw the pitchfork back into the corner and plunked his hindquarters on a barrel, burying his face in his hands. Behind his lids he could see Annie, her gray-blue eyes staring in wonder into that crate. They had lit with pleasure—he'd seen it. It made his chest feel tight seeing her light up that way. Didn't seem he had done much lately that had brought a sparkle to her eyes. Mostly he'd seen the other look—the one like when he'd said the mules were sold, the one filled with disappointment.

He stood and paced the barn. He knew he wasn't what her daddy had planned for her. Ben Elliott and his wife had put great stock in their Anna Mae, making sure she got all the book learnin' a girl's head could hold. She was supposed to go to a city somewhere and get a job as a telephone operator or a store clerk. Meet up with a fancy dude who would put her in a fine house and take her to parties and such. Old Ben had talked about all this to Harley as they'd worked the fields together—Ben had made sure Harley understood. But it hadn't changed the way Harley felt toward Anna Mae. And it hadn't changed the way she felt about him.

At least, not back then.

Harley paused in his pacing to slam his palm against the sturdy wood beam in the center of the barn. It made his hand sting, but it was nothing compared to the way his heart hurt. He'd always hoped her love for him would be enough to make her set aside those other dreams. But how many times in the past two years had he seen her staring off into the distance, her eyes all dreamy? He knew what she was thinking. And it wasn't about how happy she was here on the farm with him.

He swallowed the curse that pressed for release. Annie didn't hold with cussing any more than his own mama had. But it sure would feel good right now to let fly.

"Work it off," he mumbled to himself. He could start with that dirty straw. Spread it on the garden. Wind would probably tumble it all away before morning, but at least he'd try to keep some of that soil in place.

He pushed the manure spreader across the hard ground to the garden plot, released the lever, and watched the manure spill over the tilled ground. Despite the temper that made him want to stomp across the garden, he took care not to crush the tiny sprouts that would grow into cabbage, squash, potatoes, and peas. Too early yet for tomatoes, beans, and cucumbers, but they'd be out here soon enough.

If the garden did good this year, maybe they could sell some of the extra to townsfolk. Didn't need a mule to work the *garden,* anyway. Didn't need a mule to milk the cow or churn her cream into butter. Didn't need a mule to gather eggs. The things that brought money to the family these days— piddly amounts of money, but money all the same—why, none of 'em required mules.

He paused, looking toward the house. Of course, come Sunday, Annie might have a hard time walking the whole distance to church and back. He'd always carted her and the girls in the wagon. It was only a couple miles to the church—not too far for him, but a pretty fair distance for Annie, especially toting a baby on her hip.

Something else bothered him, too. Her asking for saltine crackers. Annie didn't like saltines. Not even with cheese or peanut butter. Said she had to eat too many of 'em when she was a little piker because her tummy was weak and her mama thought they'd make her feel better. Only time she'd asked for saltines was when—

He shook his head hard. No, couldn't be. Margie had just stopped nursing. Annie couldn't possibly be carrying another one, could she?

His stomach churned at the thought. Just what they didn't need around here—another mouth to feed, another body to clothe, another soul to care for. Harley gave the spreader a firm push to get it moving again. He loved his girls—Dottie and Margie were the best things in his life, outside of Annie. Even as hurting as they were for money, he wouldn't take a million dollars for either of his little punkins.

He snorted. "An' wouldn't give a plug nickel for another'n." The spreader flung out its last bit, and Harley pushed it out of the garden. It clanked all the way back to the barn, where he stored it in the tool lean-to. He glanced around to see what other chores needed tending. Woodpile was plenty tall. Garden didn't need hoeing. Cow would need feeding, but not for another hour or two. Nothing required his immediate attention.

He ran his thumb over his chin. He could go into the house, drink a glass of water, and tell Annie what he'd heard in town about the Works Progress Administration job over near Lindsborg in Saline County. Building a castle. Wouldn't Dottie be impressed? But he could imagine Annie's response. "A castle? What kind of fool puts a castle in the middle of Kansas?" He held on to the word *fool,* absorbed it, almost wrapped it around himself, torturing himself with its meaning.

He strode into the stall where the milk cow stood contentedly chewing her cud. As he scratched her thick neck, his thoughts continued. He hadn't gotten much book learnin'. Neither of his parents had been educated, and they hadn't seen fit to send their only offspring to school beyond the first few years. He'd come along so late in their lives, it was easier to keep him home and let him see to chores than make him traipse off to school.

But he'd learned plenty. He could use any farm implement made by man. Fix them, too, if need be. Why, he figured he could even keep one of them tractors running if he had the funds to buy one. And he had a way with animals—the cow turned and rubbed her nose against his back as if to let him know she enjoyed his scratching. Once, he'd nursed a sick raccoon back to health. His pa had thought that plenty foolish— *"Consarn critters ain't good for nothin' more'n mischief!"*—but it had pleased Harley to see the little animal scuttle into the brush on four strong legs.

"Fool, huh?" he asked the cow, giving her a final pat before turning toward the open doorway. "Well, Miz Anna Mae Phipps, these days a man's gotta do whatever he can to take care of his own, an' if you wanna call that foolish, I guess I'll just hafta set you straight." Her name might be on the title to this land, but he was still the man of the house. And he'd just march into that house and let her know once and for all she was going to have to trust him to do what was right for all of them.

Hitching up his britches, he turned his steps toward the house. Dust puffed up with every thud of his worn boots against the hard ground. He let the screen door bang behind him. He crossed the screened-in porch, wrenched the doorknob, and entered the kitchen. The crate still sat on the table, but he noticed it was empty. He smiled in satisfaction. She might've fussed, but she still put the stuff away.

Sweeping his hat from his head, he boomed, "Annie?"

She appeared in the narrow hallway, a finger on her lips. "Shh. I just got Marjorie down for her nap."

That took some of the wind out of his sail. How could he lay down the law if he had to whisper to do it? He looked around. "Where's Dottie?"

"Dorothy is outside, serving up gumdrops to her dolly and the barn cats."

Annie never could shorten up the girls' names. Seemed to stick in her craw. Stuck in his craw that she always had to be so hoity-toity. "Then come to the barn. Somethin' I gotta talk to you about."

Instead, she walked to the sink and started pumping water into the basin. "I've got dishes to do, Harley. I've been waiting for Marjorie to go to sleep so I could get some things done. She's been so fussy with those new teeth coming in, I can't put her down unless she's sleeping. Can it wait?"

He released a huff of aggravation. "No, it can't." In two long strides he was at her side. He caught her arm and made her look at him. "You can't keep ignorin' me. Don't make problems go away, pretendin' they ain't there."

She jerked her arm free and dumped a stack of plates into the sudsy water. "I'm not pretending. My problem right now is I've got an hour—maybe two—to get lunch dishes out of the way and supper started. I don't have time to go wandering out to the barn for a chat."

He leaned against the edge of the counter and crossed his arms. Annie had always been a stubborn woman. Once, when they'd only been married a few months, her stubbornness had gotten the best of him. He'd taken hold of her shoulders and shaken her good and hard. Scared her pretty good. Scared himself, too. He hadn't realized he had that much of his pa in him. He'd vowed to never again lay a hand on her in anger, but right now he was tempted to break that promise.

"Annie." He kept his voice low. "I reckon we can talk in here, but—"

"Harley—" she stared out the open window above the sink, her brow puckered up—"do you ever wonder how things would be different if Ben, Jr., hadn't died over in Europe?"

This sudden mention of her brother—a brother Harley had never met—caught him by surprise. He shook his head. "No. Can't say as I do."

"I do." Her hands stilled in the dishwater, and she continued to look out the window. "If Ben, Jr., hadn't been killed in the war, he would've come home. He would've taken over the farm when Daddy died. That's what Daddy had really wanted—for his son to have this farm, and for his daughter . . ." Finally she turned to face him. That disillusioned look was back in her eyes. "If Ben, Jr., had the farm, where would we be?"

He shrugged. In truth, if Annie's brother had lived, Harley probably never would have gotten a job on Ben Elliott's farm; he wouldn't have been needed. And he never would have met Annie.

She suddenly seemed to realize she was supposed to be washing dishes. Her hands got busy swishing a soapy cloth over one dirty plate. "Know what I miss, Harley?"

He shook his head.

She brought her elbow up to push her hair from her eyes. "The scent of rain. It's been dry for so long, I've almost forgotten what rain smells like." She closed her eyes and inhaled deeply. "Fresh, clean, burgeoning with new life." Her shoulders wilted. "Sometimes it feels like there'll never be new life around here again." Then her face pinched, and she scrubbed at the plate in her hand.

Harley stood still with his arms crossed, sorting out what she'd said. He latched on to one word: *burgeoning.* He hated it when she used fancy words like that. Sometimes he thought she did it to remind him she had more education than he did. This time, though, she seemed pretty caught up in thought.

And she was sure right about that scent of rain. More than two years had passed without a decent rainfall. If it kept up much longer, the farm wouldn't be worth keeping. Land wasn't worth plowing anymore, what with the topsoil blown into Oklahoma or Nebraska, depending on the direction of the wind. If he had to water the fields from their well, there might not be drinking water left for them. So it hadn't been foolish to sell those mules, after all, when you reasoned it all out.

"Don't know that I can do anything about rain," he finally said.

Her disappointed gaze turned in his direction for just a moment before going back to the basin of water. "I didn't expect you could. Only one who can do anything about the rain is God."

Harley scowled. "Don't bring religion into it again, Annie. Haven't you been prayin' for two years for rain? An' has anybody listened? No. No rain. Maybe that should tell you something."

Annie frowned at him. He knew she didn't like him talking about God as if He didn't exist. But what else could he do? Nobody had ever proved God's existence to him. His ma and pa lived on the same patch of ground, made the same scarce living, for fifteen years before his birth and then died early from hard work twenty years after. If there was a God, surely He could have made life easier for them in the Mississippi flatlands.

If God was as powerful as Annie liked to think, God could've kept his pa from being hateful. But God was absent during his growing-up years, and Harley saw no need to go looking for Him now that he was full grown and capable of taking care of himself.

"God has His own reasons for doing what He does, Harley. And just because He hasn't answered the way we want Him to doesn't mean He hasn't been listening. We don't have any right to think He's handling things wrong just because we think a different way."

Harley didn't care for the tone she used—the tone that said she knew more than he did. He uncrossed his arms and pressed his hands onto the worn countertop, his elbows splayed outward. "You believe your way, an' I'll believe mine. We've got along fine just lettin' one another be on that subject."

She pursed her lips and said nothing, but he could tell by her downturned mouth that she didn't like letting it go.

"I know I can't make it rain for you, but I figure I can do something about the lack of money comin' in here."

"What, Harley?" She sounded bitter. "What are you going to sell now?"

"Not selling anything." He took a deep breath, threw back his shoulders, and announced firmly, "But I ain't gonna stick around here and try to coax that ground to bring up corn that sells so low I might as well give it away. I'm leavin', Annie."

3

Leaving? He was leaving her? Anna Mae dropped the plate into the dishpan. Water and suds spattered her front. A few droplets even caught Harley on the arm. She grabbed her apron and reached to dry his shirt-sleeve.

He caught her wrist. "Annie, look at me."

But she wouldn't. As angry as she'd been at his decision to sell those mules, she hadn't meant to make him go away. If she looked at him, he'd read the begging of her heart—*Don't go! Don't go!* And she couldn't let him see that before he walked out the door.

"Annie!" His voice became insistent, although he kept it low. He released her wrist to grasp her chin between his finger and thumb and turn her face upward. But she kept her eyes averted. "Listen to me, Annie. The WPA is hiring men to build a castle over near Lindsborg. Martin at the store told me that's in Saline County—only a few hours away. The WPA pays good wages, all things considered. According to Martin, I'd qualify since the farm hasn't produced enough worth claimin' for the past two years. He says they might even put me up and feed me, an' I'd be able to send home maybe twenty-five, thirty dollars a month."

Anna Mae processed what he'd said. He wasn't leaving for good—just for a while, to take a job. At least, that was what he was telling her . . .

"Twenty-five dollars or more a month, Annie!" He gave her chin a little jerk that forced her gaze to meet his. His blue eyes—blue as the Kansas sky—captured her heart once more. "That'd see to you an' the girls' needs and then some, what with the egg and milk money that drizzles in. It'd be something to keep us going until farm prices go up again."

Anna Mae pulled loose and busied herself swiping a cloth across the cracked linoleum countertop. "A . . . a castle?" It didn't seem realistic, to build a castle in the middle of Kansas. Maybe he was making all this up—just a story to give him a reason to leave like so many other men across the country were doing.

"Yeah. Martin says it's supposed to do with some explorer that came through looking for gold."

Anna Mae glanced at him. "Coronado?" Maybe Harley was telling the truth. "Coronado was looking for a lost city of gold." She frowned, realizing the futility of that search. "No gold in Kansas, not even in corn or wheat anymore."

"An' that's all the more reason for me to go—to take this job." Harley grabbed her wrist again. The damp cloth hung from her fingers, dripping on the spot of floor between their feet. "You could see to things here for a few months, Annie. The garden chores, the chickens, and the cow—that's all that needs tendin'. Dottie's big enough now to help in the garden and do the egg gatherin'. I could see if Jack Berkley would take the eggs and milk into town, since pullin' the coaster wagon would be too much for you. You could give him . . . maybe ten percent of the money for doin' that for you. Jack'd probably even haul you to church on Sundays, if I asked."

Anna Mae swallowed. Jack would do it—she knew that. But she wasn't sure she wanted to see him three or four times a week, even just for picking up their extras. Long-buried memories tried to break free, and she covered her cheeks with her hands, determined to hold them back.

"So what'cha think?"

He had it all worked out. It hurt that he hadn't thought to ask her what she thought about any of this before making his decision. It also troubled her conscience—shouldn't they pray together about such big decisions? Shouldn't they seek the Lord's will together, the way her mama and daddy had always done? But it was typical of Harley—forge ahead, never stop to consider that she had ideas. Or that God had plans for them, too.

"Annie?"

She released a sigh. "Does it really matter what I think, Harley?"

He reared back, his jaw tightening. "'Course it does."

How could he say that when it was obvi-

ous it wasn't true? She shook her head.
"Well, I think you've made up your mind, so
I just as well oughta start putting your bag
together. You might want to take some of
the mule money, if there's any left"—she
emphasized the last four words, making
sure he knew he'd left her out of that transaction, too—"and buy yourself some decent
work boots. Your old ones won't make it
clear across Kansas."

She turned her back, took up the cloth,
and returned to her dishwashing. Harley
stood at the counter for several long seconds, watching her. She could feel his hard
stare boring into her, but she refused to look
at him. Finally he let out a huff of aggravation, pushed off from the counter, and
stomped out the door.

Lowering her head over the tepid dishwater, she felt the sting of tears. Well, he was
right about her being able to handle the
farm. She'd grown up on it, had been doing
chores from the time she was no bigger
than Dorothy. After Ben, Jr., marched off to
war, she'd been Daddy's only helper until
Harley wandered along. She knew what
needed done. It wouldn't be easy, with Mar-

jorie still so little and a new one on the way, but she could do it.

Except she didn't want to do it—not on her own. She wanted her husband working *with* her instead of just *alongside* her. Why couldn't she and Harley have what her mama and daddy had modeled—a partnership? Even though her daddy was a strong man, he hadn't been bothered by asking for Mama's thoughts on things. And when Mama talked, he listened. Why, how many times had she peeked through her parents' doorway and seen them side-by-side on their knees, praying together?

A lump formed in Anna Mae's throat. She closed her eyes and whispered, "Lord, I've prayed so hard for Harley to come to you, so we could have what Mama and Daddy had. But he still fights you. Please, Lord, please reveal yourself to Harley. Whatever it takes . . ."

A heavy sigh ended the prayer. She glanced out the window again, looking across the open expanse of prairie that seemed to stretch forever. Suddenly it felt as though the little house where she'd grown up was the only house in the world, and she the only person. Responsibility bore down on her, slumping her shoulders for a moment. Then resolve made her stand straight. She could manage things while Harley was off building his castle. Sure she could.

"As Mama always said," she told herself, turning her attention back to the dishpan to scrub at dried egg yolk on the last plate, "I can do all things through Christ who strengthens me." She looked toward the ceiling and released another sigh. "I'm counting on that promise, God. Because right now I feel about as strong as a newly hatched chick."

Harley stood beside the gate leading to the Berkley dairy farm, his forearm resting on the gate post. He sucked in breaths of hot air meant to calm him before he approached his neighbor. If a man was going to ask a favor, he shouldn't have anger in his voice when he did it. He'd done a pretty good job of learning to control his temper since he'd married Annie, but today she'd surely tried his patience.

Couldn't she see he was only doing

what he had to do to keep her farm in the family? For more than two years they'd been scratching by on next to nothing. No point in putting in a crop this year, knowing the ground wouldn't produce. But with that WPA job, he had the chance to have a steady paycheck, get the girls the things they needed, and make sure the farm would be there when the rains finally fell again so crops could grow. Why'd she have to make it so doggone difficult?

"You need Jack's help," he told himself, "so put on a smile and be friendly." He pushed off from the post and ambled across the yard, his gaze sweeping the neat grounds and freshly whitewashed outbuildings. Harley experienced the same slap of envy he always did when visiting the Berkleys. The dairy had been in Jack's family for three generations—just got handed to Jack when his pa turned sixty last year. It didn't seem fair that some people got things so easy and others had to work so hard to gain what little bit they owned.

Harley remembered working side-by-side with Annie's father, never slacking, always willing to do whatever he was asked so the old man would trust him with the farm when the time came. Ben Elliott might've left it to Annie, but in Harley's heart the farm was his. He'd work his heart out to keep it, too, even if he had to leave it and work someplace else for a while. It would be here, waiting for his return. And someday he'd give it to his girls, just like Jack's pa gave his land to Jack.

He stood between the house and the fenced pasture where cows, their udders hanging half full, stood in small clusters and eyed him with idle curiosity. He swung his gaze back and forth, seeking Jack, and suddenly from behind the barn a big border collie charged at Harley. The dog's tail wagged like a flag as the beast barked out a greeting.

"Hey, Clem." Harley gave the dog a few friendly pats. "Where's your master, huh?" The dog leaped in the air, then trotted toward the barn, looking back at Harley as if to say, "Well, come on." Harley followed and found Jack poking around beneath the hood of his Model T Ford. Another pang of jealousy struck. Now that Harley'd sold the mules, he didn't even have a wagon to his name. Jack had two wagons and a Model T.

Nope, some things just weren't fair.

Head still under the hood, Jack called, "Hey. I'll be with you in a minute. Just want to tighten this bolt good."

Harley squatted down and stroked Clem's warm back until Jack finished his task. He rose when Jack emerged. "Hey, Jack."

"Harley." Jack held out his hand, then grimaced when he spotted the grease stains. "A howdy will have to do unless you want this on you, too."

Harley grinned. "Howdy's fine." He took another step forward, Clem pushing against his legs. "Came to ask a favor."

Jack clicked the hood closed over the engine and shot Harley an interested look. "What's that?"

"I'm heading out tomorrow—taking a job in Lindsborg for a while." He briefly described the project. "That means Annie an' the girls won't have a man around."

Jack held up his hand. "Say no more, Harley. You know me and Pop will help out Anna Mae any way we can."

"She'll probably fight you." Harley shook his head, twisting his lips into a wry smile. "You know how stubborn she can be."

Jack released a hoot of laughter. "Oh, I

know. She's always been headstrong and independent. But Pop won't let her overdo."

"Thanks. I figured as much." Harley squinted against the sun. "If you'll tote our milk, cream, and eggs to the grocery, you can keep ten percent of the sale for your trouble."

"Don't want the ten percent. Wouldn't hardly amount to a hill o' beans anyway, would it?"

He grinned as he said it, but Harley's muscles tensed anyway. Hill o' beans was better than nothing, as far as Harley was concerned. But he kept his mouth shut and forced a stiff smile in return.

Jack pulled a rag from his back pocket and wiped his hands. "It's no trouble to haul yours in when I take mine to meet the milk truck. Be glad to do it."

Harley hated taking something for nothing, but he knew the Berkley and Elliott families had been friends for years—even before Annie was born. Favors among friends were acceptable. Besides that, his family could use every penny coming in. He swallowed his pride. " 'Preciate it. And if there's ever anything I can do for you—"

"No problem. Will . . ." Jack paused, the

muscles in his jaw twitching briefly. "Will your wife need help with the milking or the garden?"

"She oughta be able to handle those chores." Harley slipped his thumbs beneath his suspender straps. "Chores aren't new to her. Mostly she'll just need toting. I . . ." He ran his thumbs up and down the elastic straps. "I had to sell the mules."

Jack raised one eyebrow. "Yeah?"

Just one word, but it was enough to set Harley's hackles on edge. He released his suspenders with a slight snap. "Yeah. So . . . she'll need totin' to town and church, if you could see fit."

"I can do that." The answer came quickly. Jack slapped his hand onto the hood of the Model T, and a grin again rounded his cheeks—a sly grin. "Reckon those little girls of yours will enjoy a car ride now and then, too, huh?"

Harley pushed aside the envy Jack's comment evoked. "Reckon they will. Thanks again, Jack. I knew I could count on you."

"Anytime, Harley. Good luck at that job."

Harley gave a nod of thanks. As he walked back to his place, he felt a tingle of unease work its way down his spine. It wasn't as if he expected Jack to *resist* helping. He just wished the man hadn't seemed quite so *eager.*

4

Anna Mae kicked the sheet to the end of the bed and lay uncovered. Although she had opened both bedroom windows to allow in the night breeze, the room still felt sweltering. If spring was this hot, how would they bear the summer? A fine sheen of sweat covered every inch of her body. She'd taken a bath in the secondhand claw-foot tub Daddy had installed in the washroom tucked at one end of the back porch, but she'd need another one by morning if things didn't cool down. Pulling up the hem of her nightgown, she wiped her brow. Harley came in as she dropped the cotton cloth back across her thighs.

"Bed already?"

He'd hardly said two words all evening. It seemed odd for him to make such a casual comment in light of their earlier disagreement, but she could meet him halfway. The Good Book said you shouldn't let the sun set on your anger. "Yes. It's been a long day."

She watched Harley tug his suspenders down, then remove his shirt. Shadows played along the muscles of his shoulders as he pulled loose one sleeve, then the other. She felt mesmerized by the strength displayed in his broad shoulders. Why did he have to be such a handsome man? It would be easier sometimes if he weren't such a pleasure to look upon.

He sat on the edge of the bed, his back toward her, to remove his boots and socks. The mattress sank on his side, and she had to stiffen her body to keep from rolling toward him. Her fingers itched to reach out and touch the familiar mole that rested low on his left shoulder blade. His spine stood out like a row of pebbles, his firm skin stretched tight over muscles and ribs. He stood to remove his pants, and she shifted her gaze to the ceiling. Even after seven years of marriage, she still felt somewhat shy about this whole undressing procedure. She always tried to be in her nightclothes before Harley came to the bedroom, as her mama had taught her was proper for a lady.

Dressed only in his undershorts, Harley reached up and pulled the light cord, plunging the room into full shadow. Then he threw himself onto the mattress, making it bounce. He tucked his hands behind his head with his elbows splayed outward and let out a heavy sigh. "It *has* been a long day. The walk back from town totin' that crate plumb wore me out." He rolled his head sideways to gaze at her. "Annie?"

She stifled a sigh. How she wished he'd call her something besides that awful nickname. Daddy had called Mama *honeybunch.* It made Mama smile in a secretive way. Of course, Mama had called Daddy *sugar.* Anna Mae couldn't imagine calling Harley *sugar.*

He nudged her with his elbow. "You sleepin' already?"

She realized she hadn't answered. Shifting onto her side, she said, "No. I'm awake. What do you want?"

"You still mad at me?"

His boyish tone tugged at her heart. She wasn't mad, really. Disappointed, yes. Frustrated, too. But not angry. She answered honestly. "No. I'm not mad."

"I know you held fondness for them mules, but I just couldn't see feedin' them when it's so hard just to feed us. They can't earn their keep since I'm not plantin' this year."

He really thought it was all about mules? She swallowed hard. "I know, Harley. It's just . . ." But what could she say that he'd understand? In the past when she'd asked him to consult her, he'd gotten defensive and accused her of thinking he wasn't smart enough to run the farm. She didn't want another argument tonight.

"The job over in Saline County . . ." He went on as if she hadn't spoken, his gaze aimed at the ceiling. "That'll be a real good thing, if I can get on the crew. I like doin' with my hands—buildin' things. And a castle, Annie. A castle'll be made outta stones. Stones last. That castle will still be standin' when our Dottie and Margie are grown women—maybe even still standing when our grandbabies are grown. Gives me a real good feeling to know I'll be putting my hands to something that'll last."

Without thinking, Anna Mae stretched out her hand and placed it on Harley's bare chest. His coarse hair tickled her palm, reminding her of the whisper touch of the daisy petals from the hat he'd bought her. She blinked several times before whispering into the darkened room, "Do you worry sometimes, Harley, that this farm won't last?"

"It's gotta last." His answer came quickly, firmly. "I promised your daddy, an' I don't go back on my word."

She nodded, teasing the hair on his chest until he brought down one hand to hold hers. They lay in silence for long minutes, listening to the wind move the weeping willow branches. An owl hooted in the distance, the echo of its call drifting on the night breeze. Anna Mae yawned, her eyelids slipping closed. She hovered at that stage halfway between sleep and wake until Harley spoke again.

"You got . . . something important . . . to tell me?"

Her fuzzy mind processed the question. Something important? Then she understood. Her heart began to pound. She answered in a quavering tone. "L-like what?"

His swallow seemed loud against the night sounds. "Like why you asked for those saltines."

Fully awake now, she held her breath. She hadn't wanted to tell him yet, but she couldn't outright lie and say the saltines didn't mean anything. Instead of answering directly, she said, "Do you think they mean something?"

He released her hand to roll sideways, facing her. His right hand cupped her hip, his fingers strong and firm. "Anna Mae, are you expecting another baby?"

Suddenly she couldn't find her voice. She couldn't tell by his tone whether he was upset or hopeful.

"You are, aren't you? That's why you've looked so peaked in the mornings. That's why you asked for those saltines. You're gonna have another one, aren't you?"

There was no escaping. Her mouth was dry, and words wouldn't come. So she nodded.

A long sigh came from his side of the bed, and his hand tightened on her hip. "Are you sure?"

The hopeful tone indicated he wanted her to be wrong. Tears pricked in her eyes, but tears were a waste of precious moisture. She blinked them away. "I've missed two cycles, Harley. I'm not wrong."

His arms wrapped around her and gathered her against his chest. Although it was too hot for snuggling, she clung, welcoming the comfort found in his familiar embrace.

"I'm sorry," she choked out.

"Yeah. Me too. Even with this new job, I don't know how we'll manage to feed another one."

She pulled back slightly so she could look into his face. The scant light, coupled with his chiseled features, made his expression seem hard. She licked her lips. "Well, it won't eat right away, you know. And I've already got diapers and little gowns. If I have it at home, like I did Dorothy and Marjorie, we won't have to pay a doctor."

"You can't have a baby without at least a midwife, Annie. That takes money."

"But a midwife's cheaper than a doctor in a hospital. So it won't cost too much—not right at first." She spoke fervently, trying to convince herself as much as Harley.

"Maybe not at first, but . . . Gee, Annie. Another baby?"

That wasn't the response she had hoped for. She wanted him to tell her it was okay, that he loved the first two so much he'd surely love this one, too. She needed him to smile and laugh and spin her around the room the way he had when she'd shared that Dorothy and then Marjorie were on the way. But he just pulled her tight once more against his hot chest, his chin pressed to the top of her head, for several seconds before releasing her.

She shifted to her own half of the bed but remained on her side. She felt him groping for her hand, and she laced her fingers through his. Even if they couldn't celebrate this one's coming, they could commiserate together. That was something, at least.

"Got a name in mind?"

Thinking names already? The birth was months away. But she realized he might be gone right up until the time of this one's arrival. They probably better talk about it now.

"I like the name Rosalyn."

"Why you always thinking it'll be a girl?" Harley's rough thumb traced a pattern on the back of her hand. "And that name's too high-falutin'. What's wrong with naming this one after my mama?"

Anna Mae wrinkled her nose. "Bertha? I'm sorry, Harley, but I just couldn't name my baby Bertha."

Harley threw her hand aside and rolled away to sit on the mattress's edge. He propped his elbows on his knees and put his face in his hands. His bare back appeared white in the muted light from the moon. The muscles between his shoulder blades twitched. She'd upset him, she realized, by disdaining his mama's name. She reached out to stroke his back, but he jerked upright and swiveled to face her.

" 'My baby,' you said. Like you made that child all on your own."

His accusatory tone was like a knife in her heart. She sat up and reached for him again, but he flinched, resisting her touch. Pushing her hand into the folds of her nightgown, she swallowed the lump that rose in her throat. "Harley, I didn't mean it that way."

A harsh laugh cut through the gentle night sounds. "Oh, I think you did, Annie. Everything here—it's all yours. Your daddy left it all to you, and you're always callin' it yours. Never ours." He pointed his finger at her. "But those kids, they're mine, too. And don't you forget it."

"How could I forget it? Of course the girls are yours. Just like this new one's yours."

"It better be." The growling tone held an undercurrent that made the fine hairs on Anna Mae's neck stand up.

Anger swelled in her breast. How dare he make such an accusation? "Harley, that was uncalled for."

He didn't apologize, just turned his back and stared into the gray without speaking. His stubborn position made Anna Mae even angrier. She yanked up his pillow and whopped him across his obstinate back. She knew it didn't hurt him, but it got his attention.

"Anna Mae." A warning rumble.

She ignored the tone and railed at him. "I'm not the one running off to some *supposed* castle-building site halfway across the state. If anyone ought to be worried about somebody being unfaithful, it should be me."

He jumped up so fast the mattress springs twanged for a solid fifteen seconds. He stormed to the door, flung it open, and thumped down the hallway. Anna Mae heard the kitchen door squeak open, then thud shut. A second, softer bang—the porch door—followed.

It occurred to her he was marching around the yard in nothing but his under-drawers. The thought should have been funny. But it wasn't. It wasn't funny at all. She buried her face in her pillow and allowed the tears she'd squelched earlier to come back full force. *I'm so mixed up, God. We never fought like this before the rains stopped coming. Is this drought going to steal everything I care about?*

5

Harley awakened to birdsong. Cardinal, probably, judging by the trill. He yawned, stretching, and the back of his hand encountered something scratchy. Like hay.

Hay?

He popped his eyes open and sat up. In the murky predawn light, he made out the stall walls surrounding his makeshift bed. Rubbing his eyes, he tried to make sense of his location. Why was he in the barn? Then it all flooded back—Annie, the baby, their fight . . .

With a groan, he dropped backward against the rough blanket thrown over a pile of hay. Regret filled his middle when he remembered what he'd said. Of course the baby was his—Annie was too religious to break any laws of that Bible she spent so much time reading. He shouldn't've been so hateful, what with her carrying a child. Women got moody when they carried a child—he'd already been through it twice with her. Why'd he let himself get so upset last night?

Annie's words haunted his memory. *"My baby."* That was why he got so upset. Would anything ever belong to him?

As a boy, sharecropping with his pa, he'd owned little more than the clothes he wore. He'd realized early that those who worked their own land were better off than those working for somebody else, and he'd made the decision that he'd be a landowner someday. Well, in the eyes of the law he was. By marrying Annie right after her daddy's death, he'd become owner of the Elliott land. But if you asked Annie? Nope. This was her land, her house, her barn, her mules—and, according to what she'd said last night, *her* babies growing up on *her* farm.

Bending his legs, he rested his elbows on his widespread knees, letting his head droop low. Well, when he left, she'd have a chance to see how it felt to have everything be hers. Might even be good for her to figure out she wasn't as self-sufficient as she thought. Of course, there were lots of women managing on their own, with all the men traipsing off in search of work. Or traipsing off to escape their responsibilities.

But Harley wasn't one of *those* men. He fully recognized his responsibilities. Pushing to his feet, he set his jaw with determination. He'd promised Annie's daddy that this farm would be cared for, that it would stay in the family. He had to leave it for a spell, but he'd be back. Whether Annie admitted it or not, his own sweat was poured into this land, and that made it his.

Gooseflesh broke out over his arms and legs as he left the barn and headed across the dewy ground to the house. First time he'd felt gooseflesh since he couldn't remember when. He paused on the stoop, savoring the coolness of the morning for a few more minutes before opening the screen door and entering the porch.

When he tugged the kitchen door open, he found Annie already at the table. The tin of saltines sat open in front of her, and she held one cracker, her hand hovering midway between the tabletop and her mouth. When she saw him, her face filled with pink, and she lowered her hand to the table.

"Go ahead an' eat your saltines, Annie." His voice sounded croaky. He cleared his throat. "I'm gonna get dressed."

She gave a slight nod, her head down. He crossed to the bedroom, dressed quickly, then turned to go back to the kitchen. But Annie stood in the bedroom doorway. She twisted her toe against the wood floor, her eyes downcast. Even in her wrinkled nightgown, with her long hair all sleep-tangled, she was beautiful. Love welled up so hard it almost choked him.

They stood for long seconds without saying anything. He wanted her to speak first—it was always easier to respond to a conversation than start one. His heart bumped hard inside his chest as he waited. He hoped they wouldn't fight again. Not today. Not when he'd be leaving.

"You should say good-bye to the girls," she said quietly.

So that was how it was gonna be. Well, he wouldn't be the one to apologize first. He nodded. "Bring 'em in here."

After she'd left to wake the girls, he shimmied into his britches while he listened to the homey morning sounds of his family: Dottie's sleep-raspy voice greeting her mother, the baby's hiccupping cry, Annie's sweet voice soothing Margie. He'd miss these morning sounds.

Dottie bounced in, her hair all tousled, smelling like sweat. When he patted the bed, she clambered up and sat cross-legged beside him, her little hand on his chest.

"Morning, Daddy," she chirped, then leaned forward to give him a morning kiss.

"Mornin', Dottie-doll. Did you sleep good?"

"Uh-huh."

"Good dreams?"

"Uh-huh."

He tickled her ribs, making her squeal. Then he pulled her into a hug and kissed her hair. Annie came in carrying Margie.

"C'mere, Margie-girl." Harley held out his arms, and Margie tumbled from Annie's arms into his. He cuddled Margie in one arm and Dottie in the other. His girls . . . Dottie was big enough he didn't need to worry, but he hoped Margie wouldn't forget him.

Annie stood beside the bed, a smile on

her face. It was good to see her smile again. "I'll go get us some breakfast started."

Harley nodded. Annie left the room, and Harley played pat-a-cake with Margie while talking with Dottie. "Didja like those gumdrops, Dottie?"

"Yeah! So did Smokey."

Harley swallowed his grin. He couldn't imagine the big barn cat chewing through the rubbery gumdrops. "Oh yeah? He eat quite a few?"

"No." Dottie picked at her big toenail. "Only one. But he ate it for a long time."

Harley nearly snorted with amusement. But Dottie didn't care to be laughed at, so he kept it under control. "Well, it's real nice of you to share with Ol' Smokey."

"I know."

"Listen, Dottie-doll . . ." Margie played with his fingers, burbling to herself. He used his free arm to scoop Dottie close to his hip. "Would you like it if Daddy had money to buy you gumdrops every month?"

Dottie's blue eyes widened. "Every month?" Then her face puckered. "What is that?"

"What is what?"

"A month."

"Oh . . . a month?"

"Uh-huh."

Harley cocked one eyebrow, searching for a way to explain. "A month is about four weeks." Dottie's expression didn't clear. "You know what months are. They're on your mama's calendar in the kitchen—January, February, March . . ."

Dottie brightened. "Oh! You mean I'd get gumdrops in Janarary and Febeeary and all the months?"

Harley blew out a breath of relief. "That's right."

"I'd like that, Daddy."

Harley grinned. Good. This would be easy, then. "Well, guess what, doll? Daddy's gonna take a job that'll give us enough money for me to buy you gumdrops every month."

Dottie squealed and bounced her bottom against the bed. The noise startled Margie, whose lower lip poked out. Harley lifted her and placed her on his stomach. She toyed with his nose and lips as he spoke to Dottie. "Daddy's gonna go build a castle."

"Like in my storybook?"

Harley remembered the fairy tale book

Annie had read to the girls. "Yeah. Just like in your book."

"Can I be the princess in it? And let my hair grow real, real long like in the story?"

Harley had a hard time answering this time. Dottie's bright-eyed innocence nearly broke his heart. It would be plenty hard to walk down the road, away from his sweet-faced little girl. "Well, Dottie-doll, you're gonna have to stay here with Mama instead of livin' in that castle. The castle's pretty far away."

Dottie chewed her lower lip, and her forehead wrinkled. Finally she said, "You aren't building the castle here?"

Harley swallowed. "No."

Dottie sat up on her knees. "Where you gonna go, Daddy?"

"A place called Lindsborg. It's a far walk, but I'll be back when the castle's done."

Dottie threw herself against his chest, dislodging Margie, who set up an immediate howl of protest. "I don't need gumdrops every month, Daddy. You stay here. Okay? Okay, Daddy?" Her shrill voice pierced Harley's ears. And his heart.

If Harley had been a praying man, he'd have started seeking the Lord's help right then. Margie squalled in one ear and Dottie begged in the other while he patted and cajoled, but nothing he did seemed to help at all.

Annie rushed into the room. She took the baby, leaving Harley the task of comforting Dottie. Harley wrapped both arms around the little girl and rocked her back and forth.

"Listen to me, Dottie-doll. Daddy's only gonna be gone for a little while. An' when I come back, I'll get you those gumdrops, just like I promised, okay?"

Dottie pushed her hands against his chest, freeing herself. Hooking her heels on the edge of the mattress, she pulled herself from the bed, then stood, glaring at him. Her look of betrayal stung worse than his daddy's belt ever had. "I don't want no gumdrops!" She ran from the room.

Harley pushed himself off the mattress and took two steps toward Annie. Margie, in Annie's arms, put her fingers in her mouth. Plump tears quivered on her lower lashes. Harley toyed with the baby's hair as he stood silently beside his wife.

"Annie, I—"

"Don't talk to me, Harley." Her voice, like Dottie's, stung like a lash. "You said you were going, so just go." Without a glance in his direction, she charged down the hall, carrying Margie with her.

He stood in the middle of the floor, his hands balled into fists. *Follow her,* his thoughts urged. *Make her understand.* He swallowed his own temper and followed, but he stopped at the end of the hall and watched Annie plunk Margie into the high chair and tie a bib around the baby's neck. She yanked out a kitchen chair, seated herself, and slid a fried egg onto a plate. Using a fork, she chopped the egg into small bites—*clack! clack! clack!* He was surprised the fork didn't go clear through the table, as much pressure as she put behind it. And when she started shoving food into Margie's mouth without saying her customary prayer, Harley knew without a doubt the intensity of her anger.

She was in no mood to listen. Not to anybody. Not to anything.

He turned back to the bedroom. Digging around in the closet, he unearthed an old pillowcase that could serve as a pack. Annie had done the laundry yesterday, so he tossed in all his clean drawers, three shirts, and two pairs of dungarees. He rummaged through his socks and packed all the ones he could find that didn't have holes. He scratched his head, deciding what else he'd need, then rolled his worn jean jacket into a ball and pushed it underneath everything else. It was hotter'n blazes now, but who knew how long he'd be gone—he'd better be prepared for cooler days later.

Using an old rawhide shoelace, he tied the pack closed, then sank onto the edge of the bed, the bulky bag in his lap, listening to the scrape of the fork against the plate, Margie's jabber, and Annie's low-pitched responses. When he was sure the baby had been fed, he heaved a sigh, lifted his pack, and headed to the kitchen.

6

Margie sat in her high chair, gumming a cracker, and Annie stood at the sink, her hands on the edge of the counter, her gaze aimed out the window. When Harley cleared his throat, she jumped but didn't turn around.

Stubborn woman.

"I was thinkin' I'd take along some of those crackers, and maybe some cheese."

Annie's shoulders lifted and fell in a gesture of defeat. "Suit yourself. Cheese is in the icebox, crackers in the cupboard."

But she didn't say which cupboard, and he had to open three doors before he found them. Couldn't she help just a little bit? He held his tongue as he wrapped the cheese and crackers in a square of waxed paper. He untied his bag and dropped in the food, then tied the thing shut again. Annie still hadn't looked at him.

Leaving the pack on the floor by the door, he crossed to the high chair and kissed Margie's head. She reached her dimpled hand toward him, and he kissed her messy fingers. The back of his nose burned. She was still so little—not quite a year yet. Would she even know him when he came back? He gave her one more kiss and then straightened, his gaze sweeping around the room.

"Where'd Dottie go?"

Annie dumped the breakfast dishes into the basin, still avoiding his gaze. "I imagine she's hiding out. She'll come in when she's hungry."

Harley watched Annie lean over the sink and scrub at a plate. She scrubbed and scrubbed. No way the plate could need that much scrubbing. A part of him wanted to walk up behind her, wrap his arms around her middle, and kiss her neck. But pride kept him beside the high chair. Still, he offered softly, "I'll miss you, Annie." *You have no idea how much.*

She stiffened, her hands stilled, and her chin jerked upward. But she said nothing.

"You'll be okay?" He hadn't meant to ask it. He'd meant to say it like he believed it.

Her chin rose higher. "Of course I will." Her voice sounded tight, like she was forcing the words past a mighty lump. "I've got plenty of starch in my spine."

"And I'll stop by Jack Berkley's on my way out—remind him to check in on you."

She swallowed audibly. "It'll be nice, I suppose, to have *someone* check on us."

Harley wasn't stupid. He caught the barb. Spinning toward the door, he grated, "I gotta get goin'." He snatched up his pack and slammed through the door. One hard smack sent the porch door flying. His boots hit the packed earth, sending up a cloud of dust that coated his pant legs as he clomped across the yard toward the driveway that led to the road.

He heard the sound of pounding footsteps behind him. His heart lifted. *Annie?* But the frantic cry, "Daddy! Daddy!" identified his pursuer. He spun, dropped to one knee, and captured Dottie as she flung herself against his chest. His hat fell off and landed upside down in the dirt beside him.

The hug turned almost desperate as he cradled Dorothy's head in his wide hand and held her against his pounding heart.

"Dottie-doll, I'm gonna miss you somethin' fierce."

"Don't go, Daddy, please? I'm sorry. I won't be mean no more."

A lump filled Harley's throat, nearly choking him. "Dottie, I gotta go. An' it's got nothin' to do with you being mean. I gotta get some money for our farm. Can't grow crops without rain, an' there's no more rain in Kansas." Harley set Dottie in front of him. "But I'll be back. Maybe sooner, maybe later, but I won't be gone forever."

"Daddeeeee . . ." Dottie began to wail.

"Listen, darlin', I need you to be a big girl and help your mama while I'm gone." His fingers curled around Dottie's narrow shoulders. His chest ached with each heave of those skinny shoulders. "You remind your mama that Jack can tote the milk cans from the 'fraidy hole, and you help in the garden."

"I w-will, Daddy."

"Do you promise?"

Dottie nodded, her tangled blond hair flying around her face. Her chin quivered.

"I promise. An' you'll come back, right, Daddy?"

Harley clutched her to his chest once more, breathing in the scent of her sweaty hair. His throat convulsed. "I promise, Dottie." He cupped her head in his hands and kissed her forehead, both tear-damp cheeks, and the top of her head. Rising, he pointed to the house. "Go on, now." His voice turned gruff, roughened by emotion he could barely contain. "And be a good girl, you hear?"

Dottie nodded again, tears still raining down her pale face. She picked up Harley's hat and handed it to him. He plopped it on his head, chucked his daughter beneath the chin, and headed for the gate. When he reached the bend in the road, he heard her call, "I love you, Daddy!"

He turned to walk backward, lifting his hand in a wave. "I love you, too, Dottie-doll!"

Anna Mae heard every word between Dorothy and Harley through the open kitchen window. Her fingers gripped the sink edge so hard it hurt as she battled the urge to run outside, race down the lane, and throw herself against Harley as freely as their daughter had. But her fingers didn't let go. Not even when Harley finally turned forward again and the sight of his retreating back conjured memories of another leave-taking—her brother, Ben, marching off to join the Army. She hadn't been much older than Dorothy.

What if this was the last time she saw Harley?

Come back, Harley. Please come back.

But the words remained confined to her heart, and of course he didn't hear them. A weight pressed against her chest. Even if he heard, he wouldn't heed them. He'd made up his mind, and once Harley decided on something, there was no dissuading him. There never had been.

She found her voice and called, "Dorothy! Come on in here now and eat your breakfast!"

Dorothy released the gate post and turned slowly, shielding her eyes with her hand as she peered toward the house. Then she looked back at the road.

"Dorothy! Now!"

The stern tone set Dorothy's feet in motion, but the child scuffed slowly, head down, shoulders slumped. Anna Mae shifted her gaze so she wouldn't have to watch her daughter's heartrending journey to the house.

The moment Dorothy stepped into the kitchen, she ran across the floor and wrapped her arms around Anna Mae's middle, snuffling against her mother's apron. Anna Mae gave her a loving pat, then set her aside. "Come on, Dorothy. Let's get you cleaned up and dressed, then you need to eat some breakfast."

"Don't want breakfast. I want Daddy."

"Well, not eating doesn't fix a thing, and it sure won't bring your daddy back." Anna Mae kept her tone matter-of-fact. "So come on, now. Might as well face the day." She gave Dorothy a little push on the back of the head, and the child moved toward the bedroom. As Dorothy trudged away, Anna Mae's gaze, as if by its own will, lifted to the window and looked once more toward the road.

No sign of Harley at all.

Harley paused, bending down on one knee to retie the lace on his left boot. He gave the laces a firm jerk. Rising, he pressed

his hands to the small of his back and released a low groan. He'd left his old boots
on the porch of Martin's store after he'd
bought this new pair. Still some wear in the
old brown leathers—figured somebody
could use them. Now he wished he'd
brought them with him instead. These new
ones were so stiff they'd rubbed blisters on
both heels.

"A blessin' and a curse," he muttered
to himself. New shoes these days was a
blessing, but those blisters . . . His mumbled comment reminded him of Annie's
pregnancy. Mixed emotions concerning the
baby rolled through his gut. Guilt pressed at
him for leaving her when she was sick with
a pregnancy. "But," he reasoned aloud,
talking to himself for the lack of other company, "would it make sense to stay put
and do chores and let my family starve?
Can't sacrifice it all for the sake of that baby,
can I?"

He chose not to answer himself. Didn't
know what to say in response anyway. He
massaged the aching muscles in his back
as he scanned the horizon. Must be about
eight o'clock, he figured. He'd need to find
a place to hole up for the night pretty soon.

He'd made good distance today, following the highway. According to Martin's calculations, Lindsborg was a little less than one hundred miles northeast of Spencer. He'd walked farther in his lifetime. Of course, he'd been younger then. Seemed like the last two years, with the constant troubles, had turned him older than his twenty-nine years.

A train whistle drifted across the quiet landscape. Harley grabbed up his poke and slung it over his shoulder. Forcing his tired feet to get moving, he considered that train. Following the railroad tracks might be easier going than roadways—more direct. But he'd only walk along the tracks. He wouldn't hop the train. Although lots of fellas did that these days, he didn't feel right about riding when he couldn't pay. Plus it was too risky. Some railroad worker might catch him and clop him on the head.

"But when I get that job an' I'm makin' some money"—the sound of his own voice comforted him—"I'll buy me a ticket to go home on. It'll be cold by then, probably. Don't need to freeze my hide if I can avoid it."

Ahead and to the right, he spotted a

farmhouse with a large barn. Maybe the folks there would let him bed down in the hay. Better than sleeping on the hard ground. His stomach growled, reminding him he'd eaten everything he had packed. All this walking increased his appetite. Maybe he could work off the price of a dinner, too. Worth asking, he decided. He left the road and headed for the farm.

Two large, speckled dogs greeted him with noisy barks as he entered the yard, but they didn't seem fierce. Harley stuck out his hand and let them give him a good sniff. One ran back toward the house, but the second one trotted along beside Harley like a furry escort. By the time he reached the porch, a man stood outside, alerted by the dogs.

"Howdy." The unsmiling man looked Harley up and down as the dogs sat on their haunches at their master's side.

Harley gave a friendly nod. "Howdy. Name's Harley Phipps. I'm headin' for Lindsborg an' need a place to sleep. Wonderin' if you'd mind if I slept in your barn."

"Yup. I mind."

Harley pulled off his hat. "I'm willin' to do some work for the privilege."

"Don't need nothin' done." The man plunged his hands into his overall pockets. His sunburned face remained stoic. "Don't plan to become a stoppin'-off place for bums an' hobos. So just head on down the road."

Bums and hobos? Harley bristled at the implication. "Listen, mister—"

"No, you listen. Either you go, or I'll sic the dogs on you." The man removed one hand from his pocket and snapped his fingers. Immediately the dogs rose to their feet, teeth bared.

Harley plunked his hat on his head and gave a wave of his hand. "Fine. Have a good evenin'." Anger churned through his belly as he headed back to the road. Bum? Hobo? He wasn't either! He was a man looking to make things better for his family! What right did that ol' coot have to accuse him of being a bum?

The anger made his feet pump hard despite the throbbing pain in his heels. It carried him to another lane that ended with a two-story farmhouse. Dusk fell heavily around him; he needed sleep and shelter. Yet he hesitated. *Don't know if I can handle gettin' turned away a second time.*

Then he remembered something Annie's daddy had said when trying to decide whether to switch from wheat to corn. *"Nothing ventured, nothing gained."* A simple comment, but remembering it gave Harley the gumption to march on up to the second farmhouse. No dogs ran through this yard. The yellow glow in the windows told him folks were still awake inside. He stepped up on the porch and banged his knuckles against the door. A shadowy figure appeared behind the lace curtain shrouding the door's glass pane, then the door opened and a middle-aged woman in an apron and kerchief smiled at him.

The smile eased the ache in his heart. He swept off his hat. "Evenin', ma'am."

"Evening to you." Her eyes seemed kind.

"I'm travelin' on to Lindsborg where I got a job waiting, and I wondered if I might bed down in your barn tonight. I'm willin' to do some chores in return for the favor."

The woman looked over her shoulder. "Eldo?"

"Yeah?" a deep voice replied from somewhere in the house.

"Can you come here a minute?"

Harley peeked through the opening and

saw a tall, wiry man come from an arched doorway at the back of the sitting room. The man stopped behind the woman and looked at Harley.

"This here is—" She paused, peering up at Harley. "I didn't catch your name."

"Harley Phipps." Harley stuck out his hand.

The man shook it. "Good to meet you, Mr. Phipps."

The woman spoke again. "Mr. Phipps is traveling to a job in Lindsborg and wants to sleep in our barn tonight."

The tall man shrugged. "Sure. It's nothin' fancy, but the hay's clean. Make yourself comfortable."

Harley released a sigh of relief. "Thank you. I'll chore for you in the morning, if you like."

"Well, a pile of hay is hardly worth chores," the woman said. Her smile crinkled the corners of her eyes, reminding Harley of Annie's mother. "You plan on having some breakfast with us, young man. That'd be a good exchange for chores."

Harley couldn't stop the smile that grew on his face. "Thank you, ma'am."

"You're welcome. You get some sleep.

We'll see you in the morning." She closed the door.

Harley turned from the porch and headed across the ground to the barn. Inside, it was dark, but after a few minutes his eyes adjusted enough to find an empty stall. He sat down and tugged off his boots. Felt good to have his feet free. He wiggled his toes and stretched out full length in the sweet-smelling hay.

His eyes slipped closed, and behind his lids he reviewed his day. Faces flitted through his memory—Dottie's, tear-streaked and sad; Annie's, rigid and determined; the first farmer's, hard and unrelenting; and finally the woman's, kind and welcoming. The last one was the most pleasant to remember. He held on to the image of the woman, whose kindness warmed him from the inside out. With her crinkly smile hovering in the fringes of his mind, he drifted off to sleep.

7

Anna Mae pressed her forehead to Bossie's warm flank and willed her muscles to keep working just a little longer. Her arms burned, her fingers cramped, and all she wanted to do was quit. But the milking wouldn't get done if she didn't do it. So she set her jaw and made herself continue the squeeze-pull-squeeze-pull until every last bit of milk had been stripped.

Not even an hour into her day, and already she was tired. Her night had been restless, lonely. The bed didn't feel right without Harley in it. And funny how every little creak of the farmhouse seemed threatening with him gone. *Lord, I've got to have my rest. You're going to have to remove these fears and let me sleep nights, or I'll be just useless to the girls and this farm.*

Her muscles quivered as she slid the bucket from between Bossie's legs. Once it was safely out of reach of the cow's feet, she swiped the back of her hand across her forehead and let out a low moan. "Oh, Bossie, how am I going to do this when the baby makes my belly so big it gets in the way?"

"Well, I suppose you could ask a kind neighbor to do the milking for you."

Anna Mae spun so fast she nearly fell off the stool. A man stood in the open doorway of the barn. The rosy sun coming behind him put him completely in shadow, but she recognized him instantly. Her hands flew to her wild hair, trying to pull the strands into a tail. Then, realizing what she was doing, she balled her hands into fists and pressed them against her apron. Why should she care if she looked a sight? There was no reason to impress Jack Berkley.

She struggled to her feet, placing one hand on Bossie's broad back for support. "J-Jack. I didn't expect you to come by 'til midafternoon."

He strode forward a few feet. His features

came into view, and she could see his familiar broad, easy smile. "I figured on giving
you a hand with the milking, but I see you've
got it done. You always were one for tack-
ling whatever needed tackled."

The approval in his tone sent a coil of
warmth through Anna Mae's middle. She
pushed a hand to her stomach to remove
the feeling and responded tartly. "Not much
else I can do. Poor old Bossie here wouldn't
appreciate me leaving her untended."

Jack took one more step toward her.
Even though a good four feet still separated
them, it was too close for Anna Mae's comfort. She moved to the other side of the milk
bucket.

"Did I hear you say you're expecting another baby?" Jack's voice indicated surprise. "Harley didn't say anything about that
when he came by."

"We only just found out." Why would
Harley need to mention that to Jack anyway? It wasn't any of his business.

Jack shook his head, his sun-bleached
hair flopping down across his wide forehead. "Seems an odd time for him to be
taking off, with you expecting."

Although a part of her agreed, this wasn't

a conversation she wanted to have with Jack. She shrugged, then bent over to pick up the milk bucket. Before she could straighten, however, Jack stepped forward and took the bucket from her hands.

"You shouldn't be lifting things like that," he scolded. "Let me do it."

Anna Mae didn't have much choice except to let go. Jack was stronger, and a tussle over the bucket would only spill the milk. But she seethed with resentment. Who did he think he was, telling her what she could and couldn't do? There had been a time, maybe, when he could have demanded the right, but not now. Not anymore.

She plunked her hands on her hips and glowered at him. "Jack Berkley, I am not helpless. I am capable of carrying that bucket of milk to my kitchen."

Jack flashed a sardonic grin that brought back a rush of memories. "Feisty first thing in the morning, aren't you? Well, Harley told me you'd probably resist my help. But you shouldn't be overdoing. So . . . whether you like it or not, Anna Mae, I'm gonna be around to help."

He turned and headed toward the house. Anna Mae followed as far as the barn door, then stood, glaring at his back, until he reached the screened porch. When he stretched out his hand for the porch door, she released a squawk and raced across the ground to tug his sleeve.

"You don't just go walking into my house without permission!"

He quirked one eyebrow at her. His expression taunted her with the reminder that he'd come and gone freely through this door without knocking all through their growing-up years. Without a word, he opened the screen door, placed the bucket on the porch floor, then stepped back and allowed the door to slam shut. The door bounced twice in its frame before settling. Immediately, from inside, a baby began to wail.

Anna Mae stomped her foot against the ground. "And now you woke up Marjorie." She pointed to the road. "I know what Harley told you, but you can just listen to me! I don't need your help. I don't *want* your help. I'm a grown woman, and I can handle this farm on my own. Get out of here, Jack Berkley, and don't come back!"

* * *

Jack chuckled as he turned his team toward his own home. Marriage hadn't tamed Anna Mae one little bit. She was just as spunky and independent as she'd always been. With those snapping eyes, pert chin, and yellow hair that tumbled around her shoulders, she was every bit as appealing in womanhood as she'd been as a teenager. That Harley was a lucky man, being able to call Anna Mae his wife.

Even after all these years, Jack still carried a regret that he hadn't been able to win Anna Mae's heart. Oh, he'd tried. But somehow she'd never been able to stop seeing him as her playmate—another brother to chase and tease, a friend to laugh with and dream with. He'd been privy to all her secrets, and he'd foolishly thought that meant she loved him. But he'd found out differently when he'd asked her to marry him and she told him she'd fallen in love with her daddy's hired hand.

Jack snorted, remembering how he'd tried to talk her out of it. Harley was just a drifter, probably only wanting her daddy's land, he'd told her. And how she had argued! After that, she didn't talk to him for weeks. Not until her wedding day, when she'd thanked him for coming as impersonally as she'd greet some long-distance cousin. If she'd seen how his heart was breaking, she'd given no sign of it.

He snapped the reins, urging the team to hurry up. *She proved me wrong on Harley, that's for sure.* The man had turned out to be trustworthy. Jack couldn't fault him for the way he cared for the farm, cared for Anna Mae, and cared for those two little girls. But now Harley had up and left and entrusted his most precious possessions to Jack's care.

And boy, he'd enjoy having the excuse to see Anna Mae every day. Sure, she'd chased him off this morning, but that wouldn't stop him. He'd give her a couple of hours to cool off, to get today's milk ready to go, then he'd head back. She'd be more agreeable after she got the sleep washed from her eyes.

A wry chuckle found its way from his chest. Well, *maybe* she'd be more agreeable. But whether she was or not, he'd told Harley he'd help out. So he would. And Miz Anna Mae Phipps better just get used to it.

*   *   *

Bang!

Harley bolted upright, his feet flying from the hay with the shock of waking so abruptly. Pink morning light poured through the open doorway of the barn, and he rubbed his eyes, trying to orient himself. When he removed his hands, he got a second surprise. Directly in front of him stood a tall, husky, overall-clad man with the biggest grin Harley had ever seen. To Harley's sleep-fuzzy brain, the man appeared to be Li'l Abner, the character in a cartoon strip from the newspaper, come to life. Was he dreaming?

"Morning, mister. Sorry I woke you. The wind tore that barn door right outta my hands and slammed it against the wall." He stuck out a huge, beefy hand. "Grab hold and I'll help you up."

Harley followed the direction. The other man gave a yank that had Harley on his feet before he knew he was moving.

"Name's Dirk Farley." The man's smile stretched from ear to ear.

Harley cleared his throat. "I'm Harley—Harley Phipps."

Dirk Farley threw back his head and laughed. The cows shifted in their stalls at the raucous sound. "Well, ain't we a pair—Harley and Farley. That's pretty funny."

Harley quirked one brow. Was the man simpleminded?

"Well, c'mon, Harley." Dirk gave Harley a firm slap on the shoulder that sent him forward two feet. "Ma tells me you're willing to chore for breakfast, so I'm gonna let you do some milkin'. But first, let's splash some water on your face. You don't look full awake yet."

Harley's muscles complained as he followed the large man into the morning sunlight. He squinted into Dirk's smiling face. Outside, it became clear the man was little more than a boy—although a very large boy. Dirk couldn't be more than twenty years old. He pointed to a pump and invited, "Go splash yourself good. Get rid of the travel grit. Water'll be cold, but hard work will warm you soon enough. I'll be inside getting started on the milking." He turned and ambled back into the barn.

Harley pumped the handle on the hydrant until a steady stream of water splattered out. He stuck his head under the flow, shivering as the icy water spilled down the back of his shirt. But it felt good to get rid of the sweat and grime of yesterday's long trek.

He pushed up his shirt-sleeves and washed his arms and then stuck his feet under the water. The cold water soothed the blisters that looked angry and raw this morning. Dirk came out as Harley plunked down on the ground to tug on his socks and boots.

"Hoo-ey, Harley, those're some bad-looking sores." Sympathy underscored the overgrown boy's deep tone. "Ma's got some healing ointment you could put on them. She'd probably also give you some old sheeting to keep 'em covered so they don't get any worse." He crouched next to Harley and picked up one of his boots. "New boots?"

Harley nodded.

Dirk whistled through his teeth as he examined the boot, turning it this way and that. "Haven't seen new boots in . . . well, a coon's age, I reckon. You're a lucky man to own new boots." He grinned, handing the boot back to Harley. "Although blisters're hardly considered lucky, huh?"

Harley agreed with that. "I'd appreciate the ointment," he admitted.

"Well, head on to the back door and give a knock. Let Ma fix you up before you start that milkin'. The cows'll keep for a while yet, but those feet of yours . . ." Dirk scratched his head. "Don't know how you made it walking yesterday."

"Made it 'cause I had to." Harley pushed to his feet. "And I can milk a cow in my bare feet. I'd rather get the work done before I trouble your mother for anything."

Dirk shrugged his massive shoulders and straightened to his feet. Harley followed him into the barn. Three cows with full udders waited. Dirk pointed to the middle stall, and Harley found clean pails and a bucket of soapy water with a rag slung over its side. After cleaning the cow's udder, he grabbed a pail, straddled a small stool, and got busy. Dirk finished his cow first, then moved to the third stall. Harley finished midway through Dirk's second milking. He picked up both his and Dirk's full pails of milk. "I'll take these in," he said.

Dirk gave a nod in return, and Harley headed toward the house on bare feet, taking care not to spill a drop of milk. His thoughts drifted back to his own little farm outside of Spencer. Was Annie milking right about now? Or had Jack taken over the task? He hoped Annie wasn't so stubborn she refused Jack's help. Then again, Jack was plenty stubborn, too. He released a light chuckle, imagining the battle of wills no doubt taking place between his wife and their closest neighbor.

Harley set down one pail to knock on the back door. In a few seconds the door opened, and the smiling face Harley remembered from the night before greeted him.

"Why, come right on in, young man, and set those pails on the table there." She pointed to a scarred table that stood in the middle of the large kitchen. "Did you sleep well?"

Harley hefted the pails to the table before turning to nod at the woman. "Yes, ma'am. Real well. I was pretty tired. Probably could've slept on a bed of rocks." Then, concerned he might sound ungrateful, he added, "But I appreciate the soft hay."

"Oh, you're welcome." She bustled back to the stove and pushed a wooden spoon around in an iron skillet. An enticing aroma filled Harley's nostrils, making his stomach lurch with desire. "Got some potatoes with ham and onions cooking here, and soon as Dirk's done with the milking, he'll bring in the eggs. They'll be fried up in no time. How many eggs can you eat at a sitting?"

Harley stood uncertainly on his dusty bare feet in the middle of the floor. He wanted to answer honestly, yet didn't want to take advantage of this woman's kindness. Scratching his whisker-covered chin, he answered, "Just one'll be fine, ma'am."

She turned and looked at him with raised brows and pursed lips. "One? Just one? Now, young man, I can't imagine you've limited yourself to one egg since you grew out of knee pants."

Harley couldn't help it. A grin tugged at his cheeks. He pulled one finger along his lips to control the smile, but it kept growing.

The woman laughed. "Uh-huh, that's what I thought." She turned back to the stove. "Why don't you head out and give Dirk a hand. Breakfast'll be ready soon."

Twenty minutes later Harley sat down at the table with Dirk and his parents. The older man offered a brief prayer of thanks for the food, reminding Harley again of Annie and home. Homesickness created a hole in his middle. But fried eggs and a pile of potatoes seasoned well with ham and onions did an adequate job of filling the emptiness.

Halfway through the meal, the woman said, "So, Mr. Phipps, what kind of job do you have waiting in Lindsborg?"

Harley swallowed the last bite before answering. "Building, ma'am. WPA group's putting up a castle. I figure on helping."

"A castle?" Dirk put down his fork and stared at Harley. "You're funnin' me."

Harley shook his head. "No. They're hirin' men with strong backs to build a castle and picnic grounds. Has something to do with an explorer named Coronado."

"Coronado." The woman looked pensively across the table. "Yes, I seem to recall seeing something about that in the newspaper a while back."

"My farm's not done too well the past couple years, what with the drought. Hardly any money comin' in at all. That paycheck will be welcome to me and my family."

"You have a family, Mr. Phipps?"

A band of longing wrapped itself around Harley's chest as he thought of Dottie and Margie. "Oh yes, ma'am. Got me two pretty little girls." His lips quavered as he thought of Annie. Did she regret not seeing him off with a proper good-bye yesterday?

"Ma," Dirk interjected, "Harley's got some blisters on his heels. Can you fix him up before he heads out again?"

"Why, sure I can!" She gave Harley another crinkling smile. "You just sit tight, Mr. Phipps. We'll doctor those blisters for you, and I'll pack you a lunch to take along. Something to tide you over 'til you can get another good meal."

"Oh, but—"

"Don't you argue with me, Mr. Phipps. The Good Book instructs us to love our neighbors as ourselves. Wouldn't want my own boy here to go hungry." She turned her back on Harley and headed to the sink.

Dirk grinned in Harley's direction. "Don't argue with Ma. You can't win."

Harley shrugged. He started to answer, but the older man, who'd been silent since his prayer, interrupted.

"Boy, you figure that crew of workers would have room for one more?"

Harley turned in the older man's direction. "I . . . I don't know for sure, sir, but I don't guess it would hurt to ask. Why?"

The man rested his elbows on the table.

"We been praying for a way to keep our farm going. Haven't had a decent crop in three years. Don't know what'll happen in the next years, either, what with the topsoil blown to kingdom come. But Dirk here—he's got a strong back and willin' spirit. If that crew would take him, sure would help us out."

Dirk grinned widely. "Would you mind a travelin' partner, Harley?"

Harley looked from one man to the other. This was a strange turn of events. He offered another shrug. "I don't mind. Less lonely, I reckon."

Dirk looked toward the sink, where the woman ladled steaming water from the stove's reservoir into a dishpan. "Hey, Ma, when you pack Harley's lunch here, pack one for me, too. I'm gonna go castle buildin'!"

8

Anna Mae fed the girls their breakfast, then tied a length of braided rags, strung with several small toys, to the high chair to entertain the baby. With Marjorie's gurgling as an accompaniment, Anna Mae performed her morning household chores.

By ten o'clock, she had separated the cream from the milk and churned the cream into butter. She left a pitcher of milk in the icebox for their own drinking and cooking and hauled the extra to the cellar to join the can full from yesterday's milking. She scowled for a moment at the row of milk cans, realizing the milk and cream would spoil if it wasn't taken to town. "Jack'll have to do it," she muttered to herself, "but oh, how I hate letting him!"

Well, it would keep for a while yet. She didn't need to deal with it right now. She stomped up the steps, went back into the kitchen to retrieve Marjorie, then turned her attention to the garden. Weeding needed to be done, as well as watering. She heaved a huge sigh. So much to do! Then she remembered Harley had said Dorothy was big enough to help. She cupped one hand beside her mouth and called, "Dorothy?"

The little girl came running from her playing spot.

Anna Mae touched Dorothy's hair. "Want to help Mama?"

Dorothy squinted upward. "Do I gotta watch Marjorie?"

"No, I want you to water the garden."

"Okay!"

Anna Mae set Marjorie down in the shade of the bushes with a stern order. "You stay right here." She ran a bucket of water from the pump by the barn, hefted it to the edge of the garden plot, and plunked it on the ground where Dorothy could reach. She then instructed Dorothy on how to water the garden. She finished with, "Every little plant needs a good drink, darlin'. Can you do that?"

"Sure!" The child's enthusiasm lifted Anna Mae's spirits.

Anna Mae watched Dorothy walk with the dipper held in both hands to the rows of tiny shoots of green, splash the water onto one fledgling plant, then run to the bucket for another dipperful. The precious look of concentration on the little girl's face tugged at Anna Mae's heart. She called, "Do a good job, and Mama will fix you a treat this afternoon."

"Okay!"

Anna Mae kept one eye on Marjorie as she pulled the weeds that intruded and tried to steal nourishment from their garden plants. The weeding finished, she took the baby inside and prepared a simple lunch of bologna sandwiches and canned peaches.

Dorothy came in just as Anna Mae put the plates on the table. "Mama, I put the bucket back in the lean-to."

"Good girl." Anna Mae sent her daughter a smile. "Now climb up to the sink and get your hands washed. I think you're wearing half the dirt from the garden."

While the baby napped and Dorothy

curled up in her bed with a picture book, Anna Mae followed through on her promise to treat Dorothy. She pulled out her mama's sugar cookie recipe and got to baking. When the first batch came from the oven, mounded high with bits of sugar sparkling on the light brown tops, the aroma made her stomach growl. She smiled as she glanced out the open kitchen window. Harley could smell Mama's sugar cookies baking from a mile away. Shouldn't be long, and he'd be heading for the house, an eager grin on his face, ready to beg a fresh-baked treat.

Her smile vanished as she remembered Harley wasn't out in the barn or the fields. The smell of cookies wouldn't reach him—not with him miles down the road. Slumping forward, she fought tears.

How she disliked tears. A sign of weakness, that's all they were. Strong people didn't sit around boo-hooing over every little thing. And hadn't she always been told she was a strong person? *Lord, this crying doesn't fix anything. I know it's just because the baby's got me all mixed up inside, but I've got to be strong for my girls. Please make these tears go away.*

The brief prayer helped. Mama always said ask and you'd receive. So she asked once more for strength, straightened her shoulders, and sniffed hard. The tears dried up. She reached for the spatula to remove the cookies from the tin sheet. While that batch cooled on a wooden rack set beneath the window, she rolled balls of dough and pushed them flat with a glass dipped in sugar. She hummed as she worked, imagining Dorothy's pleased face when she came out from her rest.

Just as she leaned down, apron protecting her hands, to remove the last batch from the oven, she heard a scuffling behind her. Shaking her head, she said, "Dorothy, I told you to wait until Mama called you. What are you doing out here?"

"Sorry. Wrong again."

Anna Mae snapped upright, spinning from the oven to face the back door. A man stood in the open kitchen doorway, leaning against the doorjamb with arms crossed and one toe propped against the linoleum floor. A familiar, lazy grin lifted one side of his mouth.

Anna Mae forgot all about the cookies still inside the oven. She also forgot that she needed him to take her milk to town. Giving the oven door a slam, she spouted, "Jack Berkley, I thought I told you to git!"

Harley wiped the sweat from his brow and maintained a brisk pace. He'd lost half the morning, thanks to Mrs. Farley's insistence that he sit in on Bible reading with the family before his leave-taking. He couldn't complain—she had generously filled his poke with slices of ham, radishes and carrots, half a loaf of bread, and half a dozen boiled eggs. But if he'd left first thing, he could be a good five miles farther down the road and that much closer to his new job.

What was it with females and Bible reading? Annie would be tickled to know he'd sat through a whole chapter. She'd also have a few choice words concerning his reading with the Farley family instead of his own. How many times had she pestered him about reading the Bible with her and the girls?

Dirk strode easily beside him, his wide face creased into a permanent grin. For a big man, he sure could move. His long legs had never faltered as the two crossed a pasture to follow the railroad tracks. Dirk had agreed with Harley about following tracks rather than the road. He'd also agreed about not hitching a free ride in a boxcar.

"Be kind of like stealing, wouldn't it?" Dirk winked. "Don't know about your mama, but mine never was one for lettin' me take somethin' that didn't belong to me."

Harley released a brief laugh. "Your mama an' my wife would get along real good, what with reading the Bible every day and speaking out against stealing. Annie's got real strong ideas about right and wrong."

"Annie? That your wife?"

Harley's heart expanded as he thought about his Annie. Prettiest girl in Spencer—easily the prettiest in all of Reno County. And she'd married Harley Phipps, a drifter from Mississippi who'd hardly had two pennies to his name. "Yep. Anna Mae, but I call her Annie." He chuckled. "She doesn't much care for it, but somehow wrapping my tongue around Anna Mae just ain't easy."

Dirk nodded. "And she's a God-fearing woman?"

"Bible reading every day, church every Sunday, prayers all the time. Yep, she's

God-fearing." Harley scowled. "For what good it does her."

"What you mean by that?"

Harley sneaked a glance in Dirk's direction. For the first time, the big man's face wore no easy smile. He seemed genuinely interested in Harley's answer.

"All that prayin' . . . Asking God to bless the food, to bless the land, to bring us rain." He snorted. "Rain. Ha! Look at that sky." He flung his arm outward, gesturing toward the expanse of shimmering blue overhead. "Not so much as a cloud anywhere. See how much good her praying does?"

Dirk shrugged, shifting his pack higher on his shoulder. "Must do some good, or she wouldn't keep prayin'."

"But nobody answers!" Harley surprised himself with his vehemence.

Dirk raised one eyebrow. "Listen, Harley, I don't know how you was raised, but my ma and pa taught me that God loves me. Loves me so much He sent His Son to die on a cross just so I could have my sins forgiven. I figure a God who loves me that much has the right to decide what I need and when I need it. Sure, I'd like it to rain, too—hurts me to see plants all shriveled up and my pa watching the farm he's worked so hard on just fallin' apart."

Harley saw tears glint in the big man's eyes, and he turned away from the sight. Men and tears didn't mix. Especially not with a man the size of Dirk. Those tears gave Harley a funny feeling in the pit of his stomach.

"But seein' all that don't keep me from praying. Praying's not just to get something, Harley—praying's for what it does for you. Connects you with your Maker. Keeps you in touch. You figure your relationship with your Annie would be worth anything if you never talked to her?" He poked Harley with his elbow.

Harley grimaced but didn't reply. His and Annie's talking had slowed down too much, and Harley knew it.

Dirk chuckled. "Yep, gotta talk to keep a relationship goin'. So I talk to God. Then I trust Him to take care of me in the way that's best."

Harley couldn't stay silent. "An' you figure this drought is what's best?"

"My ways ain't God's ways." Dirk poked out his lips in thought for a moment. "In the Bible, God lets hardship bring folks around to Him. Funny how some folks keep their distance 'til they really need Him."

Harley kicked at a dirt clod.

"In the meantime," Dirk continued, seemingly oblivious to Harley's churning temper, "I'm mighty thankful for this job opportunity. Thankful to you, too, for mentionin' it. I figure you're God's messenger, Harley."

Harley nearly laughed out loud. Him? God's messenger? "You're thankin' the wrong person. I don't have nothin' to do with that job—thank President Roosevelt. He's the one thought up all these programs to help us out."

"But I wouldn't've known about it except for you. I figure God sent you along just at the time we needed the idea. Pa's been praying. God answered with you."

Harley pushed his hat brim upward and swiped at the sweat that dribbled toward his eyes. "You go ahead and believe what you want to, Dirk, an' let me believe what I want to. Long as we can agree to disagree, we'll get along fine."

Just like me and Annie.

9

"I'm tired of standing here. When're they coming, Mama?"

Anna Mae reached out and stroked Dorothy's blond curls. The little girl was always cranky on Sunday mornings. Anna Mae didn't mind Dorothy's straight, untamed hair on the weekdays, but she insisted on curls for Sunday morning church. Dorothy, however, hated sleeping on the lumpy wads of rags the night before and made sure her mother knew it.

"They'll be here soon, darlin'." Anna Mae gave her daughter a smile even though her stomach trembled. She had resigned herself to Jack Berkley's help with chores—she couldn't let her pride allow the precious milk to spoil in the cellar. But having that man march around in her yard and barn was one thing—riding in his Model T Ford as he and his father escorted her and the girls to church was another. Still, she comforted herself, having Mr. Berkley with them would keep things seemly.

"Wish they'd hurry. It's hot out here." Dorothy flapped her skirt with one hand and held her shoes in the other. Anna Mae hoped she'd be able to buy Dorothy some new shoes with Harley's first paycheck.

Anna Mae jiggled Marjorie, who fussed in her mother's arms. Both girls were irritable this morning. Anna Mae could hardly blame them. Between the heat, the wind, the dust, and no daddy to play with in the evenings, there wasn't much worth being smiley about.

"Complaining won't speed him up," Anna Mae reminded Dorothy.

The little girl scowled in reply. Then her expression turned puzzled. "Why aren'tcha wearing the hat Daddy bought you? He said it was for Sundays."

"It's too pretty to wear with my old dress," Anna Mae answered. Truth was, she had taken the hat out this morning and placed it on her head. A glance in the mirror confirmed it was a perfect hat for her cream-colored blouse and simple tan skirt. Yet she couldn't make herself keep it on. When she'd looked at the hat, she'd thought of the sold mules and the fact that Harley was halfway across Kansas. She hadn't liked the reminder. So she'd put the hat back on the closet shelf.

Anna Mae sighed and aimed her gaze toward the road. She absently smoothed a hand over her hair, which she had twisted into a knot at the back of her head. She hoped the hairpins wouldn't rattle loose on the way to church. Already the wind had pulled a few strands from their moorings, forcing her to tuck them behind her ears. Dorothy's curls looked tangled, too, and the bow Anna Mae had tied into the little girl's hair appeared bedraggled. Another sigh escaped her lips. Couldn't they at least look nice until they got to church?

A *chugga-chugga* captured Anna Mae's attention. Dorothy stood on tiptoes, watching. "There it comes!" Dorothy pointed to the Model T that turned in at the gate. She bounced off the porch and raced toward it.

"Dorothy, slow down!" Anna Mae admon-

ished. She understood the child's excitement at the chance to ride in a real automobile. Truth be known, Anna Mae looked forward to it, too. Her family had never owned
an automobile. If only Jack Berkley wasn't
the driver . . .

"Hey there, Dorothy." Jack smiled as he
stepped out of the vehicle. "You look real
pretty this morning."

Anna Mae's mother-pride welled up at
Jack's comment. Dorothy *was* pretty, even
in her flour-sack dress and bare feet. She
watched the little girl clamber into the backseat and sit on her knees to peer out the
open back window.

Jack turned his charming grin in Anna
Mae's direction. "Just as pretty as your
mama."

That comment set Anna Mae's teeth on
edge. *Compliment my girls, but leave me
out of it!* She fiddled with the hem of Marjorie's dress as she peeked inside the car.
She straightened, panic filling her chest.
"Where's your father?"

Jack rested his hand on the top of the car
door. "Gout's acting up in his big toe. He
couldn't get his shoe on. And he refused to

go to church barefooted." Jack grinned.
"Unlike your Dorothy, there."

Anna Mae felt herself blush. Sticking her
head in the car, she scolded, "Dorothy, you
get those shoes on now, you hear?"

Dorothy scowled but sat down on the
seat to force her feet into her shoes.

"Here, Anna Mae, I'll hold the baby while
you climb in."

Anna Mae looked at Jack, who held out
his hands. Should she even get in since Mr.
Berkley wasn't going? The week stretched
so long when she didn't go to church. She
needed the fellowship. With a disgruntled
huff, she held Marjorie out to Jack. The
sight of Marjorie in Jack's muscled arms unsettled her. The little girl fussed, reaching
one dimpled hand toward her mother. Jack
gave her some bounces while Anna Mae
quickly situated herself in the car's leather
seat.

Once she was settled, Jack handed Marjorie in, slammed her door, then strode
around the front of the vehicle and climbed
in on the opposite side. He sent her another
smile before putting the auto into gear and
releasing the clutch. "Here we go!" He
turned the car around and headed for the

road. Dorothy squealed from the backseat, and Jack laughed. He glanced at Anna Mae. "You look real pretty, Anna Mae, with your hair all slicked away from your face."

Dear Lord, I don't think this is a good idea to go with Jack, but how else are the girls and I going to get to church? Every other churchgoing neighbor is on the far side—it would be out of their way to come get us.

Anna Mae kept her gaze forward and didn't answer.

Jack's chuckle rumbled, matching the tone of the car's engine. "I know your mama taught you to say thank you when somebody gives you a compliment."

Anna Mae pursed her lips for a moment. Jack was too sure of himself. He always had been. What had Harley been thinking to ask him to look out for her and the girls? She finally made eye contact with him. "Jack, I appreciate your giving the girls and me a ride to church. I appreciate your help with the chores while Harley's gone. But we've got to get something straight. Our—" she licked her dry lips—"friendship . . . ended a long time ago. As far as I'm concerned, you're just a hired hand around the place 'til my husband returns. Don't try to make it into something more."

Jack ran his fingers along the edge of the steering wheel, his gaze aimed ahead. He worked his jaw back and forth. After several long seconds passed, he gave a brusque nod. "Okay, Anna Mae. I'll keep my compliments to myself." He glanced in her direction. "But I gotta say one more thing first. If I was your husband, and you were carrying my baby, I never would've walked down the road and left you behind."

Anna Mae's face felt hot. She sought words to defend Harley, but none came. To her relief, the Model T rolled into the churchyard, ending their conversation. Jack killed the engine, and the automobile heaved a rattling sigh as the motor died. Anna Mae waited until Jack came around and opened the door for her. He took her elbow as she struggled out, Marjorie's weight making her clumsy. His hand lingered a moment too long.

She sent him a warning look.

He backed off, his hands held up in a gesture of surrender. "Sorry, Anna Mae. Old habits die hard."

"C'mon, Dorothy," she said, turning her

back on him. "Let's get you to Sunday school."

After the service ended, Jack followed Anna Mae, watching the sway of her slim-fitting skirt as she made walking on high-heeled shoes look graceful even when clumping across the hard-packed earth of the churchyard.

Her hips were a little wider than they'd been in her teens—she'd always been such a willowy thing—but that was to be expected. After all, she'd borne two babies. The added curves did nothing to diminish her attractiveness, Jack acknowledged. If anything, it increased it. The woman Anna Mae had become was even more appealing than the girl she had been. And how he'd loved the girl.

They had attended this little clapboard church for as long as he could remember. In their childhood days, their families had sat together on one of the wooden pews. Anna Mae had been nine years old when she made her trek to the front of the church at the end of service to shake the minister's hand and announce her intention to be saved. Jack had waited two weeks to do the same thing—couldn't let her think he was copying—and even after all these years he remembered how she'd beamed her approval when his name had been announced as a new entry in the Lamb's Book of Life.

Only eleven years old, but he'd decided in those moments that Anna Mae Elliott had to be his someday.

Growing up on side-by-side farms with parents who were best friends had given him many opportunities to be with Anna Mae. And as they'd reached their teen years, it had been easy to see himself and Anna Mae as one. One farm, one home, one family. And then Harley had come along and disrupted everything.

But Harley was gone now. Maybe even gone for good. It wasn't unheard of in these troubling times for a man to abandon his family. Jack was back in the picture, and he liked the looks of things from this angle.

Anna Mae stopped beside the Model T and shifted her weight to balance Marjorie on her hip. She stretched her hand toward the door, but Jack dashed around and popped the handle before her fingers could close on it. Her gaze flitted upward, her expression wary. Giving a nod and smile, he gestured toward the seat and quipped, "Your chariot awaits."

"Thank you."

The words were uttered in a clipped, tight tone that didn't reflect gratitude, but Jack offered another grin and a warm, "You're quite welcome, Miz Phipps." He walked around to his side of the car, and Dorothy trailed behind him on bare feet, her shoes in her hand. She was a miniature version of her mama, and just looking at the golden-haired child opened another floodgate of memories. This child should have been his.

He winked at the little girl. "Hey there, Miss Dorothy, didja have a good time in church?"

Dorothy yawned and scratched her head, making her bow slip a little closer to her left ear. "It makes my feet tired."

"Your feet tired?" Jack could make no sense of that.

"They have to hang." The child's blue eyes blinked twice. " 'Cause the seats are too tall. And it makes them tired."

Now Jack understood. "Well, just tuck them up underneath you. Then they won't have to hang."

Dorothy pursed her lips, clearly disgusted. "Mama won't let me. Says it's not ladylike."

Jack laughed out loud. "Well, your mama's a perfect lady, so I reckon she'd know. Better do what she says. Now climb on in there."

He waited until Dorothy climbed into the backseat before kneeling beside the car and reaching beneath his seat to turn on the gas. Still on his knees, he leaned into the cab and turned the carburetor knob forward nearly a full turn, then reversed it slightly. He hid his smile at Anna Mae's curious expression as he flipped the ignition switch to the left, then moved the spark lever to its highest position. He'd learned a long time ago he wanted the spark retarded unless he wanted a good kick from the hand crank.

He had to stand to reach the throttle, and he pushed the lever down about one-third before yanking the hand brake lever to its farthest position to ensure no forward motion when the engine sparked to life. Those things accomplished, he strode to the front of the Model T and curled his hand around the crank, keeping his thumb tucked up out of the way. After two controlled forward jerks, followed by a hard shove to set the crank spinning, the auto rewarded him by roaring like a mad bull.

Quickly, he jumped inside the car and adjusted the throttle to bring the kicking and heaving under control. Once the machine reached a dull roar, he tweaked the carburetor until the roar turned into a lion's purr. Only then did he slam his door shut, release the brake, put the vehicle into reverse, and pull out of the churchyard.

On the road, dust rolling behind them, Anna Mae shook her head, her eyes wide. "You have to go through all that every time you want to drive this thing?"

Jack grinned. "Yep."

"It's a whole lot less work to hitch a horse to a buggy." She tightened her arms around a squirming Marjorie as the Model T bounced through a rut.

"That could be," Jack said, patting the steering wheel, "but it's not nearly as much fun." He glanced in the back, where Dorothy sat on her knees, bobbing up and down with the car's movements. "Right, Dorothy?"

"Right!"

Anna Mae peeked into the back, a scowl on her face. "Dorothy Mae Phipps, sit on your bottom."

"But, Mama, my feet hang!"

Anna Mae opened her mouth, but Jack intervened. "You can sit cross-legged in here, Dorothy. Won't hurt a thing."

With a triumphant grin, the little girl followed Jack's instruction. Sitting like a little Indian in front of a campfire, she craned her neck to peer out the window.

Anna Mae shot Jack a scathing look. "Don't interfere when I correct my daughter, Jack."

He shrugged. "It's my car, and her feet on the seat don't bother me a bit."

Anna Mae pinched her lips together and didn't say another word the rest of the way to her house. Jack let the car idle as he ran around to open the door for her. She pulled away from his hand when he reached to help her, turning her back on him the minute she was out.

"Come on, Dorothy, hurry up," she prodded as Dorothy took her time scooting across the seat. When Dorothy emerged, Anna Mae took her by the hand and headed for the house. She offered neither a thank-you nor a fare-thee-well in parting.

Dorothy peeked back at him from around Anna Mae's skirt as they rounded the porch, and Jack offered a smile and wave that the child returned. Then Anna Mae ushered her through the door, and the door closed with an audible *whump.*

He shook his head, unable to stop smiling. She might think she was dissuading him with her snooty attitude, but she'd forgotten just how persistent he could be. Didn't she remember that he liked a good challenge? Well, he'd just have to remind her.

Swinging back into his vehicle, he gave his door a solid yank and set the vehicle in motion. He'd be back. Not today—no reason to come back today since the milk truck didn't run on Sundays—but he'd be back. Full of smiles, helpfulness, and cheery words—and one other thing he'd noticed she needed. He'd get a thank-you out of her tomorrow for sure.

10

Mwaaaaaah.

Anna Mae waved her hand, trying to push away the intruding noise.

MwaaaAAAaaah.

It came again, more insistently. She opened her eyes, then slammed them shut against the light. Her heart lodged in her throat—the sun was up! How could she have slept so late? The poor cow must be miserable. She forced her eyes open as she threw back the sheets and leaped from the bed. The floor seemed to tilt. She grasped the iron bedpost with both hands and held on until she gained her bearings.

Mwaaaaaah.

The animal's cry tormented Anna Mae.

She pushed off from the bedpost and raced through the house and onto the porch. An arm across her churning stomach, she snatched up the clean milk bucket, which waited upside down on its shelf, and dashed across the yard. "Please, Lord, let the girls sleep a little longer," she prayed aloud. Rocks bruised the soles of her bare feet, but she ignored the pain and yanked open the barn door.

"Hey, Bossie, I'm here," she soothed as she patted the cow's hide. Bossie watched with wide, blinking brown eyes as Anna Mae grabbed the little milking stool from the corner. She placed the bucket into position, hiked her nightgown above her knees, straddled the stool, and set to work relieving Bossie of her discomfort. The cow nodded her great head, as if offering a thank-you.

After nearly a week of doing the milking, Anna Mae's arms no longer cramped with the chore. A blessing, for sure. She whispered a quick prayer of thanks for this gaining of strength. Finished, she gave Bossie another pat and said, "Okay, old girl, let me get this milk inside, then I'll come serve you your breakfast."

She rose, pulling the bucket of milk safely away from the cow's shifting feet. She returned the stool to its corner, then lifted the bucket and headed for the door. As she stepped from the barn into the yard, she heard the *clip-clop* of horses' hooves. Jack Berkley's wagon turned in from the lane. She glanced down her nightgown-covered length and released a groan. *Oh, please, not now!*

Jack brought the wagon to a stop between the barn and the back porch, cutting off her pathway. Anna Mae longed for another pair of hands to cover her glowing cheeks as he hopped down from the wagon seat and sent a lopsided smile in her direction.

"Good morning, Anna Mae." His eyes roved from her tousled hair to her bare feet, while her embarrassment increased by the second. "Late start this morning?"

"I . . . I don't have the milk ready to tote to town yet, Jack."

The customary grin grew broader. "I can see that." He strode toward her, holding out his hand. "Here, let me take that in for you."

She scuttled around the bobbing noses of the horses, her sudden movements splashing a few drops over the brim of the bucket. "No. I can do it."

Jack quirked one eyebrow and gave her a sardonic look. "I didn't say you were incapable, Anna Mae. I only offered to help." He ambled up beside her.

She hefted the bucket higher in an attempt to hide behind it. "I know. But I can do it myself. You"—she walked backward toward the porch—"just head on home and come back later." *When I'm dressed, combed, and ready to face the day.* "Okay?"

The back of her heel connected with the porch step. The jolt off-balanced her, and she jerked her arms upward, instinctively trying to save the milk. "No!" she cried as she fell backward against the closed porch door. The screen twanged in protest with her weight. She planted one elbow against the doorjamb and pushed herself free of the door, but she stumbled sideways. The bucket tipped, sloshing warm, creamy liquid down the front of her nightgown. One horse released a nervous whinny.

Jack leaped forward, grabbing her elbow with one hand and the bucket with the other. He gave a tug that should have put her back on her feet, except the ground was slippery from the milk. To her horror, her right foot slid north and her left foot south. She released the bucket to clutch Jack's shirt front with both hands. Her arm slammed into the bucket, and another wave of milk splashed out, soaking the left side of her gown and his pant leg.

Still unbalanced, she clung harder to Jack's shirt, her weight shifting as she tried to find her footing. Jack took an awkward step backward, swinging Anna Mae away from the patch of soppy ground. At last she got her feet back under her, and she was able to release his shirt.

She realized he still had hold of her elbow, and she jerked loose, spinning to turn her back on him. Her soaked nightgown clung to her front. She crossed her arms over her chest and hunkered forward. She hadn't been in such a state in front of Jack since she was eight years old and they had played in the creek together. She no longer had that little-girl body. Her face burned as she considered what he must have seen. Tears stung behind her eyes, and she clamped her jaw, determined to hold them back.

"Anna Mae, you okay?"

There was no teasing in his tone at all. If only he *would* tease. She could get good and angry at him then.

"I . . . I'm fine." She forced her voice past her tight throat. "You just go on now." A single sob found its way from her chest. She coiled tighter as she fought for control. *Don't cry! Don't cry!*

"Listen, Anna Mae, you know that old saying—no sense in crying over spilled milk."

A hint of teasing underscored his tone. But it wasn't enough to conjure anger—it only reminded her of the countless times he had cajoled her out of sour moods in her teenage years. Another sob burst out. "P-please, Jack. Just go on home, will you?"

A hand descended on her shoulder and pulled, turning her around. "I'm not going until I know you're okay."

"I'm okay!" She pressed her chin to the side, her eyes squeezed tight. She couldn't bear to look into his eyes right now. If any kindness lurked there at all, she would be completely undone.

"You're not okay."

Stubborn man! Why wouldn't he leave her alone? "P-please, Jack. . . ."

"And I don't think all this is about spilled

milk, either. You never let things like that bother you. Talk to me, Anna Mae."

"Talk to me, Anna Mae." Those words transported her back in time nearly twenty years, when the telegram had come, informing her parents that their only son, Private Benjamin Harold Elliott, Jr., had been killed in action in France. Anna Mae had been only seven, but she knew what *killed* meant—she'd buried two cats and a three-legged dog. She had run from the house to the creek, thrown herself on the bank, and sobbed her heart out because her big, handsome hero of a brother was never coming home. Jack had found her, questioned her. Even then, she'd tried to hold the hurt to herself—afraid if she talked about it, it would make it real. But he'd kept at her—*"Talk to me, Anna Mae."* And, finally, she had.

But not today. That part of their lives was over. "There's nothing to talk about. I'm— I . . . I've got to check on the girls." She darted past him, her arms still crossed over her chest, and closed herself in the kitchen. Her breath came in spurts as she waited for his wagon to rumble out the gate. But only silence greeted her ears. She pulled back the edge of the gingham curtain and peeked out. She saw him disappear into the barn.

Probably checking the cow. Holding her wet gown away from her body, she tiptoed through the kitchen and into the hallway. A glance into the girls' room confirmed both still slept soundly. Breathing a sigh of relief, she scurried to the washroom and ran water in the tub. She whisked the nightgown over her head and gave herself a quick wash, her ears perked to hear Jack if he came up on the porch.

Clean again, she headed to the bedroom and dressed, finishing with white anklets and scuffed oxfords. After running a brush through her hair and using a ribbon to hold the strands at the nape of her neck, she walked out to the kitchen and cracked the door open to peek out. The yard was clearly visible through the wire mesh of the screened-in porch. The 'fraidy hole's trapdoor gaped open, letting her know he'd carried out the milk and cream from the weekend's milkings. A glance toward the barn confirmed the wagon was gone.

Heaving a sigh of relief, she started to close the door, but something caught her eye. A box—small, rectangular, with a lid—

sat right inside the porch door. Tiptoeing, feeling like an intruder on her own porch, she crept forward and plucked the box from the floor. She lifted the lid and pressed her fingers against her lips to hold back her cry of surprise. Inside, nestled in white tissue paper, was a pair of black shiny Mary Janes.

New shoes for Dorothy.

Tears spurted into her eyes, but she couldn't decide if they were tears of gratitude or shame. She dug deep inside herself for enough anger to wash away the tears. Who did he think he was, buying shoes for Harley's daughter? Pride made her want to march across the pasture to Jack's back door and fling those little T-strap shoes right through the window. But one thing held her back.

After standing before him in a sodden nightgown, she just couldn't face Jack.

Harley wasn't sure he was ready to face the boss of this project. And it wasn't because of anything the man at the WPA office had said. It just suddenly felt . . . awkward. How long had it been since Harley had worked for anybody but himself? Not since Annie's father died seven years ago. A man could build up a lot of pride in seven years. Would he be able to take orders from someone else?

Then again, he'd been answering to Annie for those same seven years. A man with a wife ought to have no trouble answering to a boss. Still, he felt his chest tighten as he introduced himself to the foreman of the castle project.

The man, who said to call him Mr. Peterson, looked Dirk up and down and seemed pleased to have the young giant on the crew. Harley understood that, but determination to prove himself as capable as the younger man straightened his shoulders. Peterson wrote their names in a black notebook, slapped it shut, and said, "Well, gentlemen, let's get you acquainted with the project."

He walked the pair around the grounds. Harley scanned the area surrounding the castle site. As far as a person could see in any direction, there was a whole lot of nothing. Gently rolling hills, dry and brown with only a few brave yuccas providing sparse splashes of green, topped by an endlessly blue sky. A quiver of apprehension wiggled down Harley's spine. Sure was a lonely place . . .

The boss was speaking. Harley pushed aside his trepidation to focus on the man's words.

"At the top of the hill there, you can see the start of the castle itself. Small, as castles go," he admitted, stroking his chin, "but big enough to be seen from a distance. The base is constructed from blocks of shale, and we'll use sandstone at the top." He pointed to two huge piles of stone, where men swarmed like ants on a mound of bread crumbs. "The bigger stones are the shale, and the smaller ones the sandstone."

Dirk leaned forward to examine one large, roughly square-cut stone. He straightened and sent Harley a startled smile. "Hey, lookit here, Harley—there's a clam shell caught in the rock!"

Harley looked where Dirk pointed. Sure enough, a ridged half circle of dingy white was embedded in the rosy-tan stone.

Peterson chuckled. "There's bound to be water fossils trapped in the layers of rock. If you look closely, you might be able to locate the spine of a fish. All these rocks were underwater at one time."

Dirk nodded, his hands caught in the bib of his overalls. " 'Course it was underwater. Whole earth got flooded when God sent the rains in Noah's time."

Peterson swiveled in Dirk's direction, his brow creased. "Are you a preacher, boy?"

"No, sir. Just a Christian."

Peterson nodded. "You'll have Sundays off. There are a variety of churches in Lindsborg. You'll be welcome to go, if you'd like."

Dirk smiled broadly and nudged Harley's shoulder with his beefy elbow. "Hear that? I was worried I'd have to do my own services."

Harley shrugged. It was nothing to him.

Peterson started moving again, and Harley and Dirk followed as he continued the tour. "The castle will have a square turret above the door, topping its second floor." He paused, looking up at the hill where a three-foot-tall wall stood. "When it's done, a person will be able to stand in that turret and see the whole Smoky River Valley. The view should be similar to the one seen by Coronado himself when he climbed to the top of that rise, hoping to catch a glimpse of the elusive city of gold."

Harley frowned. Elusive? This man was a

puzzle. In charge of a work crew, dressed in dusty dungarees and a worn chambray shirt, a two-day growth of whiskers on his chin, yet using speech that reminded Harley of Annie. Although Peterson wore rough clothing like the other workers, he carried himself with a dignified bearing that seemed somehow out of place on this barren countryside. The man must have education. Why would he be out here, in the middle of nowhere, telling men where to pile rocks?

For long moments Peterson stood, as if transfixed by the sight of the hill. Then he whirled, bringing his attention to the men once more. He swiped his sleeve across his forehead and pointed. "Over there will be a picnic grounds. You can see where the rock wall has been started to define that area. We will build a fireplace for visitors to use, and there will also be a rock outhouse, large enough to accommodate both genders."

He took a great breath and plunged his hands into the pockets of his trousers. "So, gentlemen, the options for working are digging, hauling, or building. Can either of you read a blueprint?"

Harley and Dirk exchanged a glance. Harley surmised by the blank expression on

Dirk's face that he couldn't read a blueprint any better than Harley. Harley answered for both of them. "No, sir."

"Well, then, that leaves out building." Peterson slapped Dirk on the shoulder. "Farley, you join the men at the shale pile. Ask for Spence. He'll tell you what to do."

Dirk nodded to the boss. "See ya later, Harley." He trotted off toward the large rock pile.

Peterson turned to Harley. "And, Phipps, I assume you know which end of a shovel goes into the ground?"

Harley bristled. Was the man making fun of him? "Of course I do." The words carried a hint of resentment.

Peterson's eyebrows raised, but the boss didn't comment on Harley's indignant reply. Instead, he slapped a hand across Harley's shoulders and aimed him toward the area southwest of the picnic grounds. Harley spotted two men, leaning on shovels. "Well, then, I'm putting you to work on the pit for the outhouse. Let's get going."

Deflated, Harley moved woodenly in the direction given. A pit for the outhouse. He kicked at a clump of brittle grass and watched the brown wisps skitter across the ground. His hope of having a part in building a castle—something of value that would last—blew away like those dead bits of grass. These days, a man shouldn't even dream. Dreams were just as elusive as that city of gold Coronado never found.

11

"Mama, how come you always hide when Mr. Berkley comes over?"

Anna Mae sent Dorothy a startled look across the breakfast table. "What?" She forced her lips to form a quavery smile. "I don't *hide,* honey."

Dorothy's wide blue eyes blinked twice. "Uh-huh, you do. You run into the barn. Or you stay in the kitchen. He ask-ded me how come."

Anna Mae felt her temper building. Oh, he did, did he? Well, Jack Berkley better leave Dorothy alone. He had no right to question the child about her mother. Her temper faded, however, as she remembered that awful morning three days ago when she'd stood before him in a milk-soaked gown. Shame took anger's place. How would she ever be able to face Jack again after he'd seen . . . what he had seen?

Anna Mae rose from the table, carrying her half-full plate to the counter. She scraped the food into the slop pail as she said, "That's not hiding, Dorothy. I just have no reason to talk to Mr. Berkley. He comes to get the milk, cream, and extra eggs. He doesn't come for conversation."

Dorothy released a long sigh, her chin in her hand. "I like talking to him. He's nice, Mama."

Anna Mae closed her eyes for a moment. Yes, she remembered when she thought Jack was nice. Oh, the fun they'd had growing up together. . . . But that was before he'd turned serious and scared her with his talk of how she had to be his or he'd never survive. Nobody should ever need somebody that much.

She opened her eyes and used her fork to give the plate one more whack before dropping the plate and fork into the dishpan. "Well, you enjoy talking to him, then, but you don't need to talk about me."

Tears appeared in the corners of Dorothy's eyes.

Anna Mae sighed. She hadn't intended to be so harsh. Crossing back to the table, she gave the end of Dorothy's nose a light tap with one finger. "Surely you can find more interesting things to talk about, can't you? Like how fast does an inchworm crawl, or why do puppy dogs wag their tails?" Anna Mae deliberately chose questions Dorothy had asked in the past.

The little girl's grin returned. "You think he might know?"

Anna Mae shrugged. "You never know until you ask."

Dorothy bounced up from the table, her ponytail waving. "I'll ask him when he comes today."

"You do that." Anna Mae used a rag to clean Marjorie's hands as Dorothy headed toward the porch. "Before you scamper off to play, Dorothy, we need to water the garden. Get the bucket for Mama, please, and I'll come fill it."

Dorothy's shoulders drooped for a moment, but she didn't argue.

Anna Mae met Dorothy at the water pump and pumped water into the bucket.

Then, with Marjorie on one hip and the bucket in her free hand, she walked Dorothy to the garden, where Dorothy began her watering chores. Still hanging on to Marjorie, who attempted to eat dirt, Anna Mae knelt down and plucked weeds from between the shoots of green that she knew would one day bear vegetables.

Satisfaction filled Anna Mae's chest as she looked across the neat garden. Despite the lack of rain, despite the lack of Harley's assistance, the tiny plants flourished beneath the Kansas sun. In another couple weeks she'd drop the seeds for beans, peas, tomatoes, and corn into their waiting rows. Her mouth watered as she imagined the first taste of fresh green beans cooked with bacon and onion. At least her family wouldn't go hungry.

Dorothy splashed a dipperful of water onto the nearest cabbage plant, spattering her mother's knee. Anna Mae squealed and reached to tickle the child, and Dorothy scampered away, giggling.

Anna Mae shielded her eyes and watched Dorothy for a few minutes, sending up a silent thank-you for the little girl's willingness to help. Marjorie clunked her mother on the side of the head, and Anna Mae grabbed the baby's hand to give it a kiss. She glanced around the area where she'd been seated and said, "Well, baby girl, we've got the weeds pulled here. Let's move on."

As she struggled to her feet, she heard the familiar *clip-clop* signaling Jack's approach. Her stomach clenched, remembering Dorothy's comment from breakfast. Although she had refuted it, she knew Dorothy was right—she had been hiding. The urge to race into the house was strong.

Dorothy skipped across the garden and waved as the wagon rolled to a halt between the house and barn. "Hi, Mr. Berkley!" She returned to the bucket, humming.

"Hello there, Dorothy," Jack greeted as he jumped down. He ambled toward the garden.

Anna Mae watched him out of the corner of her eye as she rounded the row of scrawny carrot greens. She bent down, busily plucking at nonexistent weeds, her heart thumping high in her throat.

A shadow fell across the neat rows of fledgling plants. By its size, she knew it was

Jack's. She pushed her chin against her shoulder and kept her gaze low.

"Morning, Anna Mae." The soft greeting held the teasing undertone she had come to expect.

"Morning." She didn't look up. "Everything's in the 'fraidy hole, same as always." She picked up a clod of dirt and crumbled it in her hand, then patted the particles around the root of one plant.

The shadow shortened. She risked a quick glance. Jack crouched beside her, elbows on knees. "I got your empty milk cans in the back of the wagon. Do you want them on the porch?"

Marjorie leaned sideways, reaching for Jack. Anna Mae pulled her back. "Yes, thank you. That's fine."

But Jack didn't move, and she heard him release a huff of breath. "Anna Mae, how long are you going to keep this up?"

Anna Mae sent a brief, sidelong glance in his direction. "Keep what up?"

He caught her arm and rose, pulling her with him. "Hiding."

She raised her chin. "I'm not hiding. Here I am, right out in the open."

He snorted. "Yeah, all squatted down like

a roly-poly bug, hoping no one notices you there. Kinda silly, don't you think?"

Her face felt hot, but she told herself it was because the sun hit her full force. "I'm not hiding," she insisted. "I'm just too busy to chat."

He crossed his arms and looked down his nose at her for a long time. She met his gaze squarely, which wasn't easy with Marjorie squirming in her arms. Finally he shook his head. "Okay, Anna Mae, whatever you say. But keep this in mind. Harley asked me to help out around here. Harley'll be gone for quite a while. Which means I'll be coming around for quite a while. I don't expect any big thank-you from you, but the least you could do is be civil."

Anna Mae dropped her gaze, shamed by his words. Mama would be appalled. Her mother and Ginny Berkley had been best friends. Jack was right. She should be civil. She should be more than civil.

Dorothy suddenly tugged at Anna Mae's arm. "Mama, what's *civil*?"

Anna Mae felt a grin twitch at her cheeks. "Why don't you ask Mr. Berkley that while Mama carries the milk cans into the house?" She turned from Jack and headed to the back of his wagon. "And while you're at it, Dorothy, didn't you have another question or two for Mr. Berkley?"

"Oh yeah!" Dorothy turned her attention to their tall neighbor.

Anna Mae carried the milk cans one at a time to the porch, all the while listening to Jack field Dorothy's question. She had to admit, he had a great deal of patience with the child. When the cans were on the porch, she said, "Okay, Dorothy, enough now. Finish up that watering for Mama."

Dorothy puckered her face, but she lifted her hand in a wave. "Bye, Mr. Berkley. I'll see you tomorrow."

"Yeah. Tomorrow." Jack shook his head as the child scurried back to her task. Then he looked at Anna Mae, crossed to stand in front of her, and shook his finger. "That was sneaky, Anna Mae Elliott, and if your daddy were here, I'd encourage him to teach you some manners."

Anna Mae couldn't stop the giggle that found its way from her throat. "I'm sorry, Jack." She knew she didn't sound sorry at all. "But you did say you wanted to help. You just saved me some breath. I answer questions all day long, every day."

He smirked. "That's okay. It was worth it to get that smile out of you."

She felt the smile fade.

"Now, don't turn sober on me again. I declare, for a pretty girl, the faces you make could curdle milk."

"Jack . . ." She allowed her tone to send the warning.

He shook his head and blew out a breath. "Okay, okay. I'll get your milk out of the cellar and be on my way. You need anything from town?"

"Not today. Thanks for asking."

"You're welcome." He turned toward the cellar.

"Oh, and . . ." Anna Mae chewed her lower lip, holding Marjorie's small, grubby hand.

"And?" Jack waited expectantly, his eyebrows arched high.

"And thanks for those shoes." Anna Mae forced the words out through a closed throat. "Dorothy needed them."

A grin broke across his face. "Yeah, I know. You're welcome." Again, he shifted as if to move toward the cellar.

"But . . ."

The single word stopped him. He angled his gaze in her direction.

"But you shouldn't have." Anna Mae drew her shoulders back, raising her chin a notch. "Harley would've taken care of that, as soon as he got a paycheck. So as soon as his first check gets here, I'll be paying you back."

Jack shrugged. "Suit yourself."

Anna Mae nearly wilted with relief when he didn't argue, but there was a look in his eyes that she couldn't decipher. And for some reason, that look made her shiver.

"If you was home right now, Harley, what would you be doin'?" Dirk spoke around a mouthful of beans.

Third day in a row they'd had beans for dinner. Harley didn't particularly care for boiled red beans, but at seven cents they were the least expensive, most filling item on the menu at the little café where he and Dirk picked up their bucket lunch each morning on the way to work. At least this time the beans were seasoned with some pork—that helped.

Harley chewed his bite and swallowed. "I'd be sitting at my kitchen table, eating a good lunch of Annie's pickled cabbage and fried pork. I'd probably be watching Dottie hold a chunk of meat on her fork and nibble at it like an ice cream cone until Annie made her stop. And I'd be listening to Margie thump her fists on the high-chair tray and beg for her mama to feed her some more."

He closed his eyes for a moment, battling a wave of homesickness so strong he feared he might lose his beans. Each evening, as the men packed up and headed to their homes, his heart lurched with desire to head straight across Kansas back to Spencer and his own family. But instead, he and Dirk returned to the little storage shed behind the Petersons' place, where the boss had set up some cots for their use. Using that storage shed saved them the expense of a boardinghouse, and he appreciated it, but it sure was lonely without his girls. He wondered if the letter he'd sent from Lindsborg last Saturday had reached Annie yet. He hoped it had, and that she'd already written back. He didn't like the way they'd left things between them the day he'd headed out.

Harley smiled as he thought of Margie's dimpled fists and Dottie's sweet smile. How he loved his little punkins. And right now they were growing and changing, and here he was miles away. All because the rain forgot how to fall in Kansas.

Laughter broke out from a group seated a few feet away from Harley and Dirk, and one of the men cursed roundly. Dirk grimaced. A teasing voice called, "Hey, watch your language, Nelson. Preacher over there can hear you."

The hair on the back of Harley's neck bristled. Although he wasn't keen on listening to Dirk's sermonizing or recitin' of Bible verses any more than the others, he also didn't care much for the way some of the men—Nelson, especially—tormented the gentle giant. Dirk didn't do anything to deserve their mocking him. He opened his mouth to defend his friend, but Dirk cut him off.

"It's okay, Harley. They don't mean nothin' by it."

Harley snorted. "Oh yeah?"

Dirk shrugged, a weak grin lifting one side of his mouth. "Well, maybe they do. But they aren't really hurting me with that talk. They're grieving my Savior. That's why it bothers me."

Harley shook his head. "You really believe someone else is listenin' to that and cares what they say?"

Dirk's wide-eyed look reminded Harley of Dottie's innocence. "Sure I do. God's ears are always open and listening. He hears His name called whether in prayer or in curse." The big man lowered his head. "Must make His heart hurt to hear His Son's name used that way. . . ." Dirk straightened. "But every time I hear one of 'em take God's name in vain, I say a little prayer for the one doin' the cursin'. One thing about it—it's increased my prayer life somethin' fierce."

Harley hooted in laughter. "I hope someday you get to meet my Annie. I think she'd approve of you."

"That's about the best compliment I ever got." Dirk leaned sideways to prop himself up on his elbow. "I hope I get to meet that wife o' yours who's handling a whole farm on her own right now. She must be a strong woman."

Harley nodded thoughtfully. Strong. Yes, that described Annie. Had to be strong to contend with him. Harley knew he was about the most headstrong man ever put on the planet. Yet Annie stood her own against him. He smiled, remembering the early days of settling in as husband and wife. How they'd tussle. And make up. The making up was always worth the tussle.

His smile drooped as more recent memories drifted across his mind. When had her spiritedness faded? It had started even before the drought, creeping up so slow he hadn't really recognized it until she seemed more resigned than feisty. He remembered her pondering gaze aimed out the kitchen window, her sad voice asking, "Know what I miss, Harley? The scent of rain . . ."

Harley inhaled, searching for that scent. He got a snoot full of dust and sneezed.

"Bless you," Dirk said.

Despite himself, Harley chuckled. "There you go, sounding like Annie again. Never can so much as snuffle around her without hearin' those words." He scowled. "She means 'em, too."

Dirk stretched out his booted foot to nudge Harley's leg. "You miss her bad, huh?"

Harley lay back, his hands beneath his head, and stared at the quivering sun directly overhead. "Yeah." His voice sounded tight. He cleared his throat. "Yeah, I miss her bad."

"I pray for her every day, Harley."

A lump formed in the back of Harley's throat. "Y-you do?" The words came out in a croak.

"Sure I do. For protection and health for her and your little girls. For her to keep up her strength and be able to keep things goin' 'til you're home again with 'em."

Dirk's words made something sting at the back of Harley's nose. He closed his eyes. "That's nice of you, Dirk." Not that Harley believed those prayers did any good, but the idea that Dirk would do that . . . "Thanks."

"It's not a problem." Dirk remained silent for a few moments. Then his voice came again, husky and a near whisper. "Pray for you, too. 'Cause I know it's hard for you to be so far away from them you love."

Harley nodded. Yes, it was hard. But at least he'd left his wife and children in good hands. Jack was there. A living, breathing man with two strong arms and a willing spirit. Jack was better than a God Harley'd never seen. Wasn't he? Suddenly, for some reason, Harley wasn't so sure.

12

Anna Mae tipped her head sideways to better enjoy the breeze coming in through the open window of the Model T. As he'd done the previous two Sundays, Jack's father had insisted she take the front seat rather than climb in the back with the baby. Mr. Berkley had always been a chivalrous man, so she wasn't surprised by his gentlemanly gesture. She hummed "Bringing in the Sheaves," one of the hymns sung during the Sunday worship service.

"Mama?" Dorothy's voice carried from the backseat, where she sat cross-legged next to Mr. Berkley. "How come the *hes* don't get bringed in?"

"What?" Jack asked the startled question, his gaze bouncing to Anna Mae and back to the road.

Anna Mae turned backward to peer at her daughter. "Honey, I don't know what you mean."

Dorothy released a disgruntled huff. "In the song." She sang, slightly off key, " 'Bringing in the *shes*, bringing in the *shes*, we will come rejoicing, bringing in the *shes*.' " She crinkled her brow. "Only the *shes*. Where are the *hes*?"

Jack's laughter rang loud and clear.

Anna Mae bumped his arm and whispered sharply, "Shh."

He stopped, but his cheeks twitched with the effort of holding back his amusement.

Anna Mae kept an eye on him as she answered Dorothy. "The song isn't 'bringing in the *shes*,' it's 'bringing in the *sheaves*.' "

Mr. Berkley tapped Dorothy's knee. "Sheaves are bundles of wheat, honey. I bet there's a picture in your story Bible. Ask your mama to show you when you get home."

Dorothy nodded slowly. "Ohhhh, sheaves." Then her face crinkled again. "But we don't bring wheat to church. How come we sing about it?"

Jack laughed again. "Answer that one."

"You just hush." Anna Mae tried to send him a disgusted look, but she ruined it by grinning. She faced forward again, careful not to disturb Marjorie, who dozed against her shoulder. Sometimes she felt as though she'd moved backward in time—to the days when she and Jack ran barefoot along the creek bed, chattering about everything and nothing, happy just to be. And with each realization of how easy it was to be with Jack, she experienced a stab of guilt. A married woman shouldn't be so comfortable with a man other than her husband. What had Harley been thinking, asking Jack Berkley to take care of her in his absence?

The Model T rolled into her yard, and Jack left the motor idling as he came around to open the door for her. Anna Mae swung her legs out and struggled to her feet. Dorothy scrambled over Mr. Berkley's knees but then peeked back in the car to wave at the older man. "Bye, Mr. Berkley." She turned to Jack. "Bye, Mr. Berkley." Her face twisted into a scowl. "This mixes me up having two Mr. Berkleys."

Jack's father pulled himself from the backseat and touched Dorothy's head. "Well, I think I can fix that." His gaze flitted briefly in Anna Mae's direction. For some reason her heart set up a patter. "Why don't you call me Papa Berkley? Will that keep things from being mixed up?"

"Papa Berkley . . ." Dorothy seemed to test the name. She broke into a smile. "Okay."

"Good." Mr. Berkley pushed his hands into his jacket pockets and smiled at Anna Mae. The fondness in his eyes was exactly the same as it had been when she was growing up. "Papa Berkley it is."

Papa Berkley? If she and Jack had married, that might have been what their children called Ern Berkley. Anna Mae felt as if a cord had tangled around her heart; it was suddenly hard to breathe. She should protest the title, yet how could she do so graciously?

Dorothy skipped toward the porch, waving over her shoulder. "Bye, Papa Berkley! Bye, Mr. Berkley!"

"Good-bye, child." Mr. Berkley sat in the Model T's seat but left the door open.

"Bye, Dorothy." Jack's lips twitched into a smirk. "Think up some questions for your mama this afternoon, okay?"

"Okay!" The child stepped through the porch and disappeared into the house.

Jack chuckled. "She's somethin' else."

Anna Mae managed a brusque nod. "Yes, she is. Thanks for the ride, Jack." Eager to separate herself from the odd feelings churning through her middle, she headed toward the house.

"Anna Mae, wait a minute."

She turned back impatiently. "What?"

"It's Marjorie's birthday this week, isn't it?" He touched the sleeping baby's soft curls.

Jack's hand on Marjorie's head increased the discomfort in Anna Mae's stomach. She took one sideways step to put some distance between them. "That's right."

Jack shifted his weight to one hip and scratched his left ear. "Well, I was thinking. The Fox Theatre is showing a movie your girls might like—called *Dimples* with that little girl, Shirley Temple. You could come, too."

Anna Mae felt her hackles rising. "Jack Berkley, Harley might have asked you to look out for the farm, but that doesn't include taking his wife on dates!"

"Whoa! Hold on!" Jack's indignant tone

stopped her short. "I'm not taking you on a date. I'm taking the girls for a movie 'cause it's a special day and I thought they'd like it. Don't turn it into something it isn't."

Anna Mae eyed him suspiciously.

Jack tipped toward her, his hands held out in supplication. "If Harley were here, wouldn't you do something special?"

Anna Mae disliked the niggle of guilt his question raised. Was it fair to Marjorie to do nothing just because her daddy wasn't here? "I'd want to do something special, I suppose. But all the way to Hutchinson . . ." Marjorie stirred, and Anna Mae automatically rocked back and forth.

"It's the closest theater," Jack pointed out. "And I bet Dorothy's never been. I'll spring for popcorn and soda pop, too. What do you say? We'll make an afternoon of it for the kids—give them a time to remember."

Anna Mae had a hard time meeting his earnest expression. Was he truly sincere in wanting to provide a good time for the girls, or was his motivation less pure? Or was it only her own uneasy feelings creating this wariness of Jack's motives? "I don't know, Jack. . . ."

"What if," came Mr. Berkley's voice, "I went along, too?"

Both Jack and Anna Mae looked toward the Model T.

Mr. Berkley sat with his legs out of the vehicle, hands propped on knees. "Been a long time since I've seen a moving picture. I wouldn't mind a trip into Hutchinson myself."

Anna Mae considered the situation. If Jack's father went along, no one could cast aspersions at her being with Jack. Jack couldn't pull any of his shenanigans, either, with his father looking on. She'd never been to the picture show, and a desire to see the movie Jack mentioned created a strong pull. Still, she hesitated. What would Harley think?

"Mama!" Dorothy's cranky voice carried across the yard. Anna Mae turned her gaze to spot the child pressing her nose against the porch screen. "I'm hungry."

Jack cupped his mouth and called, "Dorothy, you want to go see *Dimples* at the picture show?"

Dorothy jumped up and down and clapped her hands. "Yes! Yes!"

Jack gave Anna Mae a smug look. "Say no now, Mama."

"That was underhanded," she accused. Now she had no choice except to agree to Jack's invitation. She couldn't disappoint Dorothy.

Jack grinned and rounded the Model T as his father pulled his legs back inside. Jack looked at her across the top of the car. "We'll swing by on Friday around noon and pick you up." He slid into the vehicle and reversed down the lane to the road. With a grinding of gears, the Model T hop-skipped in a forward motion, then Jack waved out the open window as the car chugged down the road.

The screen door slammed and Dorothy joined her mother in the yard. Together they watched the vehicle round the bend. Dorothy peered up at Anna Mae. "Mama, what's 'dimples at the picture show'?"

Anna Mae frowned. "A whole lot of trouble, that's what."

"Son?"

Jack barely heard his father over the chug of the Model T's engine. "You say something?"

"Yeah." Pop cleared his throat and spoke louder. "You sure you know what you're doing?"

Jack clenched the steering wheel as he guided the automobile around a large pothole in the road. He knew what his father meant, but he feigned ignorance. "Doing with what?"

His father shook his head. "Squiring Anna Mae and her girls to church is one thing—a person could see it as a Christian act of kindness. But to the picture show? Can't hardly call that a Christian act. That's purely personal."

Jack swallowed hard but didn't answer.

"You sure you're using good sense? There's a lot of history between you and Anna Mae Phipps."

Jack forced a laugh. "Listen, Pop, it's all under control. Sure there's history between Anna Mae and me, like you said. But history's in the past. So are those feelings."

Pop nibbled his mustache, his expression pensive. "Oh yeah? Then how come you haven't so much as looked at another woman since the day Harley escorted Anna Mae out of the Countryside Church?"

Jack winced. He'd lost out that day, there

was no doubt about it. And losing didn't come easy. Concentrating on driving, he slowed the acceleration and adjusted the clutch as he angled the Model T into their drive. He coasted to a stop by the back porch and waited, but Pop didn't get out.

"Jack, I'm worried about you."

Although he would have preferred to ignore his father's words, he knew his pop was stubborn enough to wait until doomsday for a reply. He took a deep breath and finally faced his father. "Look, Pop, Anna Mae never saw me as more than a replacement for the brother she lost. You think I can change that now?"

Pop lifted his shoulders in a shrug. "I'm just saying that woman and her two little girls make a pleasing package. And you seem awfully eager to claim it as your own."

"It's a package already claimed," Jack said forcefully. The truth of his words smacked him hard. "Now, are you going to get out and put our lunch on the table before it's time for evening chores?" He affected a teasing grin.

Pop sighed. "Okay, okay. Just . . ." He shook his head again. "Never mind. You're a grown man. Can't tell you what to do." As he mumbled, he opened the door and climbed out.

Jack put the Model T into gear and pulled it behind the barn. He killed the engine, then rested his forehead on the steering wheel for a moment, gaining control of his racing heart. It was easy to tell Pop he had no feelings for Anna Mae—it was another thing to mean it.

Pop was right—Jack had never looked beyond Anna Mae. No other female had ever measured up. Physically speaking, she painted a pleasing picture. Intellectually, she could match wits with anyone. She was spunky and funny and determined. Everything a man could want in a wife, Anna Mae Elliott had it. And then, of course, there was the fact that she lived right next door to his property. Together they could have created a dairy farm to best any of them. They were a perfect match.

Pop was right about all that history between him and Anna Mae. They had a connection that went back to the days of their babyhood. A person couldn't rewrite history. Jack had proposed to her, offered her the moon and stars and a fancy jar to keep them in, but she went and married Harley

Phipps, son of a sharecropper who didn't own much more than the worn-out clothes on his back. What in the world had she seen in Harley?

Nope, a person couldn't rewrite history. What was past, was past. But as for the future . . . ? That was a clean slate, and Jack had a pencil ready to write things the way he had wanted them all along.

13

Dirk leaned back in his chair and released a long, satisfied sigh. "That was good grub. Not as good as Ma's, but good." He pushed his empty plate away from the edge of the table.

Harley rubbed his stomach. "Not as good as my Annie's cooking, either, but a whole lot better than the beans we've been eating."

Dirk laughed, the sound carrying above the clatter of other café noise. "Well, you gotta admit, beans're filling, at least. Lots of people right now would appreciate even a meal of beans every day."

"I s'pose you're right about that." Harley thought about the newspaper reports of farmers protesting low prices by dumping milk on the ground or slaughtering their livestock rather than selling it to be butchered. That translated into children going hungry.

As always, thoughts of children brought an immediate rush of desire to see his own little girls. He knew Dottie and Margie were at least well fed, and with this first paycheck going home, Annie would be able to buy Dottie some new shoes. He hoped they wouldn't give her blisters.

The waitress stopped by their booth to take their empty plates. "You fellas want some pie or cake for dessert? Got peach or apple pie, and a tall chocolate cake with cherries."

Dirk's eyebrows shot up. "Chocolate cake with cherries for me. How 'bout you, Harley?"

Harley smiled, remembering how Annie had asked for a hat with cherries on it.

"That'll be two chocolate cakes, coming right up." The waitress hurried off.

Harley looked at Dirk. "Did I ask for cake?"

"Nope, but your smile did."

With a shrug, Harley admitted, "I can eat a piece of cake with no trouble."

"Whadja think of the sermon?" Dirk leaned

his elbows on the table. "Bein' a farmer, I 'specially liked the part about the sower of the seeds. Used to like that story when I was little, too."

Harley gave a brief chuckle. "I can't imagine you ever being little."

Dirk grinned. "Don't guess I ever really was. Not like most boys, anyway."

Harley frowned. "And how'd you get so big anyhow? Neither of your parents are big like you."

Dirk offered a slow shrug. " 'Cause they ain't my real parents. They took me in when I was three or four—picked me out at an orphanage in Topeka."

"You're adopted?" That explained the difference in size and appearance between the boy and his parents.

"Yep." The smile reappeared on Dirk's wide face. "Been adopted twice. Once by my ma and pa, and once by my heavenly Father."

Harley knew Dirk wanted him to question his final statement, but he remained stubbornly silent, and finally Dirk spoke again.

"You didn't answer my question about the sermon."

Harley knew that. The truth was, he'd

gone to church with Dirk just so the man wouldn't have to go alone. Harley felt sorry for Dirk, going to the church all by himself, so he'd gone along out of respect for him. But he hadn't really listened to the sermon.

"Didja understand the meaning behind the story?"

Harley looked sharply into Dirk's face. Was Dirk trying to make him feel stupid? The big man blinked in innocence. Harley pushed his temper down. Dirk wasn't capable of intentional cruelty. And that made him determined not to hurt his friend's feelings.

Keeping his voice low, he admitted, "To be honest, I didn't listen all that close. So . . . no, I s'pose I didn't understand." Dirk opened his mouth, and Harley headed him off before he could speak. "And that's okay with me. I mean, I only went 'cause you were going and I didn't want you to be alone. I didn't go to learn anything."

Dirk's eyes looked sad, but the big man chuckled softly. "That's funny, Harley—you didn't go to learn anything. Guess that makes you kind of like the seed that fell on the hard ground. You received the truth, but you chose to do nothin' with it."

Harley scowled. "Don't preach to me, Dirk."

"I'm not preachin'. I'm just telling you what I think."

"Well, quit thinking."

Dirk laughed loudly at that. "Ah, Harley, what I'm thinking right now is your wife would be awful happy to know you went to church with me this mornin', even if you didn't go to learn anything."

The waitress plopped two saucers, each holding a man-sized wedge of dark chocolate cake oozing with thick frosting and plump red cherries, on the table before rushing off again. Harley welcomed the intrusion. He picked up his fork and eagerly stabbed into his piece. Dirk did likewise, and the two ate without any conversation until every crumb was gone. The waitress brought their bill, and Dirk snatched it up.

"Lunch is on me."

Harley held out his hand. "No, Dirk. I'll pay my own tab."

But Dirk shook his head. "Nope. You favored me by goin' to church with me when you weren't truly interested. Let me favor you now by payin' for your lunch." He grinned. "Besides, don't you got a birthday present to buy with your spendin' money?"

Harley acknowledged the extra money would be helpful in finding something nice for Marjorie's first birthday. Yet it rubbed him the wrong way to have Dirk's charity. "Yeah, I do, but—"

"Then let me take care o' lunch."

Harley blew out a breath of pure aggravation. Would he ever win an argument with Dirk? "All right," he groused. "Let's get moving."

In a few minutes, they were ambling down the sidewalk to peer through windows. Lindsborg wasn't large, but it was neat, and it had nearly everything a body could want in the way of goods. Unfortunately, it being Sunday, nothing was open. But, as Dirk pointed out, Harley could find something he wanted to purchase for Marjorie's birthday and come back one evening next week to get it.

The men paused to cup their hands beside their faces and look through each store's front window, but it wasn't until they encountered a clothier's display that Harley saw something that interested him. "Dirk, lookee there." He shoved his finger against the glass, pointing at a frilly little dress of white covered all over with red dots. It made Harley think of cherries swimming in cream. A little red bow rested below the lacy collar, and more red bows decorated the puffy sleeves. "Margie's never had a store-bought dress—Annie makes all the girls' clothes. My baby girl would look sweet as sugar in that dress."

Dirk pressed his nose to the glass, squinting. "Price tag says three dollars and twenty-five cents."

Harley reared back. "That much?"

Dirk lifted his shoulders, his forehead creasing. "It's a lot."

Harley looked back at the little dress. Three dollars was half his month's spending money. As much as he wanted it, he couldn't justify paying that much for a dress that would be outgrown in two shakes of a lamb's tail. He turned from the window, regret churning through his middle. How it stung to be unable to buy something special for Margie. A baby ought to have something special for her first birthday.

"There're other stores, Harley." Dirk nudged his arm. "C'mon, let's look some more."

Harley shook his head, defeated. "Nah. I don't much feel like it anymore. Let's . . . let's just head back."

They turned toward the street leading to the Petersons' place on the edge of town. For long minutes they walked without talking, although Dirk whistled softly between his teeth. Harley ignored the tune and thought about that little dress and how sweet Margie would look in it. Maybe he should get it, even if it did cost so dear. But no, that much money could buy a week's worth of groceries—wasn't worth the expense.

His thoughts tumbled and churned until he'd worked himself into a fine temper. He kicked a rock, zinging it into the brush at the side of the street. Two birds took flight at the sudden intrusion.

Dirk sent him a sidelong glance. His whistling ended. "You mad at somebody, Harley?"

"Yeah." Harley growled the word. "I'm mad at me. Mad at me 'cause I can't even afford to buy my baby girl a decent present for her birthday. Mad at me 'cause I'm far from home—won't even be there to give her a birthday kiss or watch her bite into her first cake. Mad at me 'cause"—he gave another rock a vicious kick that left a scuff on the toe of his new boot—"nothin' ever goes right in this life."

Dirk came to a halt, but Harley marched another dozen feet before he stopped and whirled around, hands balled into fists. "Well? Are you comin' or not?"

Dirk shook his head sadly. "You're lookin' at things all backward, Harley. How can you say nothin' ever goes right? You got a wife and two little girls to love. Reckon they love you back, too. Those're sure things that are right. You got a home and a farm waitin' for you. Lots of men've lost theirs already, what with that Stock Market crash. That's somethin' else gone right. And what about this job you an' me are on? A steady paycheck, a way to take care of our families even if we do have to be away from 'em. I'd say that's three things gone right."

Harley stood silently in the middle of the road, the sun beating down on his head, his anger burning as hotly as the fireball in the sky.

Dirk walked up and put his big hand on

Harley's shoulder. "You gotta count your blessings, Harley, 'stead of always seeing the sad side of things. You'll never be happy until you do that."

Harley resisted throwing Dirk's hand away. Gritting his teeth, he admitted, "I'm not so good at counting blessings."

A sad smile played at the corners of Dirk's lips. "I know. But you won't get good at it unless you try."

Harley shook his head. Dirk was such a child at times. Counting blessings, ha! Dirk didn't know how few blessings had been in Harley's life until he met Annie and the girls were born. Then it had stopped raining, and he and Annie had grown distant, and now he was away from her. Where was the blessing in that?

Dirk gave Harley a brisk pat that set him into motion. The two walked several more yards before Dirk spoke again. "Guess I'm gonna hafta up my prayers for you, my friend. Good thing I'm on such good terms with that Sower of the Seeds. I know He'll hear me when I pray for you."

Harley snorted in response, but inwardly a little part of him hoped Dirk was right.

Ga-ooooo-gah!

Dorothy skittered to the window and peeked out. She spun back to face Anna Mae and crowed, "They're here, Mama! They're here!"

"Well, come back and let me tie your bow," Anna Mae scolded. Her fretful tone told of her inner confusion. Should she be going into Hutchinson with Jack Berkley and his father? Her hands automatically twisted the ties on Dorothy's dress into a neat bow at the base of her spine. "Now let me look at you."

Dorothy obediently stood in front of her mother, her arms held outward, a beaming smile on her pixie face. Anna Mae sighed. The dress was really too short, but it was the little girl's nicest—buttery yellow organza, full-skirted, with a peep of lace around the collar and cuffs. The short skirt showed Dorothy's scuffed knees and sagging anklets, giving her a waifish appearance that only endeared the little girl more to her mama.

"How do I look?"

Anna Mae gave Dorothy a quick hug. "You look beautiful, darlin'. Now run out and tell Mr. Berkley I'll be right there. I want to tuck an extra diaper into my purse for Marjorie."

Dorothy dashed out the door, and the child's excited chatter came through the open window. Anna Mae stood and smoothed her hands over the front of her own good Sunday skirt. It fit tightly now, uncomfortably so. The new baby was already making its presence known. It wouldn't be long and she'd need to get the maternity clothes from the box in the attic. Her hands trembled slightly as she pressed them against the gentle mound. Closing her eyes, she tried to envision the tiny babe within. No image would come.

A burst of laughter sounded from outside, deep and thunderous. Jack's. The sound sent her stomach churning with nervousness. What did she think she was doing, putting on her best dress and driving clear into Hutchinson with the man who'd proposed to her on her eighteenth birthday?

Oh, Harley, I wish you were here. If Harley were here, there'd be no need to celebrate Marjorie's first birthday with a trip into town.

If Harley were here, she'd just bake a cake. They'd watch the baby shove her little fists into the mounds of icing and laugh when she coated herself with gooey chocolate, just as they had with Dorothy.

But Harley wasn't here.

Jack was. And he was waiting.

With a resigned sigh, she stuffed another diaper into the depths of her bag, then lifted Marjorie from the high chair. She'd dressed the baby in a pink gingham sunsuit and put a little bow in the wisps of hair on the top of her head. Brown sandals covered her pudgy feet.

"I guess you'll do, too, little darlin'." She kissed Marjorie's round cheek as she headed outside.

Jack met them in the middle of the yard, and Marjorie offered a dimpled smile, waving her chubby fists in excitement. Over the weeks, the girls had become so accustomed to Jack, the baby didn't count him a stranger. Anna Mae didn't know if she considered that a good thing or an annoyance.

Jack laughed and reached for Marjorie. The baby tumbled into his arms as readily as she would have her daddy's. Anna Mae's stomach gave another jump. She turned her attention to Jack's father, who waited beside the Model T.

"Well, Miss Dimples," Mr. Berkley said, watching Jack bounce Marjorie on his broad arm, "we could save some gas and pocket change by just staying here and looking at you, couldn't we?" His gaze swept to include Dorothy. "Can't imagine Shirley Temple is any prettier than these two little girls."

Dorothy giggled. She twirled, making the skirt of her dress flare out. "Papa Berkley says we're pretty, Mama!"

Anna Mae stopped Dorothy's dance with a hand on her head. "Yes, he did, but pretty is as pretty does. Behave like a lady, please."

The little girl sighed, then skipped to the car and climbed in. Mr. Berkley got in with her.

As Anna Mae followed Jack, she asked, "Is this outing a hardship?"

He looked at her over his shoulder. His lips quirked into a one-sided grin. "A hardship? What do you mean?"

She paused beside the open car door. "Well, paying for gasoline to get us to Hutchinson, then movie tickets, and Dorothy will beg for popcorn . . . Are you sure this isn't too much?"

He shook his head. "No. I've been to several shows already at the Fox. I know exactly what I'm getting myself into, and I'm ready for it." A full grin lit his face. "But thanks for being concerned. Now get in."

14

"God, please protect me and those with me as we travel the road to Hutchinson. Give us a pleasant day. Amen." With a smile, Jack called over his shoulder, "Hold on, Dorothy! Off we go to the picture show!"

Dorothy squealed with excitement as the car headed through the gate.

For the first several miles, Anna Mae sat, stunned, unable to think of anything except the simple prayer Jack had offered for travel safety. To her shame, she realized not once had she petitioned her Father on how to respond to Jack's invitation. Thinking back, she couldn't remember the last time she'd prayed—really prayed—since Harley had left. Her mind had been so caught up in taking care of the house, taking care of the garden, taking care of the girls—and spatting with Jack—that her deep, daily communion with God had turned into snatches of time wedged between other concerns.

Tears pressed behind her lids. What was happening to her? The drought had already taken so many precious things—the crops, the mules, Harley. Would it steal the joy of her relationship with God, as well? Her heart pounded hard. She couldn't let that happen!

"Mama, look at the cows!" Dorothy's excited voice pulled Anna Mae from her thoughts.

She looked out the window. "Yes, I see them. Can you count them?"

"One, two, three . . ." Dorothy counted loudly, giggling between numbers.

Anna Mae's heart lifted. Even if she hadn't prayed about this outing, Dorothy's pleasure at rolling across the countryside on a spring day made it all worthwhile. She leaned back in the seat, determined to enjoy this birthday celebration.

It turned out to be a pleasant ride with the windows down. A steady breeze kept the passengers comfortable, although Dorothy's hair and Marjorie's ribbon were both wild by the time they reached Hutchinson. Jack parked the Model T along Main Street, and they walked around the corner to the theater. Anna Mae imagined what they must look like to the passersby on the street—a complete family with grandfather, father, mother, and children. Despite her earlier decision to simply enjoy the day, the churning began again in her stomach.

Jack stepped up to the cast-iron ticket booth, his father at his elbow, watching the transaction. Dorothy pranced in place while Anna Mae tried to finger comb the child's hair back into her ponytail. The moment Jack turned, tickets in hand, Dorothy pulled away from her mother to grab Jack's hand. Anna Mae's stomach rose into her throat at the sight.

"Dorothy, get over here with me," she ordered.

Dorothy's face puckered with hurt, but she released Jack's hand and returned to her mother. Anna Mae made a show of fussing with the child's hair some more. "Now, stay with me, and don't touch anything."

Holding Dorothy's hand and balancing Marjorie on her other arm, Anna Mae turned toward the theater doors. Jack opened the door, Mr. Berkley gestured for her to enter, and she stepped into another world.

Dorothy's mouth formed a perfect *O* as she stared in wonder at the spacious foyer with its geometric-patterned carpet and curving staircase that led to a gold-railed balcony overhead. The little girl's head turned this way and that, trying to take in everything at once. When her gaze bounced upward, she exclaimed, "Mama, there's stars on the ceiling!"

Anna Mae's gaze followed her daughter's pointing finger, and she gasped. "Oh my!" The ceiling, set with some sort of gold triangular plates, did give the appearance of stars set side-by-side. "That's the prettiest thing I've ever seen."

Then she had to rethink her statement as she examined the sparkling chandelier that sent out beams of golden light. "That thing's bigger than one of our mules!" She heard the wonder in her own tone and, for a moment, felt embarrassed by her childish exclamation, but Mr. Berkley's gentle smile eased her discomfiture. His eyes seemed to tell her to relax and enjoy, so she did.

She and Dorothy exclaimed over the gilt carvings above door openings and impossibly large, gilt-framed mirrors that hung on peach-painted walls. Dorothy skipped to the wide staircase and balanced on the first riser, resting her chin on the polished wood handrail of the gold metal railing. "Mr. Berkley, what's up there?" She pointed to the top of the stairs.

Jack crossed the floor to place his hand on Dorothy's straggly hair. "The balcony, honey. People can sit in seats up there to watch the show."

"Can we?" Dorothy's eyes sparkled with desire.

Jack shook his head. "I'm sorry, Dorothy, but warm air rises, and it'd be too hot up there today. The balcony's best for wintertime."

Dorothy's face drooped into a pout.

"But if it's okay with your mama," Jack compromised, "I can take you up and let you look down at the main floor. There's a railing up there, so you can wave down at her. How would that be?"

Dorothy's smile immediately returned. "Can I, Mama?"

Anna Mae nodded, then watched Jack and Dorothy climb the stairs together. Dorothy's small hand stayed on the handrail all the way up. When they reached the landing, Jack looked back and teased, "Well, if we're going to wave at you, you better go on in."

Anna Mae giggled self-consciously.

"C'mon," Mr. Berkley encouraged, putting his hand on the small of her back.

They walked past two uniformed, smiling young men, and entered the theater. Electric sconces along each wall gave the large room a homey glow, illuminating more gilded carvings and cream-and-peach-striped walls. Anna Mae heard Dorothy call, "Mama? Mama?"

Stepping from beneath the overhang of the balcony, she looked upward. Dorothy's happy face peered over the edge of the metal railing. The little girl waved, and Anna Mae waved back. Dorothy's giggle echoed through the room. Other moviegoers, already waiting in seats, smiled in Anna Mae's direction, and she sent them a sheepish grin.

"It's our first time at a picture show." Then she turned her gaze back up to Dorothy. "Come on down now and pick us some seats, okay?"

Dorothy gave one more wave before disappearing. In a few minutes, she and Jack joined Anna Mae in the aisle between rows of seats upholstered in a pattern similar to that in the plush carpet.

"Where do you want to sit, honey?" Mr. Berkley asked.

"Front row!" Dorothy begged.

Anna Mae needed to be where she could get out with the baby, if necessary. Jack must have read the hesitance in her expression, because he intervened with a second compromise.

"Dorothy, it's been my experience that the middle is the best place to see everything. How about right here?" He pointed to a row of seats in the center of the theater.

Dorothy nodded, her hair bouncing, and skipped to the seats. She counted as she entered the row. "One, two, three, four. You sit here, Papa Berkley." She directed him to the fourth seat in. "Then Mr. Berkley can sit by his daddy, I'll sit next, and Mama can sit on the end."

"I'll be right back," Jack said. He paused, looking down at Anna Mae. "Do you want a box of popcorn, too?"

Anna Mae hesitated. The warm, buttery smell of the popcorn tantalized her taste buds. It was so nice to be past the time of queasiness in this pregnancy. But she didn't want to be greedy. With some regret, she answered, "No, I'll just share with the girls."

Jack headed up the aisle. Dorothy entertained Marjorie with a finger game, and Anna Mae visited with Mr. Berkley while they waited for Jack to return. When he came, he balanced four boxes of aromatic popcorn on one arm, and three sweaty bottles of Royal Crown Cola dangled from his other hand.

Dorothy reached eagerly for a box of popcorn and immediately began munching.

"Jack, this is too much," Anna Mae protested when he held out a box of popcorn and bottle of soda pop.

"Nonsense. Take it."

Reluctantly, Anna Mae relieved him of the box and bottle.

"They didn't have any birthday cake," he quipped.

Anna Mae couldn't stop the smile that tugged at her lips. "No, I suppose not. But this is just as good. Thank you, Jack."

"Thank you, Mr. Berkley," Dorothy said around a mouthful of popcorn.

Jack smiled in return.

Others entered and filled in seats around

them, whispered voices and occasional muffled laughter giving the room a feeling of hushed expectancy. Anna Mae's excitement built as thick gold curtains, hung beneath an arched canopy of silver and gold gilt carvings, slid apart to reveal the movie screen. At the same time, the lights dimmed, sealing them in a murky gray that only added to the anticipation of the moment.

Dorothy released a loud gasp, perching on the edge of her seat. "Is it starting, Mr. Berkley? Is it starting?"

Jack put a finger against his lips and cautioned, "Yes, honey, it's starting. And people will want to listen, so you have to hush now, okay?"

"Okay!" Dorothy settled back, feet straight out in front of her, her gaze pinned to the screen.

From somewhere behind them booming music, as if performed by a full orchestra, filled the auditorium. Marjorie jumped, and for a moment Anna Mae feared the baby would cry and she'd be forced to take her out. But then a beam of light met the screen, capturing the baby's attention. Marjorie's wide-eyed gaze blinked as numbers flashed in quick succession. The music turned fanciful, accompanying a cartoon mouse that danced its way across the screen. Dorothy's face lit with pleasure, and baby Marjorie, with two fingers in her mouth, stared unblinking at the wondrous sights unfolding.

Laughter erupted at several points during the cartoon escapade, Anna Mae's as boisterous as Dorothy's. She couldn't help it— she'd never imagined anything as clever as drawn images becoming a lifelike, talking, prancing animal.

After the movie ended, Anna Mae couldn't decide which she'd enjoyed more—watching the story about the curly-haired street urchin or witnessing her children's enchantment with the movie. Several times she'd caught Jack's eye over the top of Dorothy's head, and the wink he sent each time told her how much he enjoyed the children's fascination. Anna Mae recognized his growing affection for the girls, and another quiver of trepidation struck hard. She pushed it aside, however, reminding herself that Harley had asked Jack to take care of them. He was only doing what Harley had requested.

Anna Mae experienced a sense of loss

when the show ended, the lights came up, and people filed past them to leave. They waited until all others were gone before falling in line. It had been an afternoon of delight, and Anna Mae understood completely when Dorothy sighed and said, "Oh, that was so wonderful my heart feels bigger."

Both girls slept all the way back to Spencer. It was past suppertime when they pulled into the yard. Dorothy sat up groggily when Jack stopped in front of the house. She hugged Mr. Berkley, then leaned over the seat to give Jack a thank-you hug before running to the house and sitting on the back porch stoop. Anna Mae climbed out of the car, cradling the still-sleeping Marjorie, and leaned slightly to peer through the open window at Jack.

"Thank you so much for the treat, Jack. The girls had a marvelous time. And . . ." She debated with herself—should she say it? He'd been exceptionally generous. He deserved the truth. After swallowing, she admitted on a breathy sigh, "So did I."

His smile lit his eyes. "Good. I'm glad." His gaze dropped to Marjorie. "I know she won't remember it, but I will. Thanks for letting us be a part of her first birthday."

A lump filled Anna Mae's throat—a lump of longing she didn't understand. Unable to speak, she nodded.

"Well, good-bye, Anna Mae. I'll be by on Sunday to take you to church."

Jack shifted gears, and the car rolled toward the gate. Dorothy wandered back to stand beside her mother and waved. When the Model T had wheezed around the corner, she looked up and asked, "Mama, can I check the mail?"

"Sure, see if anything came." Anna Mae watched as Dorothy skipped to the end of the lane, pulled down the door on the metal box, and rose on tiptoe to peek inside. The child's face broke into a smile, and she plunged her arm in almost to the elbow to withdraw an envelope. She waved it over her head as she ran back to her mother.

"Lookee, Mama! A letter! A letter from—" she examined it, scratching her head— "somebody."

Anna Mae laughed and took it. Her laughter immediately died when she saw the return address. For some reason, her heart skipped a beat and a wave of guilt washed over her. The letter was from Harley.

15

Anna Mae waited until the girls were tucked into their beds before sitting down at the kitchen table and opening Harley's letter. It had seemed wrong to read it immediately after spending time with Jack. She didn't understand why, yet she'd felt the need to clear the afternoon from her thoughts before focusing on the letter. Now they'd eaten supper, the dishes had been washed, and the girls had been bathed and settled between their sheets. The house was quiet, Dorothy's cheerful babble stilled. The picture show was tucked neatly into Anna Mae's memory bank. She could concentrate.

Before opening the envelope, she held it flat on the table and ran a finger over the messy printing that formed her name and address. Closing her eyes, she tried to envision Harley—seated on the ground, perhaps, a tablet balanced on his knee, a pencil in his work-roughened hand, face creased with concentration. A smile twitched at the corners of her mouth. How he disliked any kind of written work.

She lifted the envelope and pinched it. It was thin—probably no more than one sheet of paper resided within. She allowed herself to chuckle. He'd never be a novelist, that was certain. But she knew what she wanted to see inside. An apology. An outpouring of *I love you* and *I miss you*. Her heart swelled, making her chest feel tight, as the words she wanted to say in return rolled through her mind.

How she regretted the anger that had held her aloof his last day here. If she could go back and do it all over again, she'd run down the lane like Dorothy had, wrap him in a hug, and promise to never let anger come between them again. They'd wasted too many days allowing frustration with things that were out of their control to keep them apart. But this separation had taught Anna Mae something—her love for Harley went

deep, like a root on a willow tree. It continued to flourish despite the hardships, despite the time apart, despite the anger that
had soured their last hours before he
walked down the road.

Little wonder the Good Book advised
folks to never let the sun set on anger—the
resulting regret was a terrible burden to
carry. But she would apologize. Now that
she knew where to reach Harley, she could
tell him how sorry she was, how much she
loved him, how she longed for his return.

Eagerness to see Harley's words got the
best of her. She opened the envelope at last
and slid out a single sheet, folded in thirds.
When she unfolded it, a thin piece of paper
slipped loose and floated to the tabletop.
She picked it up, and her breath caught.
A check for $23.50. She released a huge
breath of relief. Now she could reimburse
Jack for the shoes and buy groceries and all
the other little things they needed. Harley
had said he would provide for them, and he
had. Sitting there holding that check between her fingers, she felt rich.

It took a few moments for her to remember the letter. Sliding the check back into

the envelope, she lifted the sheet of paper and read.

Dear Annie and Dottie and Margie,
How are you doing. I am fine. The work is no harder than what I did at home so I do fine. I found a friend. His name is Dirk. He's pretty green but he's a good man and we get along. Nice to have someone to talk to. He reads his bible and prays so you'd like him. Man in charge is nice enough. Names Peterson. Me and Dirk stay in a shed out behind his house. No running water. Kinda like camping. Its okay. Don't cost us nothing which is good. Take the money I sent and buy Dottie some shoes and whatever else you need then set the rest aside for taxes. Forgot to tell you they come due first of August. Not enough there to cover it all but I'll send more money later. Have Jack take you to the county courthouse to pay the bill.

Harley

She placed the letter on the table, her shoulders sagging with disappointment. Although she hadn't expected a lengthy narrative, she had hoped for something . . . personal. The apology and declaration of love she needed was notably absent. He might as well have been writing to a stranger! And his biggest concern seemed to be the farm, not the people residing on it.

No mention was made of Marjorie's birthday. Surely Harley remembered their baby's first birthday? Anger stirred in her breast, but she did her best to squelch it. She didn't want to feel angry with Harley anymore. She sought ways to allow for his brusque, impersonal communication and lapse of memory concerning Marjorie's big day. He was busy, caught up in this project—she would allow him one moment of forgetfulness.

The sentence about the man named Dirk who read the Bible caught her attention. Her heart thumped in a hopeful double beat. Harley had made a friend who must be a Christian. This pleased her: God was looking out for Harley even though Anna Mae's prayers had been sparse lately. It warmed her, reminding her of God's faithfulness. What was that verse in Psalms Mama had liked so much? It came from a short chapter—Psalm 117, Anna Mae thought. It gave

a reminder of the greatness of God's love
and enduring faithfulness. God was certainly faithful, placing a Christian man on
that work team, and Harley accepting him
as a friend.

Anna Mae folded her hands beneath her
chin and sent forth a prayer of gratitude for
Dirk. At first she struggled to find words,
prayer having been set aside far too long,
but after a few stumbling thoughts, the
words began to flow, the ease returning.
She felt the comfort of God's presence settle around her shoulders like a soft quilt as
her prayer continued. She lifted up Harley,
Dirk, herself, and her girls. She begged forgiveness for staying away so long and vowed
to do better. Then her thoughts turned to
Jack.

"I . . . I thank you, God, for Jack's friendship, for his willingness to help out here
even though I haven't always acted grateful.
Bless his kindness to us. But, God?" She
licked her lips, suddenly hesitant to express
her next thoughts, even to the One who already knew them. "Don't let me lean on him
too much. When he prayed this afternoon
before taking off for Hutchinson, it—it hurt
me. It reminded me of what Harley and I

lack. It made me long for a husband who knows you and loves you. But I married Harley, and I love Harley—I really do, God!" Her heart raced with the sincerity of her proclamation. "Don't let me look at Jack as . . . as more than the friend he was in my girlhood. Guard my heart, please. With Harley away and Jack nearby, I'm . . . I'm afraid."

Eyes closed tight, she remained silent before her God for several more minutes, absorbing the sweetness of communion. Then, with a ragged breath, she ended the prayer. "Thank you, God, for listening and answering. In your Son's name I pray. Amen."

She rose and put away the now-dry dishes that waited on a clean dish towel stretched across the counter. The task complete, she returned Harley's letter to the envelope and carried it to her room. After propping the envelope against her hairbrush on the bureau, she dressed for bed, then slipped between the sheets.

Wide-eyed and alert, she lay listening to the gentle night sounds. The wind moved the branches of the weeping willow outside her window, sending dancing shadows across the wall of the room. Crickets sang, and far away a coyote released one mournful howl. The sounds had been the same since her childhood. She took comfort in the thought that some things never changed. She wondered if the night sounds were different where Harley was. She'd have to ask when she wrote to him. Because she *would* write him. Tomorrow. A long, newsy letter, filled with her sorrow for how she'd treated him his last day and how she wished he were here.

Her thoughts drifted back over the day, images playing through her head as she stared at the flower-sprigged wallpaper covering the ceiling. Despite her disappointment with Harley's distant letter, it had been a good day. She smiled, remembering Marjorie's and Dorothy's delight at their first picture show. A feeling of warmth accompanied the memory of Jack's and Mr. Berkley's kindness, and the gratitude that, even if it was an unsatisfying letter, she'd heard from Harley. The best moment of all, though, was ending the day in prayer.

"Phipps!"

Mr. Peterson's booming voice carried over all other voices. Harley dropped his shovel and trotted across the hard ground, coming to a halt in front of the boss. Mr. Peterson thumped a box into his hand. "This came in my mail. Addressed to you."

"Thanks, sir!"

"Take a break. Open it up."

Harley smiled his thanks and gave a nod. He carried the parcel two-handed to a quiet spot away from the others. Turning his back on the throng, he plunked down on the hard ground. He crisscrossed his legs and placed the box on his ankles. It was hard to believe he'd gotten a package already. Hadn't been that long ago that he'd written to Annie so she'd know where he was and that he was doing okay.

Writing his thoughts on paper had never been something that came easy—harder, even, than saying them out loud, and that was plenty tough. He hoped she had been able to read between the feeble lines of print and see what he carried on his heart. And now he got to open a box from her. She'd be better at saying what she felt. His Annie was never short of words. His heart set up a mighty thrumming as he sat, the box weighty against his legs, enjoying the anticipation of the moment. What would Annie have sent? The box was too small to hold clothes but too large for just a letter.

Wind teased the tails of the string that held the brown paper in place. The dancing strings invited him to dive in. Rolling onto one hip, he removed his penknife from his pocket. One snip and the string fell away. He picked it up, wrapped it around his closed knife, and slipped it back in his pocket. Taking care not to rip the paper, he removed and folded it. Once it was in a neat square, he tucked it beneath his hip and finally opened the box. Slowly. His lower lip held between his teeth.

Pleasure coiled through his middle when he spotted the contents: sugar cookies. *Ah, that Annie.* He couldn't stop the smile that grew on his face. They were pretty much in pieces from their jostled journey across the state, but he picked up one sizable chunk and stuck it in his mouth. He sighed in satisfaction. It tasted like home—every bit as good as he'd remembered.

He ate two more pieces before he noticed a folded piece of waxed paper in the bottom of the box. Poking his fingers through the broken cookies, he removed the waxed paper and shook it to get the crumbs off. Tablet paper, folded into a square, was held between the layers of waxed paper. He set the box on the ground and unfolded the letter.

Dear Mr. Phipps, he read.

Huh?

He jerked his gaze to the signature. *Mrs. Eldo Farley.* His heart plummeted. The cookie turned to sawdust in his mouth. The anticipation, the joy of receiving the package, diminished until his belly felt hollow. He hadn't realized until that moment how much he wanted—needed—to hear from Annie. He pushed aside his disappointment to read what Mrs. Farley had written.

Dirk said you were getting filled by the cooking at the café, but I thought you might enjoy a little homemade treat. The cookies will probably be crumbs by the time they reach you, but they should taste the same. A crooked smile tugged at his lips. She was right—the first taste had been good. He took another piece of cookie and munched while he finished the brief letter.

Thank you again for telling us about this

job. Dirk's check was welcome, and it has given us new hope that we can keep this farm long enough for Dirk to raise his own family here someday. Bless you, Mr. Phipps. We are keeping you in our prayers. In God's love, Mrs. Eldo Farley.

In his mind, he pictured Dirk's mother—small, smiling, her eyes warm. It was kind of her to write to him and send the treat. But, he admitted as he reached for another chunk of cookie, he really just wanted to hear from Annie.

Harley rested the letter on his knee, the breeze ruffling the edges of the paper as he stared into the distance and tried to picture his farm, his family. Oh, how he missed them.

Every night, alone on his cot, he thought of Annie and wondered how she was doing—if the new baby was making her belly poke out yet, if she lay staring into the dark, thinking of him . . . He reached for another piece of cookie, but as he lifted it to his lips, an image intruded: Jack sitting at his kitchen table, holding one of Annie's sugar cookies, a smirk on his face.

Now, where did that come from? Once the

picture set in his head, he couldn't get rid of it. He threw the cookie back into the box. Two pieces bounced out and landed in the dirt. He released a soft oath as he picked them up between his finger and thumb and tried to brush off the coating of dust. Impossible. With another curse, he threw them as far as he could and lowered his head.

"Hey, Phipps!"

Harley pivoted to peer over his shoulder. One of the other workers waved at him.

"What you doin' over there? Let's get back to work."

Even though the boss had given him permission to take the unscheduled break, he didn't want to take advantage. He raised his hand in acknowledgment, and the other man turned back to his shoveling. Rising, he placed the letter and folded brown paper on top of the cookies, replaced the lid on the box, and then settled the box against his hip.

He thumped his feet hard against the earth as he headed back to the work site. With every step, one word repeated itself again and again: *Jack . . . Jack . . . Jack . . .*

"Work it off," he muttered to himself, then

released a rueful chuckle. Some things were just like being at home.

Jack tapped on the porch door, opened it, and stepped through, feeling as though he were stepping back in time ten years to the days when he'd been welcomed at the Elliott farm just like a member of the family. He paused at the kitchen door until he heard Anna Mae's call: "Come on in, Jack."

He smiled. No more "Git, Jack." Now it was "Come on in, Jack." Things were improving.

Anna Mae sat at the kitchen table. He watched as she touched glue to the flap of an envelope and pressed it down. When she finished her task, she looked up, a bright smile in her eyes.

He had to remind himself to breathe.

"Good morning. The milk's ready to go, and could I ask another favor?"

Anything, his heart said. "Sure," he said aloud, keeping his tone light.

She held the envelope toward him. "Would you mail this for me? I've got stamp money but no stamps."

He took it and looked at the name. *Harley Phipps, c/o Mr. Peterson.* He scowled, a wave of jealousy rising up inside him. "Who's Peterson?"

Anna Mae moved to the sink and stuck her hands beneath the flow of water. She spoke over her shoulder. "Harley's boss. Harley is staying in a shed behind the man's house."

"So you heard from him, huh?" Jack hoped he didn't sound as irritated as he felt.

"Yes." She dried her hands on a length of toweling, her smile soft. Digging around in a can on the windowsill, she extracted three copper coins, which she dropped in his open palm. "He's doing well, and he sent me a check. So when I go to town next, I'll be able to pay you back for those shoes you picked up for Dorothy."

"There's no hurry." He pocketed the pennies, then fingered the plump envelope, curiosity burning in his gut.

"No, it needs to be done. Even Harley said so in his letter."

Jack pinched his brows together. "How'd Harley know?"

"Oh, he didn't." Anna Mae rubbed the inside of a black cast-iron skillet with bacon fat and placed it on the stove. "He just said to buy her some shoes with his paycheck.

Since they're already bought—" striking a match, she opened the side door to the fuel chamber and dropped it on the waiting kindling—"I just need to pay you back." Facing him, she pressed a finger to her lips and looked at him thoughtfully. "When are you heading to town?"

Jack slid her letter into his shirt pocket. The bulk felt odd against his chest. "Why?"

"I'd like to get things taken care of as soon as possible."

It rankled that she was so eager to rid herself of her perceived debt—like she couldn't be beholden to him for something as small as the cost of a pair of shoes. "I'm heading there now."

Her face fell. "Oh. I couldn't go now. The girls are still sleeping." She peeked into the fuel chamber and added two scoops of coal from a half-full bucket sitting next to the stove. "I guess I won't be able to go today, then. Will you go some other time this week?"

Jack nodded slowly. "I'll go in on Wednesday."

"May we go with you?"

He shrugged. "Sure. We'll have to take the wagon, though, since I'll be transporting milk to meet the truck."

"That's fine." The grease in the skillet began to sizzle. Reaching for a basket of eggs on the edge of the counter, she asked brightly, "Have you had breakfast?"

He hadn't, but he had other pressing business. As much as he wanted to sit and have fried eggs with Anna Mae, there was something else he needed to do more. "Yes," he lied, "but thanks anyway. I'll grab the milk and head out."

"All right. Bye, Jack." She flashed another smile. "Thanks for taking that letter."

Her attention turned to the breaking of eggs, and he slipped out the door. He loaded the milk as quickly as possible, climbed in the wagon, and slapped the reins down hard. The horses jolted forward, clanking the two milk cans together. He relaxed his hands on the reins and intoned, "Eeeeasy, there, boys. Let's go easy." No need to spill Anna Mae's milk.

Halfway between his house and the Phipps' place, he gave a tug on the reins that brought the horses to a halt. Then he reached into his pocket, removed the letter Anna Mae had asked him to mail, and tore it open.

16

Jack resisted the urge to peek over his shoulder as he removed the letter intended for Harley from its envelope. There wasn't anybody looking, and even if there were, they'd just assume he was reading his own mail. But he still fought the need to check. There was no pang of guilt—just a worry of being caught.

The glue was still damp, and he got goo on his finger. He grunted and wiped it on his pant leg, then unfolded the pages, bringing Anna Mae's neat lines of script into view. He angled the pages away from the sun and began to read, a scowl pinching his face.

Dear Harley, I was pleased to receive your letter and to know how to reach you. I can't believe it's been a whole month since you left. Our last day, and our fight, has weighed so heavily on my heart. If I could do things over, Harley, I wouldn't have sent you off in anger. I hope you will forgive me. It's been so lonely here without you.

Lonely, huh? Jack's lips twitched. Well, maybe he'd better come around more often and take care of that little problem.

The girls and I miss you terribly, but I'm glad to know you are safe and working and have found a place to stay. Jack—his heart gave a lurch seeing his own name scripted by Anna Mae's hand—*has been by every day to see to the milk and cream and extra eggs. The penny bank on the windowsill jingles when I shake it. It's a good feeling, knowing the amount is growing. I'm thinking I'll use it to pay Mrs. Connelly when the time comes. The baby is already making the waist on my clothes pinch. I'll need to get out my maternity skirts soon.*

Jack frowned. All he'd done, and she couldn't let Harley know how much she appreciated his assistance? Then his gaze swept over the words *maternity skirts*. The reminder of the new baby set him back for a moment. How he wished it wasn't Harley's baby making her waistband tight. Jealousy smacked him hard, tightening his fingers on the pages firmly enough to leave creases behind. He pushed the emotion aside and read on.

Marjorie had a good birthday even though I didn't bake her a cake. We'll save that for when you come home. With a snort, Jack slapped the letter against his knee. She could've baked that cake and asked him to join her! Jerking the pages back into position, he continued to read. *Jack and his father took the girls and me into Hutchinson and we saw a picture show.* The description of the theater and the moving picture took up more than half a page. Jack's chest got so tight he found it hard to breathe. He'd paid for her tickets, her popcorn and soda, and all she could talk about was the theater. Why was she being so ungrateful?

Taking a deep breath, he reminded himself she was writing this letter to Harley. How could she pour out her gratitude toward Jack in a letter to her husband? Of course she couldn't. But he'd heard it in her voice this morning as she'd welcomed him. He'd seen it in her eyes as she'd thanked him for being willing to take her to town.

And he knew when it had blossomed. Friday, in the car, when he'd prayed before leaving for Hutchinson. Harley's lack of faith had been a sore spot for Anna Mae for a long time; Jack had overheard his father advising Anna Mae's father on the subject, and Ern Berkley continued to pray daily for Harley's salvation. Jack released a wry chuckle. He'd offered that prayer out of habit—Pop expected it—but the look on Anna Mae's face had told him it had a deeper implication for her. It was the turning point in her trusting him again.

Oh yes, Anna Mae's gratitude was there. It just needed to stay between the two of them—Harley couldn't know.

His thoughts calmed, and he flattened the pages against his lap, using his finger to underline the words as he read. *Now that your paycheck has arrived, I'll ask Jack to take me into town so I can buy flour, sugar, and some other groceries. I promised Dorothy she could pick out the flour sack, and I'll make her an apron from the fabric. I'll also pay for some shoes.* Jack smirked. What a clever way of wording it. It wasn't a lie, yet it hid the fact that Jack had already purchased shoes. It pleased him to have a secret between himself and Anna Mae.

Thank you for telling me about the taxes. I'll be cautious not to spend too much and set as much aside as I can. I'm sure Jack will take me to the courthouse to pay our tax bill.

Hmm. Another drive all the way to Hutchinson with Anna Mae. Maybe they'd take in another picture show, only this time they'd leave the girls with his father and go alone— just the two of them. He sucked in a breath of anticipation, his gaze aimed unseeingly across the dusty landscape, before turning back to the pages in his hand.

The letter went on, telling about how the garden fared, Margie's new tooth, Ol' Smokey's capture of a barn swallow and Dottie's horror at witnessing it, as well as other little items that were more important to women than men. And finally, the letter came to a close.

We miss you, Harley, and eagerly anticipate your return. Please greet your friend Dirk for me. I'm so pleased you've found someone to spend time with while you're away. It helps to have a friend. Could those words hint about the time she'd spent with him? *Do you know when the castle might be finished so you can come home? We're managing, but it will be nice when we are all together again. Take care of yourself, Harley. My prayers are with you even if I can't be. I love you, Anna Mae.*

The closing tightened Jack's chest with an envy so deep it almost frightened him. How often had he hoped to hear "I love you" from Anna Mae's lips? His whole life, it seemed. And there they were, staring up at him in black lead on white paper, but they were meant for someone else.

Without a thought, he crushed the pages in his fist until they were nothing but a mangled ball. He threw the wad as hard as he could into the brown weeds beside the road. "Git up there," he commanded, slapping the reins on the horses' backs once more. A few yards farther, he ripped the envelope to shreds and disposed of it the same way. The pennies sat heavily in his pocket, reminding him of his traitorous act, but he reasoned he could use those coins to buy some candy for Dorothy and Marjorie; then it wouldn't be wasted.

"Jack, what are you doing?" His father's

question echoed in his mind. But Jack played dumb and refused to answer.

Anna Mae hummed as she served Marjorie and Dorothy their breakfast. A lightness filled her heart—a happiness that bubbled upward. She examined herself for the root of her joy and discovered making peace with Harley had allowed her to make peace with herself. Even if his letter hadn't overflowed with proclamations of love, it had felt good to tell him how she felt. *Do unto others as you would have them do unto you* had always been the rule when she was growing up, and she realized that doing right just made a body feel good all the way to her toes.

What would Harley think when he got her letter? Would all his frustration with her melt away with the reading of her loving thoughts? She hoped so. Even with him miles away, she didn't want him to stay angry with her. Maybe this time apart would prove good for both of them—make them realize how much they meant to each other. There was so much to admire in Harley—his desire to take care of her and the girls as well as the farm, his honesty, his innate sense of

fairness. Those were the things that had ap-
pealed to her from the beginning.

The drought, the lack of money, and
Harley's stubborn refusal to believe in God
had pulled her focus away from the positive
aspects of her relationship with her husband. She remembered when Mama fell ill,
and the doctor had said there was no hope.
Anna Mae had cried a river of tears, but
then Mama had said it was time to stop
looking at the dark underside of the cloud
and try to see the silver lining—heaven just
around the bend. The peaceful look on
Mama's face as she'd slipped away had assured Anna Mae the silver lining had become reality for her.

Well, now Anna Mae needed the glimpse
of a silver lining, and the only way she'd see
it was to look for it. She made the determination to look, and she found it in the security of a steady paycheck, Harley's promise
to Dorothy to return, and her own prayers.
When Harley came back, they'd make more
of an effort to hold frustration at bay and
really work together as a team. She offered
a prayer for that to occur.

"Whatever it takes, Lord," she prayed under her breath as she cleared the breakfast

table, "to pull us together and give us strong roots to weather any storm. . . ."

"Mama, who're you talkin' to?" Dorothy's face scrunched in query.

Anna Mae sent a smile in her daughter's direction as she scrubbed at a plate. "I was talking to my Father God, darlin'."

"You were praying?" The child sounded shocked.

"Yes, I was."

"But your eyes were open!"

Anna Mae released a light laugh. "Well, God doesn't mind if we talk to Him with our eyes open, Dorothy. Just as long as we talk to Him at all, He's happy."

Dorothy tipped her head, obviously deep in thought. "Then how come my Sunday school teacher got so mad at me when she saw me peeking during a prayer?"

Anna Mae coughed to cover her laugh. Sometimes Dorothy asked the funniest questions. "In church we should always close our eyes when we pray. But you don't have to when you're doing dishes."

Satisfied by the answer, Dorothy hopped down from the table. "I'm goin' out to play with Ol' Smokey."

"Stay close," Anna Mae admonished, "since we'll need to water the garden soon."

"Okay."

Once the kitchen was clean again, and the garden had received a thorough watering, Anna Mae joined Dorothy and Marjorie under the weeping willow tree for a tea party. Those moments in the dappled shade provided by the slender, nearly luminous leaves of the willow transported Anna Mae back to the simple days of her own childhood. She wondered if someday Dorothy would serve dirt clods on slabs of bark to her own little girls under this very same tree.

Sitting there giggling with Dorothy while Marjorie squirmed in her lap, she wondered how she could have ever considered leaving the farmstead. This was her home, the place that held all of her growing-up memories as well as those of her brother, mother, and father. A feeling of belonging welled up and filled her, and tears pricked the corners of her eyes. This was home, and it always would be. The realization increased the lightness of her heart, and she offered a silent prayer of gratitude for the job Harley had found and the means to keep this farm. The silver lining she'd sought earlier lengthened, hiding a bit more of the cloud's gray underside.

Sliding Marjorie from her lap for a moment, she struggled to her feet. "Okay, darlin'," she told Dorothy, "this has been fun, but lunchtime is just around the corner, so I'm going to have to go in."

Dorothy heaved a sigh. "Okay." She pushed her straggly bangs away from her eyes. "Can I stay out here a little longer? Please?"

"Yes, but you come when I call you for lunch."

Dorothy nodded her agreement and turned her attention back to the odds and ends that served as plates and cups.

Anna Mae scooped up Marjorie and headed for the house. While Marjorie banged on the tray of the high chair, Anna Mae prepared their lunch. Dorothy came running when called, and they munched cheese sandwiches and pickled beets, drowning it all with glasses of milk. Midway through eating, Anna Mae released the buttons at her waistband. The pinching had become nearly unbearable.

Dorothy pointed. "How come you did that?"

"My dresses are too tight." Anna Mae winked at Dorothy. "There's a new baby growing inside of Mama, and it's taking up more room than my clothes will allow."

Dorothy's blue eyes grew so wide Anna Mae thought they might pop from her head. "Really, Mama? A baby?" At her mother's nod, she exploded, "A girl baby or a boy baby? When will it get here? Can I name it?" She clapped her hands, bouncing in her chair.

Anna Mae laughed. Dorothy's unbridled enthusiasm gave her the first real taste of excitement concerning this new life. "We won't know if it's a brother or a sister until it makes its appearance, and that's a ways off yet. As for naming it . . . You'll have to ask your daddy about that when he gets home." She pushed aside the unhappy memory of the night she and Harley fought about the baby's name, choosing to focus instead on Dorothy's happiness. "And as soon as Marjorie is down for her nap, I'm going to get my maternity clothes from the attic so the baby will have room to grow."

Dorothy trailed behind her mother as Anna Mae changed Marjorie's diaper and placed her in her crib. Back in the kitchen, the little girl tugged her mother's skirt. "Get the 'ternity clothes now, Mama, so my new baby can grow."

Anna Mae tweaked Dorothy's nose, then grabbed hold of the rope attached to the overhead stairway in the corner of the kitchen. It took three tugs to pull the stairway free of its frame. With a creak, the ladder unfolded until the shoes of the side rails met the floor. Anna Mae placed one foot on the bottom rung and peered upward through the hole that led to the attic. She took a deep breath. How she hated these steep stairs! But she had to have those clothes. If only Harley were here to go after them for her. Maybe she should wait and ask Jack to . . . No, Jack had done enough already. She could retrieve her own maternity clothes.

Dorothy stood beside her mother, her little face creased with concentration. "Mama, how're you gonna carry the box down?"

"I'm not," Anna Mae replied. "I'll just drop it from the hole. Nothing in it can break. But you stand back. I don't want it to land on you." She managed a smile. "It would squash you like a bug."

Dorothy scuttled behind the table. "I'll stay over here."

"Good girl." Anna Mae took hold of the side rails and made her way slowly up the rungs, one by one. Her palms began to sweat when her head popped through the attic floor and stuffy air slapped her face. This was the part she hated. There was nothing to hold on to for the last three steps. Dizziness made her head spin as she released the side rails. With a silent prayer, she managed the last few steps. Relief washed over her when her feet stood securely on the wood floor of the attic. The dead air, laden with dust motes, made her nose twitch, and she sneezed.

"Mama?" Dorothy's voice sounded hollow. "Can you see?"

"Yes, darlin', I'm fine." The dust-encrusted windows at either end of the attic allowed in enough murky light for Anna Mae to locate the box of maternity clothes. She pushed it to the opening, then called down, "Dorothy, stay back. Here it comes." With a grunt, she sent the box through the opening. It bounced against the ladder halfway down. The box popped open and tipped upon impact, spilling its contents across the kitchen floor.

Anna Mae groaned. Another mess to clean

up. *Oh well, they're down where I can get to them, at least.*

Dorothy appeared at the base of the ladder. "Mama, want me to pick these up?"

"Yes, that would be a big help. Thank you, darlin'."

"You're welcome," the child chirped.

Kneeling at the opening, Anna Mae lowered one foot through the hole and found a rung. Her hands on the sturdy floor, she put her other foot through and began the downward climb. As she connected with the fourth rung, the ladder seemed to shudder. She heard an odd sound—like a twig snapping—and then, to her horror, the ladder gave way.

She grabbed frantically for the frame of the opening overhead. Her nails tore at the floorboards as her fingers slid along the wood. She experienced one panicked moment—Dorothy stood beneath the ladder—and she heard her daughter's shriek of fear. Her body connected hard with the kitchen floor. She registered pain as she heard the thud of her head against the linoleum, and then . . . nothing.

17

"Phipps, you got some kind of death wish?"

Harley paused, the shovel ready for another thrust, and glanced over his shoulder at Nelson. The man stood with his weight balanced on one hip, glowering in Harley's direction. Harley propped his elbow on the end of the shovel handle. "Whadd'ya mean by that?"

Nelson's squinting gaze flitted to the clear sky and then back to Harley. "It's close to noon—hottest time of day. An' you're shovin' that metal in the ground like there's no tomorrow. You thinkin' you gotta get this job done right now? You're gonna kill yourself, hot as it is."

Nelson's comment made the searing heat

that baked Harley's scalp and shoulders seem to increase in intensity. But he only snorted and turned back to his task. He forced the shovel into the hard ground and strained, popping loose another clump of grassless sod.

"I said, you're gonna kill yourself." Nelson bumped the back of Harley's leg with the blade of his shovel.

Harley spun and shot the man a warning look. "I was hired to do a job," he grated through clenched teeth, "an' I intend to earn my keep."

Nelson strode forward and curled his fingers around Harley's shovel handle. "Slow down, Phipps." The tone prickled the hairs on the back of Harley's neck. "You're makin' the rest of us look bad. 'Sides that, it ain't safe to work this hard when the sun's so high. Give yourself heat stroke."

Harley jerked the shovel free of Nelson's grasp. "I reckon that's my own business."

Nelson backed up a step, shaking his head. "You are by far the most stubborn cuss I've ever encountered. Fine. Drop dead out here. But don't expect none of us to cry over your grave." Nelson stomped several feet away, threw down his shovel, snatched up a water jug, and took a long draw.

Harley swiped his hand across his forehead. His throat felt parched. A drink would be welcome. But perhaps the drink would do more than soothe his dry mouth—it would cool his anger. And Harley wasn't ready to let loose of that yet.

He'd never been a man prone to flights of imagination, but the pictures tormenting his mind wouldn't leave him alone. Some of them sprang from the directions he'd given Jack: Jack sitting next to Annie on the leather seat of his Model T or beside her on a wooden church pew. Others were pure conjecture: Jack at the table in the kitchen, laughing while he ate a snack, or working side-by-side with Annie in the garden.

Harley drove the shovel blade into the ground with such force the handle vibrated, stinging his palms. Sweat dribbled down his forehead, stinging his eyes. Images of Jack and Annie haunted his mind, stinging his heart.

He yanked at the shovel, trying to dislodge it from the dirt, but it refused to budge. With a loud oath, he slapped the handle and spun around. Yanking off his hat, he flung it on the ground, then turned his gaze to the sky.

The sun wavered against the backdrop of blue, appearing to grow larger as Harley stared, panting. The anger grew within his chest until it became a fury he wasn't sure he could contain.

"What's a matter, Phipps? Finally wearin' down?"

Harley swiveled to meet Nelson's sardonic expression. Here was a target for his temper—a means to dispel some of the frustration. Balling his fists, he took two steps in Nelson's direction.

"Phipps!"

The authority in the tone stopped Harley in his tracks. He looked over his shoulder. Mr. Peterson strode toward him, a stern look on his lined face.

Harley released his fists and straightened his shoulders, willing himself to calm.

Mr. Peterson came to a stop not more than twelve inches from Harley. "What do you think you're doing?" Although the man's voice was low, intended only for Harley's ears, Harley didn't miss the admonition in the tone.

Harley clenched his jaw for a moment. He

considered telling the truth—saying he intended to pummel Nelson into the ground—but in the end he barked out one word. "Nothin'."

"It sure looked like something," Mr. Peterson countered. His gaze bored into Harley's, his expression communicating that he knew exactly what Harley had been planning. "You are aware that fighting is grounds for dismissal."

Harley gave a brusque nod. More sweat dribbled into his eyes, but he kept his arms at his sides, welcoming the distracting smart of pain. Took his mind off the ache in his heart.

Mr. Peterson stood, silent, looking hard into Harley's eyes for another few moments. Harley waited, contributing nothing, his gaze pinned to his boss's face yet keenly aware of Nelson standing a stone's throw away. Finally the boss sighed and threw an arm around Harley's shoulders, guiding him away from the pit.

"Listen, Phipps, you've been going at it hard and strong this morning. Take off a little early for lunch—go sit in the shade, get a good drink, *cool off*."

Harley recognized the message beneath the words. He nodded again.

"You're a good worker. I don't want to lose you on the project, and I certainly don't want to see you lose the income. I suspect your family can use it."

Again, Harley understood the warning. He forced himself to answer calmly. "You're right, sir. Thank you."

The boss headed back toward his shack, and Harley turned to scoop up his hat, careful not to look in Nelson's direction. If the man so much as smirked, Harley knew he'd barrel into him whether it meant a lost job or not. Besides, he thought as he settled into the shade cast by the towering pile of shale, if he got fired, he could go home. He could find out what Jack had been up to. And if it was anything like his mind told him, what he planned for Nelson would seem like pat-a-cake compared to what he'd do to Jack.

"Now, you're going to have to stop that crying. It's not helping anything."

The voice drifted through the blackness as if from a distance. Familiar, warm, bringing with it a rush of disjointed memories from earlier years. But Anna Mae didn't understand the message. She wasn't crying. Or was she? A second voice sobbed, "Mama, mama . . ." Was it her own voice? "Mamaaaa." She wished her mama were here. Mama would be able to make sense of all this confusion.

Puckering her face, Anna Mae struggled to break through the dark cloud that held her captive. Her mother's voice came softly, tenderly, whispering a soothing message: *"And the light shineth in darkness; and the darkness comprehended it not."*

What did it mean? Her eyelids felt weighted, but with great effort, she managed to force them open. Light hit her eyes, striking her with a wave of pain so intense she gasped. She felt her face contract with the abrupt slamming of her lids, but in the blackness she found blessed escape from the pain.

She chose to remain in the dark void.

Harley waited until the other two workers moved away from the boss's shack. The shack reminded Harley of a roadside vegetable stand—the top half of each wall folded down to flop against the bottom half, creating large window openings. The roof overhead protected Mr. Peterson from the relentless sun, but the boss could see the entire work site thanks to the wide-open windows. The man now glanced up from the table that sat inside the shack and gestured for Harley to enter. Harley yanked off his hat as he ducked through the doorway.

"Phipps. You cooled off now?"

Funny how Peterson could ask something like that and make it almost teasing. If Nelson had asked the question, Harley would be tempted to take the man's head off. But he heard no animosity in the boss's tone, so he gave a nod in return and said what he'd been waiting to say. "Thanks for suggesting that break. Helped me get my . . . heat . . . under control."

The older man's lips twitched. "Glad to hear it. I'd like to keep you on this project."

Harley nodded again, his head down.

Mr. Peterson rested his elbows on the table. "Listen, Harley, I know Nelson's got a big mouth. Most of the men haven't welcomed you and Farley with open arms. There's a reason for that: you took two positions that might have been filled by local men." When Harley would have spoken, Peterson held up his hands, staying his words.

"I'm not defending them—you have just as much right to this job as any of them—I'm trying to help you understand the animosity."

Harley nodded. "I understand. I'm willing to look past it. But Farley . . ." He grimaced. "Farley's pretty defenseless against it."

Peterson leaned back, his elbow draped over the ladder back of the chair. "I know Nelson ribs poor ol' Dirk constantly. But I need Nelson on this project. He's got a grasp of bedrock and bucking that exceeds anyone else on the team."

Harley wasn't sure what the boss meant by bedrock and bucking, but he understood the underlying message: Nelson wasn't going anywhere, so Harley might as well learn to get along with him. "Yes, sir." Without meaning to, his gaze lit on the drawn plans stretched across the desktop, and he pointed. "That what the castle'll look like when it's done?"

Peterson flicked his fingers at Harley, a silent invitation to come near. When Harley stood on the opposite side of the table, the man flipped the drawing around so Harley could look at it right side up.

"A fascinating thing, a blueprint," Mr. Peterson mused. "A map, really, of how to put materials together into a three-dimensional form. See here?" He pointed. "By reading these marks, a person can determine the height, width, and depth of the structure, as well as placement of windows and doors. If the building were wired for electricity or required pipes for plumbing, there would be separate plans to show where light sockets belong and plumbing lines run. The drawings work together to show how the whole building will be constructed."

Harley looked at the crisscrossing of lines, the tiny numbers indicating feet and inches, and he walked his fingers up the drawing of the enclosed stairway. "It's somethin', all right. How does a body learn to draw one of these things?"

"Where does anybody learn anything? School, Phipps." The man tipped his head, his brows coming down into a thoughtful expression. "That interest you?"

Harley chuckled, rubbing his finger under his nose. "Oh no, sir. I'm just a farmer. Couldn't make it in school. Couldn't afford it, either."

Peterson leaned back in his chair. "Well, I used to teach at the university in Kansas

City—world history. There's a lot to learn about architecture when studying the different cultures of the world, so I picked up things here and there. You're right that it costs to go to school, but it's worth it. Might be something to think about."

Harley shook his head. "I'm only a farmer," he insisted.

"Okay." Peterson glanced at a pocket watch that lay on the table. "It's nearly quitting time. Do you and Dirk want to join the missus and me for supper tonight?"

Harley blinked twice, taking an awkward step backward. Although Mrs. Peterson had occasionally carried out a plate of food to the shed in the evening, never had Harley or Dirk been invited into the house. A gust of wind gave him a whiff of his own body, and that was enough to convince him he had no business sitting across a dinner table from Peterson and his missus.

"Thank you for the invitation, sir, but I reckon Dirk and me will just grab us a bite at the café."

Peterson shrugged. "Suit yourself."

Harley turned toward the door, but just as he was ready to step through, Peterson called his name. He looked back over his shoulder.

"If you change your mind about that blue-print reading, just say so. Learning new things can be good for a man."

Harley nodded, slapped his hat on his head, and clopped toward the shale pile where Dirk was finishing up. *"Learning new things can be good for a man."* The words replayed themselves in his head, and for a moment he fought the temptation to go back and tell Mr. Peterson he'd like to learn about blueprints. Just then, off to his right, a meadowlark burst from a clump of brown brush and shot into the sky. Harley watched it go, recollecting times he'd startled up a bird from the cornfields at home. The reminder of the cornfields was all it took to help him remember that he had a farm waiting for him in Spencer. A farm he'd promised to care for.

Harley wasn't here to learn new things. He was here to save the farm. Better to keep focused on his original goal. And he'd best keep his temper under control, too.

"Our goal at this point is to keep her still and comfortable. . . ."

Doc Warren's droning voice carried from the bedroom to the kitchen, where Jack and Pop sat on opposite sides of the table, each holding one of Anna Mae's girls. Pop cradled Marjorie, who dozed against his shoulder, too young to be concerned about her mother. Jack held Dorothy in his lap as he listened to the doctor's instructions to Mrs. Stevenson.

Dorothy had hardly left Jack's side since she came panting into the yard earlier today, her frantic cry scaring Jack out of ten years of his life. And when he and Pop had come through the back door to see Anna Mae sprawled across the kitchen floor, white and silent, he'd lost another dozen years. These Phipps females would be the death of him yet.

Thank goodness Doc Warren had been in his office when Jack had called. He'd agreed to drive out immediately. The man hardly made house calls anymore, with his advancing years and the arthritis slowing him down, but he'd delivered Anna Mae, and it was obvious in the way he'd hovered over her bed that he took a real interest in keeping her healthy.

At first he'd said he wanted Anna Mae in

the hospital, but then he'd asked where Harley was. Little Dorothy had piped up, "Daddy's away building a castle." The doctor had sent Jack a knowing look and instead instructed Jack to go back to town and fetch Mrs. Stevenson. She was a fair-to-middlin' nurse, he'd said, and she could give Anna Mae care while keeping an eye on the little girls, too.

Mrs. Stevenson, a widow with a bulky frame and two chins, came at once when Jack explained the situation. Her only stipulation was that she must also bring her cat. To Jack's knowledge, Anna Mae had never had an animal in the house, but given the circumstances, he wasn't in a position to argue. Anna Mae needed help. The fuzzy black-and-white critter now curled in a ball next to the stove, its purr providing a background hum to Doc's endless list of to-do's.

Doc entered the kitchen and stopped at the table. His gaze on Dorothy, he said, "Let me peek at your face, young lady."

Dorothy shrank back against Jack, so the doctor leaned forward to examine the little girl's injury. When he pressed his fingers to the large bruise on her forehead, she whimpered but didn't pull away.

Finally Doc smiled. "You'll be fine, Dorothy. That bump'll give you a headache, but it's nothing serious. In fact, it should be easily cured with a—" he dug in his bag and withdrew a pink-and-white-striped candy stick—"peppermint stick."

"Thank you!" Dorothy stuck the candy in her mouth at once.

"And Anna Mae?" Jack asked, holding his breath.

Doc's smile faded. "I'll be back tomorrow morning first thing. Mrs. Stevenson knows what to do. I told her to have you call me if something should change."

Jack shifted Dorothy to the floor, gave her a pat and a whispered order to stay put, then walked the doctor out to his car. Outside of earshot of the girls, he asked, "Will she be okay?"

Doc scratched his chin. "Anna Mae will survive, but I can't say the same about her baby just yet."

Jack felt like someone had punched him in the gut. "You mean she could lose the baby?"

Doc shrugged, tossing his bag into the seat. "That's really not up to me at this point, Jack."

"Then who?"

Wordlessly, Doc Warren pointed skyward, lifting his brows. Then he climbed into his vehicle.

Jack watched him drive away. When the doc was out of sight, he lifted his gaze to the blue sky overhead. A chill went down his spine.

18

A jumble of voices—one deep, one high-pitched, one babbling—forced their way through Anna Mae's subconscious. She frowned, slapping her hand at the sound.

Hush now, I want to sleep.

Soft laughter, more talking.

If you're going to talk, at least talk clear enough for me to understand you. If you can't do that, then hush!

Another burst of laughter followed by a fierce "Shhh!" from a new voice stirred Anna Mae to full awareness. Although she kept her eyes closed, sealing herself in a cocoon of comforting gray, her other senses were keenly aware. She recognized the firm softness of the mattress supporting her body, the cradle of a fluffy feather pillow beneath her head, a teasing breeze from an open window, the sweet trill of birdsong, the smells of morning—fresh dew and pungent barn and spicy bacon . . .

And pain.

She was acutely aware of pain. In her head, shoulders, and hips. Yet she found it bearable, unlike her last memory of a deep, stabbing pain that had sent her scuttling for blessed disconnection.

"Now sit up here and eat," came the deep voice that had awakened her. Even though it still came from a distance, she could understand the words. "Say your prayers first."

"Okay, Papa Berkley," was Dorothy's cheerful concurrence, then, "God is great, God is good . . ."

Anna Mae twisted her head against the pillow, struggling to make sense of what she'd heard. Why was Jack's father here, cooking breakfast? Why was she still in bed? She should be up. She shifted her body, an effort to pull herself into a seated position, but before she could accomplish it, two hands clamped on her shoulders.

"Don't you do that, Mrs. Phipps," a

waspish voice scolded. "You stay right there in that bed. I'll fetch Doc."

Doc? Doc Warren? He was here, too? Something must be seriously wrong! She needed to open her eyes. But the remembrance of pain made her scrunch them more tightly shut instead.

"Doc! Doc, come in here." The offending voice blared in Anna Mae's ear. "She's wakin' up, and I don't know if I can hold her down."

Footsteps—more than one set—thundered close, then a warm, soft palm pressed to Anna Mae's forehead. "Anna Mae, can you hear me?" Doc's voice—how well Anna Mae knew it.

She opened her mouth, willing her dry tongue to form words. All she emitted was a low moan.

Something slapped her cheek twice. The motion made her headache increase. She grunted and moved her head to avoid the contact.

A low chuckle filled her ears. "Oh, get feisty now, that's what we need to see."

Pat, pat on her cheek again. She shifted. The hand followed.

Pat, pat, pat. With a rush of irritation, she

opened her eyes, focused blearily on Doc Warren's face, which loomed over the bed, and rasped, "Stop that. It hurts."

Doc burst out laughing and looked toward the foot of the bed. "She's okay. If she's complaining, she's okay."

Anna Mae squinted at the figures lined up behind the iron footboard. Jack Berkley, Ern Berkley, Dorothy, and Mrs. Stevenson from church, all grinning at her like fools. "What—what's everybody doing here?"

"Dorothy fetched Jack when you fell. He put you to bed and left his father to stand guard, then he called me. I had him fetch Mrs. Stevenson to take care of the girls." Doc's calm voice filled in the gaps.

When I fell . . . ? Confusion clouded her brain. And then she remembered—fetching the maternity clothes, climbing down from the attic, the breaking ladder, and landing hard on the floor.

Dorothy had gone for Jack? What a brave girl . . . Anna Mae tried to send the little girl a smile, but when she focused on her daughter, all she could do was frown. The child had an ugly bruise on her forehead. "Dorothy, what happened to your head?"

Jack put his arm around Dorothy and

tucked her against his side. "She told me when you came down, your feet pushed her into the table. It looks worse than it is, right, honey?"

Dorothy beamed upward. "It don't hurt much, Mama. I'm okay. Mr. Berkley says I'm a trooper."

Yes, she remembered Dorothy picking up the scattered clothes from beneath the ladder. She should have told her to wait. She should not have fallen on her child. Tears stung her eyes—how foolish she had been to endanger her daughter!

"Tell me where it hurts, Anna Mae," Doc prompted, pulling her attention back to him.

"Head . . ." It was so difficult to form words—her tongue felt swollen and dry. "Hips. Shoulders . . ." She grimaced as the pain pounded through her head. She pressed her hands to her hips, and her fingers brushed across her belly. Fear raised her from the bed. "My baby!"

"Shhh." Doc's hands caught her shoulders, gently pushing her back onto her pillow. "Now, don't fret about that."

"Did I—um, did I—?" She couldn't ask the question. Not until that moment had she realized how very much she wanted this new baby. What if her carelessness took the life of her unborn child?

"You didn't lose it." Doc's soft assurance cast a wave of relief through Anna Mae's aching body. But his next word pierced her with fear once more. "Yet."

A bitter taste filled Anna Mae's mouth. "Yet? You mean, I . . . I could still—?"

Doc took her hand. "You took a hard fall. You've had some bleeding, but it's under control now. Still, I want you to take it easy for a week at least, limit your activity. It'll be the best chance for keeping that baby where it belongs."

Although she'd struggled so hard to open her eyes, all Anna Mae wanted to do at that moment was close them and pretend none of this had happened. She had a farm to care for—she couldn't be lazing around in bed. What would she say to Harley if the garden failed? All the things that needed doing had to be done by her. When Harley heard about this, he'd be home in an instant. But then there would be no money coming in. And they would be back where they started, living with the constant threat of losing the farm.

"B-but," she argued weakly, "Harley's not here, and I have to—"

"You have to stay in bed." Doc's firm tone rose in volume with each word. "There's nothing more important than the life of your baby, Anna Mae. Remember that."

The farm's more important. Did she say the words or only think them? If Harley were here, he'd say them. The farm—keeping the farm—was more important to him than anything else. That's why he was gone right now. But Doc had said nothing was more important than the baby. Was he right, or was Harley right? The dull ache in her head became a throbbing pain. She turned her face away from Doc and closed her eyes. A hand squeezed her shoulder.

"That's right, Anna Mae." Doc's voice soothed the tattered edges of worry from Anna Mae's mind. "You sleep. Your body needs the rest. So sleep."

Anna Mae allowed herself to drift away.

"Papa Berkley, what'cha doing?"

Ern Berkley looked up from the writing tablet. Dorothy peered across the table, her chin and fingertips resting on the wooden edge. The bruise on her forehead had perfectly matched her blue eyes the day after Anna Mae's fall, but over the past week it had changed to an angry yellowish green, the color of a frog's underbelly. He shifted his gaze from the bruise to the child's eyes. "I'm writing a letter to your daddy. Your mama asked me to let him know she got hurt."

Dorothy pulled out a chair and climbed up, pressing her palms to the tabletop. "Is Mama hurt real bad?"

Ern glanced toward the bedroom doorway. He could hear Mrs. Stevenson's plodding footsteps as she puttered around the room. For a week now, the woman had been spoon-feeding Anna Mae, giving her sponge baths, and waiting for her to regain her strength. Anna Mae had always been a fighter, but lying on that bed, pale and weak, she didn't appear to have much fight left in her.

"Papa Berkley, I said is Mama hurt real bad?" Dorothy's voice rose, a hint of panic underscoring the childish tone.

He reached across the table to tap the end of her nose. "Your mama's just tuck-ered, Dorothy. She needs a nice, long nap. But she'll be fine."

"Are you sure?"

Ern tipped his head and wiggled his mustache. "Well, now, haven't we been praying for just that? You think God isn't listening?"

Dorothy didn't smile. "Daddy says God doesn't hear prayers."

Ern swallowed the disappointment that rose with Dorothy's innocent comment. Harley should have more sense than to trample a child's faith. But he managed another smile and said, "Well, your daddy's right in most things, honey, but this time I think he's wrong. I've been saying prayers since I was littler than you, and I know God answers. So you just trust your mama is going to be okay, will you do that?"

Dorothy released a long sigh. She scraped her thumbnail at a bit of loose paint on the table's edge. "I'll try."

"Good girl. Now, can you do something for me?"

"What?"

"Can you go get your color crayons from your room without waking Marjorie? I think your daddy would like a picture from you in this letter."

The child's eyes lit up. "I'll draw him a rainbow! We talked about rainbows in Sunday school yesterday."

"That's a good idea." He tugged a piece of paper loose from the tablet. "Here's some paper. Go fetch your crayons and get started. I'll make sure it gets mailed."

"Thanks, Papa Berkley!" The little girl scooted off the chair and tiptoed to the bedroom. In minutes she was back, a battered Crayola box in her hand. Kneeling on the chair, she dumped the well-used crayons out on the table and got busy creating shaggy arches of bright color.

Ern watched for a few minutes, smiling as Dorothy's tongue poked out on the left side of her mouth while she worked. Anna Mae had done the same thing when she was little. She just wasn't concentrating hard if the tip of her tongue wasn't showing. She'd poked it out while doing her homework, when lost in thought, or when reasoning something out.

The rumble of a wagon interrupted his thoughts. Dorothy raised her head, looking toward the open kitchen window. "Somebody's here," she said. She hopped down from the table, raced to the porch, then careened back in, a panicked look on her face. "The mailman's out at the box! An' my picture's not done!"

Ern pointed to the crayons. "It's okay, Dorothy. He comes every day. We'll send your picture tomorrow. I don't have the letter ready to go anyway, so it will have to wait until tomorrow."

Dorothy's face twisted into a pout. "I wanted to send it *now*."

Ern said in a reasonable tone, "Well, you don't want to send half a rainbow, do you?"

Her lower lip poking out, Dorothy shook her head.

"Well, then, finish that up. I'll finish your daddy's letter, and I'll put everything in the mail tomorrow."

With a great heaving of shoulders, Dorothy climbed back into the chair and picked up the red crayon. Ern waited until she was thoroughly engrossed in her coloring before finishing his letter. His wording was concise and carefully avoided any suggestions regarding what Harley should do—it simply stated the facts: Anna Mae had injured herself in a fall, she and the baby were fine, and the chores were being seen to by Jack.

Harley would have to decide for himself what to do with the information.

"All done!" Dorothy held up the drawing of a crooked rainbow, its colors running together as if the sun had melted it. The pride on her face made Ern smile.

"Very good," he praised, taking it and folding it to fit the envelope. He slipped it in with his letter and sealed the envelope with a dab of glue. He gave the envelope a pat. "There now! I'll put a stamp on it when I get home and send it off tomorrow, okay?"

"Okay!"

The kitchen door opened and Jack stepped through. He glanced at the table as he headed for the sink. "What're you doin', Pop?"

Ern spoke over the sound of running water while Jack washed his hands. "I wrote a letter to Harley. Anna Mae asked me to let him know about her accident."

Jack's shoulders stiffened. "She tell you to ask him to come back?"

Ern felt a prickle of trepidation. Jack's tone was too disinterested to be sincere. "No. Just lettin' him know what's going on here. Why?"

"No reason." The answer came fast. Too

fast. Jack turned around, wiped his hands on his pant legs, and offered a broad smile that didn't reach his eyes. "Want me to stamp it and get it sent?"

Ern rose. He tucked the envelope in his shirt pocket, but he couldn't tuck away the odd sensation that Jack was hiding something. "That's fine, son. I've got stamps at home. I'll put it out in the box for tomorrow's pickup." He tousled Dorothy's hair, giving the child a smile. "Dorothy here included a picture of a rainbow for her daddy, too."

"That so?" Jack scooped Dorothy from the floor and bounced her in the air a couple of times, making her squeal. "You drew a rainbow? How come?"

Between giggles, Dorothy explained. "My Sunday school teacher says rainbows is s'posed to help us remember promises. I promised to be good, an' my daddy promised to come home. So I drawed him a promise rainbow."

Ern watched Jack's lips form a grim line. Jack set Dorothy on the floor and turned back to the sink. He seemed to gaze out the window, lost in thought. Watching him, Ern experienced another uneasy feeling. *What's going on in your heart these days, son? You've been a tower of strength and a source of helpfulness to Anna Mae. If only I didn't feel you were up to no good.*

19

Jack paused by the back door, hand on the doorknob, ear tuned to his father's footsteps as the old man climbed the stairs to his bedroom. At the click of the bedroom door, Jack's breath released in a *whoosh*. He hadn't even realized he'd been holding it back.

He rotated his shoulders, tension creating a knot between his shoulder blades. The letter Pop had written to Harley was stamped and waiting for pickup in the mailbox at the end of the drive. The drive could clearly be seen from Pop's bedroom window. And Pop was in his bedroom. Jack tipped his head, trying to detect any movement from upstairs. If Pop was wandering around, he might look out the window and catch Jack in the act. But if he were in bed . . .

Squeak.

Jack smiled. The old springs on Pop's bed gave him away. He was no doubt stretched out for his after-breakfast Bible reading. It was safe. Jack held tight to the door, easing it closed without a sound. He tiptoed across the porch, avoiding the creaky middle board, then broke into a run across the yard and slid to a stop beside the mailbox. A quick glance up and down the road confirmed no one was around. He removed the letter, folded it in half, and jammed it into his back pocket. He'd deal with it later.

Interfering with mail was a federal offense, he knew. And he'd interfered with more mail in the past several weeks than he could keep track of, sneaking off with every letter Anna Mae tried to send to Harley, as well as an envelope that came from Lindsborg addressed to Anna Mae in sloppy handwriting. If Pop found the stash of letters underneath the long johns in Jack's bureau drawer, he'd be pretty upset. But what else could Jack do? Harley couldn't know about Anna Mae's accident. If he knew, he would come home. If he came home, Jack wouldn't be needed over there anymore. And Jack wasn't ready to give up his position of being needed.

Harley lifted his gaze as Mr. Peterson's truck rolled onto the work site and rattled to a stop beside the boss's shack. Must be nice to be able to go home to a wife and a home-cooked lunch every day. Harley watched the boss step out. Then the man reached back inside the cab for something. Harley squinted, his heart thumping hopefully. Yep, Peterson held a package. Harley's hands curled around the shovel handle, ready to drop it and trot over when his name was called.

Peterson shielded his eyes with his hand, scanning the grounds, and his gaze went right past Harley. The rise of expectation was crushed by a wave of envy when he heard the boss call out Dirk's name. Giving the shovel a jerk, he spun from the sight of Dirk jogging to the boss's side. That made three packages in addition to the letters that arrived twice weekly for the young man. Harley hadn't yet heard from Annie. Not once. She knew she could reach him at Peterson's place—why didn't she write? She must still be powerful mad to hold out this long.

"Hey, Harley!"

Harley turned slowly to face Dirk, who bounded across the dry landscape. "Lookee here. Ma sent me clean socks and a loaf of pumpkin bread loaded with cinnamon and pecans." He laughed, his face nearly split from his grin. "Bread's purty well smashed, but reckon it'll taste the same. We'll have us quite a treat for our supper tonight. Just can't beat Ma's pumpkin bread."

Harley tried, but he couldn't muster so much as a smile in response.

Dirk pointed to a crumpled note in the bottom of the box. "Ma says to give you one of these pairs o' socks"—he held out a gray pair with red toes and heels—"and to tell you thanks again." Dirk shook his head. "This paycheck's been a real help, Harley. Don't know what we would've done if you hadn't happened along."

Harley fingered the socks, his calluses catching on the soft woven cotton. "You don't need to keep thankin' me. I'm just glad it worked out for both of us."

Dirk's smile faded. He nudged Harley with his elbow. "Hey. What's wrong?"

Harley angled his gaze past Dirk's shoulder. The empty landscape appeared as lonesome today as it had when he'd first arrived. The lonely ache in his heart hadn't gone away, either. "How long we been here now?"

Dirk shifted the box to his hip and scratched his head. "Gotta be eight weeks at least, 'cause we just sent off our second paychecks to home."

Harley nodded slowly, squinting against the high sun. "Long time."

Understanding dawned across Dirk's face. "You ain't heard from Annie, have you?"

Harley swallowed. "Nope."

"Worried something's wrong?"

Harley released a short huff. "I reckon she's still mad at me for goin'. 'Course, she was mad about some other things before I left. Reckon she's just . . . mad."

Dirk shook his head, sadness drooping his face. "Aw, I'm sorry."

Harley forced a wry chuckle. "What you sorry for? You didn't have anything to do with our fussing. That's just what Annie and me do—fuss." Although he tried to make light of it, the truth of his statement struck hard. Why had he and Annie turned to fussing so much? His folks had fussed at each other. A lot. He'd never liked listening to it, and he'd always sworn he'd avoid it if he was ever lucky enough to have a family. Yet he fussed at Annie, and she fussed at him. Their peaceful times ended when the rains went away. Would it change if the rains started falling again?

Dirk rocked back on his heels, his eyes narrowed thoughtfully. "Well, I ain't got a wife, but I guess I've learned from watchin' my folks that fussin' just happens sometimes, mostly when a body's tired. And I'd have to say hardship makes a body tired. Can't hardly live with somebody without fussin' now and again. But . . ." He scrunched his lips to one side, his forehead crinkled. "Gotta be careful that the fuss doesn't turn into a grudge. Grudges are harder to set aside."

Harley nodded. For a young man, Dirk had a lot of wisdom.

Dirk gave Harley a firm clap on the shoulder. "Listen, don't let it get you down. You're busy here—reckon she's busy there. Probably just busyness that keeps her from writin'."

Harley scuffed his toe in the dirt. "You're probably right. Busy. Yeah." Although, what did she have to do besides care for the few animals and the garden? Maybe she was busy with things that had nothing to do with the farm. Like spending time with her neighbor.

Harley's chin shot up, his gaze colliding with Dirk's. "Dirk, you . . . you said you'd been prayin' for Annie?"

Dirk nodded, his hair flopping. "Every day."

Harley swallowed again, his dry throat making it hard to form words. "Could you maybe add a prayer for her to . . . to forgive me? So maybe she'd write and let me know for sure how she and the girls are doing?"

"Sure, I'll do that. But"—Dirk clamped a big hand over Harley's shoulder—"you know you can talk to God yourself. God's ears are open to the prayers of every man."

Harley shook his head, releasing a mirthless chuckle. "Can't imagine why God would want to hear from me. I'm not so much."

Dirk's hand tightened. "To Him, you're everything, Harley. You're so much, He let

His only Son Jesus be nailed to a cross just to take on your sins. That's a love that can't be measured."

Dirk's serious tone and fervent expression made Harley squirm. "Well . . ." He shifted, pulling himself away from Dirk's warm hand. "Since you're already on a first-name basis with Him, I guess I'll leave the prayin' to you." He bent over and picked up his shovel, ignoring the worried look on Dirk's face.

"Farley!"

The angry voice made both Harley and Dirk turn quickly. They looked toward the half-built castle, where Nelson stood, hands on hips.

"What're you doin'? Lunch break is over! Stop yammering and get to work!"

Harley's hackles rose. Who put Nelson in charge?

Dirk offered a brief wave in Harley's direction. "Catch ya later, Harley." He back-pedaled toward the castle. "I'll be prayin' for your wife, but remember what I said—you can talk to God yourself. It's a good thing to be able to talk to God."

"Farley!"

"Comin'!" Dirk spun around and took off at a trot.

Harley watched him for a moment before turning back to his shoveling. Dirk's words replayed in his head as he forced the metal blade into the hard ground. *"To Him, you're everything."* Harley broke loose a clump of sod and tossed it aside. Everything, huh? No-account son of a whiskey-drinking sharecropper was everything to God? That didn't make sense.

Harley paused, a band clamping painfully around his heart. Might be nice to think of being loved that much, loved so much someone was willing to die for you. But he didn't even know God. God surely didn't know him. Why would God care? No, it was better to let Dirk do the praying if there was any hope of prayers being heard. Harley'd spent too many years denying God's existence for God to pay him any mind now.

Still, as Harley jammed the shovel into the ground, a part of him wished he could be wrong about God.

"Still nothing?"

Anna Mae clapped a hand over her

mouth. She hadn't intended to voice the question aloud, and Jack's quirked eyebrow magnified her embarrassment. She should have known the answer since he returned from the mailbox empty-handed. Why hadn't Harley responded to her letters? She wrote faithfully every week. It was too much to expect he'd write lengthy letters in return, but couldn't he send a note? Something to let her know how he was? To let her know he thought about her, was worried about her recent accident, or happy she hadn't lost the baby after all?

And why hadn't another paycheck arrived? More than enough time had passed for him to have received a second check. In one more month the taxes would be due. After paying Doc Warren for his visits and paying Mrs. Stevenson for her care, Anna Mae had nearly used up the money Harley had sent the first time. Even if she used every cent from the bank on the windowsill, there still wouldn't be enough. They needed his paycheck, and soon.

Tiredness sagged her shoulders. It seemed as though, despite all the resting she'd been forced to do since her tumble from the ladder four weeks ago, she couldn't get her energy back. Disappointment was a weight too heavy to carry on top of all that tiredness. Jack slid his hands into his pockets, his shoulders high. "I'm sorry, but I can't give you anything today."

"I know." She sighed, turning toward the stove to stir a thick, bubbling vegetable stew. "I just hoped by now . . ."

Warm hands closed around her upper arms, the touch intimate. "Anna Mae, can I say something without you getting upset?" Jack's voice, whisper soft, stirred the hair behind her left ear.

Anna Mae's hand on the wooden spoon stilled, and she held her breath. "W-what?"

"It's about Harley."

She felt Jack's chin brush against the side of her head. A prickle of awareness shot down her spine. Releasing the spoon, she twisted away from the stove and walked to the sink. From this safer distance, she asked again, "What?"

Jack leaned his weight on one hip, slipping a hand into his pocket. With the other hand, he clasped the back of his neck. The pose gave the impression of great worry, and Anna Mae's heartbeat accelerated.

Jack drew in a deep breath. "Do you remember when you told me you were going to marry Harley?"

Frowning, she nodded.

"I tried to talk you out of it, remember?"

She gave another nod.

"Why?"

Because you were jealous. But she couldn't say that out loud. Instead, she pressed her memory, trying to come up with the words he'd used. It didn't take a great deal of effort to find them; he'd made her so angry that day. "You said Harley was a no-good drifter only after my daddy's land." Even after all the time that had passed, repeating his statement made her angry all over again.

Jack must have seen her temper rising, because he raised his palm toward her as if to head her off at the pass. "Now, I don't want to upset you, but I just wonder . . . Is it possible Harley has drifted off? It's too hard to make a living here, so he's decided to move on?"

Anna Mae raised her chin, her jaw jutting forward. "Without the girls and me?"

Jack held out his hands in a gesture of surrender. "Don't get riled. It's an honest question."

Anna Mae plunked her fists on her hips. "How so?"

Jack's lips quirked. "He's been gone . . . what, now? Over two months? How often have you heard from him? Once?"

"So?" The defensiveness came automatically. *You've got no right to be putting down Harley, Jack.*

"So Harley wasn't raised like you and me, Anna Mae." Jack lowered his tone, taking a step forward. If he stretched out his hand he'd be able to graze her cheek with his fingertips. She watched his hand to be sure he kept it to himself. "He wasn't brought up in the church, or with any kind of real tie to anything. Sharecroppers are a different lot; they don't own anything, so they never learn pride of ownership. Doesn't hurt them to walk away."

"That's not true." Anna Mae shook her head wildly. "Harley takes a great deal of pride in this farm. He—he takes care of it like it has always been his." Jack hadn't seen Harley the day he'd walked away.

Anna Mae had. It had hurt him. It had hurt him a lot.

"Yeah . . . he took care of it while it was producing." Jack's words came out slowly, deliberately, cutting Anna Mae like a knife. "But now that he can't get anything out of it, what's he done? Took off for parts unknown."

"He had to!" Her vehemence made her chest hurt. "We need the money. And he isn't gone to *parts unknown*. He's right across Kansas, at a job site in Saline County."

"Are you sure?"

"Of course I'm sure. Why shouldn't I be?"

"Don't you think, if he were there, he'd be answering your letters? You were hurt, Anna Mae, and he didn't come home or even write to check on you? Maybe he's moved on, so he's not even getting your letters. Is it possible?"

The question brought her up short. Was it possible? She hated that Jack made her wonder, made her think for even one second Harley might not be where he said he would be, doing what he said he would do, earning money to take care of his family. She pointed to the door. "Get out of here, Jack."

"Anna Mae—"

She hardened her heart to his pleading look and jabbed her finger toward the door. "Get. Out. Now." She kept her voice low, but the tone held conviction. "And don't come back until you're ready to apologize for slandering Harley. He's my husband. I love him. I trust him. He's out there working at some lonely place so he can provide for me and our girls, and I won't have you putting thoughts in my head to the contrary. Out!"

He had the audacity to chuckle. "Okay, then. Sorry I made you mad. I'll go, but I'll be back tomorrow to see to the chores, like I've been doing ever since the husband you love and trust decided to walk down the road."

She still held her finger, aimed at the door, like a pistol. It trembled. "Sometimes I hate you, Jack Berkley."

He raised one eyebrow, his smile sardonic. "Be careful, Anna Mae. Hate and love are both fiery passions, and they're only a hairsbreadth apart."

She picked up an enamel plate from the shelf beside the sink and threw it at him. It clanged off the door as he slipped through and closed it behind him. Marjorie's startled wail carried from the bedroom, and Dorothy came running from the parlor, her doll tucked under her arm.

"Mama, what was that noise?"

Anna Mae pointed to the plate, which rolled underneath the table and twirled to a halt. "Mama dropped a plate, darlin'. No need to worry." She brushed past Dorothy to enter the bedroom and lifted Marjorie from her crib.

Dorothy padded along beside her. "You dropped it clear across the room?"

"Yes." The word clipped out. Anna Mae patted Marjorie, bringing the baby's crying under control.

For the remainder of the evening, Jack's comments caused a lingering question to haunt Anna Mae's mind. While she talked with the girls, cleaned up dishes, and read bedtime stories, it never left her. Even as she remembered her adamant support of Harley's actions and thought of more things she wished she'd said to Jack, the question whispered through her mind. And even as she lay in bed, her arm thrown across the empty slice of mattress where Harley used to lie, missing his presence with an intensity that hurt, one question hovered on the fringes of her subconscious.

What if Jack is right?

20

Harley leaned against the castle wall, the patch of shade a welcome change from the boiling sun. He stretched out his legs, crossed his ankles, and set the lunch bucket in his lap. Dirk sat beside him, big hands folded in prayer. Harley waited until Dirk opened his eyes before carrying his own spoonful of beans to his mouth.

Neither man spoke as they ate. It was too hot for conversation. Harley reckoned the heat sucked the life out of a person. Just the act of chewing took more energy than he felt he had left in him. Was it this hot back in Spencer? If so, it would take a heap of watering to keep the garden alive. By now the new baby was probably making

Annie awkward. Had she asked Jack to take care of watering chores for her?

His hand stopped midway to his mouth as another unwelcome picture filled his mind: Jack in the garden with his Annie. He plunked the spoon in the beans and slapped the can onto the ground next to his hip, his appetite gone.

Why had he asked Jack to step in and help? There were lots of reasons. 'Cause he was the closest neighbor. 'Cause Jack was his friend. 'Cause Jack's folks and Annie's folks had been friends for all of Annie's life. 'Cause he trusted him. So why all these odd thoughts now?

He remembered Annie's reaction when he'd told her Jack would be helping out. She'd tensed up—he'd seen it. At the time, he'd just figured she was irritated about his leaving. But now that he really thought about it, he'd seen that reaction at other times when Jack's name came up or the man wandered over for some reason. She'd never cottoned to Jack. Why?

An ugly idea struck. Could it be, all along, Annie had harbored feelings for Jack? Maybe her reaction was her way of fighting those feelings.

Harley didn't like the way his mind was running. He turned toward Dirk, ready to ask Dirk to pray for somebody else to come along who could help out at the farm, but Dirk was leaning back against the rough rock, his eyes closed and mouth slack. Napping. Harley didn't have the heart to wake him.

Facing forward again, he wondered: should he go home? Only a couple more weeks, he'd have his third paycheck. He could go home with money in his pocket, at least. He'd earned enough to cover the tax bill for the year—no need to worry over that anymore. Maybe he should just take that next check and go home.

"Hey, Harley, thinkin' about home?"

The question took Harley by surprise. He jerked around to find Nelson at the other end of the wall, enjoying the shade and a thick sandwich of roast beef on white bread. Harley's mouth watered at the sight of that sandwich.

"Why you think that?" he asked, his gaze on the roast beef.

Nelson laughed. "The look in your eyes an' the beans in the pot. A man who don't eat must have somethin' more important on his mind. So . . . you thinkin' of home?"

Harley wasn't interested in engaging in a conversation with Nelson. He shrugged in response.

Nelson nodded as if Harley had said a mouthful. "Yeah. Thought so." His voice boomed out, impossible to ignore. "So, you a family man?"

Dirk stirred. Harley resumed eating while he contemplated giving Nelson an answer.

"How many kids?"

Harley guessed Nelson wasn't going to let the subject drop. He sighed. If he answered, maybe the man would go away. "I got two kids, two girls." A knot formed in his throat as he thought of Dottie and Margie getting bigger there on the farm without him. And the new baby, too, making Annie grow bigger. " 'Nother baby comin', too."

"That so?" Nelson sounded genuinely interested. "Think this one'll be a boy?"

Harley felt his lips twitch as a smile threatened. A boy would be nice. Somebody to show how to plant and plow and care for animals . . . Annie seemed to be thinking girl, but who knew? This one could be a boy, couldn't it?

"Yes, sir, must be tough to be here when you got a wife, two little girls, and a new baby comin' at home." Nelson's tone turned thoughtful. He took a big bite of his sandwich and chewed with his jaw working back and forth, his gaze aimed outward. Swallowing, he kept his gaze away from Harley. "Now, me, if I had somethin' like that at home, I wouldn't be miles away. I'd stick close, where I could take care o' my own." Choking out a chuckle, he finally sent a cocky look in Harley's direction. "But that's me."

Harley didn't answer. Kept his jaw clamped shut on the angry words that wanted release. Nelson didn't have any business telling Harley what to do. Harley was taking care of his own the best way he knew how.

Nelson popped the last bite of his sandwich into his mouth and heaved to his feet. "Gonna go get a drink. See you fellas later." He ambled away.

Dirk squinted at Nelson's retreating back, then looked at Harley. "You makin' friends with Nelson?"

"Nah." Harley lifted the bean pot and took a bite. The beans were nearly tasteless, but he needed something in his stomach. "Can't imagine ever bein' friends with that man." He took another bite, then admitted, "Funny, though, how he was talkin' about just what I had been thinkin'."

Dirk raised his eyebrows. "Oh? What's that?"

"Goin' home."

Dirk offered a slow-motion nod. "I can see why you'd want to go. Got good reasons."

"Good reasons?" Harley nearly barked the question.

Dirk blinked, his expression innocent. "Well, sure. Annie an' your little girls. Those're good reasons to go home."

Harley made himself relax. He needed to quit reading things into every comment; of course Dirk wouldn't suspect anything about Jack. "Yeah . . . Yeah, I got good reasons."

"I'd miss you," Dirk said, lifting his broad shoulders in a shrug, "but I'd understand if you was to leave. And I guess that would make an opening for that friend of Nelson's."

Harley scowled. "Friend of Nelson's?"

Dirk nodded. "Yep. Heard him askin' the boss about it yesterday. He's got some friend from town needin' work, but Mr. Peterson said the crew's full. Only way he could hire another'n is if somebody up and left."

So that was it. Harley nodded, his brows low and lips puckered. Nelson was trying to make Harley homesick enough to leave so somebody else could get his paycheck. Well, it wouldn't work. This job belonged to Harley. It was the only security his family had right now. He chomped another bite of beans, determination filling him. He'd stay on 'til the task was done. Nelson wasn't going to run him off. And neither were these ridiculous worries about Jack with Annie.

Jack poured the remainder of the water on the tomato plants, then headed for the shed to put the bucket back where he'd found it. So far, despite nature's best efforts to destroy Anna Mae's garden, he'd managed to keep the plants alive. They looked sad, and they weren't overflowing with bounty, but there were beans, cukes, and tomatoes to pick every day, so at least her family wouldn't starve.

He glanced across the yard. Anna Mae sat under the weeping willow on an old patchwork quilt that she'd spread out on the grassless ground. A chuckle found its way from his chest. Seeing her there took him back about a dozen years, to when she was still a young girl and he was bent on tormenting her. It was always the best way to get her attention.

She'd been under the tree, like she was now, only with a book in her lap. He'd sneaked up behind her and stuck a garden snake under her nose. My, how she could shriek! And she ran faster than most girls, too. He could still recall the exhilaration of the chase, her bare feet pounding behind him, his laugh not quite covering her threats to get even. When he was sure she was right on his heels, he'd spun around, captured her in his arms, and planted a kiss directly on her surprised mouth.

He touched the side of his head, remembering how the clop she gave him had made his ears ring. But it had been worth it. Ah, she'd always been a feisty thing. He thumped the bucket on the shelf, then remained hidden in shadow, enjoying the opportunity to secretly observe her.

She was so graceful looking with her feet tucked to the side, her skirt smoothed over her knees. Her soft smile as she watched Marjorie bang a rag doll on the quilt made his heart thud with desire for her to look at him in that same way. Anna Mae's beauty was eye-catching, even with the obvious rounding of her belly showing the growth of Harley's child inside of her.

As he watched, Dorothy scampered to her mother's side. The little girl held out a cluster of wilted wild flowers, and Anna Mae took them with a smile, lifting them to her nose and making a great show of inhaling their fragrance. Suddenly she jerked upright, an expression of surprise on her face. Jack took a hesitant step forward, worry striking. But Anna Mae caught Dorothy's hand and placed it on her stomach.

Jack watched the child's eyes grow wide, her smile huge, and his worry faded. Dorothy's giggle carried across the yard to Jack's ears, stirring a longing in his soul to be a part of the circle the mother and children created. What would Anna Mae do if he strode across the grounds, pulled aside those drooping branches, placed his hand on her belly to feel the movement of her child, and kissed her while the babe kicked inside?

He snorted. He knew. She'd smack him good, for sure. Rubbing his chin with one finger, he contemplated doing it anyway. Might be worth it. It had been a long time since he'd stolen a kiss from Anna Mae.

Only the remembrance of her throwing that plate at his head three weeks ago kept him planted in the shed. Even though he'd come faithfully each day to see to the milking, egg collecting, and gardening, and had carted her to church each Sunday, she hadn't softened toward him. But she'd have to set her anger aside here pretty soon. Her tax deadline was coming up. She'd need him to take her to the county courthouse to pay that bill. And since she didn't have the money to cover it, he'd have to step in and help. How could she stay mad at somebody who saved the farm for her?

She couldn't. Jack was banking on that.

Anna Mae kept an eye on the shed where Jack had disappeared a few minutes ago. What was he doing in there? It didn't take but a second or two to put the bucket away. He must have found something out of place. She wished he'd emerge so she could say what needed saying and be done with it.

Her throat felt tight, knowing she'd have

to talk to him. The past weeks had been so awkward, with him showing up, caring for things like nothing had happened. But after what he'd said, everything had changed. She couldn't look at him without wondering if he was right about Harley. His words had plagued her constantly, creating a knot of tension between her shoulder blades that never went away, not even when she prayed. She had no desire to approach Jack, but what choice did she have? There was no other way to get to Hutchinson except to walk. And she couldn't do that.

Dorothy sat down on the quilt with Marjorie and danced the rag doll across Marjorie's dimpled knees, making the baby giggle. Anna Mae touched Dorothy's hair. "Darlin'? Would you stay here with Marjorie for just a minute?"

Dorothy flashed a quick smile. "Sure, Mama." Turning back to the baby, she sang, "Margie-pargie, puddin' an' pie . . ."

Anna Mae struggled to her feet, one hand beneath her belly, and headed across the hard ground toward the shed. Wind tossed her hair across her face, and she pushed the strands aside, focusing on her destination. A movement near the wide doorway—

a shifting of shadows—made her pause for a moment as a chill wiggled down her spine. Pressing a hand to the small of her back, she wondered about the odd sensation. She shook her head, reasoning that the sudden change from shade to sun was making her light-headed, and she pushed her feet to move forward.

When she reached the shed, she stopped in the slice of deep shade outside the doorway and called, "Jack?"

He emerged from the shadows, a smile on his face. "Well, hey, Anna Mae. I've been organizing Harley's tools in here, makin' sure everything still works right."

Her next thought chilled her. Iron tools clanked when used, and she hadn't heard a thing. She forced the peculiar feeling away and pasted on a stiff smile. "Thanks. I . . . I need to ask a favor."

"Anything." The word came quickly and carried an intimate tone.

Anna Mae took one shuffling step backward. "Property taxes come due August first, so I need to go into the courthouse and pay them."

Jack scratched behind his left ear. "And you want me to take you?"

She swallowed. "Yes, please."

He winked. "Sure, I'd be proud to cart you in to Hutchinson. Let's see, the first is a Saturday. Probably would be better to pay the taxes early rather than late, so let's plan to go in on the last day of July. That suit you?"

That gave Harley nearly two weeks to get another paycheck to her. Oh, how she prayed the money would be here in time! But if it wasn't, she'd have to make some sort of arrangement to pay part of the bill now and the rest when his check did arrive.

"Anna Mae? You okay?"

Anna Mae jerked, suddenly aware Jack had been waiting for an answer. She squirmed. "Yes. Yes, I'm okay. We can go in that last Friday."

Jack's grin spread. "Good. Let's leave midmorning, and we can grab a bite to eat at a cafe´ in town, celebrate getting those taxes paid, huh?"

Anna Mae cringed. "I don't have money for that, Jack."

"No problem. My treat."

"But . . . I don't have gas money to give you, either."

Jack's hand crept out, his fingers brushing down the length of her arm. "Honey, don't worry about that. Friends do favors for each other. I told Harley I'd cart you around as needed, and that's what I'll do. As many times and as many places as you want to go."

To Anna Mae's chagrin, tears spurted into her eyes. *Honey.* The endearment washed her in longing for the days when a glance from Harley made her feel cherished and loved. How she wished Harley were here to hold her and tell her she didn't need to worry—he'd take care of that tax bill and the garden and everything else.

She turned to go back to the girls, but Jack's hand on her arm stopped her.

"Anna Mae, I want you to know somethin'—and this is a promise. You don't have to worry. You'll be cared for. Do you understand?"

Woodenly, meeting Jack's eyes, Anna Mae nodded. Oh yes. She understood perfectly what Jack was saying. She sucked in a huge breath of hot air, jerked her arm free, and ran back to the sheltering limbs of the weeping willow.

21

"I'm sorry, Mrs. Phipps, but the law is clear. If you don't pay your taxes, you don't keep your land."

Anna Mae wiped her sweaty palms on her skirt and blinked rapidly, a feeble attempt to hold back tears of frustration. "But I can pay some of it now," she said, her voice weak in her own ears. "And the rest as soon as my husband's paycheck arrives. He's got a job—with the WPA, steady work—but for some reason—"

"Mrs. Phipps." The man's stern expression and raised palm brought Anna Mae's words to a halt. "I sympathize with your situation. Truly I do."

Anna Mae saw no evidence of sympathy in either his face or his vocal tone.

"But you must understand that taxes are required. If, within the next thirty days, this tax bill is not paid in full, there will be no other choice but to sell the property at auction. Do you understand?"

She wanted to ask that smug man behind the desk where she and her children would go if the government took her home away. But the cotton that filled her mouth made a reply impossible. She gave a miserable nod and rose, moving on stiff legs to the hallway, where she collapsed on a bench outside the county treasurer's door.

"Oh, Harley, why haven't you sent any more money?" she murmured, tears stinging the corners of her eyes. "You love that land so much . . . surely you didn't leave it. . . ."

"Hey, Anna Mae."

Jack's cheery voice jerked Anna Mae's gaze around. Dorothy skipped toward her with Jack behind her, moving more slowly since Marjorie held to his index finger, toddling along on pudgy legs. The sight of Jack with her girls made her heart flip-flop in her chest. His words—*"You'll be cared for"*—re-

turned to haunt her. She shoved them aside
and pushed herself to her feet.

"Did you get everything done?"

Although she hadn't accomplished what
she'd hoped, she'd done all she could do.
She answered in a dull tone, "Yes. Yes, it's
done."

"Good." Jack flipped Dorothy's ponytail.
"Then let's go get some lunch."

Anna Mae knew she wouldn't be able to
eat a bite, but Dorothy's squeal of pleasure
stifled her suggestion that they just go
home. Jack reached down and lifted Marjorie, who giggled in his arms as he headed
back toward the main lobby. Dorothy gal-
loped beside him, chattering away. How
easily the girls had accepted Jack's presence. Sometimes it seemed as if they'd forgotten they had a daddy named Harley
Phipps.

Jack paused at the end of the hall, peering back at Anna Mae with a smile on his
face. "Hey? You comin'?"

Anna Mae drew in a fortifying breath. She
set her feet in motion. "Yes. I'm coming."
She joined her daughters and Jack, taking
Dorothy's hand and offering a smile when
the child beamed upward. But her smile

faded when Jack slipped his hand beneath her elbow and guided her toward the double doors leading outside.

The girls may have forgotten about Harley, but she hadn't. And she wouldn't. She *wouldn't.*

Jack decided to allow Anna Mae to sit in silence as they drove from Hutchinson to Spencer. All through lunch, he'd done his best to engage her in conversation, but her answers were monosyllabic at best, lacking any enthusiasm. And he was tired of trying to draw her out. Let her sit there and brood, then.

She glanced into the backseat, and a whisper of a smile crossed her lips. He peeked, too, and spotted Dorothy and Marjorie coiled together on the seat, asleep. The wind coursing through the open windows stirred their blond hair. Cute kids— really cute kids—even if they were Harley's. He felt a smile tug at his cheeks. But when his gaze caught Anna Mae's, her smile died, and she turned toward the window without a word.

He tightened his fingers on the steering wheel. Her moodiness was becoming a real thorn in his side. Everything he did for her, and she couldn't offer a smile and some casual conversation? Or better yet, a genuine show of appreciation? What was it going to take to get her to understand how much he cared for her?

Jack bit down on the inside of his cheek. At least he knew what the moodiness was all about. The tax bill. She couldn't cover it. There was no way she could cover it. He'd seen how much money she'd handed the doctor and Mrs. Stevenson, he'd seen what she'd paid at the store, and he knew what she'd given him for Dorothy's shoes. He'd also seen what was left, and there was no way she could have paid that tax bill without the other check from Harley.

What aggravated him was that she just sat there and stewed without opening her mouth and asking him for help. All she had to do was say the word and he'd pay that bill in a heartbeat. Hadn't he told her he'd take care of her? Hadn't he proven it by being there every day since Harley had gone? Hadn't she learned that he wouldn't abandon her the way her no-account drifter of a husband had done? He had Harley's paycheck squirreled away, snatched from her mailbox, giving him the perfect opportunity to prove his dependability. And still she didn't ask. . . .

He flicked a glance in her direction. She remained with her face turned away, watching the countryside slide past. Wind tossed her hair, fine tendrils dancing along her delicate jawline. His fingers itched with the desire to smooth those strands back into place, to rest his hand along her cheek and cup her chin with this thumb, to turn her face toward him. His hand left the steering wheel, inching toward Anna Mae, but a dip in the road jerked the vehicle, forcing him to grab hold with both hands again.

Releasing a mild oath under his breath, he returned his focus to the road. Anna Mae might not ask for his help, but that didn't mean he wouldn't give it. Soon as they were home, he'd call the courthouse, find out what was needed for her bill, and send a check in the mail. He'd save that farm for her whether she liked it or not.

He could do it, too. He wasn't hurting for money like so many other area farmers were. Even though milk brought in a lot less these days, the steers he sold still earned a pretty good sum, as did the pecans. And if what he'd overheard while he was waiting for Anna Mae to finish her appointment proved accurate, he stood to make even more money.

Oil. The very thought made his heart race with eagerness. Just six miles from his land, they'd found oil. If they'd found it on Jensen's property, they might find it on his. It would only take a telephone call to bring the surveyors out, then a small investment to get wells put up, and he'd be bringing in money. Lots of money. Enough for himself, Pop, Anna Mae, and her children.

An idea struck so hard he jerked the steering wheel. Anna Mae tipped toward him, her elbow bouncing off his. He put out his hand to steady her, but she latched on to the window ledge with both hands, keeping herself secure in the seat. Not once did she look in his direction. He frowned. Yes, it was time to get her attention good and proper. The only reason she didn't depend on him now was because she still had a place to call her own. She'd keep hanging on to that farm as long as she could, for Harley. But what if she didn't have the farm? She'd have no choice but to look elsewhere for help. And he knew where he wanted her to look.

What if he paid that tax bill—but not right away? What if he waited until the property went delinquent and she was forced to let it go? With those two little girls and another one on the way, with no husband in the picture, she'd have no choice but to turn to Jack for help. He could invite her and the girls to move in with him and Pop, and with her under his roof, completely dependent on him, he'd finally have the chance to win her once and for all. Once she'd been convinced that she couldn't get along without him, he'd secretly pay for the property and surprise her with it, telling her they'd keep it for Ben Elliott's grandchildren. He smiled, thinking of the hug and kiss she'd bestow with the presentation of that gift.

A deep sigh came from the other side of the seat. A sad sigh, a sigh filled with worry. For a moment Jack faltered. Should he offer to give her the money now?

No. He hardened his heart with resolve. If he did it now, she'd have no need to lean on him in the future. He'd have to wait.

Harley had never been right for her; she'd see that as soon as all of this was done. It was a matter of being cruel to be kind. It might sting for the moment, but in the long run, she'd be better off.

"Well, men, it's good to have that project done, isn't it?"

Harley nodded in agreement with Peterson's words. If he never lifted a shovel again in his lifetime, it would suit him just fine. But he had to admit, there was a sense of satisfaction in having completed the difficult task. That sod was as hard as sunbaked bricks, but he'd broken it. He'd pleased his boss, earned a paycheck that was keeping his family fed and housed, and for the most part held his temper despite Nelson's frequent attempts to rile him. Yep, Harley felt pretty good.

"But now I've got to decide what to do with you." Mr. Peterson pinched his chin between his thumb and forefinger.

Harley waited beside the other two diggers, sweat dribbling down his forehead and between his shoulder blades. His gaze drifted to the castle, where a crane lifted a block of rock. The rumble of the engine sent vibrations down the backs of Harley's legs, and he held his breath, watching as the crane operator guided the rock above the existing wall. Two men, standing on scaffolding, reached out with gloved hands to bring the block into position. Once the block rested in its proper location, the men released the chain, and the crane swung away for another block.

Harley never tired of watching the erection of the walls. Over the weeks, the castle had slowly taken shape, with doorways a man could walk through and windows a man could peer out of and a staircase a man could climb to an observation loft. Instead of just a line of rocks on a hilltop, the structure had begun to look like the drawings on Mr. Peterson's desk. Although he wouldn't admit it out loud, it fascinated Harley. He'd used a scrap of paper to recreate the blueprint, and he planned to build a smaller replica of the castle on his own property when he got home, a play castle for Dottie and Margie.

"Phipps!"

Harley set aside his daydreaming to focus on the boss.

"I'm gonna have you work with Farley on sorting blocks."

Harley swallowed his yell of triumph. He'd

have a hand in building the castle after all!
"Yes, sir."

Peterson gave directions to the other two
men, too, but Harley didn't wait around to
listen. He took off at a jog to join Dirk at the
shale pile. "Hey, Dirk! Gonna be workin' with
you now."

Dirk welcomed him with a broad smile
and clap on the back.

Harley wiped the sweat from his forehead. "So tell me what to do."

The afternoon passed quickly. Worn out,
Harley lay flat on his back in the bed of
Peterson's truck as the man transported
him and Dirk to town. The metal bed was
far from comfortable, but Harley was too
pooped to care. He closed his eyes, a smile
on his face, reliving the hours of wrapping
chain around blocks of rock, then watching
them rise above his head, carried by the
crane. The grinding thud as they fell into position was as beautiful as music.

He memorized the position of each rock
his hands touched. Someday he'd bring the
girls back here, and he'd point and say,
"See there? That's the ones Daddy added
to the castle."

Sitting up, he reached into his pocket and

withdrew the drawing he'd made. Too bad he didn't have a ruler—the lines would be straighter, the dimensions more accurate. He examined it, picturing the finished product in his mind. He was so wrapped up in his plans, he didn't notice when the truck heaved to a halt. Suddenly Peterson was beside the bed, smiling in at him.

"Planning to climb out of there, Harley?"

At the work site, Mr. Peterson called him Phipps. But at the house, it was Harley. The man's friendliness gave Harley the courage to do something he wouldn't ordinarily do. Thrusting the drawing toward his boss, he asked, "Do you think this could be built?"

Mr. Peterson took it as Harley scooted out of the truck. Dirk peered over the boss's shoulder, his heavy brows pulled down in concentration. Mr. Peterson worked his jaw back and forth for a moment before raising his gaze to Harley.

"You drew this?"

Harley nodded. "Tried to make it like the castle on the hill, but smaller. Probably won't put a second story on it since it'll just be a play castle, but I'd like a little balcony, at least. That's what this is." He pointed.

Peterson nodded. "Yes. I could tell. This

is crude but very doable, Harley. You have a natural inclination for balance and space."

"Really?"

Peterson laughed, leaning against the dusty side of the truck. "Yes, really. Maybe you should consider that schooling after all."

Harley took the paper back, folded it, and stuck it in his back pocket. "Nah, don't think so. I'm a farmer. But I think it'll be fun to put that thing together for my girls."

Peterson nodded. "No doubt your girls will love it." He pushed off from the truck, heading for the house. "Have a good evening, fellas."

Dirk and Harley ambled to the water hydrant at the back of the property. A few minutes with the cold water revived them enough to walk to town for supper. Dirk ordered a hamburger, but Harley asked for the special: a thick ham steak, fried potatoes, and corn on the cob. For some reason, he felt like celebrating. Peterson's complimentary words about his drawing, on top of the exhilaration of assisting with the castle's construction, filled him with a sense of well-being. He wished Anna Mae were sitting across the table from him so he could tell her all about it.

Scooping up a forkful of potatoes, Harley said, "Gonna write to Annie tonight. Tell her I helped put up blocks of stone today, and tell her to show the girls the drawing of their new playhouse." His excitement faltered. He still hadn't received a letter from Annie. The miles between them seemed to grow longer with each day that passed without word from home.

"Betcha your little girls'll be tickled to see what their daddy's got planned," Dirk said.

"Yeah. Yeah, I hope they will."

Dirk reached across the table and tapped the hand holding Harley's fork where the bite of potatoes waited, uneaten. "Hey? What's wrong?"

Harley shook his head. "Nothin'. Just thinkin' about how long it's been, an' no word from Annie."

Dirk took another bite, chewed, and swallowed before answering. "You're bound to hear soon, Harley. In fact"—he put the remainder of his hamburger on his plate and folded his hands—"I'll just pray about that right now." He bowed his head. "Dear Lord, Harley here is lonesome for his wife an' children. Could you please see fit to prod Annie to send him some word that things're okay at home? He'd feel a lot better. Thank you, Lord. Amen." He opened his eyes, picked up his hamburger, and took another bite.

Harley sat, unmoving.

Dirk poked him again. "Eat. I prayed. God'll answer. You gotta trust."

Harley chuckled. He finally put the bite of potatoes in his mouth. Talking around the lump, he said, "Sometimes, Dirk, you don't act no older than Dottie."

Dirk grinned. "I'm gonna take that as a compliment, my friend, 'cause the Bible tells us to trust like little children."

Well, Harley thought as he stabbed his fork back into the mound of potatoes on his plate, *I'm gonna keep writing to Annie until she sees fit to write back to me.* In the back of his mind, a tiny ray of hope flickered that Dirk's prayer would be answered.

22

At the whoosh-thud of the machine's first thrust, Jack felt as though his heart rushed to the top of his head. He counted the heaves of the pump, imagining the extraction of gallons of oil. It was worth standing in the broiling sun, being pelted with dust by the gusting wind, just to see the pump in action.

"I'm glad you contacted us, Berkley." Floyd Tompkins slapped Jack's shoulder, his smile wide. Jack had located the man at the Stamey Hotel in Hutchinson, where the oilmen all seemed to gather, and Tompkins had been pleased to come out and oversee the placement of Jack's pumps. Now, having spent two hours in the pasture with

Jack, getting the machines all running, the man's face was shiny from sweat, his blue-and-white-striped shirt blotchy at the chest and under the arms. But he still looked happy. "This will prove lucrative for both of us."

Jack nodded. Oh yes, four oil pumps on his property would surely prove lucrative. In more ways than one. He glanced at the scraggly row of cottonwoods that separated his land from Anna Mae's. His heart picked up its tempo. How could she possibly turn away from someone who could provide financial security for her and her children? A smile tugged at his lips. She couldn't.

His gaze shifted to the fifth oil pump, the one that sat over the edge of his property line, on Anna Mae's land. Sun glinted off the sleek black pump, making Jack squint, but he didn't turn away. He'd had to do some string-pulling to get that one in place. But nothing he'd told the surveyors was untrue—the land was going delinquent due to nonpayment of taxes, and he would be snatching it up the moment that happened. So, in theory, it was already his land. Anna Mae stood to gain from that oil pump, so how could anybody think he'd done wrong by authorizing its placement there?

Remembering Pop's sad look when he'd seen the map and the Xs that indicated the pumps' locations, Jack felt a small prickle of unease. Pop knew that fifth well wasn't on their land. Pop thought Jack'd done wrong, but Pop didn't understand how business worked. You had to strike when the opportunity arose or stand to lose. Once the money was rolling in, and once Anna Mae was living under Pop's roof, he'd be glad Jack had moved ahead with these plans. Pop had always loved Anna Mae, and being Grandpa to those little girls would surely bring him a great deal of pleasure.

"Well, they're all workin' fine." Tompkins lifted his toolbox and turned toward his waiting pickup truck. "I'll be back end of the week to check the output. See you then."

"Bye," Jack said. He watched the truck bounce across the pasture, dust kicked up by its tires. Cows shifted, turning their curious stares to follow the truck's passage, then moved back into clusters. The animals kept a wide berth around the wells. Jack surmised they didn't like the noise. That was okay—he didn't want one of them getting hurt. Doctoring the cows was one of his least favorite chores.

He couldn't stop his smile from growing. Might be that he could sell off his stock and give up the dairying completely, depending on how much oil was pumped from the ground. He set his feet in motion toward the house, plans tumbling through his mind. Yes sir, no more early morning trips to the barn to line up sleepy cows, no more meeting the milk truck, no more doctoring sick cows or wrestling calves, no more work or worry. Just let the pumps do their job and carry the bags of money to the bank.

The bank. Jack glanced at his watch. Yep, there was still time to get in to Hutchinson and check the amount in his savings account. Then he needed to make a little visit to Robert Syler at the courthouse. Anna Mae's land would go delinquent in less than two weeks. He'd better be ready.

Anna Mae kneeled beside the claw-foot tub, one hand on Marjorie's waist. She scooped a cup of cool water and poured it down Dorothy's bare back. The child squealed, arching backward, then begged for her mama to do it again. Smiling, Anna Mae followed Dorothy's directions, but her thoughts were miles away from the bathtub and the two naked little girls who sat in four inches of water, their mama's way of keeping them cool on this unbearably hot day.

Right now, in Hutchinson at the courthouse, her land was being declared delinquent. Well, she conceded as she splashed water over Marjorie's chubby knees, it might not be happening right that minute. But the exact time didn't matter so much. What mattered was that after today, the land that had been in her family's possession since her granddaddy homesteaded back in 1862 would no longer be hers.

Her heart ached at the thought. She was glad her father wasn't here to see this day. Her gaze moved slowly around the small room, examining the evidence of her daddy's handiwork. She smiled, remembering how he'd carried Mama over the threshold of the bathroom when the hot water heater was set up. His voice boomed in her memory: *"Now you can take you a hot bath without heating pots on the stove. Ain't that somethin', honey bunch?"*

It had taken Daddy two weeks of late evenings to turn half the porch into a bathing room, his hammer-banging keeping her and Mama from sleep, but it had been a small price to pay for the pride she witnessed on his face. Daddy had always taken such pride in this property. Who would own it now? Would the new owners even care about the split-rail fence Daddy had built using trees from their own hedgerow? Would they appreciate the tall ceiling of the lean-to on the side of the barn, set high so a man could wear his hat in there without bumping against the rafters? And all those acres of land that Daddy had so tenderly tilled and planted and sown. Would the person who took over the land care as much about it as Daddy had, letting one plot go fallow each planting season so the soil could renew itself?

She felt tears gather in her eyes, and she splashed a little water on her own face to hide them. Now that the land was being taken away, she couldn't imagine why she'd ever considered leaving it. This was her home.

"Mama?" Dorothy's voice interrupted

Anna Mae's thoughts. "Can we open the window? It's *snuffly* in here."

Despite herself, Anna Mae released a short laugh. "Darlin', I think you mean *stuffy*."

Dorothy made a face. "It's hot. Can we?"

Anna Mae shook her head. "The window's closed to keep out the dust. The wind is really strong today." She spattered Dorothy with water. "If I opened the window now, the dust would stick to all your wet places, and you'd be black as coal."

The child shrugged, grinning. She flicked her wet fingers at Anna Mae, then laughed when her mother pretended to sputter.

"Mama? Can we have bologna samwiches for lunch?"

Again, Anna Mae had to shake her head. "I'm sorry, darlin'. The bologna is all gone. How about jelly-bread sandwiches instead?"

Dorothy sighed. "Okay. But I sure like bologna samwiches. Daddy does, too." She hummed as she ran her fingers through the cool water.

Anna Mae's heart lurched. How long had it been since Dorothy had mentioned her daddy? Weeks. Anna Mae thought of Harley

every day, but she'd stopped talking about
him to the girls, just in case.

She forced a close to the thought. He
would come back. He *would* come home.
But when? And why didn't he answer her
letters? Why didn't he send money, as he'd
said he would?

And then reality struck hard. Come home
to what? The farm would no longer be
theirs. What was the point of Harley returning now? He'd be coming back to nothing.
She didn't know where she and the girls
would go when the county treasurer banged
on the door and told her to git. Even if
Harley did come back, where would he find
her?

Oh, Lord, what's going to happen to us?
Are you watching? Do you even care?

A mighty gust of wind roared, slapping the
branches of the weeping willow hard against
the wood siding. When she was a little girl,
maybe ten or eleven years old, Anna Mae
had asked her mother how she could be
so certain God was there. Her mother had
smiled softly, taken her by the hand, and led
her to the willow tree. Her sweet reply, using
the willow as a living example of her words,
had given Anna Mae all the security she'd

needed to trust completely that God was there and that He cared.

The branches slashed again, more fiercely this time. Marjorie, eyes wide, reached for her mama. Anna Mae scooped her up, cradling the wet baby against her breast, and soothed, "It's okay, angel-baby. That was just God's way of reminding me He's listening."

Dorothy scrunched her face in puzzlement. "Huh?"

Anna Mae smiled. "You see, darlin', the roots on a willow tree run deep, clear under the ground to the source of water. That's what keeps it alive even when everything around it is drying out. Faith works the same way. It runs way down deep through our souls to the Source—to God—and keeps us going when things get hard."

Anna Mae could tell by the look on Dorothy's face that she didn't understand what her mama had said. But it didn't matter. Anna Mae understood, and that was enough. Reaching for a towel, she said, "You two are going to look like little prunes if you don't get out. Let's dry off and have some lunch now, okay?"

Dorothy grumbled, but she stood and

took the towel. Anna Mae struggled to her feet, wrapped a towel around Marjorie, and headed to the bedroom to dress the baby. Another slap on the siding made her smile.

"When do you think it'll stop?"

Harley shot an impatient look in Dirk's direction. He squelched a sharp retort. This wind and heat were making him cranky. No need to take it out on Dirk. "Don't rightly know. I hope soon."

"Yeah." Dirk closed the shed door against the blowing dust. "Me too. Don't much like being cooped up in here."

Harley didn't, either. He felt trapped, like a chicken in a crate. They had to keep the door closed so they wouldn't suffocate from breathing dust, but with the shed closed up, they nearly suffocated from the heat. The small building had no windows, so the only light sneaked through cracks between the weathered boards. Dust motes swam on slivers of light, and just watching them made Harley want to sneeze.

They'd been stuck in this shed for two days now. The wind blew so much dust, a person could hardly see his hand in front of his face. Mr. Peterson had decided it was too dangerous to work the machinery when visibility was so poor, so he'd brought the project to a halt until this dust storm passed. Harley worried about home. What kind of soil would he have to work with when winter passed and he was ready to plant again? Surely the wind had carried away every bit of fertile topsoil by now.

Dirk had been praying for their farms and for the windstorm to pass quickly, and Harley had caught himself echoing Dirk's words in his heart. Took him by surprise, because it was mighty close to talking to God. Funny how Dirk's habit of prayer was rubbing off on him when Annie's never had. He pondered the reason for this, and even though he couldn't come up with a solid reason, he suspected it had to do with strength.

Annie was a female. Strong in spirit, perhaps, but weak in body. A weak body needed to rely on someone else's strength. But Dirk wasn't weak—not in spirit or in body. Yet he leaned into the strength of a higher power. Seeing the strong man on his knees in prayer humbled Harley—made him realize that maybe sometimes a man could benefit from a little bolstering.

Dirk returned to his cot, sat down, and

picked up his Bible. Seemed like all Dirk had done for the past two days was read that book. Sometimes he read out loud in his halting speech, stumbling now and then with the *thee*s and *therefore*s. At first Harley had prickled—too much like sitting in church—but at least it had been something to do. And some of it . . . Harley scratched his head. Well, some of it sounded kind of good and reminded him of things Annie'd said in the past.

He'd liked the reminder of Annie.

He lay back on his own cot, the canvas squeaking with his weight, and closed his eyes for a moment, allowing pictures of Annie to fill his head. Less than two more months and he'd be seeing her again. Peterson predicted they'd be done with the castle by mid-October. He'd be home even before the snow flew. Peterson would be moving farther west in the county to put up some bridges, and he'd invited Dirk and Harley to go with the crew. Dirk was planning to go, but Harley just figured on going home.

They'd have to pinch their pennies to get through the winter, but if the rains came back by springtime, and if the bank would loan him money for seed, and if the depression would lift, then things would go back to normal. He chuckled to himself. That was a lot of *if*s. Ask Dirk, and he'd say God could take on those *if*s. Harley wouldn't ask Dirk.

Rolling to his side, he reached beneath his cot and picked up his tablet. He propped himself up on one elbow and flopped the tablet open. The first few pages held crude drawings: bird's-eye views of his house, his barn and lean-to, the grounds. He was sure they weren't accurate, but he wasn't a bird and couldn't fly over to see. Plus he didn't have any tools to measure feet. Still, he didn't think they looked too bad. He'd made a few from his imagination, too: a bigger house, with separate bedrooms for each of the girls and a bathroom that held more than a tub and sink. It had a real flush toilet, so there'd be no need for the outhouse.

Not that he figured he'd ever be able to afford such a place, and not because he was unhappy with the house he had. It just gave him something to do. And it was satisfying. Almost as satisfying as dropping seeds in the earth and looking forward to the day the stalks would shoot for the sky and grow thick with plump ears of corn. He squinted as he struggled to read the pencil lines in the dim light. What would that house look like all tall and proud with white-painted siding and green trim?

"Gonna write to Annie again?"

Harley gave a start. The pad slipped from his hand and hit the dirt floor with a soft *flump.* He picked it up, shook the dust free, and put it back on the cot. "Why you ask that?"

Dirk pointed. "Got your writin' pad out."

Harley swung his feet over the edge of the cot and sat up. Sweat trickled down the center of his back. He squirmed at the tickle. "Guess I could. Nothin' else to do."

"Heard from her yet?"

"You seen me get any mail?" Harley hadn't intended to snarl, but it came out that way.

Dirk ducked his head. "No, I reckon I haven't."

Harley blew out an aggravated breath. Apologizing was hard, and he couldn't make himself do it even though he knew he should. Instead, he flipped to a clean sheet of paper, licked the end of his pencil, and held the pad to capture one of the stray beams of flickering sunlight. *Dear Annie . . .*

And there he stopped. What could he say? *I'm holed up in a shed waiting out a dust storm and decided to write to you.* Oh, she'd love that. *I miss you and the girls.* He'd written that already at least three times. Had it done him any good? *How's the farm?* She'd interpret that as him caring more for the land than for her. *Bet the new baby's making your stomach grow.*

He yanked out the paper, wadded it up, and threw it under the cot. There wasn't anything he could say that was worth saying. Not until he heard from her. He needed something to respond to. He'd never been good at starting conversations, and it was worse on paper when there was no give-and-take at all.

Flopping back onto the cot, he unbuttoned his shirt and let it hang open. Dust blew in from the crack above his head and settled on his chest and belly, leaving black specks on his sweaty skin. He didn't even bother to try to wipe it away. Just closed his eyes. *Please let me sleep. Let me . . . sleep.*

He didn't consider that a prayer.

23

Jack popped open Anna Mae's mailbox and removed a single envelope—a long one like businesses used, boasting the Reno County Courthouse address in the upper left-hand corner. This was it. His heart pounded.

What would Anna Mae do when she opened the letter? Would she cry? If she cried, he'd hold her, let her get his whole shirt front wet if she needed to. Then, when she'd dispelled all that sorrow, he'd give her the good news—she was welcome to stay at his house in one of the upstairs bedrooms. She could stay as long as she liked, she and the girls. And with her under his roof, with more contact between the two of them, he'd finally be able to convince her that they were meant to be together.

He pulled himself back into the wagon and urged the horses forward, then brought the wagon to a stop at her back door. He hopped down, strode to the screen door, and walked right on in.

Anna Mae stood beside the kitchen table, running a soapy rag over the oilcloth table cover. When he stopped in the doorway, she looked up. She opened her mouth, but before any words came out he held up the envelope. He watched her gaze jump to the rectangle of paper. Her eyes grew wide, and the rag dropped from her hand. Wiping her hands on her apron, she approached slowly, her lower lip tucked between her teeth.

One hand extended to take the letter from him, and she stared a long time at the address. He waited for the tears to start, but her eyes remained dry. Finally, still without opening the envelope, she raised her eyes to meet his. The calm acceptance reflected in her gray-blue eyes took him by surprise.

"I knew it would be coming, just didn't expect it so soon. I guess they don't waste any time."

Jack stuck his hands in his pockets. He guessed he wouldn't need to wrap his arms around her. At least not yet. Remembering he was supposed to be ignorant about her unpaid tax bill, he formed a question. "That your tax receipt?"

She cringed, and his hands convulsed in his pockets, ready to grab her in a hug the moment she needed it. Her head moved back and forth, and a sad smile tipped up the corners of her lips. "Not a receipt . . ."

Turning her back, she lowered her head over the envelope. Her shoulders rose and fell, and then her fingers finally moved to peel back the flap. Jack shifted forward a few inches to peer over her shoulder as she read the official statement of delinquency.

Dear Mrs. Harley Phipps,

This letter is to inform you that, as of September 1, 1936, taxes on the property located in Reno County Township, Section 24, which were due August 1 of same year, remain unpaid. According to the laws of Reno County, a 30-day grace period is allowed. As of September 1, the 30-day grace period has

ended and the property has been de-
clared delinquent. Land and structural
holdings, minus personal effects be-
longing to the residents, will be made
available for public purchase.

Therefore, please allow this letter to
serve as your notice that the aforemen-
tioned property will be placed for auc-
tion on October 1, 1936.

Sincerely,
Henry Jones Wright
Reno County Secretary

Jack knew when she reached the end, because another sigh raised her shoulders. He clamped his hands around her upper arms and squeezed. "You okay, Anna Mae?"

She spun around, dislodging his hands. "This is wonderful news."

Jack scowled. "Wonderful? How do you figure that?"

"I thought this letter would tell me I had to get out immediately. But it's thirty more days before it goes to auction. Surely that will give Harley time to get money to us, and I'll be able to pay the taxes and stop the auction. Or I can buy the property myself."

Jack felt heat climb from his neck to his

hairline. His hands balled into fists, and he gritted his teeth as he fought the urge to explode at her naïveté. When would she finally accept the fact that Harley was not the answer to her problems? The man was so stupid he couldn't figure out to send money to a bank account instead of to a home address where anything could happen to it. She didn't need Harley; she had Jack!

Anna Mae turned and headed to the hallway that led to the bedrooms. She disappeared from view, but he could hear a drawer squeak open, then click closed. When she came back into the kitchen, she wore a smile. "Three days ago I told God I wouldn't give up. Today He's given me a reason to keep hoping. Isn't He good, Jack?"

Jack swallowed his frustration, forced his lips into a grim smile, and gave the answer he knew she expected. "Yeah. Yeah, He's real good, Anna Mae."

She scooped up the rag she'd left on the table, carried it to the sink, and then faced him again. "I didn't even ask why you came by. Did you need something?"

"No." He stepped closer to the table and

clamped his fingers over the top rung of a chair's back. "Just saw the mail wagon go by and decided to bring your mail in."

She smiled. "I could have done that. The walk to the mailbox isn't long. You've kind of become my own personal mail deliverer."

Her teasing tone removed a tinge of Jack's frustration. "Anything I can do to help." He hoped his vocal inflection provided enough innuendo for her to catch on.

Leaning her hips against the counter, she tipped her head, her sweet smile sending a coil of warmth through Jack's middle. "You've been very helpful, Jack. I don't know how the girls and I would have kept things going after my accident if you hadn't been willing to come by every day. And all the chores you've done for me, even helping with canning vegetables, which I know you didn't enjoy. We've argued a lot, but—"

"You know I'd do anything for you, Anna Mae." His voice turned husky as his fingers tightened on the chair. He wished he could reach out to her, draw her near.

"You've done more than enough." Pushing off from the counter, she said, "But if you'd like to do one more thing . . . ?"

He released the chair and took a step toward her. "Sure."

"If you don't have anything pressing to do, could you just stay here for a half hour or so? Both girls are napping—neither have been sleeping well with the wind and heat— and I'd really like to take a walk. Just stretch my legs good. Would you mind?"

A strand of hair slipped free of its tail and fell along her jaw. Jack pushed his hand into his pocket before it reached out and put that strand back in place. "I don't mind at all. But I gotta tell you—" he grinned, cocking one eyebrow high—"no walk's gonna work off that belly of yours."

She blushed crimson, but she laughed, tucking her hands beneath the mound. The tug of fabric accentuated the roundness. "No, I suppose not. But it'll still feel good to get out a bit." She headed for the kitchen door, but when she reached his side she paused for a moment. "Thanks, Jack. You— you've become a good friend in the last few weeks."

She moved on then, before he could answer, but it wouldn't have mattered. He wouldn't have been able to find enough words to express what her statement meant.

In his heart, the words reverberated, taking on a deep meaning.

Anna Mae will be mine.

Harley slapped the block of shale and hollered, "Good to go, Ted!"

The crane operator gave a nod, and the machine roared into action. Harley watched the chain go taut and the rock rise as the boom lifted. He stayed in the block's shadow as he walked toward the wall, his gaze following the progress of the rock. It was sure good to be back on the job. Three more rows of blocks all the way around, completion of the turret, and the castle would be finished, and he would be on his way home. Harley's chest expanded in eagerness.

Two men stood on the second-story floor, waiting to catch hold and guide the block into position. At the base of the wall in a wide patch of shade, Dirk chatted with Mr. Peterson, but their words were lost on Harley. He focused on the placement of the next piece of the wall. A shiver went down his spine, and he licked his lips in anticipation of the moment when the rock would become a part of the castle. It was like watching a huge puzzle piece slip into place.

From the west, Nelson charged up the hill, coming to a halt directly in front of the boss. "Peterson, I gotta talk to you about the doorways on the privy. Hendricks says—"

The roar of the crane swallowed the rest of Nelson's statement. That was fine with Harley; he didn't much care to listen to Nelson talk. The rock dangled directly over the castle wall, ready for its descent. The men on top raised their arms, reaching toward the rock. But then—Harley couldn't be sure why—the rock slipped sideways in its chain.

"Look out!"

The cry came from one of the men on the scaffolding. Both men dove backward, away from the boom's chain. The boom jerked, and the rock fell free, hitting the wall of the castle with a crack that seemed to echo through Harley's gut. To his horror, the wall shuddered, a section seeming to take a huge breath as it shifted forward.

Peterson bolted down the hill to safety, but Harley stood, watching, frozen by fear.

"Harley, move!" Dirk's voice, frantic. A pair of hands smacked Harley on the back, knocking him flat on his face. He rolled, shifting his gaze in time to see Dirk lunge toward Nelson, who stared stupidly upward, his jaw slack. Dirk tackled Nelson, shielding the man with his body.

Harley screamed Dirk's name as a chunk of wall fell, hitting Dirk squarely in the back. Harley scrambled to his knees. But another block fell and caught him on the left leg, right below his hips. He screamed again—this time in pain—and collapsed, smacking his chin in the dirt. Nausea attacked, his whole body breaking out in a cold sweat. Though his eyes were open, darkness descended, leaving only a shallow tube through which he could see. The scene filled his throat with bile.

Dirk, sprawled on Nelson. Nelson, arms and legs flailing. But Dirk . . . no movement. No movement at all.

Dirk . . . Dirk, no . . . God, please no . . .

The tube narrowed, the light dimmed, and Harley was blanketed in darkness.

Anna Mae stooped down and plucked a cluster of goldenrod from its thick stem. She smiled, sliding her finger along the outer edges of the delicate petals on a dime-sized blossom. Raising her gaze to the sky, she

said, "You've tried, old sun, to make everything shrivel. But look at this—wild flowers
as fiery orange as your face at sunset, still
managing to bloom."

She chuckled to herself as she began
walking again. As a little girl, she'd often
taken long walks and talked to whatever
she encountered—the bane, she supposed,
of spending so much time alone. In childhood, her desire to escape solitude had often sent her scampering across the property line to Jack's place, to beg him to come
out and play. Yet it was comforting somehow on this day to visit with the sun, to pick
a wild flower, to amble across the empty
fields with only herself for company.

Although September had arrived, the
summer-hot weather continued. She sought
the shade offered by the scraggly clusters
of trees along the edge of the property.
Wind whistled, interrupted occasionally by
an odd whiz and thump she'd never heard
in all of her childhood meanderings. She
tipped her head, straining to identify the
sound. She wasn't certain of the source, but
she surmised it came from somewhere
ahead and to the right, off behind the wind-

break of cottonwoods and hedge apples. Curious, she headed toward the sound.

It took her a while to find a place to ease through the windbreak. Dead branches caught at her clothes and hair, and she grunted when she encountered a spider web. Yet onward she pressed, determined to discover the source of the strange sound. And she found it: some odd, bucking black monster.

An oil pump?

Looking across the expanse of Berkley land, she spotted at least three more. Her brow furrowed as she stared, unable to believe what she was seeing. Oil? In Spencer? She'd heard of it being found on the other side of Hutchinson, but she never dreamed it was this close. Why hadn't Jack said anything?

Her gaze shot back to the closest well. Her scalp pricked. She turned and looked toward the spot of land where her own house rested. Exactly where did the property line fall between her land and the Berkleys' holdings? If she was correct in her estimation, this well stood on her land.

Now that she knew what made the sound, her curiosity should have been satisfied. Instead, it was piqued. A dozen questions crowded her mind. Who put the well here? Why? How long had it been pumping? Had anyone gained anything from it? If so, where was the money? Could it be used to pay the tax bill and keep the land from going to auction?

Anna Mae needed answers to those questions. She broke back through the windbreak and headed toward the house, huffing as she pushed herself in the blistering heat. By the time she reached the back porch, she was drenched in sweat and she had a cramp in her side, but she ignored the discomfort and burst into the kitchen. Jack and Dorothy sat at the table, glasses of milk and slices of bread spread with sandplum jelly in front of them.

"Hi, Mama," Dorothy chirped with a bright smile.

Anna Mae gave her daughter a brief hello, then turned to Jack. "I just found oil pumps. And I think one of them is on my property. Do you know anything about that?"

Jack grimaced, ducking his head for a moment. Anna Mae held her breath, waiting for his reply.

"Yeah. I know about that."

She pulled out a chair and seated herself stiffly, her hands clasped in her lap. "You put them up?"

"Yeah."

"All of them?"

"Yeah."

She collapsed against the chair's back. "Why didn't you tell me?"

Jack shrugged—a slow, embarrassed gesture. "I didn't want to get your hopes up."

"My hopes up? Jack, oil—"

He held up a hand. "Listen, Anna Mae. It's a pump, okay? I had surveyors come out, and since your land is so close, I had them prospect yours, too. We put up the pumps, but there's no guarantee anything of worth'll be found. It's just a . . . a gamble."

Anna Mae scowled, her thoughts running willy-nilly. A gamble? Oil pumps cost money to put up. She didn't know a lot about drilling, but she suspected no one would go to that expense unless they were reasonably certain they'd get a return on the investment. But there was something else more pressing to understand. "So you paid for my pump?"

His lips pressed together for a moment, as if he were irritated. "Yeah, I did."

Another debt she couldn't repay. "Who gave you permission to put one on my property?"

Again, that slow shrug. He didn't quite meet her gaze. "Didn't take too much to get it arranged. I hoped . . . Well, that I could surprise you. But you ruined it."

A little pang of guilt struck. Small wonder he was irritated—he'd tried to do something kind for her, and all she could do was interrogate him. She reached across the table and placed her hand over his. "I'm sorry."

He looked fully into her face. An odd smile—almost conniving—curled his lips. Anna Mae went to move her hand, but he captured her fingers and held on.

"I'd forgive you anything, Anna Mae."

"Th-thank you, Jack."

"You're welcome." He lifted her hand to his lips and kissed her fingertips. "Just remember, honey—whatever I do, it's for your own good."

She pulled her hand free. Her fingers tingled. She wrapped her hands into fists and buried them in her apron. He smiled again—

another smile that gave her a shiver of un-ease.

"Good-bye, Miss Dorothy." He bowed toward the child who sat with jelly on her cheeks, sent a wink in Anna Mae's direction, and then slipped out the back door.

Anna Mae stared at the empty doorway, confusion making her stomach clench. *"Whatever I do, it's for your own good."* Why did words that should be reassuring make her feel so unsettled?

Pain like fire shot through Harley's hips into his back, bringing him to full conscious-ness. He gasped, and a hand clamped on his shoulder.

"Easy, there, we're going to help you."

The soothing voice was unfamiliar. Harley squinted. The face, hovering only inches above him, looked fuzzy, the features un-defined. Who? He tried to grab hold of the man's shirt front to pull him close enough to see clearly, but his weak fingers missed their target and fell to his side.

"Don't bother with me. Help Dirk. My friend . . . Dirk . . ." The words came in spurts, his breathing erratic.

The hand squeezed. "Mr. Phipps, all that

can be done was done for your friend. Don't you worry now." The hand left his shoulder. "Lift."

The ground beneath him jerked, and Harley felt himself floating. No, not floating—being carried. Every slight movement brought stabs of agonizing pain, and he breathed as shallowly as possible, a feeble attempt to control the pain.

"Where . . . where are you taking me?" All he could manage was a hoarse whisper.

"To the hospital, buddy." The same voice, calm, soothing. "Just hang in there."

"Take my friend, too." Harley grimaced as the stretcher thumped onto the floor of the ambulance. "My friend . . . Take care of my friend."

Doors slammed behind his head. The thud startled him, made him jerk, and the pain stabbed again. With a deep gasp, he squeezed his eyes shut and gave in to the darkness.

24

"At the castle site? Are you sure?"

The General Merchandise owner leaned his elbows on the high counter and gave a firm nod. "The salesman who came through here said he heard it straight from the project boss's mouth—a man was killed. An' he said the man came from Spencer, Kansas." Martin tipped his head, his eyebrows high. "You know anybody besides Harley Phipps who was workin' on a castle?"

Jack ran his hand through his hair, his forehead pinched, his chest tight with the heavy beats of his heart. "No. Nobody but Harley."

Martin sighed, straightening to reach beneath the counter and retrieve a feather duster. "Yes sir, a sad thing. Mighty sad thing. Anna Mae with those two little girls an' another'n on the way . . . Don't know what she'll do now."

Jack knew. He caught hold of Martin's arm, bringing the swish of the turkey feathers to a halt. "Listen, Martin, this is gonna hit Anna Mae hard. It'd be better if . . . well, if it came from a friend. Do me a favor and don't say anything to anybody else. At least until I've had a chance to talk to Anna Mae, okay?"

Martin's eyes widened, and he held up both hands as if in surrender. "Sure thing, Jack. I wouldn't want to bring no extra heartache to Anna Mae. I've known her since she was no higher than a horse's kneecap." He shook his head, his lined face sad. "Just such a sad thing to have happen."

"Yeah, sad . . ." Jack lifted a hand in good-bye and hurried from the store, his shopping forgotten. He and Pop could do without that cornmeal and sauerkraut, and Anna Mae'd survive without bluing for another day or two. He had to get to Anna Mae's place before word reached her another way. He had to be the one to tell her.

He drove his Model T like it had never been driven before over the dirt roads, hitting potholes so hard the car left the roadway a time or two. But it didn't matter. Nothing mattered but one thing: Harley was dead. Out of the picture. He was never coming back. And that meant there was no barrier standing between himself and Anna Mae.

All the years of Anna Mae's marriage to Harley, he'd stuck close around, befriending Harley so he could keep an eye on him, remaining under his father's roof so he'd be near if Anna Mae needed him for anything, going to sleep every night with images of Harley lying next to her in that feather bed in the front bedroom of her little house. For years he'd tried to erase Harley from the picture in his mind, and finally it was done.

He hit another pothole and the car jerked so fiercely, he nearly lost control. "Slow down," he murmured, following his own direction. No need to kill himself—that would be plenty foolish right on the verge of having his long-held dreams come true. Anna Mae wasn't going anywhere—except where he took her.

*   *   *

"Maa-ma!" Dorothy's singsong voice carried through the kitchen window. "Mr. Berkley's Model T is comin'."

Anna Mae glanced out the window. A cloud of dust indicated the vehicle's approach. She moved the soup pot from the stove and headed outside to wait with Dorothy for the car to pull into the drive. She'd given Jack a dime for a bottle of Mrs. Stewart's bluing, and the laundry waited its arrival.

The moment the auto heaved to a halt, Jack leaped from the driver's seat and rushed at her, arms outstretched. Before she knew what was happening, he captured her in a firm embrace. Jack's hand cupped her head, holding it tight against his shoulder, and his other arm curled around her waist. Too stunned to struggle, she remained motionless within the circle of his arms.

Dorothy giggled. "Mr. Berkley, why're you hugging Mama?"

Jack pulled loose by inches and glanced down at Dorothy. His hand reached out to tousle her hair, and a weak smile creased his face. "Just thought your mama might need a hug, honey. Do you need one, too?"

With a huge grin, Dorothy catapulted into

Jack's arms. He met Anna Mae's gaze over Dorothy's blond head, and something in his expression made Anna Mae's knees feel weak.

"J-Jack?"

He put Dorothy on the ground and took hold of Anna Mae's upper arm. His thumb stroked in a gentle caress. Looking at Anna Mae, he said, "Dorothy, get the watering bucket, would you? I'll be back in a minute or two to help you water the tomatoes."

"Okay, Mr. Berkley."

Dorothy skipped in the direction of the shed. Anna Mae allowed Jack to guide her to the house and push her into a chair. Shaky as she felt, she welcomed the solid wooden seat beneath her. He crouched before her and took her hands.

"Anna Mae, I . . . I gotta tell you somethin', and it's not gonna be easy for you."

Anna Mae broke out in goose bumps. Her hands trembled, and she felt Jack tighten his grip. "What is it? Is it about the farm?"

He shook his head, his gaze sorrowful. "No, honey. It's about Harley."

Her shoulders jerked back, fear striking as hard as a blow from a stick. Her mouth went dry, and her tongue seemed to stick to the roof of her mouth. She sat, silent, waiting for the second blow.

"Martin at the store . . ." Jack ducked his head for a moment, as if gathering his thoughts. "He said a salesman traveled through from Salina and told him that there was a death at the castle site." His voice was soft, gentle, in direct opposition to the hard grip he kept on her fingers. "He . . . he said the salesman mentioned a man from the city of Spencer."

Anna Mae yanked her hands loose to cover her mouth. Her fingers held back the cry that built in her throat.

Jack gathered her in his arms. She allowed his embrace while her hands remained firmly over her mouth, her eyes wide, her heart pounding. Harley . . . gone? It couldn't be. Oh, Lord, it couldn't be.

Anna Mae had no idea how long she and Jack remained frozen in that position—she in the chair, he on the floor with his arms wrapped around her and his cheek against her hair—before Dorothy burst through the porch and into the kitchen. The screen door slammed behind her. From the bedroom, Marjorie began to wail.

"Mr. Berkley? When're you gonna come

pump the water?" Dorothy hollered over the baby's cry.

Anna Mae lowered her hands to push Jack away. "Go help Dorothy. I'm okay." She heard her own voice, its normal delivery. How could her voice sound so calm when a storm raged through her insides?

Jack rose to his feet, his worried gaze pinned on her face. "You sure?"

Marjorie's screams intensified.

She nodded—a jerky, uncontrolled movement. "I'm sure. I . . . I'll take care of the baby. You take care of the tomatoes. Then I'll—" She'd what? She didn't know. She'd been through deaths before—Ben's and Daddy's and Mama's—but at those times she'd had people around her to help her make decisions. She had no idea what she'd do now.

Without another word, she moved to the girls' bedroom. She closed the door behind her and crossed to the crib where Marjorie stood on her mattress, her little face red and tearstained, her pudgy arms reaching to be held. But Anna Mae didn't pick up the baby. Instead, she stood beside the crib and closed her eyes, shutting out the sight of Marjorie's distress.

While Marjorie continue to wail, she added her own cries to those of her daughter.

Jack killed the motor and let the Model T roll to a stop in the yard outside the back door of his house. Clem ran over to greet him, sniffing his pant leg as he climbed out of the car. Jack turned to inspect the Model T's tires. His wild ride from town to Anna Mae's might have done some damage. He bent over, ran his hand along the right front tire to feel for bulges, then straightened. Pop stood silently on the opposite side of the hood. Jack startled.

"Pop, don't sneak up on me like that." He took in his father's serious expression and scowled. "You need something?"

"Had a phone call about an hour ago."

"About Harley?" Jack's heart picked up speed.

Pop's face twisted into a frown of confusion. "No. From Robert Somebody-or-Other at the Reno County Courthouse."

Jack's heart thumped double hard.

"Wanted me to tell you the auction'll take place first of October, and you can turn in your bid anytime before that date." Pop's forehead turned into a series of creases.

"What auction, son? What are you planning to buy?"

Jack walked around the vehicle and put his hand on Pop's shoulder. "Don't worry about it. There's something more pressin' you need to know." Briefly, he recounted his conversation with Martin.

Pop's face drooped with sorrow, and tears appeared in the corners of his faded eyes. "Do we know for sure?"

Jack held out his hands. "Well, Martin said the salesman mentioned Spencer by name."

Pop shook his head. "Ah, poor Anna Mae. Too bad she doesn't at least have letters from Harley to hold on to. Those letters, they'd be her last words from him and would mean an awful lot. Might ease the pain."

Jack shot his father a sharp look. What was he intimating? Did he know that Jack had stolen the letters? Jack swallowed. "Yeah."

Pop remained silent for a long time while Jack ignored him, busying himself by using his shirt cuff to clean a splattered moth from the headlight. At last Pop sighed and asked, "What's she gonna do?"

Jack shrugged and leaned down to check the left tire. "Don't know she knows for sure yet." But she'd know soon. He'd help her make all the decisions. She'd be okay soon.

Pop slipped a handkerchief from the rear pocket of his overalls and blew his nose. "I should go over. Sit with her. She doesn't have a dad to do that for her."

"She'd probably appreciate it." Jack offered his father a brief smile.

"I'll go in about an hour. Take her some muffins or somethin'. I can make pretty good muffins." Pop followed Jack as he moved to the back of the auto. "But, son, about that auction . . ."

Jack forced a laugh. "Now, Pop, don't get all worked up. I'm not leaving you." He turned back to the tire.

Pop followed. "That ain't what I asked."

Jack skimmed his hand along the black rubber, keeping his tone casual. "I'm just picking up another piece of property, that's all. Call it an investment. A man can't go wrong buying land, can he?"

"Where is the property?"

Jack released a huff of annoyance and swung around to face his father. "What difference does it make? It's my money and my decision. I'm a grown man, Pop. Do I need your permission?"

Pop took a hesitant step backward. His quavering hand rose to rest on the hood of the car, as if he needed support. "No, of course not, son. It's just—"

Jack shook his head. "Look, Pop, I know what I'm doing, and we both stand to benefit from this acquisition."

Pop shrugged, gave the Model T a pat, and then stuck his hands in his overall pockets.

Jack headed around to check the last tire. From the corner of his eye, he spotted Pop still standing beside the car, watching him with an odd expression on his tired face. He shook his head. Pop had no reason to worry. In a few more days, he'd be celebrating just like Jack, having Anna Mae and her little girls livening up the place.

Patience, Pop. Just trust me. I have it all worked out.

Ern Berkley bounced his knuckles off the porch door's frame a few times. He'd walked over; only a quarter mile separated his farmhouse from the Elliotts' if you took the shortcut across the pasture. It reminded him of old times, trekking across the dried grass while dusk settled around the landscape.

How many times had he and Ginny, arm-in-arm, made the cross-pasture journey to enjoy a cup of coffee and a time of fellowship with Ben and Margaret Elliott? He sighed. The sting of losing Ginny had lessened over the years, but a part of his heart would never be the same again. And now Anna Mae—Ben and Margaret's little girl— was feeling that same hurt.

The kitchen door stood open, just as it had in years past, and through it he could see the table, still scattered with dishes from the supper Anna Mae had prepared. He shook his head at the sad sight of those abandoned dishes. Anna Mae had been taught to clean up the table right away, so if she left that mess behind, her heart was in a sorry state for sure. At least she'd cooked. He hoped she'd also eaten. She'd need her strength to face the days ahead.

He balanced the bulky, paper-wrapped package in one hand and gave a second light knock. Although lights were on all through the house, except for the back corner where Anna Mae's bedroom used to be, he got no response to his gentle knock, so he tried again, harder, rattling the screen door in its frame. And this time Anna Mae appeared from the little hallway that led to the bedrooms. Ern could tell from her red, blotchy face that she'd been crying, and a paternal swell rose in his heart. *Lord, why'd you have to take Harley away from this girl?*

Anna Mae pushed against the screen door, the discordant squeak of its springs a harsh contrast to the soft sounds of evening. "Mr. Berkley . . . come in."

He smiled and touched her cheek as he stepped past her. Placing the packet of fresh-baked muffins in an empty patch on the messy table, he said, "I brought you a little somethin' to munch for breakfast tomorrow. Some honey-bran muffins. Baked 'em myself with Ginny's recipe."

Anna Mae moved beside him and touched the paper-wrapped bundle. "Thank you. You didn't need to do that." Her voice, usually so expressive, sounded flat.

Ern took hold of her shoulders, turning her to face him. "It's not so much, Anna Mae. It's a lot less than I'd like to do."

Tears flooded bloodshot eyes that were already puffy and sore looking. She ducked her head, swept away the moisture with shaking fingertips, and whispered in a ragged tone, "I don't know what to do."

Ern gave her shoulders a pat. "Well, I do. First of all, let's get this table cleared off. I'll wash; you dry. Then we'll sit and chat, okay? Get things sorted out in your head."

She nodded.

He glanced toward the hallway. "Are your girls sleepin'?"

"Yes. I know it's early, but . . ." She lifted her gaze. "I need to tell Dorothy, at least. Marjorie's too little—it wouldn't mean anything to her—but Dorothy needs to know. And I just can't—" Her face crumpled.

Ern followed his instincts. He pulled her tight beneath his chin in a fatherly embrace, rubbed her quaking shoulders, and murmured soothing words into her ear. And all the while, he prayed inwardly. While putting away laundry last week, he'd found something unexpected in Jack's bureau drawer: letters. Letters that appeared to be meant for Harley and Anna Mae. *Lord, I don't know what my foolish son is up to, but please prompt him to give those letters to Anna Mae.*

25

Harley winced as he stretched to place his half-empty plate on the table beside his hospital bed. Any movement at all, despite the thick cast wrapped around his left leg and the stabilizing straps that elevated his foot twelve inches above the crisp sheets, brought stabs of pain. The doctor had explained it was good that he felt pain—it meant the nerves were mending themselves despite the bone-crushing blow from the block of shale—but Harley wished he could escape it.

And the pain in his leg was nothing compared to the pain in his heart. He couldn't get away from that, either. The knowledge ate at him like a cancer, stealing his appetite and tormenting his dreams.

Dirk was dead. The memory of Dirk's final minutes made Harley's stomach roll until he feared he'd lose the little bit of supper he'd managed to swallow. Kind, gentle, smiling Dirk. Dead. It wasn't fair!

Harley threw his arm over his eyes as hot tears stung behind his lids. Why had Dirk done it? Why had he stayed beside that wall and pushed Harley aside? Why had he protected Nelson? Nelson had never done anything to warrant Dirk's protection. Dirk should've saved himself, not Nelson.

"Harley?"

Harley dropped his arm, tipping his chin down to peer toward the door. Mr. Peterson stood framed in the doorway, his hat in his hands.

"You up to some company?"

Harley nodded even though he preferred to be alone. Talking took energy he didn't have.

Mr. Peterson grabbed a metal chair and dragged it over beside the bed. The screech of chair legs against the tiled floor sent a chill up Harley's spine. There were so many unpleasant sounds in this place—and smells. A part of him longed for the day he'd be released, and a part of him dreaded it. He had no idea what the future held for him now.

Peterson seated himself, resting his hat on one knee, and gave Harley a sad smile. "So, are they treating you okay? Feeding you well?"

Harley glanced at the plate. The sight of congealed gravy made his stomach churn. "Feedin' me, but the cooks could take a lesson or two from my wife. They don't seem to know what a salt shaker's for."

Peterson chuckled softly. "Yes, well, lots of upset stomachs in hospitals, so they have to keep things bland."

"I reckon." Harley shifted a bit, grimacing with the throb of pain in his hip. Where was that nurse with her little pills that sent him back to dreamless sleep?

"Here." Peterson leaned forward, giving a tug on Harley's pillow that brought it more beneath his shoulders. "Better?"

Harley nodded.

"Now, tell me what the doctor says about your leg."

The throb increased as Harley's muscles tightened. He swallowed hard. "Doctor says the surgeon did the best he could to repair the break. They're gonna keep me strapped up like this for another week yet to let everything heal. Says it's good that the leg tingles and hurts 'cause it means the nerves are healing. But the bone . . ." He licked his lips, reliving the terror-filled moment when that rock slammed him to the ground. "The bone was pretty much shattered. There's no promise on how the leg'll work. I . . . I don't know if I'll be able to farm—" His voice broke as he considered the magnitude of his admission.

Mr. Peterson nodded. "I'm sorry."

The men sat in silence for a long while, their breathing an accompaniment to the unique sounds of the hospital floor—rolling carts, soft voices, occasional moans, the *rattle-swish* of curtains on iron runners. Each sound pierced Harley. He might not ever walk normally again, but he was alive and able to hear, thanks to Dirk's quick actions. But Dirk . . .

"I brought something from the men." Mr. Peterson's voice intruded into Harley's private thoughts.

Harley opened his eyes and watched Mr.

Peterson slide a thick envelope from a pocket inside his jacket. When he didn't reach for it, Mr. Peterson placed the envelope on the mattress next to Harley's hip.

"We took up a collection. The government will pay your hospital bills, but we figure there will be other expenses—a train ride home, bills to pay while you gain your strength so you can start working again . . ." The man swallowed, his expression mournful.

Harley shook his head. "I don't want it. Give it to Dirk's family. They'll need it worse than I will."

"We did the same thing for Dirk. I sent it the day after the accident, and I got a thank-you from his mother today." Mr. Peterson reached into his jacket again and withdrew a sheet of paper, folded down into quarters. "She included this for you."

Harley didn't reach for that letter, either. His heart pounded. How could he bear to read words penned by the mother of the man who died in Harley's place? She would certainly condemn him, but no more than he'd already condemned himself. "I . . . I don't want it."

Mr. Peterson slid the letter underneath the envelope, one corner sticking out, inviting investigation. "I understand. But in case you change your mind, I'll leave it, along with the collection from the men."

"No, please . . ." Harley didn't want that letter or the money left here. "Take it. Please, just take it."

Mr. Peterson frowned. "Don't you think your family can use it?"

Harley considered this. As much as it hurt his pride, he knew he wouldn't be much use to Annie and the farm. Not for a long while, if ever. She could use that money. He released a huffing breath. "Can you—can you send it to my wife?"

"Do you want to write a letter to go with it?"

Harley shook his head. He had no idea what to say to Annie now.

"Do you want me to put in a note?"

Very slowly, Harley nodded. "Yeah. But . . . don't tell her I'm hurt."

The boss's eyebrows formed a sharp *V*. "You haven't let her know about the accident?"

"No." Harley swallowed. "She can't do

nothing about it. It'll just worry her, an' she's expectin' a baby. She doesn't need the worry. Can you . . . can you think of some reason to send it?"

"I'll see what I can do. But I won't lie to her."

"Wouldn't ask you to."

Mr. Peterson nodded. "All right, then. I've got the address in your paperwork at the job site." He rose, putting his hand on Harley's shoulder. "I'll come by and see you again, Harley. You take care."

Harley nodded and watched the man leave the room, his hat still in his hand. A nurse bustled in and picked up the plate from the table. She shook her head. "Mr. Phipps, how do you possibly hope to regain your strength if you don't eat? I've not seen you finish one meal all week."

Harley scowled. "Bring me somethin' that tastes good, an' I'll eat it." He slumped back against the pillow, clenching his teeth against the pain that shot through his hip and into his leg. The letter Mr. Peterson had left behind slid off the bed onto the floor, and the nurse reached for it and handed it to Harley. He held it between his thumb and forefinger, his heart thudding, then laid it on his chest.

Now to find the courage to read it.

Anna Mae placed the last plate on the shelf and turned to Mr. Berkley. "Thank you so much for your help."

His eyes crinkled with his smile. "You're welcome. And now we can sit, sip some coffee, and talk." He poured himself a cup and settled himself at the table.

Anna Mae didn't want coffee, but she sat down across from him and fiddled with the edge of the oilcloth cover on the table. "A part of me just can't believe it. Harley . . . dead." She whispered the last word, unable to utter it aloud. Shaking her head, she met his gaze. "Shouldn't I have felt it somehow? How can I love someone so much and not know when he slipped away?"

Ern Berkley reached across the table to take her hand. "Honey, don't torture yourself. The good Lord is the only one who can know such things."

But Anna Mae shook her head. "No. It was like that for Mama and Daddy. The day Daddy had his attack, he was out in the field, and Mama was at the sink, washing dishes. I remember all of a sudden, she straightened and put her hand against her heart. A couple minutes later, Harley came running into the yard, hollering that something had happened to Daddy."

Tears distorted her vision, making Mr. Berkley appear fuzzy. "She knew, Mr. Berkley. She felt the pain of Daddy leaving her. But I—" A sob pressed up, and she clamped her hand over her mouth, holding it back, her head low. "It's because Harley and I never had what Mama and Daddy had. Jack was right . . . Jack was right."

Mr. Berkley tugged her hand, and her gaze met his. His grim expression startled her. "You listen to me, Anna Mae. What your mama and daddy had was a whole lot of love and commitment—and that's just what you and Harley had. He loved you and those little girls with all his heart. And his commitment to this land? Why, I never saw a body work so hard to provide for his family. Don't you go puttin' down what you and Harley had. It might not've been perfect, but it was a whole lot more'n a lot of people ever get to experience in a lifetime."

Anna Mae swallowed her tears. "But he

didn't have faith, Mr. Berkley. We didn't share that. And now—"

"You leave that in God's hands." The older man's voice quivered with conviction. "Stewin' about it won't change it now anyway. It'll only sour your stomach."

He was right about that. All the worry of the afternoon had created a pain in her middle that wouldn't go away. "I just wish—"

"Wishing is a waste of time." The words were brusque, but the gentle tone removed any hurt. "What's past is past, honey. What we've got to do now is look ahead, make plans for your future."

Reality caved in around Anna Mae. What kind of future would she have now? No home, no husband, and two—no, three— other lives depending on her for their survival. How would she meet the needs of her children when she didn't even have a roof to put over their heads? How could she work while nursing a baby?

"Oh, why did God let this happen? Why, Mr. Berkley? Why?" Her questions turned to wails, and she laid her head on the table as she fought against giving way to another binge of weeping.

Mr. Berkley's warm hand rubbed her

shoulder. "Sometimes God's ways are so mysterious, our human minds can't grasp the why. This is one of those times, honey. But that's where faith comes in. We just have to trust He can work this all out to His glory and your good."

"My good?" Anna Mae lifted her head, fixing her gaze on the older man's. "How can Harley's death and the loss of my house do me any good?"

Mr. Berkley's bushy brows came down. "Loss of your house?"

Anna Mae nodded. "Yes. I couldn't pay the tax bill. Harley didn't send money—" Suddenly an idea struck. "Maybe he couldn't because he's been gone for a long time." Her chin quivered, tears filling her eyes again. She swiped her fingers across her eyes, removing the traces of tears. "At least, if he was dead, I know he didn't deliberately abandon me." She found a small measure of comfort in the realization. "But it doesn't fix anything. I had no money to pay the bill, so the county is taking my land. It goes to auction the first of October."

She watched Mr. Berkley's expression turn hard, his dark eyes snapping. Fear rose in her throat. What had she said that angered him so? Before she could question him, he ducked his head, sucking in a deep breath that wiped the anger from his face. When he looked at her again, the gentleness was back.

"Honey, let's tackle one problem at a time, okay? The first thing is helpin' your Dorothy understand what's happened to her daddy."

Anna Mae's chest tightened. "It'll be so hard."

"Yes, but keepin' it from her won't help a thing." He gave her shoulder a squeeze. "Do you want me to tell her?"

Anna Mae considered his offer. It would be easier on her, most certainly, to allow someone else to assume that responsibility. And Dorothy admired Mr. Berkley so much—she'd surely listen to the older man. But was it fair to ask it of him? She knew it wasn't. Dorothy was her child. She needed to be the one to tell her. "I appreciate your willingness to do that for me," she finally said, "but I think I need to be the one to tell Dorothy."

Mr. Berkley nodded, admiration in his eyes. "That's my brave girl. I can be with you, if you'd like."

"Tell me what, Mama?"

The little voice brought both Anna Mae and Mr. Berkley up short. They looked toward the hallway where Dorothy stood, her hair on end, rubbing her eyes with her fists.

Anna Mae stretched a hand toward her. "I'm sorry, sweetheart. Did I wake you up?"

The little girl scampered to her mother's side and laid her head on Anna Mae's shoulder. "I heared Papa Berkley talking, and I wanted to tell him hello." Her lips curved into a sleepy smile. "Hi, Papa Berkley."

"Hi, honey."

Dorothy lifted her head and put her hands on Anna Mae's cheeks. "You still cryin'?"

Anna Mae choked back a sob. The child's sweetness was like salt in an open wound. How could she bear to tell this little girl that her daddy was gone forever? Gathering Dorothy into her arms, Anna Mae whispered against her hair, "A little bit."

Dorothy wiggled loose and sent Mr. Berkley a knowing look. "Mama was sad at supper. She kept cryin'." She turned again to her mother. "How come you're sad, Mama?"

Anna Mae opened her mouth, but no words came out. How could she explain death to the child in a way she would understand? Anna Mae looked at Mr. Berkley. He closed his eyes briefly, as if offering a silent prayer. When he opened his eyes, he gave her a slight nod, reaching across the table to clasp her hand. The moment his fingers closed around hers, she found the words.

"Darlin', do you remember when Ol' Smokey caught the birdie in the barn?"

Dorothy nodded, her blue eyes wide. "Yes. Poor birdie . . . I wanted you to make him fly again."

Anna Mae smoothed Dorothy's hair from her forehead. "I know, but I couldn't. Do you remember why?"

"Uh-huh. You said Smokey squeezed the spirit out of the birdie, and the spirit went up to heaven. With no spirit, the birdie couldn't fly anymore. So we buried it under the bushes."

"That's right." Anna Mae took a deep breath, finding strength in the comforting pressure of Mr. Berkley's hand. "Sometimes the spirit gets squeezed out of people, too. And when that happens, the person's body dies, and they can't be with us on earth anymore."

"Like your mama and daddy?"

Anna Mae nodded. "Like my mama and daddy. And . . ." She felt her heart beat in her temple as she forced the words out. "Dorothy, I'm sad because that's what has happened to your daddy. His body died—his spirit went away—so he isn't going to be able to come back to us."

Dorothy's brows pinched together. "Daddy went to heaven like the birdie?"

Oh, how Anna Mae hoped he had! She managed a slight nod.

The child shook her head, her expression innocent. "No, he didn't."

Anna Mae's heart caught. She couldn't let Dorothy think her father wasn't in heaven. "Yes, sweetheart, Daddy is in heaven."

But Dorothy took a step backward. "Daddy's *not* in heaven. Daddy is building a castle, and then he'll be back. He *promised*." The child's matter-of-fact tone nearly broke her mother's heart. "He'll be back. You'll see."

Without another word, Dorothy turned and headed for the bedroom. She paused at the hallway opening, peeking over her shoulder. "Good-night, Papa Berkley." She skipped around the corner and closed the bedroom door.

Anna Mae looked at Mr. Berkley. There were tears in the older man's eyes.

26

Tears filled Harley's eyes. The words on the page blurred together. He crushed the letter to his chest and closed his eyes, his throat convulsing, as the salutation reverberated through his mind.

Our dear Mr. Phipps . . . Our dear Mr. Phipps . . .

How could Dirk's parents call Harley dear after what he'd done? He'd shown up at their place, hauled away their son—the son they'd specially chosen from an orphanage—and let him die because he'd been too stupid to jump out of the way of a falling block. They knew what had happened. Yet the letter opened with *Our dear Mr. Phipps . . .*

Several minutes passed before Harley gained enough control to read the rest of the letter. He dried his eyes with the backs of his wrists, lifted the page, and pushed himself past the greeting.

I'm sorry you're hurt and laid up. Mr. Peterson told us you were hurt in the accident, but I'm thankful it wasn't worse. Your little girls need their daddy to come home again. Thank the Lord, you'll be able to do that.

Mr. Phipps, you're probably feeling guilty about what happened with Dirk. Don't. It isn't your fault. Dirk did what Dirk's always done—took care of others. We knew when we brought him home seventeen years ago that he was a special boy. We accepted that he was a gift from the Lord. The Lord giveth and the Lord taketh away. He's with his heavenly Father now, and although it pains us to say good-bye, we know he's happy.

Dirk thought a lot of you, Mr. Phipps. He considered you a friend. He asked us to pray for your family and for you. He especially wanted you to find a rela-

*tionship with God through Jesus. We
will continue to pray that for you. I hope
you will keep in touch with us. It will be
quiet here without Dirk, but the Lord
will see us through.*

Take care of yourself, Mr. Phipps.
In Christ's love,
(Mr. and) Mrs. Eldo Farley

Harley laid the letter back on his chest, folded his hands on top of it, and closed his eyes. What a dear woman. Her heart must be breaking, but she took time to comfort Harley, to reassure Harley, to tell Harley she'd be praying for him. Emotion filled his throat with the need to cry. And something else pressed at him, too—a need for . . . something.

His mind drifted back to conversations with Dirk. The big man had told Harley more than once that God loved him—loved him enough to let His Son die for Harley's sins. Harley had questioned that—how could someone he didn't even know give His life for him? It hadn't made sense . . . until now. Seeing Dirk wrap his arms around Nelson, throw him to the ground and offer the protection of his body, painted a picture of sacrifice.

Nelson had never been nice to Dirk. He'd needled Dirk and tormented him until Harley wanted to punch the man right in the nose. Yet Dirk had sacrificed his own life to keep Nelson from being harmed.

Just like Jesus had done.

I reckon I'd like to know a man like that. I'd like to know Jesus. The need increased, building pressure around Harley's chest that threatened to squeeze the air from his lungs. He couldn't hold back his sobs. One burst out, followed by a second. Harley crossed both arms over his face and gave vent to the pain of loss and the power of need. The bed shook with the violence of his crying, sending spasms of pain through his hip and leg, but he ignored the physical discomfort and continued to cry in huge, hiccupping sobs that echoed through the room.

Footsteps approached, and a hand touched his shoulder. "Mr. Phipps? Mr. Phipps, is it the pain? I have a pill for you. Here . . ."

Harley shook his head behind the shield of his arms. "I don't need a pill. I . . . I need to talk to someone. A minister. I need to talk to a minister."

The hand offered a gentle pat. "Yes, sir. You hold on. I'll make a call right now."

Anna Mae walked to the end of the lane where the mailbox stood lonely sentinel. Her legs felt weak, and she paused for a moment to grab hold of a fence post and rest. She'd hardly slept and had eaten next to nothing since last week when Jack had careened into the yard, leaped out of his Model T, swept her up in a hug, and delivered the news. Her appetite, as well as her ability to sleep, had slipped away with the knowledge of Harley's death.

Jack and his father came by every day to see to things, to check on her. She knew they worried about her. Mr. Berkley even thought she should go see the doctor. But what could Doc Warren do? Could he turn back time, bring back the rains and her husband so the farm would prosper once more? She lifted her eyes to the blue sky. A desire to talk to God—to lay all of her worries at His feet—welled up inside of her, but she pushed it aside. Fear that He wouldn't answer silenced her prayer.

A gust of wind tangled her skirt around her knees and tossed her uncombed hair across her cheek. Inside her belly, Harley's baby shifted, a tiny foot pressing into Anna Mae's ribs. She pushed the heel of her hand to the spot, sorrow striking anew. What kind of life would this child lead with no daddy, no home, and a mama who was fast losing hope?

"Oh, Lord, I'm so tired." The words found their way from her broken heart, slipping out in a whisper. Another gust struck, and fleetingly Anna Mae wondered if her simple statement would be carried by the wind to heaven, to God's ears, and He would send rest. How she needed rest.

Pushing off from the post, she walked the final few feet to the mailbox and looked inside. One thick envelope leaned against the side of the tin tube. She plucked it out, frowning at the unfamiliar handwriting. Holding it in front of her, she scuffed her way back to the house. The branches of the weeping willow swayed in the wind, as if beckoning her to draw near. She sidestepped past the tree and entered the house.

It was quiet. Marjorie and Dorothy both napped. She sank down at the table, brushed a few crumbs from lunch aside, and used her thumb to pop loose the flap on the envelope.

Money spilled across the oilcloth. She reared back in surprise. Bills—several ones, a few fives, a ten . . . Her hands shook as she counted it. Money enough to pay the tax bill? Hope set up a patter in her heart. Among the bills was a sheet of paper torn from a note pad. She snatched it up.

Dear Mrs. Phipps,

Enclosed is a small token of affection collected in honor of Harley and his family by the workers of the Coronado Heights Castle project. It is our hope this will lighten your load as you cope with Harley's absence. Please use these funds as needed. If there is anything I can do to assist you, please do not hesitate to contact me.

God bless you.
James Peterson

Anna Mae dropped the brief note. Holding the evidence of Harley's death burned her fingers. She stared at the paper lying on top of the pile of bills, her mind racing.

There was so much she wished to know—how the accident had happened, if Harley had suffered, where he was buried. None of that was addressed in the few lines of text.

But Mr. Peterson had invited her to contact him if she needed assistance. She sprang from the chair and raced to the parlor, to Mama's bow-front secretary. Behind the fold-down desk lid she saw the writing paper and envelopes.

Mr. Peterson had offered to assist her. Anna Mae was going to ask.

Jack reached into the back of his wagon and lifted out the large crate. He grunted as he cleared the side of the wagon—the box was heavy. It smacked against his thighs, sending him backward a step. But he managed to keep his grip and his footing. With a muffled curse, he hefted the box a little higher and headed, in stumbling steps, toward the back porch of Anna Mae's house.

Through the open kitchen doorway, he spotted her at the table, hunched forward over something. With no free hand to knock, he called through the screen, "Anna Mae? Come get the door, huh?"

She straightened in the seat, scowling as

she turned in his direction. Then the scowl turned to an expression of surprise. She dashed across the porch and swung the door wide, pressing herself backward to clear the way for his passage.

"Ooph!" He thumped the box onto the table, covering several sheets of paper that were scattered across the tabletop.

Anna Mae stood at his elbow, her puzzled gaze aimed into the crate. "What's all this?"

Jack swiped his arm across his forehead, removing the beads of perspiration from his exertion. "Collection from town. Folks've been dropping stuff in this box when they shop at Martin's. It got full, so Martin asked me to bring it on out."

Anna Mae rested her fingertips on the edge of the crate, her eyes bright with unshed tears. "That's so nice of everyone."

Jack gave her shoulders a quick rub. "People care, Anna Mae."

She nodded. Stepping away from him, she rounded the table and tried to tug loose the papers from underneath the crate. He tipped it up to help her. She slid them all free, tamped them into a stack, then carried them into the parlor. She returned empty-handed. For several seconds, she stood across the table, staring at the crate, an unreadable expression in her gray-blue eyes.

"Want me to help you put this all away?" Jack offered, taking out a five-pound sack of flour. "Looks like there's enough to keep you goin' for a while."

When she didn't answer, he looked at her again. One lone tear slid down her cheek. She did nothing to stop it, just stood silent and staring, allowing the tear to fall. In those moments, Jack experienced a tiny niggle of regret that Harley wasn't coming back. He hated to see Anna Mae so forlorn. "Hey? You okay?"

She gave a start, and her gaze bounced up to meet his. "Yes. I . . . I was just thinking about Harley. His last day here, he carted in a crate like that—only smaller—full of groceries. I . . . I didn't really thank him for it." Her voice dropped to a whisper. "And now I can't."

Jack circled the table and put his arms loosely around her. She pressed her cheek to his chest. But when he tightened his grip, she pulled free and moved to the table.

"I'll need to post a thank-you note at the store—let people know how much this is appreciated." She reached into the crate and began removing items, stacking them on the table.

Jack didn't say anything, just helped unload, and then watched as she put things away in the cupboards.

When she'd placed the last can of beans on a shelf, she turned with a sigh. "Feels good to have full cupboards again. Especially since it looks like maybe I won't have to move after all."

Jack's brows jerked downward. "You won't?"

She shook her head, a slight smile tipped up her lips. "Harley's boss—Mr. Peterson—took up a collection at the job site and sent it to me. If I can pay my taxes, surely the auction will be stopped, won't it?"

Jack's legs turned to rubber. He pulled out a chair and sat down.

She crossed to the table and sat in the chair next to his. "I've got to at least try. Even if I can't keep farming here, I need to have claim to the property. I may need to sell it for money to buy a place in town—maybe Hutchinson—where I can work and provide for the girls. With Harley gone for good . . ." The tears welled again, but she brushed them aside and continued. "The girls are depending on me now. I can't let them down."

Jack shook his head. Hadn't she listened to anything he'd said over the past few months? His voice grated out, "The girls don't have to depend only on you. I told you, Anna Mae—you'll be cared for. *I'll* take care of you."

She ducked her head for a moment, making a steeple of her hands in her lap. "I know what you said, Jack, but we aren't your responsibility. It shouldn't be left to you to take care of us."

"Didn't I tell Harley I would?"

Her gaze shot up. "Yes, but that was for the milk—not for his wife and children."

Jack took hold of her hand and squeezed gently. "Anna Mae, don't you know my promise went deeper than taking care of the cow?" He leaned forward, bringing his face within inches of hers. "Why do you think I took over all the chores after you got hurt? Why did I put that oil pump out on your property? Why have I taken you and your girls to church and to the store and to the courthouse? It's because I care about you. Haven't you figured that out by now?"

Anna Mae gave a little tug on her hand,

slipping it from his grasp. She cupped the rounded curve of her stomach with both hands and released a sigh. "I know you care, Jack, but . . ."

"But what?" He tempered the fervency of his tone with a forced smile.

"But it would be wrong for me to lean on you now. It would be out of desperation, not love."

Jack shot straight up, bringing his spine against the spindled back of the chair. He felt heat fill his face, and it was all he could do to keep a rein on his temper. After everything he'd done for her, her ingratitude was like a slap. All the time and money he'd poured into her since her husband headed off . . . She should be kissing his hands and thanking him.

He took several deep breaths, trying to calm himself. "I guess it's no secret I love you." He heard his own clipped, flat tone. He saw her face turn white, but he didn't care. "And I won't lie right now. I can't imagine why you're still clinging to Harley's memory. But you're going to have to let go. You think you can run this farm on your own? You're wrong. You think you can find a job in town and still take care of your little girls? Wrong again. Whether you realize it or not, Anna Mae, you need somebody. You need *me*."

He rose, looking down at her pale face through narrowed eyes. "When you come to your senses, you'll know where to find me—out in the barn, taking care of your cow. My offer stands—I'll take you and the girls in, be a provider to all of you, including that new baby. I've got room, and I can afford to do it. But I won't beg."

He started for the door but then turned back, deciding she needed to hear one more thing. "And I also won't keep this up forever. You're right—it's not fair to me to keep hanging around here, seeing to your farm, when I don't get anything in return. So decide what you really want, Anna Mae—to be taken care of, or to be on your own." He stomped through the porch, allowing the screen door to slam behind him.

Back in the wagon, rolling out the gate, he felt a smile climb his cheeks. Laying out that ultimatum was the smartest thing he'd done so far. She'd come running now for sure. She'd never make it on that farm without him.

27

Anna Mae leaned forward and kissed Dorothy's cheek. She smoothed the hair from the child's face, smiling as Dorothy's eyes slipped closed and she nestled into her pillow. Turning from Dorothy, she peeked into Marjorie's crib. Marjorie lay flat on her back, arms up over her head, her lower lip puckered out in a pout. A mixture of love and protectiveness welled up inside Anna Mae's breast. The baby looked so innocent.

She crept from the room, pulled the door closed behind her, then headed to the parlor. Opening the drop-down desk on the secretary, she removed the letter she'd written to Mr. Peterson and scanned it, frowning a bit as Jack's words interfered with her focus. Carrying the letter with her, she crossed to the sofa, tugged the chain on the standing lamp, and sank down in the soft circle of yellow light. She set the letter on the cushion beside her and rested her head against the high back of the sofa, replaying the afternoon conversation with Jack in her mind.

Although she had said little in response to his proclamations of love and his promise to care for her and the girls, he had certainly created a reaction in her heart. She had tried not to think about it over the years, but underneath she'd always suspected Jack still loved her. He'd never dated anyone after she turned down his proposal. When he'd come by the house, presumably to talk to Harley, he'd always made it a point to find her, greet her, ask how she was doing. She had kept her distance so she wouldn't give him any encouragement, but over the past months she knew Jack had encouraged himself.

His time in her barn, her garden, her fields. His carting her to church, to Spencer, to Hutchinson. His fetching the doctor, the groceries, the mail. All of these things had combined to make him feel like he was part of her life. She couldn't blame him for thinking it was right to step in now and assume responsibility for her permanently—he'd had a taste of family life, and he'd obviously found it pleasurable.

She shifted on the cushion as the baby moved, creating a pressure against her right side. This child was sure an active one. She rubbed her belly absently as memories continued to unfold. So many of her childhood remembrances included Jack. He'd been an annoyance much of the time, but they'd also had fun. Especially after Ben, Jr., went away, she'd relied on Jack for companionship. She cared for him as a dear friend, a brother in Christ, but she'd never loved him. Not the way he claimed to love her.

Now she wondered: Could she grow to love Jack in that way? It would solve so many problems. She would have no financial worries, and the girls would have someone to call Daddy. Ern Berkley would certainly welcome them into his family. She smiled as she recalled the older man's delivery of muffins, his tender hug, and his fatherly words of advice. He would be a wonderful grandfather for the girls, something they'd never known.

A deep sigh escaped, and she opened her eyes. The wind had calmed, but a gentle breeze ruffled the lace curtains. In the distance, a coyote released one long howl. A second one replied, and then the two together gave a series of yips. Anna Mae imagined the two creatures frolicking in the empty field, happy for companionship. Her heart lurched. She needed companionship. Despite the presence of the girls, she felt so lonely. How she missed Harley.

She wouldn't need to feel lonely if she did what Jack suggested. If she married him, she would have companionship again, other adults around. Even if she didn't love him like she'd loved Harley, having a helpmate would be good, wouldn't it?

Leaning forward, she rested her elbows on her knees and covered her face with both hands. She groaned. "Oh, what do I do?"

Come to me, all ye who are heavy-laden, and I will give you rest.

The words came as clearly as if uttered aloud. Anna Mae jerked upright and looked around the room. She was the only one there, yet she knew without doubt she was not alone. Tears flooded her eyes. Slipping from the cushion, she knelt beside the sofa and clasped her hands together beneath her chin.

"Thank you, Lord, for reminding me that you are here. You're trying to take care of me, aren't you? By sending the money from Harley's boss, and the groceries that came from town. I'm sorry I've been so focused on what I lost that I couldn't see what I have—your presence in my life." She swallowed, listening for a moment to the gentle whistle of the wind through the willow branches. "I told you I wouldn't give up on my faith, but I need your strength right now. I'm scared, God. I don't know what to do. Show me, please, where I should go."

She sat in silence for several minutes, absorbing the peacefulness of the moment, relishing being in God's holy presence. Slowly, her muscles relaxed, a calm filling her soul. She knew what she would do.

She would send her letter to Mr. Peterson. When she had her answers, she would somehow travel to Harley's grave site and say her good-byes. Before she could move forward, she needed to bring closure to her past.

*   *   *

Harley closed the book in his lap and sighed, a deep sigh of satisfaction. Still trapped in this bed, still battling pain, still far away from his farm, his girls, his wife, and yet, somehow, Harley was happier than he'd ever been before.

He wasn't sure he understood the lightness in his heart. But he realized he didn't need to understand it to celebrate it. The minister had been right: with the acceptance of Jesus into his heart, his perspective had changed. From the outside, everything was the same, but inside . . . Ah, inside Harley was a new man.

This evening he had read portions from the third chapter of Colossians. So many of the verses held deep meaning for him. He needed to set aside anger, he needed to build his knowledge of God, he needed to forgive those who had hurt him. Including Nelson. He swallowed, realizing how difficult it would be. Yet he was sure he could do it, with God's help. He closed his eyes and whispered a prayer.

"Lord, let your peace rule my heart. Let me please you with my thoughts."

A shuffle sounded from the doorway, and he opened his eyes, expecting to see the night nurse. It was time for lights-out. But instead, Mr. Peterson's head and shoulders poked through the doorway.

"Did I wake you?"

Harley shook his head and gestured with one hand. "No. Come on in. But aren't visiting hours over?"

The man entered the room, crossing to stand beside Harley's bed. A bulky burlap bag dangled from his hand. "Yes, but the nurse said I could come up if I only stayed a minute. I wanted to bring you something."

Harley smiled. "You've brought me enough. The food was great, but . . ." He lifted the Bible. "This is the best. Thank you. Never had a book of my own before."

Peterson's face lit up. "I'm pleased to see you're reading it."

"Every day. Learnin' a lot, too." Harley frowned, regret striking. "Don't know why it took me so long to start listening to God. My wife—she preached it at me for years, but I just couldn't see it. Not until Dirk . . ." The picture of Dirk's still form sprawled in the dirt flashed through his mind. He pushed the image aside, replacing it with one of Jesus with outstretched arms. The minister who had come at the nurse's call last week had given him the suggestion of replacing unpleasant images with a picture of Christ. It helped.

Peterson gave Harley's shoulder a pat. "I know your wife will be thrilled to hear of your conversion. My wife and I celebrate it with you, too."

Harley managed a wobbly smile. He'd had no idea how many people had prayed for him: Dirk and his parents, Annie, the Petersons. God had used so many people to bring his heart around. The knowledge of God's love washed over him again, bringing the sting of tears to his eyes.

"Have you written to your wife to let her know what happened?"

Mr. Peterson's question sent a stab of guilt through Harley's chest.

"No, sir. I . . . ." He shook his head. "I wrote to her lots of times, but she's never written back. Not once. I . . . I don't rightly know where I stand with Annie anymore. I'm afraid . . . Well, I'm thinkin' she might've decided to carve out a life without me."

Mr. Peterson frowned. "That doesn't make much sense."

Harley shrugged. "I don't know what else to think. Why wouldn't she ever send me any word? We . . . we'd been strugglin' for quite a while before I left. Might be she's just decided things're a lot easier without me." He forced a light chuckle. "Might be she doesn't want me back."

Mr. Peterson hefted the bag to the edge of the mattress, propping it next to Harley's hip. Peeling back the top flap, he revealed several books. "Remember we talked about you learning to draw blueprints?"

Harley nodded, his eyes on the books.

"I gathered up a few used textbooks. They aren't new ones, but I think you'll still get some benefit from them. According to the doctor, it will be at least another week before they let you try out your leg." The man's gaze flitted to Harley's cast for a moment. "Just in case you aren't able to farm again, I thought you might want to explore an alternate way to take care of your family."

Harley's heart picked up its tempo. He reached for the books. "Do you really think I could learn all this?" He flopped one book open, and his eyes widened at the columns of words and complicated diagrams. "I'm just a stupid farmer who never got much schoolin'."

Mr. Peterson gave a snort. "Now, don't

defeat yourself before you begin. A stupid person can't be a successful farmer. And schooling has nothing to do with intelligence. Believe me, son—from what I've observed, you've got the intelligence; now you need the training."

Harley fingered the books, his eyes scanning the blue cover of the top book. Peterson's words of praise made Harley's chest fill with pride. No one had ever told him he was smart before. He didn't know what to say.

"Well . . ." Peterson glanced toward the door. "I better leave before the nurse throws me out." He smiled down at Harley. "Enjoy that reading."

Harley met the man's gaze and held out his hand. He found his voice. "Thank you, sir, for everything you've done for me."

Harley spent a few minutes after Mr. Peterson left just looking at the stack of books. Then, with some difficulty, he rolled slightly to his side and turned the little snap on the bedside lamp. He pulled out one of the textbooks, propped it on his belly, and turned to the first chapter: "Drawing to Scale."

* * *

Ern Berkley lay with his hands behind his head, staring at the ceiling. He needed to repair that one long crack that ran from the center of the room to the northeast corner. He'd cracked the plaster when installing the electric light two years before Ginny's death. Turned the screw on the ceramic plate too tight on one side. It took a whole year for the crack to wiggle its way clear to the corner. Funny—it had happened so slow he hardly noticed it until it was too long to ignore.

Kind of like sin.

Ern grimaced. Jack . . . When had his son started changing? The crack probably began the day Anna Mae said "I do" to Harley. That was the day Jack developed a veneer. Ern had ignored it, thinking Jack would come back around when the pain lessened, and return to being the lighthearted, happy-go-lucky boy he'd always been.

But instead, Jack had nursed the pain—never looked elsewhere for a wife, stayed in his childhood home where he'd be close to Anna Mae, kept an eye on Harley. Watching, always watching. It hadn't been healthy, but Ern hadn't realized how wide the crack had grown until the day Harley headed down the road, trusting Jack to check in on his family.

Ern brought down his hands, thumping his fists against the mattress. Jack's choices in the past months had created a barrier between father and son, but more than that, they'd created a chasm between Jack and the God of his childhood faith. The relationship needed to be repaired. Jack needed to be convicted.

But how? Ern wasn't even sure where Jack was right now, at ten o'clock on a Saturday night. He should be in bed, sleeping, resting up for services tomorrow. But Jack probably wouldn't go. He'd avoided church for the past four weeks, giving some excuse about a cow that needed attention or a pump that needed adjusting or something. Always something.

Ern knew the truth. Jack was avoiding God. He was avoiding his conscience. He'd been raised to know right from wrong; he knew he was walking in the wrong, but he wanted to keep doing it.

Instead of anger, only sorrow pressed against Ern's chest. "Oh, Lord, I want to help my son." The depth of his sadness pushed him from the mattress to his knees at the side of the bed. He prayed, pouring out his concern for Jack and his concern for Anna Mae. When he finished, he felt better, but he was still restless.

He padded to the quiet hallway. Across from his own room, Jack's bedroom door faced him. Closed. Another change. Jack had never closed the door to the room before Harley left. Ern's heart beat a rapid tattoo. He knew what Jack was hiding, and he also knew Anna Mae had a right to know.

Jack could return at any minute and catch him, but Ern decided it was worth the risk. Eventually Jack would need to be confronted anyway. If he came in and found his father rustling through his things, it would give Ern an opportunity to tell him it was time to 'fess up. Ern could no longer carry the burden of guilt. It was past time to set things to right.

Moving forward on bare feet, he stretched out his hand and curled his fingers around the doorknob. He needed to retrieve the letters Jack had been hiding and show them to Anna Mae. "Lord," he prayed, "please forgive my son."

28

Mr. Berkley helped Anna Mae down from the wagon seat and then reached into the back to lift Marjorie and Dorothy from the bed. He swung the girls high in the air before plunking them on the ground, making them both giggle.

Dorothy took hold of Marjorie's hand and guided her toward the porch. "Bye, Papa Berkley!" Dorothy waved with her free hand.

A fond smile lined Mr. Berkley's face as he watched the children climb the single step and enter the porch. When he turned to face Anna Mae, his expression sobered.

Anna Mae puckered her brow. "Is everything okay? You were so quiet on the ride home."

The older man lowered his head for a moment. "Honey, I'm bothered about something. Jack—"

"Where is Jack?" Anna Mae hugged her Bible against her chest. "He's missed church now . . . what? Three Sundays?"

"Four." Mr. Berkley's mouth formed a grim line. "I—" He shook his head, his eyes sorrowful. "I don't know what's going on with my son these days, Anna Mae."

The sadness in his eyes pierced Anna Mae's heart. She touched his arm. "I'm sure he's okay. Just busy. He's responsible for your dairy farm, his oil wells, and my chores, too. He's carrying a heavy load."

He frowned. "Yes . . . a heavy load."

Worry about Jack pressed at Anna Mae, too. He'd said he would wait for her to approach him, and he'd kept his word. He came each day to do the milking, but he didn't come to the house for conversation like he used to; he just performed the chores and headed out. It hurt Dorothy's feelings, and it bothered Anna Mae more than she cared to admit. She felt as though something else of importance was slipping away from her. She'd lost her crops, her house, and Harley. Jack's friendship took on a greater meaning in light of those other losses. Did she want to forfeit that, too?

She forced her lips into a bright smile even though her heart ached. "Don't worry, Mr. Berkley. I'm sure things will settle down soon." Her words sounded lame even to her ears.

Mr. Berkley released a deep sigh, his eyes closing for a moment. When he opened them again, he offered her a weak smile. "Honey, there is something I need to talk to you about. Do you suppose—?"

"Mama!" Dorothy stood inside the porch, her nose and both palms pressed to the screen.

"Dorothy, don't push on the screen," Anna Mae said. "You'll loosen it up." Harley knew how to reset the screen; Anna Mae didn't.

Dorothy took an obedient step backward, but her face crunched into a scowl. "Marjorie an' me are hungry."

Anna Mae sent Mr. Berkley an apologetic look. "Could we talk later? I do need to get lunch on the table."

He nodded, smoothing his hand over his balding head. "Yeah. Yeah, that'd be okay. I'll maybe come by this evening?"

"Yes, that would be fine. Come at supper-time and you can have some stew with us. Jack is welcome, as well."

"No." The word burst out forcefully, startling Anna Mae. Mr. Berkley appeared surprised, too. He took a backward step, his eyes widening. Then, drawing his hand down his face, he cleared his expression. "I . . . I'm sure Jack will be choring. Cows need to be milked, you know. It'll just be me."

Trepidation struck. Mr. Berkley was hiding something, but from Anna Mae or Jack? She couldn't be sure. She forced another quavering smile. "All right, then. Just you. I'll bake some of Mama's buttery baking soda biscuits. I know you like those."

The smile made him appear much more relaxed. "Oh yeah, your mama was a good cook."

Anna Mae nodded, a longing for her mother washing over her. Growing up, she'd had her parents plus Ern and Ginny Berkley in her life. Now all that was left was Mr. Berkley. The thought made her want to give the man a hug. Instead, she clutched her Bible tighter. "I'll see you this evening."

After another quick smile, he pulled himself into the wagon and slapped the reins down. The horses obeyed, and the wagon turned a neat circle and rolled out the gate. Anna Mae stood for a moment, watching after him. Heat that had nothing to do with the noonday sun filled her chest.

"Mama?" Dorothy's voice sounded more curious than fretful now. "You comin'?"

"Yes, darlin'." Anna Mae turned toward the house, but her gaze followed the wagon and Mr. Berkley's slope-shouldered position on the seat. Something worried the man. She hoped there wasn't something wrong with Jack. She couldn't face one more piece of bad news.

Ern entered the house through the back service porch. He found Jack at the kitchen table with a sandwich in his hands. Stopping in the doorway, he watched his son lift the sandwich to his mouth and take a bite. He shook his head, disappointment striking.

Jack raised his head to look toward the doorway. Around the bite, he said, "What?"

"Did you pray before you ate?"

Jack dropped the sandwich and slumped back in the chair. He swallowed. "It's just a sandwich, Pop. Not that big of a deal."

Ern pushed himself forward, tiredness making him move slowly. He stopped at the table and shoved his hands into his jacket pockets. "Just like it's not a big deal that you've missed church these past Sundays?"

Jack screeched the chair backward and rose, stomping to the icebox, where he pulled out a pitcher of milk. He splashed milk into a cup and took a long swig before answering. "Look, Pop, I've been busy. Lots to do here now with those oil pumps. Gotta keep 'em primed and running at full throttle to meet the demands. You like the money coming in, don't you?"

Ern couldn't deny they were blessed. Many in these troubled times didn't have a steady source of income. He felt good dropping that tithe into the offering plate each Sunday. "'Course I'm pleased we don't have money worries, son, but—"

"But what?" Jack returned to the table, sat, and snatched up his sandwich. "With everything I got going, something's got to be sacrificed. Missing a few church services is a small price to pay for everything we're gaining."

"And what exactly are we gaining?"

Jack scowled, shooting his father an impatient look. "That's a dumb question."

Ern shrugged. "I don't think so. What are we gaining, son? We were doin' just fine with the dairy. Didn't need more money. House is paid for, got a good source of income between the milk and the beef. Got a whole lot more than most do these days. Seems to me we could've been satisfied. Why'd we need more?"

Jack's huff of laughter chilled Ern's heart. "Pop, you're hopeless." He took another bite, shaking his head.

Ern tugged out a chair and sat. Drawing in a deep breath, he whispered a silent prayer for strength and addressed the issue he knew would have to be shared with Anna Mae. "Son, I know what you've been doin', the tricks you've been playin' to gain more."

Jack's gaze jerked upward. He swallowed, his Adam's apple bobbing visibly. "What're you talking about?" The words were more a growl than a question.

Ern folded his hands together to control their tremor. "I found the letters."

Jack sat straight up, his expression turning to a fierce scowl. "You went in my room?"

"Your room's in my house." Ern kept his tone calm. No sense in having a shouting match. "And what I did was a whole lot less wrong than what you did. Jack, you stole."

Jack slapped his sandwich onto the plate. The layers bounced apart, the bread sending crumbs across the table. "You had no right!"

"No right?" Ern shook his head slowly. "Jack, you shouldn't be hollerin' about me havin' no right. You should be lookin' at yourself. What right did you have to take those letters? They were private, between Harley and Anna Mae. You know how it's hurt her, thinkin' Harley didn't care enough to write. And poor Harley on the other side of Kansas, wonderin' why his wife didn't write to him. Can't you see how wrong you've been?"

Jack leaped from the table, stormed toward the sink, then paced back. The veins in his temples pulsed purple as his face reddened. He clenched his fists, bringing them outward, and for a moment Ern feared his son might strike him. But Jack stayed on the opposite side of the table.

Slowly, Jack opened his hands and pressed both palms to the tabletop. His voice rattled with anger as he said, "I'm not wrong, Pop. Everything I've done has been for Anna Mae's good."

Disbelief at his son's statement sagged Ern's shoulders. "How?"

Jack waved a hand as if shooing away Ern's question. "Harley was never right for her, we all know that. Her old man didn't even approve of him. Ben Elliott wanted her to marry me. But she turned stubborn, married Harley against everyone's advice, and she's never been happy. All I did was set things to right."

Ern could have argued that Anna Mae had been happy. He'd seen enough of the couple to know, despite their differences when it came to faith, they'd found happiness together. Anna Mae's sorrow at Harley's loss also showed evidence of how deeply she cared. But instead of arguing, Ern pointed out, "Since when do a pile of wrongs turn into a right?"

Jack huffed. "A pile of wrongs?"

Ern nodded. "You've been doin' wrong for weeks: stealing letters, puttin' up oil pumps on property that doesn't belong to you, robbin' Anna Mae of that income—"

"Whoa, Pop!" Jack thrust his hand upward, stopping his father's words. "I haven't robbed Anna Mae of any income. I've been putting that aside for us. When she marries me, she'll benefit from it."

"And if she doesn't marry you?"

"She has to." Jack's tone turned hard. "She can't stay on that farm by herself. How can she keep it going without a man? It's what should have happened seven years ago—what *would* have happened if Harley hadn't wandered onto their place and asked for a job. Now Harley's gone, and I'm just setting things back to right. If I have to do a little finagling to make her see the light, then so be it."

Ern rose to his feet and turned toward the door. "I was plannin' to wait until evening, but she has to know all this, Jack. She has to know what you've been up to."

Jack's pounding feet on the floor brought Ern to a stop before the hand grabbed onto his arm. "Oh, no you're not. You're not going to mess this up for me."

Ern jerked his arm free. He looked into his son's hate-filled face and felt as though he were looking at a stranger. Where Jack's fingers had cut in, an ache formed. But it couldn't compare to the pain that stabbed Ern's heart.

"Stay out of it," Jack said, his tone ominous. "If you walk out, I'm locking the door behind you. You won't be welcomed back in."

Ern frowned, his heart pounding. "What do you mean?"

A sly smile crept up Jack's face. "You signed this place over to me, remember? It's mine, Pop. I let you stay here, but . . . that could change. You own the cows, but I own the land. If you go, the cows go. I don't need 'em. I got money coming in by the barrel. So before you march on over to tattle to Anna Mae, you might think about all those dumb animals in the pasture. Where you gonna keep them if you can't stay here anymore?"

Ern stuck out his chin. "I'll take them to Anna Mae's place. Milk 'em myself."

One sharp blast of laughter pierced Ern's ears. "Oh yeah. Milk 'em yourself. With no machines, with your arthritic hands? Besides that, Anna Mae's lost her land. She didn't have enough to pay the tax bill, so it's going to auction. And I've got it on good authority that her land will be my land." He chuckled, a mirthless sound. "Don't fool yourself, Pop. You need me. Just like Anna Mae needs me." He smiled again, a smile that sent a chill straight through Ern's chest. "Have a sandwich. Then go upstairs and take a nap. You're beat."

For long moments Ern remained rooted in place, staring into the face of a son he no longer recognized, trying to decide what to do. The ache in his chest was nearly unbearable. For the moment, Jack did have him beat. He broke eye contact first, and Jack's low chuckle as he turned and headed for the stairs sent a new shaft of pain through his heart.

He plodded upstairs, his steps heavy, his head low. *Dear heavenly Father, help me reach my son.*

29

"I thought you said Papa Berkley was comin' for supper."

Dorothy scowled across the table at her mother. Anna Mae put down her spoon and offered Dorothy an apologetic smile.

"He was invited. I don't know what happened." She hoped her calm tone masked the worry underneath. Ern Berkley had seemed so burdened this morning. There was certainly something he needed to discuss with her—something important. Why hadn't he come?

She hoped he hadn't fallen ill. How she wished she had a telephone so she could call and check on him.

Dorothy sighed, resting her chin in her

hand. "I wanted him to come. I wanted him to tell me stories. Nobody comes anymore. Not Daddy, not Mr. Berkley, not Papa Berkley . . ."

Anna Mae reached across the table and stroked Dorothy's hair. "I know it's a disappointment, darlin', but I'll read you stories tonight, okay?"

Dorothy sighed again. Her face twisted into a pout. "It's not the same."

No, Anna Mae supposed it wasn't. The presence of a man in a child's life was so important. As a little girl, she had endlessly trailed behind her father, getting in the way of his work and asking questions that he had answered patiently—she smiled in remembrance—most of the time. She'd adored her mother, too, but there was something different about being with her father. A father-to-child relationship was the first glimpse of a Father God-to-child relationship, she realized. Where would Dorothy, Marjorie, and the new baby get that glimpse now?

Anna Mae stifled the sigh she longed to release. She tapped Dorothy's arm and said, "I'm sorry you're sad, but you still need to eat. Finish up that stew, and then we'll have some canned cherries for dessert, okay?"

"Not hungry." Dorothy turned stubborn, the thrust of her lower jaw reminding Anna Mae of Harley.

A mingling of fond recollections and deep loneliness struck Anna Mae with the reminder. She swallowed, blinking to hold back tears. "If you don't want to eat, that's fine," she said, forcing a reasonable tone. "You'll probably have a tummy ache in the morning if you go to bed with an empty stomach, but you go ahead and get down if you want to."

Dorothy looked at her mother, her head tipped and lips pursed in thought. After several long seconds, she blew out a breath of aggravation that imitated her father perfectly, picked up her spoon, and took another bite.

Marjorie banged her hand on the highchair tray, reminding her mother that she was ready for another bite, too. Anna Mae carried a spoonful of stew to the baby's eager mouth, her hand trembling slightly. Mr. Berkley's peculiar absence added one more worry to a list already too long. Where was he?

*   *   *

Harley drew in a deep breath and held it while the doctor ran a small silver instrument from the heel of his bare foot to the underside of his toes.

"Do you feel that?"

Harley jerked his head in a brief nod, blowing out air through his nose. "Yep. Tickles. Don't much like it."

The doctor chuckled. "Well, you should be thankful. That tickle tells me the nerves have healed."

"And that's good?"

"It's very good." The doctor slipped the instrument into his pocket and patted Harley's cast.

"So I'll be able to walk without problems?"

"Well . . ."

Harley held his breath again.

"Based on my observations, the bone is mending, but it was shattered. We weren't able to line things up perfectly, which means it lost some of its length." The doctor looked at Harley straight on. "I'm afraid the leg will never be one hundred percent again."

Harley waited for anger to strike within his chest. It didn't. He released the breath on a sigh. "So what can I expect?"

Another pat. "You can expect to have less strength in your left leg. You can expect to walk, but with a limp." The man's brows tipped downward as he glanced at Harley's chart. "You were a farmer?"

"Yes, sir."

"Did you use motorized equipment?"

Harley allowed a rueful chuckle to escape. "No, sir. I used mules and walked behind 'em."

The doctor grimaced. "Well, you might be able to continue farming with motorized equipment, but I don't think you'll be up to walking behind mules again."

Harley shrugged. "Sold 'em anyway." The day rushed back—his pleasure at buying groceries and that flowered hat for Annie, Annie's reaction, their fight, sleeping in the barn . . . Swallowing, he pushed his shoulders into another shrug. "With the drought, farmin's not gone so good. That's why I was workin' at the castle site."

The doctor nodded. His gaze drifted to the bedside table and the stack of books. He tapped the top one. "Are you considering a different vocation?"

Harley wasn't familiar with the word *vocation,* but he figured it had something to do with jobs. He nodded. "Yes, sir. My boss from the castle site—Mr. Peterson—brought me those books to study on."

Picking up the top book, the doctor flipped it open and glanced at a few pages. His eyebrows shot high. "Intriguing. And I would imagine there will always be a need for draftsmen, considering how the country continues to grow and change." He closed the book and put it back on the stack. "I wish you success in your new venture."

The doctor's high-falutin' talk gave Harley a reminder of Annie. His heart twisted painfully. What would it do to Annie, finding out he could no longer work her land? How could he expect her to give up her childhood home? 'Specially when there was no guarantee he'd be able to get schoolin' and learn to draw blueprints. There wasn't money lying around for things like school.

"Would you like me to send your family an update on your situation?"

Harley shook his head. "No. My wife'll only worry if she knows I'm hurt. It's better she don't know about this . . . yet. I need to find a way to tell her myself, when I've figured out for sure how I'm gonna take care of things. I need to pray about it some first."

Despite the situation, a smile tugged at his lips. Hearing himself state the need to pray wasn't something he ever figured on. Yet the reality of it fit as neatly as a good pair of boots. But unlike boots, which must eventually be kicked off, he felt certain the need to pray would be a part of him from now on.

"Very well, then." The doctor took a step toward the open door. "I'll leave you to rest. I'll be in next week to get you up on your feet and practicing with a crutch."

Anticipation filled Harley's chest. "It'll be good to be up and moving again."

The doctor smiled, backpedaling toward the door. "I'm sure it will. But in the meantime, rest. Gain strength." He pointed. "Read your books." Pausing in the doorway, he smiled. "And pray."

Harley nodded. The moment the doctor rounded the corner, Harley closed his eyes and began. *Dear God, about Annie an' the farm . . .*

Dear God, what should I do about Anna Mae and her farm? Ern paced in his room. Jack fully intended to steal Anna Mae's land from her. That's what it amounted to. Surely those checks from Harley would have covered the tax bill, but Jack didn't let her have them. How hurtful Jack had been, letting Anna Mae believe her husband had abandoned her. Never, despite his son's faults, would Ern have believed Jack's selfishness would stretch to these lengths.

He left his room and stalked to the end of the hallway. Pushing back the lace curtains, he looked across the grounds toward the Elliotts' land. If he squinted, he could glimpse the lights of Anna Mae's house. Had she delayed supper waiting for him to show, or had she gone ahead and fed the girls? He hoped she hadn't made the girls wait. No doubt it worried her when he hadn't turned up as he'd said. Another burden on a heart already overburdened.

Sighing, he returned to his bedroom. He'd come up without eating lunch and he hadn't gone down for supper. A rock filled his belly—there was no room for food. And he could hear Jack prowling around down there. He couldn't face his son, even if he were hungry.

What could he do besides hide up here? Until he figured out a way to counter Jack's threats, he was stuck. He'd seen fury in his son's eyes. Jack had meant what he'd said.

He'd throw his father out of the house and set the cows loose. Ern needed a firm plan in place. A few fuzzy ideas danced through his mind, but nothing he could firmly grasp. He slapped his hand down on his scarred dresser top, bouncing the framed photograph that rested there. He caught the frame before it tipped.

Rather than putting it back, he cradled the oval, filigreed frame in his hands. His eyes filled with tears as he gazed into the black-and-white image of his Ginny's sweet face. "Oh, Mother, how disappointed you would be in the choices our son is making." One child. All the hopes and dreams pinned on one child. All the training that went into forming the child into a man who would serve the Lord. Had they failed somehow? Was Jack's fall from grace the result of something his parents neglected?

Looking into Ginny's face, Ern was washed with a sense of peace. No, he and Ginny had done right when raising Jack. The Bible promised that if a person raised up a child in the way he should go, he would not depart from it when he was old. Well, Jack still had some growing to do, but Ern made the decision to trust that Jack's childhood training would bring him back on the right pathway again.

He placed Ginny's picture on the dresser, crossed to the bed, and dropped to his knees. Folding his hands, he once again petitioned his Father in prayer.

"Here you go, Mama!" Dorothy held up a damp dress.

Anna Mae took the garment, gave it several brisk snaps to shake out the wrinkles, then clipped it to the line. Her hands shook, and she glanced toward the barn, wondering when Jack would reappear. She wanted to call out to him, ask why his father hadn't shown up for supper last night, but the grim look on his face as he'd jumped down from the wagon seat and stomped across the ground to the barn without offering even a hello suppressed her question.

"And another one!"

Dorothy's impish grin soothed the edges of Anna Mae's frayed nerves. "Thank you, darlin'." She secured the apron with clothespins and then peeked at the empty basket. "And that's it. Now, we can—"

Suddenly the horses raised their heads and snorted, rolling their eyes. One stamped the ground, and both released nervous whinnies. An unfamiliar noise intruded—a rolling growl similar to thunder, but from a far distance. Anna Mae scanned the horizon. Not a cloud in sight. What on earth? The horses pawed the dust, snorting and tossing their manes.

An odd sensation crept from the soles of Anna Mae's feet up her legs. She froze, uncertain what had created the vibration. Was she going to faint? She looked at Dorothy. The child stood with her arms out from her sides, her face holding a wide-eyed look of terror. Dorothy's frightened pose, combined with the horses' strange behavior, convinced Anna Mae the sensation wasn't hers alone.

"Mama?" The single-word question quavered on a note of fear.

Anna Mae took two stumbling steps forward to wrap Dorothy in her arms. From the blanket under the weeping willow, Marjorie set up a wail. The baby pushed herself to her feet and toddled toward her mother, arms reaching. Anna Mae shuffled sideways, Dorothy pinned to her side, then dropped to her knees and gathered Marjorie near.

The three huddled together, both children panting in beat with Anna Mae's rapid pulse, for what seemed hours until the odd quivering beneath their feet ended. The moment the gentle rumble stopped, Jack rushed out of the barn straight to the hugging group. He fell to his knees beside them, touching each in turn, his face white. "Are you all right? Were you hurt?"

"We're fine," Anna Mae gasped, her heart beating so hard she feared she might lose her breath. "What was that?"

"I don't know, but we need to find out. C'mon." He rose, tugged Anna Mae's hands to help her to her feet, and then scooped up Marjorie. "Let's go get Pop and we'll go to town in the Model T."

The drive was made in tense silence. Jack's knuckles glowed white as he gripped the steering wheel with both hands, his brows pulled down in a scowl of concerned concentration. In the backseat, Mr. Berkley tucked Dorothy and Marjorie snug beneath his arms. He offered an encouraging smile each time Anna Mae peeked into the backseat, but the pallor of his face filled Anna Mae's heart with fear. First the drought and the heat and the wind, now that curious shaking of the ground. What else would go wrong in Kansas?

Jack was forced to bring the vehicle to a crawl when they reached Spencer. The streets teemed with activity—people talking in excited, nervous voices; cars and wagons entering from all directions; dogs running between vehicles, barking. The combined cacophony created a discordant chorus of confusion.

Jack stopped the car in front of the mercantile, where a cluster of townspeople milled on the porch. He jumped out and hollered over the din, "What's going on? Does anyone know what happened?"

Anna Mae opened her door, stepped out, and folded the seat forward so Mr. Berkley and the girls could climb out. Anna Mae lifted Marjorie to her hip. Dorothy pressed against Mr. Berkley's side, her blue eyes wide.

A man—Rev. Tompkins—separated himself from the group on the porch and called an answer to Jack's query. "Earthquake. It was an earthquake. Telegraph message said it came clear from Arizona."

Marjorie complained and wriggled in her mother's arms. Anna Mae tightened her grip. "Shhh, darlin'," she whispered, taking comfort herself in soothing the baby.

From the back of the mumbling group, a woman's strident voice carried. "It's because of sin! All the things of nature going wrong around us—it's because someone has sinned, and the Lord is exacting His punishment!"

The reverend turned back to the crowd. "Now, we can't be certain of that—"

"I'm certain!" The woman forced her way to the front. Fierce determination reddened her face. "The Lord can't tolerate sin, and He says it will be meted with judgment. This quakin' was proof of that! Someone needs to be awakened to his sins and set things right before his Maker!"

The crowd's murmurings increased, and the reverend raised his arms, his calm voice calling for reason. Anna Mae shifted to ask Mr. Berkley what he thought, but as she turned, her gaze drifted across Jack's face. The expression there chilled her. Fear—and guilt—showed clearly in Jack's colorless skin and wild eyes.

Anna Mae felt a chill of apprehension wiggle down her spine. *What sin is Jack hiding?*

30

A rumbling . . . faint at first, like the purr of a contented cat, then growing louder, turning into an old man's snore. A trembling . . . first a quiver, then a rattle that shakes the house. Jack holds to the window frame, a futile attempt to still the shaking of his home. Beside him, a plate falls from a shelf and shatters on the wood floor. He remains mute, frozen by fear, as the ground begins to crack. The wide mouth of the crack rushes toward him, zigzagging like a snake, widening as it nears. It is coming for him.

The shaking grows severe, threatening to topple him. He tightens his grip on the sill as his heart pounds and his body sweats. No! No! But the words remain unspoken, so great is his fear. In a rush and roar, the crack broadens to encompass the entire width of the house, and Jack feels himself falling . . . falling . . . into the black chasm.

A voice speaks, "Sins will be meted with judgment!"

"No!" The hoarse cry awakened Jack. He sat bolt upright, his hands gripping the soggy sheets of his bed. Only then did he realize the frightened cry had been his own.

A dream. It was only a dream. The relief struck with such force, Jack collapsed against his pillows, completely limp. He stared at the ceiling, waiting for his heartbeat to return to normal, while snatches of the dream replayed in his head. The condemning voice echoed: *"Sins will be meted with judgment! Sins will be meted with judgment!"*

Jack shook his head, fresh sweat breaking out on his already-soaked body. Sure, he knew God was a God of judgment. Of wrath. But that earthquake—that wasn't because of anyone's sin. It was just . . . nature. Nature had run amok in the past few years. No rains falling, winds trying to blow one county into another, the extreme heat . . . That earthquake was just another bit of evi-

dence showing how nature was all confused right now. It didn't have anything to
do with somebody's sin.

Did it?

Jack swallowed. He kicked his sheets to
the foot of the bed and lay uncovered, blinking into the muted shadows of his quiet
room. Across the hall, Pop snuffled in his
sleep. Jack wondered if Pop blamed him for
the earthquake. Probably not—Pop wasn't
a finger-pointer. Although he'd come mighty
close to finger-pointing last Sunday.

Pop wanted Anna Mae to know everything Jack had been doing. Jack wanted
Anna Mae to know, too—to know how he'd
put that oil pump in place so she'd be making money, how he'd arranged to be the
winning bidder for her daddy's farm. He
wanted her to keep count of how many
times he milked her cow, weeded her garden, picked her tomatoes, answered her
daughter's questions. Those were the things
that counted—the helpful things he'd done.
All that other stuff didn't matter in light of
the good it would do her in the end.

He reasoned with himself, the dream slipping away as he balanced his actions on a
scale of right and wrong. Sure, he'd kept a

few letters from going back and forth, but what had that really hurt? Harley was dead—he wasn't coming back—and those letters would just be a painful reminder. Anna Mae needed to look to the future, a future with Jack. Focusing on the past was just a waste of time.

And that earthquake was in the past, too. Nobody could change the fact that the ground shook in Kansas. So it was silly to lie awake, worrying over its cause. Instead of worrying, he should be planning. Planning his trip to Hutchinson to get that land deal finalized. His bid was in, and he'd been assured no one else had expressed any interest in the property. Now it was just a matter of stopping by the courthouse and making good on his bid.

While in town, he should visit a jewelry store, pick up a ring. Anna Mae would accept his wedding proposal given time. He needed to be ready. It might be best to wait until after the new baby was born before making things official; it would look better to others in the community if they didn't rush things. But it was so hard to wait. He'd already waited a lifetime for Anna Mae.

His heart settled back into a comfortable

beat. The fear that had been so overwhelming only minutes ago slipped away. Jack took in a deep breath and released it slowly, his body relaxing. It would be okay. Everything would be okay. *Don't lose sight of the goal. Anna Mae will be yours.*

"Pop?"

Ern paused in the middle of buttoning his shirt and cocked an ear toward the open bedroom door. "Yeah?" The smell of bacon and eggs drifted up from the kitchen, letting Ern know Jack had finished the milking. He always milked first, then ate breakfast.

Jack's voice came again from the kitchen. "There's a plate in the hob for you. I'm headin' over to Anna Mae's. Gonna milk her cow and then meet the milk truck. I'll see you around noon."

Ern's heart thumped. Noon. Would that be enough time? "Sure, son. Thanks."

The slam of the kitchen door let Ern know Jack had left. He slipped his suspenders over his shoulders, releasing them with a light snap, then snatched up his shoes. Downstairs, he peeked into the hob. The eggs and bacon smelled good, but if he took the time to eat, he might not get his errands finished. His stomach cramped with hunger, but he chose to ignore it. Sitting in a kitchen chair, he grunted as he tugged his shoes over thick gray socks. His shoes tied, he grabbed his jacket from the hook by the door.

His knees trembled a bit as he crossed the yard to the barn where the Model T waited. He'd only driven the auto a few times—Jack usually drove—but he whispered a silent prayer for God's help. He had to get to Hutchinson, take care of his errands, and be back before Jack returned with the wagon. He'd have to take the roads on the far side of Spencer, too; he couldn't risk meeting Jack on the road. If Jack came home and found the automobile missing . . .

Ern shook his head, sadness striking. How it bothered him to sneak around, to be fearful of his own son. But he couldn't predict what Jack would do anymore. Despite his worries, he would follow through with his plans. If Jack threw him out, he'd survive. God would provide. Ern had to trust that somehow all this would turn out to good.

He fumbled a bit as he pressed his memory to recall all the necessary steps to get the Model T's engine running. A prayer of gratitude formed itself in his heart when the motor roared to life. He slipped behind the wheel, slammed the door, and shifted the car into gear.

"Now, Lord, keep me safe as I travel, and let all the doors I need open wide for my entry. I'm countin' on your help here, Father."

"Mr. Phipps?"

Harley jumped, startled from his nap. He yawned, rubbed his eyes, and focused on the nurse who stood in the doorway. He mumbled, "Yeah? Suppertime already?"

The nurse smiled. "No. You have visitors. May I bring them in?"

Harley pressed his hands to the mattress, pushing himself higher on his pillows. He scratched his whiskery chin. "Long as they ain't offended easy, they're welcome to come in."

The nurse laughed. She gestured toward the door. "Come on in, folks."

Harley's eyes widened as his company entered the room. Mr. and Mrs. Farley! Immediately a pang of guilt ripped across his middle. Despite the letter, which had been so kind, he still carried a burden of responsibility for Dirk's untimely death. He waited, unable to speak, as the couple approached. Mr. Farley guided his wife with a hand on her back. They appeared more frail, older, than the last time he'd seen them, yet the same joyful light he remembered still shone in the woman's eyes.

Mrs. Farley reached her slim, wrinkled hand toward Harley, closing her warm fingers around his. "Mr. Phipps. How good to see you looking so well."

Harley held back the nervous chuckle that formed in his throat. Looking well? With his leg wrapped in plaster and elevated above the bed, his hair a mess, his face covered with a growth of whiskers, and him dressed in a hospital gown? Mrs. Farley surely owned a pair of those rose-colored glasses Dirk had been fond of wearing.

He cleared his throat and formed a reply. "Thank you, ma'am. It's—it's kind of you to come."

"We had to."

Mr. Farley nodded firmly at Mrs. Farley's simple reply.

She went on. "We needed to see where our son spent his last months, get a look at the castle he helped build, meet the men he talked about in his letters." Her eyes brightened with unshed tears. "And we needed to see you. You're our last link to Dirk. Couldn't rest until we knew for sure you were going to be all right."

A huge lump filled Harley's throat. Their last link to their son. Could he carry that responsibility? "I . . . I'm so sorry . . . about Dirk . . ." The words choked out.

The woman sandwiched his hand between hers, leaning close. Behind her, Mr. Farley reached out to clamp Harley's shoulder with one hand while the other curled around his wife's slender waist. Harley felt his own shoulders heave with suppressed sobs. For long moments they remained silent, mourning together.

After swallowing a dozen or so times, Harley finally found his voice and said what his heart felt. "Dirk was the finest man I've ever known. You raised him right, an' he lived what you taught him. I . . . I was proud to call him my friend."

Tears rolled down Mrs. Farley's cheeks. Her hands pressed tighter for a moment, then slipped away. She straightened, leaning against her husband. "Dirk was proud to call you a friend, too. He talked about you in his letters to us. We brought them." She

looked upward at her husband, and he nodded. From inside his jacket, he withdrew a
packet of envelopes, tied together with
string. Mrs. Farley took them and handed
them to Harley. "You read them. Then"—she
suddenly looked shy—"you give them back.
That'll give you an excuse to visit us."

Harley offered a quavering smile. He'd
visit them. He owed them that. But there
was something else they needed to know. "I
gotta tell you . . . Dirk talked a lot about
God. More than talk, he lived what he believed. I—" He scratched his head, uncertain how they'd react to his confession. "I
had a hard time buyin' everything he said.
Even though my wife had preached the
same thing at me for years, it still just didn't
seem . . . well, *real*. How could some Jesus
I didn't even know love me enough to die for
me? I'm not so sure my own father would've
made that choice if it had come down to his
life or mine."

The day of Dirk's death pressed his memory, causing him to wince. His voice faltered.
"But then . . . when the rock fell . . . and
Dirk . . ." Tears stung his eyes. He closed
them, his chin quivering. "When Dirk used
his own body as a shield . . ." He opened his

eyes, looking directly into Mrs. Farley's stricken face. "I got a glimpse of Jesus. And now . . . now I know Him for myself."

Mrs. Farley covered her face with her hands. For one long moment she seemed to freeze, then sobs broke loose that shook her slight body. Mr. Farley rubbed her shoulders, resting his chin against the top of her head. Tears glittered in his eyes, his face contorting with the effort of holding back his own sobs.

Harley battled tears himself at their grief-filled reaction. He reached out and touched the woman's elbow. "I'm so sorry, ma'am. I didn't mean to upset you."

She shook her head, lowering her hands. Although her face was wet with tears, her eyes glowed with happiness. "Oh, please, don't apologize. Don't you see?" She looked up at her husband once more, and they exchanged a look of—what? Acceptance? Satisfaction? Harley couldn't be sure. Looking back at Harley, she smiled and said, "If you've found the Lord, then Dirk didn't die in vain. Your salvation makes his death worthwhile. Thank you, Mr. Phipps, for this gift."

Harley had a hard time absorbing all of

the emotions that tumbled through his heart at that simple statement. With the woman's words, some of the guilt he carried crumbled and fell away.

Mr. Farley offered his wife a handkerchief. While she cleaned her face, he turned to Harley. "We went out to see that castle. It's a proud thing, there on the hill. Understand why Dirk got such pleasure in its buildin'."

Harley nodded. "Yeah. Dirk had more of a hand in the castle than I did. I did more diggin', but it gives me pride to know that castle'll be standin' out there years from now."

Mr. Farley leaned against the edge of the bed, making the springs squeak. "We got to see all the places where Dirk worked. A Mr. Nelson showed us around."

Harley stiffened at that name. He clamped his teeth on his tongue to hold back angry words.

"Nice man, humble. I know Dirk prayed for him a lot. He said so in his letters."

Nice man? Humble? Nelson? Dirk had left an impact on more than just one person, it seemed. He pushed his own resentment toward Nelson aside. If Dirk could pray for the man who'd been so unkind to him, then Harley could forgive him, too.

"Our train leaves in less than an hour. We better go." Mrs. Farley reached once more for Harley's hands. "You will come see us, won't you?"

Harley nodded, giving the wrinkled hands a gentle squeeze. "Of course I will. I'll bring my wife an' little girls, too, if you'd like."

"Oh, we would like that." Mrs. Farley's face crinkled with her smile. "Been since Dirk was a little boy that we've had a child laughing on the place."

She'd make a wonderful grandmother, Harley thought. It saddened him to realize that Dirk's death removed the possibility of grandchildren. It made him all the more determined to include this couple in his life from now on. He'd adopt them, just like they'd adopted Dirk.

They left then, leaving a heavy silence in their stead. Harley shifted his attention to the little packet of letters. An image of Dirk—big, laughing, open Dirk—appeared in Harley's memory. What would Dirk have said about Harley? Nothing bad, he knew that for sure. Dirk wasn't capable of speaking ill of anyone. Suddenly eager to connect once more with his friend, Harley tugged loose the restraining string, opened the first letter, and began to read.

31

Anna Mae turned the calendar to October and drew in a big breath. She stared at the little square representing the first day of the month—the day her property would transfer to someone else's hands—and said a little prayer of thankfulness.

It surprised her to discover there were several things for which she was grateful. Her father wasn't alive to see the land change ownership. Since bids were turned in at the courthouse, she had been spared the humiliation of a public auction. And Harley didn't have to experience this heartache with her.

As difficult as it would be to leave—and she still didn't know where she would go—

there were silver linings around each gray cloud. She chose to focus on those silver linings as she broke eggs into flour and stirred up Dorothy's favorite breakfast— waffles flavored with vanilla and cinnamon. If this were to be one of the last days in her childhood home, she wanted to build happy memories of the time.

Dorothy's squeal of joy when she spotted the waffles and strawberry jam on the table gave Anna Mae's heart another lift. Marjorie hollered from her crib, and Anna Mae strapped her into the high chair, laughing as the baby banged her hands on the tray in excitement. "Eat, eat, eat," she jabbered while Anna Mae broke a waffle into pieces for the baby to pick up.

As soon as Marjorie was able to eat, eat, eat, the kitchen grew quiet except for the sizzle of the waffle iron, the burble of perco- lating coffee, and the scrape of Dorothy's fork against her plate. Anna Mae absorbed the peaceful morning scene: her daughters in their places at the oilcloth-draped table, a splash of sun painting a yellow carpet across the faded linoleum floor, the gentle lift and fall of the gingham curtains her mama had sewn for the kitchen window. She turned from one sight to another, burning the memories into her brain.

Through the kitchen window, Anna Mae watched Jack's wagon pull into the yard. It rolled to a stop between the house and barn, and the sun glinted on his hair as he leapt from the wagon to the ground. He headed straight for the barn, as he'd done every day for the past week. She turned back to her waffle making, hoping Dorothy wouldn't hear him moving around out there. The child missed his visits, and Anna Mae didn't want any unhappiness to ruin this cheerful start to the day.

She poured herself a cup of coffee and stood at the counter, munching her waffle while waiting for another one to cook. Jack ambled out of the barn, milk pail in hand. She expected him to slosh most of the milk into a can in the wagon and then leave the remainder on the back porch for her use as he'd been doing since he stated his ultimatum. But instead, he came right on into the kitchen and placed the bucket on the counter next to her.

She offered a hesitant smile. "G-good morning, Jack."

He tipped his head and winked. "Good morning to you."

Apparently he'd decided to let things return to normal—another little silver lining. She felt her smile grow. "Would you like a waffle?"

He sniffed the air. "Mmm, those smell great." He grinned at Dorothy, who forked another waffle onto her plate and spooned out jam. "You gonna leave some for anybody else?"

The little girl giggled. "Daddy says I'm a waffle-piggy."

Anna Mae's heart caught, and she noticed Jack's jaw tighten at Dorothy's comment. Dorothy still refused to believe her father was gone. In the days since Anna Mae had told her about Harley's death, the child had spoken of him more than she had in all the previous weeks of separation. Anna Mae feared the child was trying to keep her daddy alive, and she worried about the effect it would have on Dorothy's faith when Harley didn't return.

Jack cleared his throat. "Well, since you're the piggy, I'll let you go ahead and gobble." He turned toward Anna Mae.

"Thanks for the invitation, but I've got some errands to run today, so I need to hurry."

The urgency in his tone raised Anna Mae's eyebrows. "Everything okay?"

A smile formed quickly. "Oh yeah. Everything's fine and dandy. And promising to get better every minute."

Anna Mae took in a sharp breath, her eyes widening in wonder. Was Jack experiencing the same rush of blessings that she'd felt this morning? She opened her mouth to question him, but he stepped forward and planted a kiss on her cheek, shocking her into silence.

"Take care, Anna Mae. I aim to bring you a surprise back from Hutchinson."

Dorothy clapped her hands. "Me too! Bring me a surprise, too!"

Jack swung his grin in the little girl's direction. "Sure thing, Miss Dorothy. Now be good for your mama, you hear?" With a wink, he headed out the door with long, sure strides.

"What'cha think he's gonna bring us, Mama?" Dorothy's eyes sparkled with anticipation.

"I don't know, darlin'." Anna Mae touched her cheek where his lips had pressed for one possessive second. Jack's familiarity threw a different cast on her day, leaving her feeling weak and almost queasy.

"I hope it's a doll. Or a new dress. Or a book." Dorothy chattered as she stabbed her fork into her waffle and raised another bite. "It'll be somethin' good, though, I betcha."

Anna Mae managed a small smile for Dorothy's sake and tousled her hair. "I'm sure you're right. Now finish up there, and try to get the jam into your mouth instead of on your face."

Dorothy hunched her shoulders and giggled. "Yes, Mama."

Anna Mae poured the last of the batter onto the waffle iron and closed the lid with shaking fingers. Steam whooshed from the edges of the iron, scenting the air with vanilla. Anna Mae inhaled, hoping the smell of the waffle would drive the smell of Jack's skin from her memory. She pressed her mind for a silver lining to the gray cloud his intimacy had created over her head, but for the first time that morning, silver linings escaped her. She could find no good in Jack's impromptu act of ownership.

*　*　*

"What do you mean someone outbid me?" Jack attempted to keep his tone controlled, but the anger welled up, forcing the words out harshly.

The clerk scowled. "Exactly what I said. Bids were accepted through five o'clock Wednesday, September thirtieth. You were outbid."

"But that can't be!" Jack put out his hand. "Let me see the bids."

The clerk pulled the file against his chest. "I can't let you see. Closed-auction bids are called closed because that's exactly what they are—and they are not a matter of public record."

Jack waited, his jaw clenched and hand extended toward the man on the other side of the counter. "Well, I'm not going to believe you unless I see it for myself. Hand it over."

"No, sir." The clerk raised his chin a notch, too. "You're just going to have to—"

"What is going on out here?" A second, authoritative voice intruded.

Jack looked beyond the clerk to spot the county treasurer, Robert Syler, marching toward the counter. Jack pointed an accusing finger at the man's chest. "That land was supposed to be mine. You told me last week I was the only bidder and I shouldn't worry."

Syler frowned as the clerk shot a speculative look in his direction. He kept his voice low, but Jack didn't miss the warning growl in the tone. "You know very well that would be privileged information. You must be mistaken."

Jack felt heat rush to his face. He needed to be careful. No sense in ostracizing the very person who could get this whole mess turned around. If the bids weren't publically recorded, then surely anyone could be announced as the winning bidder. He took a deep breath.

"I believe there has been an error. The clerk here—" he jerked his gaze briefly toward the man—"seems to be reading the bids wrong."

"I assure you I am not—" The clerk's blustering reply was cut short by a firm look from Syler.

The county treasurer held out his hand. "Let me see the file."

The clerk released it, but his lips formed a grim line of annoyance.

"Thank you, Lester. I'll take care of this."

Muttering under his breath, the clerk

moved away. Syler leaned across the counter, dropping his voice. "Look, Jack, I did what I could. I can't help that someone came in here yesterday, right before five, and made a bid that was higher than yours."

"So adjust mine," Jack said. "Can't be that hard to change a number. Land still gets sold, which is what you want. Who's it gonna hurt?"

Syler shook his head. "I can't do that. Others have seen these bids. There's not a thing I can do to reverse it now."

"Switch the names!" Jack grated the command. "Put my name on his bid and his on mine. Who's gonna remember who bid what? I'll pay the higher bid, whatever it is. I've got to have that land!"

Taking a step backward, Syler lowered the file to his side. "Can't do that. I don't know what your interest is in this deal, but I won't put my job and reputation on the line for you." He raised his voice so it carried throughout the office. "What you'll have to do is wait until the new owner takes control of the property. Then you can talk to him about buying it. There's nothing more I can do."

Jack smacked the counter with his fist.

"Fine. Just fine. But when elections come around again, don't be countin' on my vote."

Syler didn't reply, raising Jack's ire. He spun from the counter and stomped down the hallway, his steps echoing in his ears. Couldn't trust anybody these days. The man had told him not to worry, no one else was interested in the land. Just hold tight until the first of October and it would be his. And Jack had believed him.

He reached the lobby. Ramming both palms against the outside door, he swung it wide and stormed through. Warm air smacked him, and he paused on the steps, catching his breath.

Now what? He'd counted on being the new owner of that land. On showing Anna Mae the title, offering it along with his marriage proposal and using it as proof of how he was taking care of her. The loss of that bid ruined everything!

He thumped down the concrete steps, his scowl so tight his forehead hurt. By the time he'd reached his Model T, he'd come to some conclusions. So he couldn't keep her land and the money from the oil being pumped there. But that didn't mean he was licked. Somebody had bought the property, so Anna Mae was going to have to vacate the land now. She had no place to go. He could at least take care of that.

And he might as well run that other errand he'd planned. He'd promised her a surprise, and despite that backstabbing county treasurer, she'd have one. It wouldn't be the title to her land, but it was better. He'd give her the title to his heart.

Harley scrawled his signature on the bottom of the letter, placed the pencil on the bedside table, and leaned back against his pillows with a smile. He glanced at the pages in his lap. Longest letter he'd ever written. A chuckle sounded as he clenched and unclenched his fist, working his fingers. He'd probably have a cramp in his hand tomorrow, but it had been worth it to get all those thoughts down.

There was so much Anna Mae needed to know. What would she think, having a husband who drew plans for buildings? Would it make her proud to have Harley get some schooling? He hoped so—he wanted her to be proud of him.

In his letter, he'd told Anna Mae about

trusting God to find a way for him to provide for his family, about trusting God to take care of her and the girls until he got back. He knew whatever anger she might still harbor would wash away when she read about how he was trusting God. She'd wanted that for so long.

Regret struck. Harley'd wasted so much time fighting through life on his own strength. He wished it hadn't taken something so hard—Dirk's death—to awaken him to the reality of God's love. He shook his head, forcing away the thought. He couldn't go backward; he could only move forward. And he'd make sure all of his tomorrows included leaning on God's strength.

"Well, did you get your letter all finished?" The nurse bustled in, lunch tray in hand.

Harley shifted a bit, moving the letter to the table. "Yes, ma'am. It's ready for an envelope."

"I'll get one for you right after you eat." She settled the tray across his lap. "And then the doctor is coming in with your crutches. We'll see how good you are on three legs."

Harley laughed. "I was plenty clumsy on two. Three oughta be downright ridiculous."

The nurse grinned. "Enjoy your meal." She left.

Harley bowed his head. "Thank you for this food, Lord. May it nourish my body so I can be strong enough to do your will. Amen."

The food tasted no better than it had the first days of his hospitalization, but he ate without complaint. If he ate, he'd gain strength. If he gained strength, he'd heal. If he healed, he could go home.

32

A light tap at the back door roused Anna Mae. She stretched, trying to wake herself. In the last weeks of her pregnancy, she often grew tired midafternoon. She tried to nap when Marjorie napped, catching a few minutes of rest in the big, overstuffed chair that had been her daddy's. Pushing herself clumsily to her feet, she plodded through the parlor to the kitchen and to the back porch. Her heart lifted when she spotted Mr. Berkley waiting on the small stoop.

"Mr. Berkley." She pushed the screen open. "Come in. Dorothy will be so pleased to see you."

He grinned and stepped through, sweeping off his hat as he crossed the threshold.

"I made watermelon-rind pickles and thought you might like some."

Anna Mae took the jar of jewel-toned rinds. "Why, thank you. What a treat!" Anna Mae suddenly felt the desire to recall things from the past, knowing that soon she would be far away from this home. Pausing in the porch, she shared, "I remember Mama used to make these before Ben, Jr., left. After he died, though, we never grew melons."

He gave a solemn nod. "Yes, honey. I know."

She smiled fondly. Of course he knew. He knew most everything about her family. With a smile, she headed into the kitchen.

He followed her. "Girls napping?"

"Marjorie is. Dorothy's out in the barn, playing with Ol' Smokey." She laughed lightly. "I wanted her to nap, but she's watching for Jack. He promised a surprise earlier today, and she's waiting for it."

Mr. Berkley didn't smile. "A surprise?"

Anna Mae nodded. "Yes. He was in a good mood this morning. Came right in the house and visited with me for the first time in . . . well, a while. I'm glad." She remembered the kiss, and she frowned briefly. Then, seeing Mr. Berkley's concerned expression, she forced a smile to her lips. "I'm sure he'll be by here before too much longer. Do you want to have some coffee and visit with me while we wait for the surprise?"

Mr. Berkley seated himself. "That sounds good. I'm curious about this surprise, too."

They chatted amiably while sipping coffee, and Anna Mae laughed at the stories he recalled about her little-girl years. Listening to him reminded her of listening to her own parents reminisce, and she made a determination that, no matter where she and the girls ended up in the next months, they would not lose contact with Ern Berkley.

As Anna Mae rose to fill his cup, the wheeze of the Model T intruded. She peeked out the window in time to see the car heave to a halt beside the house. Dorothy ran from the barn to greet Jack.

"Jack's here," Anna Mae said, but Mr. Berkley was already out the porch door and heading around the corner.

Anna Mae watched Jack give Dorothy a large picture book. Her own heart lifted as the child's face lit with pleasure. Immediately the little girl grabbed Mr. Berkley's hand and tugged, pulling him toward the house. In moments the three of them came through the back porch, Dorothy calling, "Mama! Mama!"

"Shh!" Anna Mae stooped over and touched Dorothy's lips with her fingers. "Your sister is sleeping. Don't wake her."

"Mama." Dorothy lowered her voice to an excited whisper. "Look what Mr. Berkley got me. *The House That Jack Built*. See?"

Anna Mae took the book and admired it for a moment, flashing a quick smile in Jack's direction. "Oh, lucky you. Do you want to go read it now?"

Dorothy took the book and sent Ern Berkley a hopeful look. "Papa Berkley, will you read it to me? Please?"

The old man's eyes crinkled with his grin. "I'd be glad to, honey. Want to go outside and sit under the tree?"

"Yes!" The child danced to the door. "C'mon! C'mon!"

With a chuckle, Mr. Berkley followed her. He glanced back at Anna Mae and Jack. "I'll be out here with Dorothy if you need me."

Anna Mae noticed Jack's face crease into a brief scowl, but when he caught her looking, the scowl faded. He pointed to the parlor doorway. "Shall we go sit, too? Dorothy got her surprise. Now it's your turn."

Remembering the way he had caught her off guard with that kiss this morning, she wasn't sure she wanted to be alone in the parlor with Jack. But Mr. Berkley was right outside. Surely Jack would behave. She nodded. "All right."

Choosing the overstuffed chair, she lowered herself awkwardly onto the soft cushion. Jack stood in the middle of the floor for a moment, sending her an odd look, before crossing to the sofa and sitting on the end closest to her. The silence turned tense while she waited for him to speak, reminding her of times when she and Harley had been at an impasse. The thought brought a rush of sadness and loneliness, and she ducked her head, curving her hands around her extended belly.

"Anna Mae?"

Jack's soft voice brought her head up. "Yes?"

He sighed. "I've waited for you to come let me know if you were ready for my help. You haven't come."

She nodded slowly. "I know. I . . . I haven't known what to say."

He sucked in his lips, his brows crunching downward. Finally he nodded. "I know. I was hard on you. But you have to know I didn't do it to hurt you." He scooted forward to the edge of the cushion and stretched out his hand. His fingertips brushed her arm. "Do you believe me?"

She really wasn't sure if she believed him or not. Jack had become so unpredictable. She offered no reply. Several seconds ticked by, and he removed his hand, clamping it over his own knee.

"I was hopin', when I left here this morning, that I'd have some good news when I returned." His voice sounded tight, underscored with frustration. "You see, I went to Hutchinson to the courthouse. I planned to take ownership of your property."

Anna Mae's eyes widened. "You put a bid on my land?"

"Yep. I did." He rubbed the underside of his nose and sniffed. "I wanted to offer it to you . . . along with me." His hand slipped into his jacket pocket, and when he pulled it out, he held something in his fist. "I hoped we could combine our properties, put up more oil pumps—the surveyors figure there's more oil under the ground—and . . . well, combine our lives, Anna Mae."

Slipping from the sofa, he knelt before her. "You know I love you. I've said all along I'd take care of you. Will you let me, Anna Mae? I can't give you back your land, but I can offer you my home and my heart." He uncurled his fingers. A small box rested on his palm.

Anna Mae stared at the box. The gold ring on her finger seemed to tighten as she stared at the box Jack held. How could Jack do this now, with Harley dead less than a month and her belly swollen with Harley's child? Couldn't he see how hurtful it was to think she could replace her husband so quickly? Her heart pounded, nearly covering the sound of Jack's voice.

"I know you're still mourning Harley, but circumstances bein' what they are, we can't wait. You're losin' your home. You've got no place to go. But if you say yes, you can move in with me and Pop. You and your girls, you'll be cared for."

"You—you really tried to buy my land . . . for me?" Anna Mae struggled to make sense of everything Jack had said.

"I tried, but someone outbid me." Jack's

face twisted into a horrible scowl, and for a moment he tightened his fist around the ring box.

Anna Mae thought of the cheerful morning she'd shared with the girls. A lump formed in her throat. Soon someone else would be building memories in her house. "Do you know who?"

"I can tell you who bought the place."

Jack jerked to his feet and spun toward the parlor doorway. Mr. Berkley stood in the arched opening, his hands shoved deep into the pockets of his faded overalls, his weathered face stoic.

"Where's Dorothy?" Jack asked.

Mr. Berkley poked his elbow toward the outside. "Still under the tree, readin' her new storybook to that big ol' gray cat. She'll be busy for a while." He took a forward step. "So we can talk freely." When his gaze settled on Anna Mae, she detected a deep sorrow that made her heartbeat pick up in sudden worry. "You want to know who bought your land, Anna Mae?"

She licked her lips and gave a hesitant nod.

"I did."

Jack's face turned bright red, and his

neck muscles bulged. "You, Pop? Why would you do that to me? Betray me like that?"

"Betray you?" Mr. Berkley removed his hands from his pockets and took another step into the room, the color in his cheeks rising. "You're a fine one to talk betrayal. Why don't you tell Anna Mae here why she never got any more letters or money from Harley?"

"Pop . . ."

The word held an undercurrent of warning that prickled the hairs on Anna Mae's neck. She struggled to her feet, her gaze on Jack, her heart pounding with trepidation. "Jack? What's he talking about?"

"Nothing." Jack snapped out the word and then grasped Anna Mae by the upper arm. "Come on. He's getting old, goin' over the edge. Let's get out of here where we can talk in private."

Mr. Berkley stepped into Jack's pathway, his palm against his son's shirt front. "You aren't going anyplace, son, until you've told her the truth."

The hold on Anna Mae's arm constricted painfully. She wrenched herself free.

Jack slapped his father's hand down and growled, "I'm warning you, Pop."

"No, I'm warning *you,* son. I got the evidence in my back pocket right now."

Jack bristled, straining toward his father, his fist clenched. Anna Mae stepped between them, one hand raised to each man. "Please. I don't know what this is all about, but I don't want you fighting with each other. Please just calm down and—"

Jack grabbed her again and pushed her aside. She cried out, grabbing her belly as a cramp caught her low on the left. Jack whirled on his father.

"See what you made me do!" Immediately his expression became concerned as he put an arm around Anna Mae's waist and guided her toward the sofa. "Are you all right, honey? Here, sit down." He pressed her into the middle cushion and then sat beside her, holding her hand.

Mr. Berkley, shaking his head, looked on. "You're not gonna get away with it, son. I couldn't let you continue in your sin."

Jack scowled fiercely at him. "Takin' care of Anna Mae? That's sinful?"

"Yes, it is, the way you been doin' it. Sneakin' around, tellin' her lies, makin' her believe her husband abandoned her while all the while you was—"

Jack was on his feet and across the room before Anna Mae could release a breath. "You better keep silent, old man!"

But Mr. Berkley raised his chin a notch and glared back, equally fierce. "Or what, Jack? What'll you do? Can't be nothin' worse than I've wanted to do to myself, standing aside and letting you go on deceiving her. But no more. I won't be a party to it no more."

Pushing past his son, he crossed the room to stand, shamefaced, before Anna Mae. "I bought your land, Anna Mae, but I don't intend to keep it. Soon as I have the title in hand, I'll sign it right back over to you. Shouldn't have been taken in the first place, and it wouldn't've been had Harley's checks got through to you. So your land—that's my first gift to you. As for the second . . ." He reached behind his back and then brought his hand around. He offered her a cluster of envelopes, tied together with dirty white string.

Anna Mae reached for the packet, her hands trembling. When she realized what she held, her jaw dropped open, but she was too stunned for words.

Mr. Berkley nodded, his expression grim. "The letters you sent to Harley and the letters he sent to you—far as I know, they're all in there." He glanced over his shoulder at Jack, who remained in the middle of the floor, his expression still angry, but also defeated. "Found 'em in Jack's bureau drawer. He's been keepin' 'em from you. He oughta be the one to tell you why, but he probably won't do it. So . . . I'll try. And when I'm done, I hope you'll forgive me."

33

The veins in Jack's temples throbbed visibly. With his gaze aimed through the parlor doorway, he remained stubbornly silent.

Watching his son, Ern took a deep breath. "Well, at least tell Anna Mae how much that oil from her property has made and promise to pay her back."

Jack spun toward him, his eyes narrowed to slits. "I never touched one penny of that money! It's all set aside. I never planned to keep it!"

"Good. That's one small right in a heap o' wrongs. And I intend for Anna Mae to know every one of those wrongs done." Ern crossed his arms. "You planning to stick around while I tell her?"

With a thrust of his jaw, Jack made his answer clear.

"Fine, then. Go get her money and bring it over here. I oughta be done by the time you get back."

Jack stormed through the parlor door. In seconds, the slam of the kitchen door signaled his departure. Ern sighed, his heart heavy. He turned slowly to face Anna Mae, who sat white-faced and silent in the middle of the sofa where Jack had left her. Ern's knees felt suddenly weak, and he sank down next to her, allowing his head to droop low.

He sighed. "Where to begin?"

Anna Mae touched his knee. Her fingers trembled. "Maybe start with these letters . . . and how they didn't reach their destinations."

Ern nodded. He started with the letters, telling how Jack apparently took them and hoarded them in his bureau drawer. Next he shared how Jack convinced the oilmen to place that pump on her property by assuring them the land would be his in a few more weeks. He finished by telling her about Jack bidding on her land. "And, honey, I suspect he wasn't planning to tell you he'd bought it—at least, not at first. I think he really wanted you to have to lean on him." Ern felt worn out by the time he had laid everything out. His heart ached for his son's deceitfulness.

Anna Mae shook her head. "I really feared Harley had just *left,* and all that time . . ." She drew in a deep breath and released it slowly, still shaking her head in disbelief. "There were moments when I would get a feeling . . . I can't describe it, but I told myself I was being silly—that Jack would never do anything to hurt me."

Ern took her hand and gave it a squeeze. "Jack did lots of things wrong in the past months, that's for sure. Hurtful, selfish things."

"But why?" Anna Mae's forehead crinkled. "He told me over and over again that he cares for me. Why would he do all that sneaking around, things he knew would be hurtful, if he cares for me?"

Ern closed his eyes for a moment and prayed for guidance. Father-instinct made him want to defend Jack, yet he knew he needed to be honest. Meeting Anna Mae's gaze, he formed his answer. "Honey, I believe deep down Jack does care for you.

You were his first love, and he's never really let it go. When he saw the chance to have you in his life, he set all reason aside and went after you. It didn't matter if it was God's will, or if it was best for you, he just wanted what he thought was best for himself." He paused, swallowed, and finished quietly. "Jack convinced himself he was doin' all this for your own good, but it wasn't. It was for *his* own good. A body should never get so self-focused that others and their feelings cease to matter."

Anna Mae nodded, a pensive look on her face. Her hand still in his, she asked, "But you bought my land instead?"

"Yes, I did. Couldn't let Jack get it. I had to disrupt his plans somehow, and it was the only thing I could think of."

"But where did you get the money? I thought Jack owned your property now."

Ern allowed a small smile to creep up his cheeks. "Well, Jack has title to the land, that's true. But I own the cows." He shrugged. "I sold off some of my stock to a dairyman from eastern Oklahoma. Enough, at least, to put in a good bid for your place." Her look of dismay brought a chuckle from his throat. "Now, honey, don't look so stricken. Old man like me doesn't need a big ol' herd mooin' around, takin' up his time." He walked to the front door and peered down the road. "Jack's been gone more'n long enough to fetch that oil money. I wonder what's keeping him."

Anna Mae pushed to her feet. It looked like it took some effort, with her extra bulk out front. She stood beside him. "Do you want to go check on him?"

He frowned. "I don't want to leave you right now. You just got quite a shock."

"I'm fine." She touched his arm. "Really, Mr. Berkley. Go check on Jack. He—he may need you right now."

Ern gave Anna Mae a gentle hug, his throat convulsing. "You're a good girl, Anna Mae." He grasped her shoulders. "And don't you worry. I know I'm old, but I'll do what I can to help you out around here. You won't be left unattended."

Her quavering smile cheered him. "If there's one thing I've learned since Harley left for that castle site, it's that I'm never alone. God's always with me, and He'll meet my needs."

He wrapped her in one more quick hug before heading to the back door. He called a good-bye to Dorothy, waved once more to Anna Mae, and then cut across the pasture toward his home. His heart pounded harder the nearer he got to his old farmhouse. He didn't know what would happen when he faced Jack. He prayed Jack would ask forgiveness and work to make things right with both Anna Mae and his father.

Jack threw the third suitcase into the backseat of the Model T and slammed the door. He still wasn't sure where he was going, he just knew he couldn't stay here. He couldn't face Anna Mae again, and he had no desire to speak to his father.

As he stomped around the hood of the car, his gaze swept across the pasture, the barn, and the contented cows. For a moment he faltered, his steps slowing. How would Pop get the milking done when his rheumatism acted up? He hadn't been fully in charge of the chores for over five years. But then Jack set his jaw and hurried the final few feet to the driver's door.

Going through the necessary motions to get the vehicle running, Jack kept a one-sided conversation going with himself. *Pop should've thought of all that before he hu-*

miliated me in front of Anna Mae. If Pop had just kept his mouth shut, I could've stayed. I could've married Anna Mae and given him grandchildren. Everything would've been fine. Pop did this to himself.

By the time the Model T chugged to life, Jack had himself convinced.

He backed up the car and yanked the wheel to turn toward the road, and out of the corner of his eye he spotted Pop stepping from the windbreak between the Phipps and Berkley properties. Pop raised both hands and waved, trotting across the brown grass toward the car.

Jack's hands twitched, ready to barrel out of the yard, but the look on his father's face—combined panic and yearning—gave him pause. Pop stopped outside the passenger door and swung it open. He didn't slide in, but he bent down and put his head into the car. His gaze flitted to the backseat, and his face twisted in disappointment. "Son, what're you doin'?"

"What does it look like? I'm headin' out. Leavin'."

Tears glittered in Pop's eyes. "You don't have to do that."

Jack forced out a harsh snort of laughter. "Oh yes, I do. You made sure of that."

Pop shook his head. The old man seemed to grow older with each passing minute. "I know you're angry at me, but—"

"Angry?" Jack slapped the steering wheel. "Angry, Pop? You took my chance for happiness—the chance that got stolen from me by Harley Phipps years ago—and you trampled it into the ground. Anna Mae'll never accept me now. She'll never understand that I did all that to protect her!"

Pop's forehead turned into a series of deep wrinkles. "You really believe that, son?"

Jack clenched his jaw and jerked his gaze forward. There was no reasoning with Pop. Jack shifted gears. "I left Anna Mae's oil money on the table. Money from cashing Harley's checks is there, too. Left the name of the surveyor who came out so she can contact him about puttin' up more pumps. Likely she'll need the income since I won't be taking care of her." He risked a quick glance at Pop. The look of intense sorrow in his father's eyes made something hot and heavy press Jack's middle. "I gotta go."

But Pop didn't back out, didn't close the door. Instead, he leaned a little farther in and put his hand on Jack's arm. The weathered hand, warm and familiar, burned Jack's skin. "Back door'll always be open." The words came out in a pained whisper.

A lump filled Jack's throat. He knew he wouldn't be able to answer. He jerked his head up and down in a quick nod of acknowledgment, and finally Pop backed out. The moment he slammed the door, Jack popped the clutch and the Model T hopped forward.

Jack gripped the steering wheel and brought the car under control, slowing it to make the turn onto the road. As he yanked the wheel to the right, he glanced in the little mirror above the dashboard and got a brief glimpse of Pop, still in the middle of the smooth driveway, hand lifted in goodbye, tears running in rivulets down his age-wrinkled cheeks.

Jack wished he hadn't looked back. He feared that image of his father would be pressed in his memory for the rest of his life.

Anna Mae, holding Marjorie's hand, walked to the storage shed. She hoped she'd be able to locate the basket they'd used as a bassinet when the girls were tiny. Her fingers itched to create little sheets and flannel blankets for the new baby, but she couldn't remember the exact size of the basket.

"I hope no mousie has decided to make a home out of that thing," she told Marjorie. If Harley had wrapped it good in burlap and hung it up high, it might have been safe from any little critters.

Marjorie looked upward and blinked, her long eyelashes throwing a shadow across her round cheeks. "No moufie," she repeated.

Anna Mae laughed. "That's right. No mousie."

A rumble intruded, and for a moment she froze, remembering the earthquake. But then she recognized the sound—the motor on Jack's Model T. She spun to face the road, her gaze pinned on the opening of the drive to the house, anticipation rising in her chest. She wasn't sure what she would say to Jack when she saw him, but the need to see him, to settle things between them, was strong.

The Model T roared past the drive without stopping.

Anna Mae's shoulders slumped.

Dorothy ran up beside her. "Mama, was that Mr. Berkley?"

Anna Mae nodded, numb. Her knees felt weak. That odd sensation was back, and she feared she'd just seen Jack for the last time. Despite his duplicity, she mourned for him.

"How come he didn't stop?" Dorothy's tone reflected her hurt feelings.

Anna Mae took Marjorie's hand again and forced a smile. "I don't know, darlin'. He must have been in a hurry."

Anna Mae watched Dorothy for a moment, her heart heavy. If what she suspected was true, and Jack didn't return, it would be one more loss for Dorothy. The little girl adored Jack. Even with all the wrong things he'd done, he'd been good to the child. Anna Mae's mother-heart ached for the unhappy confusion Jack's departure would create for her daughter.

With a sigh, she said, "Come on, Marjorie." She located the basket, freed it of its covering of burlap held in place with thick strands of rope—Harley had made it a real challenge for a mouse to break through— and carried it to the back porch. Marjorie and Dorothy trailed behind her. She left the basket on the porch while she fixed supper, and not until the girls had been tucked into bed did she haul it into the house.

Placing it on the table, she dipped a rag in a bowl filled with soapy water and gave the basket a thorough wash. It was a mindless, automatic task, and her mind wandered as she ran the rag over the woven strips of painted wood. What a day of discovery it had been. Jack's marriage proposal followed by Mr. Berkley's revelations, the fear of losing her home erased by Mr. Berkley's sacrifice, being given letters penned by Harley. After pining for word from her husband, she hadn't been able to make herself read the letters. She had, instead, placed them in a trunk in her room with other precious keepsakes. Someday soon she would take them out and read them carefully, but for some reason she didn't clearly understand, she needed to wait.

Although she'd kept her ear tuned toward the road, she hadn't heard the Model T return. She wondered if Mr. Berkley was watching, waiting, hoping. It saddened her to think of the old man sitting in his house, alone, feeling guilty. Certainly he would blame himself for Jack's leave-taking.

She owed Mr. Berkley a huge debt of gratitude for saving her property. How much it must have cost him to go against his own son. She scrubbed hard at a soiled place on the rim of the basket, vowing that she would repay the man. He wouldn't let her pay him in money, but she would do it with time. Especially if Jack didn't return, he would need company. She could provide it. It would benefit both of them. The girls needed a grandfather figure, and he needed someone to look after. They'd take care of each other, she and Mr. Berkley.

The basket shone, the grime erased. For a moment, she peered into the basket's depth, remembering how sweet Dorothy and Marjorie had looked, nestled on a fluffy pillow, little faces puckered in sleep. She tried but was unable to conjure a picture of the new baby. Even as the nesting instinct began, and her extended belly shifted with the movement of the child, the pregnancy still had a feeling of unreality at times. Was it because she was facing this child's delivery alone?

She was too tired to reason it out. Dropping the rag, she pressed her hands to her lower back. Her gaze found the open kitchen window, and she released a deep sigh as contentment washed over her. Dusk had fallen, evening shadows turning the barn into a rectangle of gray. The whisper of the willow tree branches had become a gentle *clack-clack* now that the leaves were starting to fall away. And she would still be here in the spring, to see new leaves bud, to hear the lullaby of the willows another season.

"Thank you, God, for letting me keep my home." She spoke aloud to the quiet room.

Leaving the basket on the table to dry, she entered the parlor and sat in the over-stuffed chair. The moment she sat, she pictured Jack on his knee with a little box held on his open palm. She never even saw the box's contents. Twisting the plain gold band on her finger, she realized she was glad the box had remained closed. No ring could ever take the place of the one Harley had slipped onto her finger.

Closing her eyes, she allowed her mind to drift over snippets of time with Harley. Their marriage had been far from perfect, yet there were many good times on which to dwell, and she deliberately drew on every tender, funny, heartwarming minute. "Oh, Father God, if only I could see him one more time . . ."

An idea struck. Anna Mae sat up, eyes wide, as the plan unfolded almost without her cooperation. Mr. Berkley had intimated she would have a tidy sum of money from the oil. If there was enough, she could buy a bus ticket—maybe even a train ticket—and travel to Lindsborg. She had the address for Harley's boss, Mr. Peterson. She would go to his house and ask him to take her to where Harley was buried.

Surely if she were able to put a headstone at the site, say some prayers, and talk to Harley, it would be easier to move forward. Mr. Berkley would stay with the girls if she asked, and she'd only be gone a couple of days, three at most. And when she returned, she'd be able to plan for her future. But first she needed to settle her past.

Rising, she hurried to her bedroom and slipped into a nightgown. She gave the string above the bed a tug to turn out the light and pulled the sheet to her chin. Eyes closed, she willed sleep to come quickly. She had a big day ahead of her tomorrow, and she needed energy to see it through.

34

Wind rushed through a crack at the top of the bus window, tousling Anna Mae's hair and whistling in her ears. She used her handkerchief to rub away the dust from the glass, clearing an area about six inches square. The window clean, she squinted out at the landscape of brown grasses, stretches of nearly treeless prairie, and gently lifting rises interrupted occasionally with thick clusters of yucca. This, then, must have been what Harley observed as he walked toward Lindsborg six months ago. She pressed closer to the glass, her gaze seeking, determined to memorize everything so she could tell Dorothy, Marjorie, and Mr. Berkley about it when she returned.

She smiled as she remembered Mr. Berkley's delight at keeping the girls. He'd insisted they come to his place, though, because he had the cows to care for. They had even hitched Bossie to the back of his wagon and taken her over to his pasture. The cow had seemed confused at first, looking at the others as if she didn't realize she was a bovine, too, but Dorothy was sure Bossie would make friends and be happier with company. Anna Mae hoped the little girl was right. She wasn't worried about the girls—she knew Mr. Berkley would take excellent care of them—but she missed them.

Turning to face forward once more, she rubbed her belly with both hands. *Little one, maybe it will be easier to think about you being real after I've dealt with your father's death. I hope so. I want to look forward to your arrival, not dread it.* How she longed for the unbridled anticipation that had accompanied the months she'd been pregnant with Dorothy and Marjorie. *Help me, Lord, be both Mama and Daddy to this baby as well as Dorothy and Marjorie. I know I can do all things through your strength, so strengthen me, please.*

"Well, folks, Lindsborg's around the next bend," the bus driver called.

In unison, the few passengers sat up, peeking over seat backs to look down the road for their first glimpse of the city. Anna Mae reached under her seat and tugged her bag free. Lifting it to the empty seat beside her, she unsnapped the flap and took out her comb and compact. She removed her hat—the straw hat with daisies around the brim that was more suitable for summer than fall, yet was somehow appropriate for this journey—and used the comb to slick her hair back into the bun at the nape of her neck. After replacing the hat, she examined herself critically in the little round mirror.

The reflection looked the same, yet somehow different. She'd aged in these past months. Although she was still a young woman, maturity tinged her features. She supposed that was all right.

She dropped the comb and mirror back in the bag, snapped it, and sat up just as the driver stopped the bus outside the Redland Midwest Bus Depot. Anna Mae waited until all other passengers had cleared the bus before picking up her bag and following. She paused beside the driver.

"Sir? Could you tell me where to find Coronado Avenue?"

The driver grabbed the brim of his hat and shifted it back and forth, his face pursed in thought. "I believe that's on the western edge of town. A walk of maybe seven or eight blocks." He gave her a worried look, his gaze bouncing to the evidence of her pregnancy before meeting her eyes again. "You up to that?"

Anna Mae smiled at this concern. "Yes, sir. I am. Thank you for the directions."

On the sidewalk, she moved out of the way of new passengers pushing toward the bus. The city, although not large, bustled with Saturday morning activity. From somewhere on the block, she got a whiff of fresh bread baking, and her stomach cramped, reminding her that breakfast had been hours ago.

But she didn't want to take the time to eat. She needed to find the Peterson place, find out where Harley was buried. After she'd made her peace with his death, she would see to her physical needs. With a deep sigh, she adjusted her grip on her bag and turned west.

Anna Mae stopped on the street and stared at the little building crouching well behind the house. The one letter Jack hadn't filched had said Harley stayed in a little shed on Mr. Peterson's property. That little building, then, must have been Harley's home here in Lindsborg. Desire to go to the shed, peek inside, and touch the things that Harley had last touched, pulled hard. But fear of being accused of trespassing kept her feet on the street.

The Petersons would surely allow her to explore once they knew who she was. She'd have to see them first. Leaving her bag at the end of the walking path that led to the porch, she made her way to the front door. A brass knocker centered the painted door. She used the knocker, clanking it down with force, then waited. But no one came. She knocked again, harder and longer, tipping her head to listen for any sound from inside. Nothing.

Turning a slow half circle, she examined the grounds. There was no sign of activity anywhere. Worry struck. What if they'd gone away for the weekend? Had she come all this way for nothing? Then she remembered the busyness on the downtown streets. Perhaps the Petersons had gone in to do shopping. She shrugged, sighing. They'd have to return eventually. She'd wait.

Sitting on the top step of the porch, she ignored her parched throat and growling stomach and watched the street. A tabby cat stretched its way from under the porch and coiled around Anna Mae's feet, arching its back in pleasure when Anna Mae scratched its ears. She petted the cat, appreciative of the company. She and the cat spent a pleasant half hour getting well-acquainted. The feline, its trust gained, started to climb into Anna Mae's lap, but suddenly it tensed, fur on end, and darted back under the porch.

"Hey, what's the matter?" Anna Mae asked, looking after it, but the approach of a pickup truck captured her attention. Pushing to her feet, she smoothed her skirt down and watched the truck pull into the driveway beside the house.

Two people—a man and woman who appeared to be in their mid-fifties—stepped out of the pickup. The woman sent Anna Mae a puzzled but friendly look. "Hello. May I help you?"

Anna Mae crossed the dried grass to meet them. "Are you the Petersons?"

The man rounded the truck's hood. "Yes, we are. And who might you be?"

Anna Mae clasped her hands at her waist. "I'm Anna Mae Phipps. My husband, Harley, worked on the castle project. You sent me a letter."

Recognition dawned across the man's face, and he immediately reached for Anna Mae's hand. "Mrs. Phipps, yes. It's so good to meet you." Squeezing her hand between his palms, he said, "I'm so sorry about Harley's accident."

Anna Mae blinked back tears, touched by the kind sincerity in the man's voice. "Thank you. I . . . I'm sorry to just show up this way. I hope it's not an imposition."

"Don't apologize. I'm glad you were able to come."

Mrs. Peterson interrupted. "Let's get these groceries inside, Jim. And Mrs. Phipps, I bet you could use a cool drink, couldn't you?"

Anna Mae nodded. Her tongue felt stuck to the roof of her mouth. Each of the Petersons removed a bag from the back of the truck, and then she followed them inside to a cheerful kitchen. Mrs. Peterson bustled around, pouring tea into glasses filled with crystal ice chips. Anna Mae and Mr. Peterson sat at the table, and he waited until Anna Mae had downed her glass of tea before speaking again.

"Did you receive the money I sent?"

Anna Mae nodded. "Yes, sir, and I thank you for it."

He waved a hand as if shooing flies. "No need for that. It was the least we could do, considering the circumstances."

Swallowing, Anna Mae dropped her gaze for a moment. "Yes. It's been hard, with Harley gone, and now that the paychecks have stopped . . ." She looked at him again, forcing a smile. "But that money was a big help to my girls and me."

"As I said, the least we could do. Especially since Harley won't be doing any more farming."

Anna Mae cringed, looking at the tabletop. His last words, uttered so kindly, felt like a slap in the face. "N-no. Of course he won't."

"But I'm sure he told you he's been

studying textbooks on drafting. That would be a good career for him if he can get the money to go to school."

Anna Mae's gaze bounced up, meeting Mr. Peterson's. She could make no sense of what he'd said. "You mean before his accident, Harley was studying?"

Mr. Peterson shook his head. "No. Since his accident."

The room spun. Anna Mae grabbed the tabletop for support, knocking her glass sideways. Half-melted ice slivers skidded across the table. One slipped over the edge and hit the floor beside her foot. Mrs. Peterson scurried to clean up the mess.

"W-what do you mean *since* his accident?" Anna Mae's voice sounded hollow in her ears, as if it came from far away.

Mr. Peterson frowned. "Well, while he's been in the hospital."

Harley was in the hospital? But that would mean— She shook her head, her heart pounding. Mr. Peterson's words planted a seed of hope in her heart, yet she was desperately afraid of letting the hope take root.

Mrs. Peterson stopped beside Anna Mae's

chair and grasped her shoulder. "Mrs. Phipps, are you all right?"

Anna Mae looked from one to the other, struggling to comprehend what she'd just heard. Was it possible that it had all been a mistake? That Harley was alive? "You . . . you said Harley was . . . was in the hospital?"

Mr. Peterson nodded. "Yes. He's been there for several weeks."

Anna Mae's heart thumped so hard she thought she might pass out. "But—but a salesman came . . . he said a man had been killed." She pressed her fingers to her temples, trying to put the pieces together. "He said a man from Spencer had been killed, and Harley was the only man from Spencer on the crew."

"Oh, you poor girl." Mrs. Peterson sat beside her, continuing to pat her shoulder. "What you must have gone through these past weeks."

Mr. Peterson leaned forward, his elbows on the table. "Mrs. Phipps, a man *was* killed. A man named Dirk Farley. The salesman must have gotten his facts turned around."

Dirk Farley? Harley's friend, Anna Mae remembered, the one Harley said read his Bible. Her heart ached for Harley. She understood the loss he must have experienced at Dirk's death. Holding trembling fingers to her lips, she fought to gain control of her emotions. When she felt secure, she pushed herself to her feet and stood on shaky legs. "I . . . I need to see my husband. Where is the hospital?"

Mr. Peterson rose. "Yes. I'll take you there, then you can spend the night here, with us."

"Oh, but—"

Mrs. Peterson cut in, "No arguments, Mrs. Phipps. Go now. You've got some making up to do."

Although Anna Mae knew the woman referred to making up lost time, there was a deeper meaning in her heart. *Thank you, God, for the opportunity to make things right!*

Harley propped his crutches in the corner and hopped on one foot back to his bed. His everyday practice of walking around the room had strengthened his leg and given him confidence. The doctor had told him that he would be able to go home in another few days.

Home. That had to be one of the best words in the English language.

He glanced at the stack of books Mr. Peterson had brought. If he had limited time left, he'd better take advantage of it. Settling on the edge of the mattress, he reached for *Drafting Fundamentals.* As he opened the book to the sixth chapter, someone entered the room. He glanced up, expecting the nurse with his supper tray.

He rubbed his eyes, certain he was imagining things. But when he looked again, the vision was the same. Annie, with a circle of daisies on her head, stood framed in the doorway. He thought his heart might shoot from his chest through the wall. He grinned with uncontrollable joy. "Annie!"

She raced across the floor, the daisy-laden hat flying off and landing on the floor. Her arms slipped around his torso, and she buried her face against his neck. His bulky cast—and her bulky form—created a barrier, but he wrapped both arms around her and held her as tight as he could. The way he'd longed to hold her for months. The way he wanted to hold her forever.

Her tears wet his skin, and he couldn't hold back a teasing comment. "I hope those're happy tears."

"Oh, Harley," she choked, burrowing into his shoulder. "Harley . . . Harley." She pulled free, and her hands roamed, touching his shoulders, cheeks, mouth, hair. Her face wore an expression of wonder he didn't understand, but he sensed her need to explore, so he remained silent and waiting, his hands on her thick waist. Her inspection finished, she melted into his arms again. He held her, allowing her to cry, while a lump filled his throat.

At long last she pulled loose and stood before him, holding both of his hands as if afraid to let him go. Her eyes, red-rimmed from tears, shone with a happiness Harley hadn't seen in a long while.

He sighed. "Ah, Annie, honey, I've missed you so much. I'm so glad you're here." He looked toward the door, his heart hopeful. "Did you bring the girls?"

"No. They're with Ern Berkley."

Ern? "And Jack?"

"No, not Jack." She shook her head, her face clouding for a moment. "Harley, I have so much to tell you."

He twisted his face into a mock scowl, giving her hands a tug. "I know. It's been months, and you never wrote."

She ducked her head, biting down on her lower lip. When she raised her gaze again, she said softly, "We've got a lot of catching up to do. But first, could we just . . . sit together? I need to feel your arms around me."

There was something in her eyes he couldn't read—something she wasn't yet ready to share. Although curious, Harley could wait. He shifted himself fully onto the mattress and leaned against the pillows, scooting to the edge of the bed. He held out his arms, and she climbed awkwardly into the bed beside him, curling sideways to nestle her head against his shoulder. He'd almost forgotten how neatly she fit into the crook of his arm.

35

Harley bounced Margie on his good knee, relishing the sound of the baby's chortle. Dottie stood nearby, hands clasped beneath her chin, blue eyes sparkling. "Me next, Daddy! Me next!" He slipped Margie to the sofa beside him, hefted Dottie onto his knee, and bounced her wildly enough to make her ponytail dance.

A week home and it felt like he'd never left. So much was familiar—same barn in the yard with the same old cow needing milked every dawn, same squeaky porch door, same morning sounds—with a few additions. Muffled clanks drifting from the pasture on the morning breeze let him know the oilmen were setting up those new pumps. His jaw had nearly hit the ground when Annie showed him how much money one pump had brought in. With four, they'd be set just fine. Better than fine. God was meeting their needs beyond anything Harley could have imagined.

"Are my pony and pony riders ready for breakfast?"

Annie stood in the parlor doorway, her hands in her apron, a soft smile lighting her face. The sweetness in her expression every time she peeked in his direction nearly melted him. She couldn't pass him without stopping to run a hand through his hair, tweak his ear, or kiss his cheek or his lips.

"Waffles!" Dottie crowed, slipping from her father's knee and racing for the door.

Harley lifted Margie from the sofa and watched her toddle after her sister. It gave him a twinge of sadness to see how much Margie had grown and changed when he wasn't looking. But now he was here and he was staying, Lord willing, and he wouldn't miss even one more minute of changes.

Grabbing his crutches, he hobbled toward Annie, who slipped her fingers beneath one of his elbows and escorted him to the table. He settled himself while she put Margie in the high chair. Dottie waited, hands folded, until Annie sat down. Then she looked at Harley.

"Pray, Daddy."

A lump filled Harley's throat. Such a simple command, yet what an effect it had on Harley's heart. *"Pray, Daddy,"* like she'd said it a hundred times before. It was the way it should have been all along, with him leading his family in prayer and Bible reading and church attendance.

At first he'd felt embarrassed, praying out loud. But when he remembered Dirk's ease in addressing God, it gave him courage. Closing his eyes, he licked his lips and began. "Thank you, Lord, for this food. Thank you for Annie, who fixed it for us. Let this food bless our bodies so we can be strong to do your will. Amen."

"Amen!" Dottie echoed, then snatched a waffle from the steaming plate in the middle of the table.

Breakfast passed with the baby's babbles and Dottie's cheerful chatter. When they'd eaten their fill, Annie cleaned Margie's face with a rag and lifted her from the high chair. "All right, Dorothy. Take your sister to your room, and you two get dressed. I laid out your clothes for today."

"Okay, Mama." Dottie took hold of Margie's hand and led her from the room.

Harley watched them go and then looked at Annie. "You've been lettin' Dottie dress Margie all week. That something new?"

Annie stacked dirty plates. "With this new one coming, I'll need her help. She can do it; she's getting to be a big girl."

Harley pushed his plate toward Annie and watched her carry it to the sink. The new baby had certainly made its presence known. Annie's gracefulness had slipped away with the expansion of her middle, but she was still the prettiest thing in Reno County. He reminded her, "I'll be around to help, too, y'know."

She glanced at him over her shoulder. "No, you won't."

"I won't?"

Turning around, she grinned. "No, you won't."

Crooking his elbow over the back of the chair rungs, he frowned slightly. "Where am I gonna be?"

A giggle spilled out. She reached into her

apron pocket and thrust a piece of paper at him. "In school."

Harley took the paper and unfolded it. It was a brochure about Salt City Business College. His gaze bounced back to Annie's smiling face. She sat at the table and flicked the brochure with one fingertip.

"I had it mailed to me. I wanted to see what courses they offered. You can take classes there for drawing blueprints, Harley."

The enthusiasm in her voice reminded him of the celebration when he'd told her he'd asked Jesus to be his Lord and Savior. She'd babbled something about praying "whatever it took" and being sorry it took so much, yet the joy in her voice had made him want to celebrate all over again. He had the same lift in his heart now, looking into her smiling face and hearing the bubble of excitement.

He hated to put a damper on things, but he had to be practical. "Annie, I don't even have a high school diploma. They probably won't let me in."

She shook her head, pointing to a paragraph in the brochure. "They'll give you a test, and if you pass it, you can enroll."

"But—"

She took his hand. "Harley, you can't farm."

Her gentle voice didn't sting a bit.

"Even if you could, the ground won't produce, not without rain. There's no guarantee when rain will come again. The oil pumps will be working, though, so we'll have money for you to go school and for us to live on. Then, if the oil dries up, you'll have a skill you can use to take care of us." Her eyes sparkled. "Don't you see? It's God's way of working things out."

Harley wouldn't argue that point. But he did see a small problem. "But that school—it's in Hutchinson. That's a good twenty-mile drive. And we don't even have a wagon to get me there since I sold the mules. Who's gonna take me every day?"

She bit her lower lip. "Well, Mr. Berkley and I talked about that a couple days ago. He came up with an idea."

Harley's curiosity grew. Ern Berkley had done so much to help his family—even at the expense of losing his own son. Harley trusted the man to have good ideas. "What is it?"

"He said maybe we should use some of

the oil money to buy a car—not a brand-new one, but an older one that wouldn't cost so much—and then rent a house in Hutchinson so you'd be close to the college."

Harley sat back, his jaw open. "You want to leave the farm?"

A hint of sadness appeared in Annie's eyes. "Of course I don't." She rested her elbows on the table, fitting her thumbnails together. "But we wouldn't need to sell it, as long as the pumps are producing. Mr. Berkley said he'd keep an eye on things for us, even take care of Bossie. Then, when your schooling is done, we could come back here and live, or we could think about selling if you need to be in a city to do your blueprint drawing."

Harley thought about what she'd said while he fingered the brochure. He wouldn't deny the eagerness that rose in his chest when presented with the chance to get schooling. Thinking about not being on this farm put a little tinge of sadness around the edges, but it wouldn't have to be forever. And maybe they could drive out on weekends, attend the little church where Annie'd grown up, invite Ern Berkley over for dinner . . .

He looked at Annie. "You think I could learn to drive a car?"

Annie smiled. "Harley, you helped build a castle in the middle of Kansas. I think you can do anything you set your mind to."

Anna Mae glanced at Harley, and she felt a smile creep up her cheeks. He wore his driving face: proud expression, chin angled high, eyes bright. When he'd spotted the late-1920s Oldsmobile in the back corner of Felix Haskell's small car lot, his eyes had lit with pleasure. The once bright-red paint had faded to a rusty reddish orange, and the chrome bore some gray smudges, but Anna Mae had known at once this was the automobile they'd buy.

She'd learned to drive first. With Harley's cast, he couldn't work the pedals. How they'd laughed at her first attempts! But she'd mastered it, earning Harley's admiration. And then she'd taught him, giving them more reasons for laughter. He now looked as at ease behind the wheel of his Oldsmobile as he had behind the handles of his plow. And how it pleased her to have her husband driving her home from church after sitting beside her in her familiar pew, hearing his voice raised in song, seeing his head bowed in prayer. They'd stayed a few minutes after the service today to talk to the minister and arrange Harley's baptism now that his cast was off. Anna Mae had never been happier.

So many things had fallen into place. Harley had passed his test for entrance into the Salt City Business School, and he'd start school in January. They'd found a little house on Avenue C in Hutchinson, just a few blocks from the college, to rent. When Dorothy had explored and found a fairly young weeping willow tree on the far corner of the backyard, Anna Mae had known it was the house for them. They would move in after Christmas, and the oil money would take care of their financial needs until Harley finished his classes and found a job.

Harley had blossomed so much in the past month. Love for her husband overflowed, making her chest feel tight. How could she have wondered for even one minute whether he was the man for her? It seemed so foolish now, remembering how Jack had made her question it. Her love for

Harley ran as deep as a willow's root, as deep as the roots of her faith, which he now shared. She knew their faith in God and each other would continue to grow.

Another twinge caught her in the back, making her squirm in the seat. Those twinges had started early this morning, awakening her. They'd gotten stronger during the long sermon, and twice Harley had sent her curious looks when she'd straightened in the pew. But she knew from past experience babies took their time about coming. They'd be home, comfortable, long before this baby wiggled its way into the world.

And Harley would be here to welcome it, to love it, to raise it in the knowledge and love of the Lord. Anna Mae swiped at the tears that formed in her eyes.

Harley's brows came down as he glanced at her. "You okay?"

She nodded, sending him a secretive smile. "I'm okay. But instead of taking the girls home, let's drop them off at Mr. Berkley's—see if he'll keep them this afternoon."

"Papa Berkley! Papa Berkley!" Dorothy bounced in the backseat, clapping her hands.

Marjorie echoed, "Papa Berk'ey!"

Harley's frown deepened. "You got some reason you want the girls out of the—" And then his eyebrows shot high. "You mean—?"

Anna Mae nodded, but then a twinge—stronger than any of the others—seized her, making her catch her breath.

Harley adjusted the accelerator, zooming the car along the road. Anna Mae stayed in the car while Harley walked the girls to the house. His limp, a permanent reminder of his accident, endeared him even more to Anna Mae. He'd overcome a great deal, all without complaint. She clutched her belly and whispered, "You've got an extra special daddy, little one. And you'll get to meet him soon."

She looked out the window for Harley, and something—something she hadn't seen for months—captured her attention. Clouds. Dark clouds building in the east. "Lord, can it be?" she wondered aloud.

Harley slammed the door open and fell in behind the wheel. "Ern says he'll keep the girls as long as we need him to. Now let's get you back to Spencer an'—"

"No, Harley, no time to go back to

Spencer." A pressure down low told Anna Mae things were moving faster than they had with her first two. She stared hard at the clouds, hope building in her heart. "We'd better just go home."

"But I can't deliver a baby!"

Anna Mae finally looked at him. "Well, of course not in a *car*. But at home, in my own bed, we can do it. Let's go, Harley."

He sat, his mouth hanging open.

"Harley, let's go," she said again, using a tone she reserved for her sternest moments. "I will not have this baby in Mr. Berkley's driveway!"

Harley put the auto in drive and headed for the house. He guided her inside, his touch as gentle as if she were made of fine china, and helped her into her nightgown. Lying back in the bed, Anna Mae sighed. In her house, with the willow tree dancing in the fresh, scented breeze that had sprung up, she knew everything would be fine.

"Go ahead and get things ready, Harley. Boil water to sterilize scissors and string, get the clean towels from the shelf, and get some newspaper to put underneath me so I don't soil the mattress."

He stood near the bed, worry creasing his

brow. "Annie, honey, I'm not so sure about this. . . ."

Anna Mae gave a firm nod. "I'm sure. We can do it. And it'll be so special, Harley, you and me welcoming this baby together."

"But, Annie, what if—"

"I'll be fine."

Anna Mae found reason to question her blithe statement as the afternoon wore on and the pains drew closer together, lasted longer, and the intensity increased. She held her breath through the hardest ones, almost forgetting to breathe, but Harley's hand on her head and encouraging whispers got her through. And finally the moment arrived. Through a blur of pain, she heard Harley's exultant shout: "It's a girl! Glory be! Annie, we got a girl!"

She thought groggily, *He should name this one. Gloria Beatrice . . . that's pretty . . . and he can call her Glory Bea if he wants to.*

She heard the snip of the scissors, and then Harley lay the infant across her chest. The baby girl waved miniscule fists and crunched her face into a horrible scowl. The baby's fury at being thrust into the world brought a gentle laugh from her mama. "Hey, there, baby," she soothed, wrapping a towel around the scrawny body, "you're okay. Mama's got you."

The baby's weak wail filled the room, competing with a different sound—a rumble that had been so long absent, Anna Mae didn't recognize it at first. But then she remembered the clouds, remembered the cause of the noise, and a smile found its way to her parched lips.

"Harley, is it raining on our baby's birthday?"

Through drooping lids, she saw Harley cross to the window and peek out. He spun around, his smile wide. "Look here, Annie! See that on the window? Spatters! It *is* rain! The drought is over!" He returned to the bed as fast as his limp would allow and scooped the baby into his hands. Back at the window, he kissed the baby's red cheek, avoiding a tiny flailing fist, and held her up to the window. "Look at that, little darlin'. Rain. It's as much a sight for sore eyes as you are."

Cradling the baby in one arm, he flung the window open, and a sweet scent washed into the room. Anna Mae inhaled, filling her senses with the fragrance of rain. She closed her eyes, listening to Harley's soft voice.

"Little baby, lookee out there. Those rain-drops comin' down'll water all the plants, quench those thirsty leaves, and water'll be stored up underneath the ground again. See that big ol' willow tree? It has the good sense to send roots way down under the earth to reach the deep-down water. That's why it's been growin' so well all this time. That's what I'm gonna teach you to do, dar-lin' girl. You're gonna learn to send your roots to the deep source of God's love, so you can grow in Him. My friend Dirk taught me 'bout that."

Anna Mae felt warm tears wash down her face. Hearing her husband speak of God with such familiarity while rain gently pat-tered the roof was a pleasure beyond any-thing she'd experienced before.

Harley's voice fell silent, the baby's soft hiccups calming, as well.

"Bring her over here, Harley," Anna Mae begged.

Harley turned, his face lit with a smile. He carried the baby to the bed and placed her in Anna Mae's waiting arms. The baby nuz-zled against her mother's neck, bringing a rush of pure love.

Harley pressed his palms on either side of

Anna Mae's shoulders and planted a tender kiss on her forehead. Smiling into her face, he whispered, "It's perfect, isn't it?"

Anna Mae lifted her chin to kiss Harley's lips. Perfect, yes. Their faith had blossomed just like a willow tree, despite hardship and drought. When Harley shifted to sit on the edge of the mattress, Anna Mae gasped. Through the open window, a rainbow appeared, its bright bands of color shimmering against the deep blue of the clearing sky. Harley slipped his arm behind Anna Mae's shoulders, lifting her so she could see more clearly.

"God's just rainin' down blessings, Annie," Harley whispered into her ear.

She didn't answer. She didn't need to. She knew her smile said it all.

Acknowledgments

Writing a book is not a one-person undertaking—and I'm deeply grateful to the following people for their assistance.

Mom and Daddy—You've encouraged my writing for as long as I can remember. Your belief in me helped me believe in myself. God blessed me extra good when He gave me you.

Don—Thanks for telling me you're proud of me. The only sweeter words are when you tell me you love me.

Kristian, Kaitlyn, and Kamryn—You three are always in the back of my mind as I write. I pray your God-planted dreams will find fulfillment and you will always seek His face no matter where you go or what you do.

Connor, Ethan, and Rylin—Gramma loves you so much! Thank you for providing comic relief and smiles and hugs. What did we ever do without you?

Mr. Harvey Kohr—Thank you for telling me about your father's leadership on the castle-building site. I appreciate your willingness to answer the questions of a stranger. I feel as though I made a friend.

Ron Loomis—The hayrack ride at your place in October 2004 planted the seed of this story. Thank you for allowing me to come back in the light of day to explore the old farmhouse. The sunshine of that afternoon brought the seed to life.

Kathy, Don, Ann, and the choir members of First Southern Baptist—Your prayers and words of support are invaluable to me. Thank you for your continued interest in what I'm up to.

Eileen, Margie, Crystal, Jill, Staci, and Ramona—You ladies take my words, tweak them, and make them better than they were before. I think I've got the best bunch of "critters" around.

Charlene and the staff at Bethany House—What a privilege and honor it is to work with you! Thank you for all you do.

Finally, and most importantly, praise be to God—I feel so close to You when I'm at the keyboard, creating the stories You place on my heart. Thank You for Your steadfast presence in my life. May any praise or glory be reflected directly back to You.

KIM VOGEL SAWYER is fond of C words like *children, cats,* and *chocolate.* She is the author of nine novels, including the best-selling *Waiting for Summer's Return.* She is active in her church, where she teaches adult Sunday School and participates in both voice and bell choirs. In her spare time, she enjoys drama, quilting, and calligraphy. Kim and her husband, Don, reside in Hutchinson, Kansas, and have three daughters and three grandsons.